THE TRANSFORMATION

Few witnessed what happened next. Few would be able to testify to it. Lisa saw. Her eyes were fixed on the young woman chained to the stake, and they never left her.

The chains fell. The woman dropped away from the stake, and in dropping she metamorphosed into a great, lean gray wolf. In a bound, she leaped from the platform and crossed the narrow ground toward the platform where Peter Binsfeld remained seated under a canopy that sheltered him from the downpour. The wolf leaped to the platform and lunged at the suffragan bishop.

Peter Binsfeld screamed. . . .

The Summoned

MEGAN MARKLIN

POCKET BOOKS

New York   London   Toronto   Sydney   Tokyo   Singapore

This book is a work of fiction. Names, characters, places and incidents are either products of the author's imagination or are used fictitiously. Any resemblance to actual events or locales or persons, living or dead, is entirely coincidental.

An *Original* Publication of POCKET BOOKS

POCKET BOOKS, a division of Simon & Schuster Inc.
1230 Avenue of the Americas, New York, NY 10020

ISBN: 0-671-76098-X

First Pocket Books printing March 1993

10 9 8 7 6 5 4 3 2 1

POCKET and colophon are registered trademarks of Simon & Schuster Inc.

Cover art by Vince Natale

Printed in the U.S.A.

"Be sober, be vigilant; because your adversary the devil, as a roaring lion, walketh about, seeking whom he may devour."

—1 Peter 5:8

"It must be remembered that we have heard only one side of the case. God has written all the books."

—Samuel Butler

"The devil is merely a fallen angel, and when God lost Satan he lost one of his best lieutenants."

—Walter Lippmann

The Descent of Lisa Hamilton

(★The Most Powerful Witches)

Elizabeth (Lisa) Catherine O'Neil (1951–   ) [m. Benjamin O. Hamilton]. Lisa is the daughter of . . .

Mary Kathleen Horan (1925–   ) and John C. O'Neil. Mary is the daughter of . . .

Elizabeth Catherine Kennedy (1899–1977) and Patrick Horan. Elizabeth was the daughter of . . .

★ **Elizabeth Mary Spencer** (1868–1951) and Sean Kennedy. Elizabeth was the daughter of . . .

Angelina Tatum (1829–68) and **Jonathan Roper.** Angelina was the daughter of . . .

Honor Trowbridge (1810–99) and Josiah Tatum. Honor was the daughter of . . .

Honor Osborne (1781–1826) and John Trowbridge. Honor was the daughter of . . .

★ **Moll Douglas** (1763–1821) and Samuel Osborne. Moll was the daughter of . . .

Amelia McClintock (1724–90) [m. William Douglas] and **Jonathan Roper.** Amelia was the daughter of . . .

Katherine McNeill (1705–68) and George McClintock. Katherine was the daughter of . . .

Patience Hollister (1672–1749) and Foster McNeill. Patience was the daughter of . . .

★ **Charity McDougal** (1651–1747) and William Hollister. Charity was the daughter of . . .

Anna Baltussen (1634–88) [m. Angus McDougal] and **Jonathan Roper.** Anna was the daughter of . . .

Anje Bittrich (1616–61) and **Willem Baltussen.** Anje was the daughter of . . .

Eva van Wildbad (1599–1666) and **Friederich Bittrich.** Eva was the daughter of . . .

★ **Mathilde Seiler** (1578–1676) and **Henricus van Wildbad.** Mathilde was the daughter of . . .

Angélique Cordier (1558–96) [m. Philippe Robeus] and **Johann Seiler.** Angélique was the daughter of . . .

Jacqueline d'Alembert (1541–59) and **Jean Cordier**

The Summoned

1

MANY IMPORTANT THINGS BEGIN WITH DREAMS.

Abraham Lincoln dreamed he would be assassinated, and it happened.

Jacob dreamed of the ladder to heaven. God appeared to him in that dream and promised him his family would be numerous and would scatter over the earth, always under His special protection. And it happened.

Joseph's dreams nearly cost him his life at the hands of his brothers, and yet what he dreamed happened: he achieved wealth and power and dominion over them.

Pharaoh dreamed of the fat and lean cattle and the full and withered ears. Joseph interpreted those dreams to mean years of plenty and years of famine, and they happened.

King Nebuchadnezzar dreamed, and from his dream Daniel foretold the history of the world.

The Angel of the Lord appeared to Joseph in a dream, telling him not to set aside his marriage contract but to take Mary to wife, even though she was pregnant, for she was pregnant by the Holy Spirit. The Angel told Joseph that Jesus would save his people, and it happened.

The Emperor Augustus analyzed his dreams assiduously, never doubting that they were meaningful. Livy, Plutarch,

1

and Galen believed that much was to be learned by analyzing dreams. Eminent men of all faiths—Christians, Jews, and Muslims—long studied the meaning of dreams.

It was only when the world committed itself to "science" that mankind began to doubt the significance of dreams—until Dr. Sigmund Freud turned the rationalist community around and made the world once again recognize the importance of dreams.

What happened to Lisa Hamilton began with a dream.

One dream. Then another. And then another. At first she was only amused by them, for they were erotic dreams, and she would awake afterward with a pleasant sensation that she had shared a satisfying experience with her husband just before they went to sleep. Realizing after a moment awake that she'd had no such experience at eleven or midnight, she wondered how she could feel so warmly satiated, just from a dream.

Her satisfaction was not corporeal and yet not purely incorporeal either. It was of a dream, suffused with erotic elation and limited to illusion; yet there was more; an elusive ache in the private parts of her body insisted she had been invaded in her sleep, not just in the dream sense but really. Her sense of having been erotically exercised was so compelling that several times she rose from her bed and went to the bathroom to examine herself for evidence of sexual intrusion. A flush of color she saw in a hand mirror argued that she had been entered, really.

She had no sense at all of who her dream partner was. In the dreams, he came and went, shadowy, with no features that might identify him.

He was not unwelcome. He was not a stranger, not an intruder. Certainly he was not a rapist. She was always glad to receive him. He was tender, a skillful lover, a lover who left her satisfied. In the dreams she was never curious as to who he was. It was as though she knew.

Only when she was awake did she want to know who he had been. Only then did she feel violated.

One thing was certain. He was not her husband. Nothing about the way he made love to her was anything like the way Ben did it. Or had ever done it. Something else was certain. He was not one of the three men with whom she had been intimate before her marriage. Her dream lover was . . . He was not of her experience. She was reluctant to say it, but he was a better lover than any man she had ever wakefully experienced.

The dreams were very much alike. They did not begin with seduction or love-play. The shadowy figure simply appeared at her bed, in which she was apparently alone, Ben not beside her, and she welcomed him to lie down with her. He was always welcome. She did not fear him. He never spoke. He caressed her briefly, then disposed her body to receive him and entered, filling her and exciting everything within her that could be excited. The experience was supreme, always.

Supreme . . . That would have been difficult to explain, if she'd had to explain it. It would in fact have been impossible to explain why in each dream she found utter satiation in joining herself, without foreplay, without so much as a suggestion of love, with a mysterious anonymous being who came for one purpose, achieved that purpose, then disappeared.

That was what he did: he disappeared afterward. He said nothing. She had no idea if he was satisfied. He never spoke. He made no gesture. He entered her bed and entered her. That was the total of it.

Sure. It was the erotic fantasy of a woman who had ceased even occasionally to reach even the edge of satiation with her husband. Once there had been ecstasy. A few times, anyway. No more. Something pleasant now and again. Nothing better. Okay. That was what these dreams were: self-therapy, what a man would call a wet dream. Why not? Why not just enjoy?

Maybe she could have. Except . . .

Except that she found herself growing drowsy in midafternoon, so drowsy she was compelled to nap; and the dream

3

came to her also in those afternoon naps. Her dream lover came while she was asleep on the couch in her study.

The nap dreams were different. He came in daylight. The dreams were never of a different time and place, so in daytime dreams he came in daylight. Yet, seen in the light, he was no more distinct, no more recognizable. She simply could not make out anything about him. Or if she could, she couldn't remember when she woke.

She did remember one thing that she did not remember from his visits to her dark bedroom: in the daylight she could see that he was stark naked. She remembered wondering when and where he had undressed, also where his clothes were and where he would dress again.

The nap dreams were different in another way: he wouldn't make love to her on the couch. He was strong, and he gently lifted her and positioned her on the floor.

And that drastically changed her perception of what was happening to her, transformed it from amused curiosity to cold fear.

She woke from the third nap dream to discover she had not just dreamed of being on the floor; she *had* been on the floor. She had really been on the floor. For sure. She could tell. The proof was plain.

Meaning to try to stay awake, she had carried the Sunday *New York Times* with her to the couch in her study, intending to try to complete the crossword puzzle she had begun on Sunday evening. Too drowsy to solve more than two or three more clues, she let the paper fall to the floor. Now, waking after her dream, she found the newspaper wrinkled and torn. Not only that. Ballpoint ink was smeared across the puzzle!

Jolted, Lisa scrambled to her feet, pulled down her jeans, then her panties. Stained! Blue. The ballpoint ink was on her skin and on the inside of her panties!

Elizabeth Catherine Hamilton hardly responded to the name Elizabeth. From her earliest memory she had been called Lisa. Her mother had called her that, and so had everyone else. She pronounced it "Leess-a" and became downright testy when someone called her "Lye-za."

At forty-one Lisa did not see that she was much different from the girl she had been at nineteen. She had always been what was euphemistically called a big-boned woman—unkindly spoken of as horsy. She was tall, five-feet-ten, and possessed of broad shoulders and hips. She weighed no more than was appropriate for a woman of her height and build, but people tended to overestimate her weight and think of her as stout. A better word for her was husky. She had curly dark-brown hair and thick brows. Her eyes were blue. Her face was unmemorable, because it was in no way flawed and yet not strikingly beautiful. She had generous breasts, a visible but not protruding belly, and good legs. She was, in short, an attractive, pleasant woman who made friends easily and was disliked by no one.

She would have described her life before the dreams began as prosaic, if not downright dull. Looking back over her life for satisfaction—that is, for elements or experiences she was proud of or in which she had found special pleasure—she could think of only a few.

One highlight was the day when Professor Mosley approached her on the campus at Smith College and, smiling, handed her an envelope containing the notice that she had been elected to Phi Beta Kappa.

Another was the evening when she and Ben, five years married, walked through a Venetian archway and had their first sight of the gleaming, rain-drenched Piazza San Marco.

Still another was when they bought this house: to be able to afford it, as well as having had the good fortune to find it.

The birth of their only child, Ben Junior, had not been a highlight of her life, for she had suffered much pain giving birth and had been terrified.

Once born, though, Ben Junior—Benny—had become a source of warm satisfaction. His little triumphs—a gold seal affixed by a teacher to one of his crayon drawings, an all-A report card, a medal for junior-high swimming, his induction into National Honor Society—had been little triumphs for her, too. She had been careful not to become an obsessive mother; still, mother was a major element of her self-identification.

She was proud of Benny, who was a freshman at the college there in Marietta. Though he attended the college in his hometown, he did not live at home but in his fraternity house. She saw him no more than once or twice a week.

She was proud of Ben, too, and would say if anyone asked that they had a good marriage.

Ben was an uncomplicated man who had always been moved by an uncomplicated ambition: to find the right company and then work his way up in it, as high as possible. His company was American Cyanamid. He was the manager of its plant at Waverly, West Virginia. To have achieved that managership at his age was not an outstanding achievement, yet it bespoke success; he was regarded in his company as a competent, reliable man, not a star but a man who had earned promotions and would earn more. Ben was content with that. Lisa had no choice but to accept it.

When she learned they were to move to West Virginia, of all places, she thought the world had come to an end. They had flown out to look around, had found the rural Ohio Valley all she had feared, and then had discovered, a few miles down the Ohio River from the plant, the town of Marietta, Ohio. It was New England transplanted, with tree-shaded brick streets, old churches, many fine old houses, a cemetery filled with the graves of Revolutionary soldiers, and a superb small college.

She had led Ben in exploring the oddly situated town. Her interest had turned to fascination. It was distinguished by an odd, even unique, mixture of contradictory characteristics: midwestern town, river town, farm town, industrial town, college town, secure and insecure, ugly and beautiful, provincial and urbane—all, of course, in constant conflict.

Behind wrought-iron fences, on high terraces above brick-paved Fourth Street, stood several nineteenth-century houses, looming big houses with towers and wrought-iron gingerbread on the peaks of their slate roofs. Two or three of these had been lovingly restored. The others were in good repair. When Lisa saw these houses, she insisted Ben stop at a realtor's office, though this was only a preliminary visit to their new location.

The realtor was pessimistic. Those houses, he said, never came on the market. But two weeks later they received a telegram. Because of a sudden corporate transfer, one of the Victorian houses was up for sale.

Ben called the style of the house Gothic Grotesque, but since it would make a move to the Ohio Valley more palatable for Lisa, he agreed to make a bid for it. Real estate prices in Marietta were surprisingly low for people used to East Coast prices. To their surprise, Lisa and Ben found themselves the owners of the best-restored of the splendid old homes.

So they had come to Marietta, and she had fit herself into this town as she had fit herself into the three towns where the company had sent the family before. She was a company wife and well practiced at it. First you joined the PTA, then the American Association of University Women and the League of Women Voters. These were organizations that accepted every applicant, gladly. Ben was of course invited to join the Rotary Club; every plant manager in the area was courted by the self-anointed cream of service clubs. From these contacts came the invitation to play as a substitute at the Thursday-afternoon bridge club, followed in a few months by an offer of full membership. Then of course the country club.

Lisa tried to avoid, even in thought, the cliché that this was not the life she had envisioned when she was a Big Woman on Campus at Smith. She had made her choice and was living with it.

She had majored in literature and art, with a vague idea she would find a position in the creative section of an advertising agency. She had in fact interviewed with three agencies while she was still on campus. Before the time for second interviews she was planning her wedding. Ben was not working in New York. She did not apply for second interviews. She knew, though, that some of her classmates envied her. Her life was all but free of challenges, also all but free of tension. Here in Marietta, as in other towns, she was liked and respected, thought of as a caring, giving, generous person.

If nothing more, she was comfortable. Or had been until she found the blue ink on her skin and panties.

As Lisa would learn later, the town had viewed the Hamiltons' purchase of the house with some apprehension. They were afraid of what this pair of easterners would do to it. They did not guess that Lisa had probably a clearer appreciation of the history of the house than they did. She and Ben installed air conditioning in two bedrooms and in Lisa's private retreat in the tower, but the units were chosen and installed so that they were almost invisible from within and without. Fortunately the previous owners had been willing to sell much of their furniture, some of which they had bought from their own predecessors. The house was not pure 1870—the Hamiltons were not fanatic about preservation—but it was close to pure, and Lisa loved it and was proud of it. She was in fact so much in love with the house and so proud of it that Ben dreaded the day when the company would want him to move somewhere else.

The central tower at the front of the house was octagonal and had a crenellated roofline. The octagonal room at the top, entered in the middle by way of a cast-iron spiral staircase, was Lisa's study and her personal retreat. From her eight tall windows she could see a panoramic view of the town and its two rivers, which she said distracted her from the work she tried to do at her desk.

Two more towers were too slender to contain rooms and were purely decorative. A double chimney stood to the south of Lisa's tower, and its bricks were set in flamboyant patterns. All the rooms on the front of the house had floor-to-ceiling windows, and the ceilings were twelve feet high. The windows to the south of the grand front door were in the shade of a deep porch. The windows to the north were not shaded—or hadn't been until the trees grew so large—and the north room had once been regarded as a solarium.

Of course, everything was adorned with gingerbread. The man who had built the house, in the late 1860s, must have abhorred straight lines.

A Korean boxwood hedge suffused the summer air with its distinct spicy perfume. A carpet of pine needles, covering much of the front yard, shed its own sweet odor all year 'round. In the autumn, the sharp, pleasant smell of fallen oak leaves overwhelmed the other fragrances. Inside, the house had the special air of age: of old wood, of some rot, of damp in the stone-walled cellar. To Lisa, all of it was delicious.

She'd had a garden built in the back yard—"built" because each separate bed was a heavy oak frame containing black topsoil and manure, in which she grew a few tomatoes and some asparagus but mostly herbs and flowers. The mint, basil and rosemary, oregano, tarragon and dill, parsley, thyme, and sage that she used in her kitchen came from her own garden, as did the flowers on her table. Her friends marveled at her asparagus and at the quantity of strawberries she harvested from a layered conical bed. She covered her beds with clear plastic in early spring, and by late spring, when she removed the plastic, her little plants were healthy and well ahead of anyone else's.

She had gained such a reputation as an herb and flower gardener that she was invited to write a column for the Marietta *Times*. It appeared on Saturday every two weeks from early spring through early autumn.

Her octagonal study in the central tower was a center of her life, a very private place where she invited none of her friends, where even Ben and Benny rarely came.

The furniture she could have there was limited by the narrow spiral stairs. She had a dilapidated but comfortable couch and as many bookcases as she could cram into the space. Her desk was a table dominated by a big electric typewriter and cluttered with files and loose papers. This was where she wrote her gardening column. Also, since she had become known as a quick and articulate writer, she was appointed to write news releases and newsletters for every organization she joined, plus some she had never joined.

She had in past years struggled her way through two short stories, both of which had produced rejection slips, not even letters of encouragement. A New York friend had told her it was far more difficult to place a short story in a magazine than to publish a novel. So for the past four years she had been working desultorily on a novel, trying to incorporate the two short stories so the work she had done on them would not be wasted, then to expand and connect them to produce an account of a year in the life of a woman devoted to her family and home and friends and garden.

She felt inhibited in writing her novel. It would be called autobiographical, inevitably, and for that reason she had to give her heroine a life that she, Lisa, did not have. She could not portray a marriage that was now nothing better than habit, that was only comfortable, which was the best she could say for it. She could not write of a woman alone in her tower study, wiping tears of frustration from her cheeks with clenched fists. She could not write of a woman struggling to sublimate her disillusionment. She couldn't write what she felt. She wrote only desultorily because she had decided the novel could never be true so could never amount to much.

She was thinking of trying a mystery.

The tower study. A snug hideaway. But . . . Blue ink. The blue ink . . .

"Father, forgive me, for I have sinned."

"Yes, my daughter."

"Father, I tell you this first in the confidentiality of the confessional. It may be that I will need counseling or help beyond the confessional."

"We can perhaps share in making that judgment."

"Yes . . . I don't know how to start, how to describe—"

"In simple words. I will try to understand."

"Father, I think I am being visited by a demon."

"Describe the experience."

"It happens in my dreams. At first it was only at night. I dream that I am having carnal connection with a strange man, someone I don't know and can't identify. Then I wake, and I am certain he has been there with me, *really* there with me. I can feel it physically."

"This is not unusual. Are you married?"

"Yes. In fact, my husband is there with me in the bed when these dreams happen."

"These are fantasies. I believe you are only experiencing carnal fantasies that manifest themselves as vivid dreams. It is nothing terribly unusual. It is not even unusual that a woman should awake and retain in her body a palpable sense of having been violated. The mind and body are one, after all. The body often feels what the mind signals it should feel."

"I analyzed the problem the same way, Father. But there is more. I become drowsy in the middle of the afternoon. I am all but compelled to take a nap. I lie down on my couch. And he comes. He will not join me on the couch but lifts me off and puts me on the floor. Yesterday afternoon there were newspapers on the floor. I had used a ballpoint pen to work on the crossword puzzle. When I woke up, the newspaper was all wrinkled and torn, and the ink was smeared. Father, I found ink stains on my skin and on the inside of my underclothes."

"Yes . . . So you rolled off the couch and—"

"Father! I nap with my clothes on. The ballpoint ink was on my skin! Did I undress, roll on the floor, and dress again in my sleep?"

"It is not impossible. Sleepwalkers—"

"Undress? Lie on the floor and mimic the motions of sexual intercourse? Dress again?"

"I am searching for a rational explanation, something other than demonic possession."

"So am I, Father. So am I."

"Wear a crucifix when you sleep. I shall give you a little

holy water. Dab it on yourself, on your sexual parts especially, before you sleep."

"Yes, Father."

Lisa did as the priest at Saint Mary's said. That night the dream did not come. But since it didn't come every night, she did not take that as terribly significant. The next day she did not feel drowsy and did not take an afternoon nap. Again, it wasn't significant, because the experience did not come every day.

And the next night, still again, it didn't happen.

Thursday afternoon she played bridge at the Betsy Mills Club, a women's club occupying a handsome brick house at the edge of the college campus. She walked home. At four-thirty she was sleepy. Ben would not be home before six-thirty, so she went to her study and her couch to nap. Before she lay down, she dabbed holy water on her mouth and breasts and crotch. She wore her crucifix on a thin gold chain around her neck.

The dream came. The sex she dreamed was exhausting but totally satisfying, given with new vigor, demanding new vigor, and she gave her shadowy lover all he wordlessly demanded. She woke euphoric, glad to have known such joy.

Her crucifix— It hung on its chain from the lamp beside her desk, gently swinging, as if it had been touched and set in motion only a moment before. The little flask of holy water was empty.

Her euphoria turned to horror.

"You're here," she said as calmly as she could. "You must be here. What do you want? And why do you want it from *me?* Why me?"

"This thing hasn't hurt you, as I understand it. I mean . . . not physically."

"What about spiritually, Father?"

"Your soul remains in the hands of God, who holds you

12

blameless for what you cannot prevent, especially since you have not only confessed but have sought guidance. Have you spoken with your husband about this?"

"Of course I haven't told my husband. Except for the secrecy of the confessional, I wouldn't talk to *you.*"

"He would suggest what I am going to suggest."

"That I see a shrink. Forget it."

"You may need professional help."

"That's why I came to you. I am thinking of an exorcism."

"That is all but impossible."

"Father . . . In the circumstances, it would make more sense than psychoanalysis."

"I would need the permission of the bishop."

"Then get it."

"That may not be so easy. I am sure you know that the Church does not favor exorcisms. They are too . . . too—"

"Theatrical."

"Theatrical. Thank you. His Eminence will be most reluctant to grant to me the authority to perform an exorcism."

"Try, Father. I am as much interested as His Eminence must be in keeping the matter private, confidential. I don't want a public spectacle any more than he does."

"It will take time."

"I may not have much time."

"Surely—"

"I . . . may . . . not . . . have . . . much . . . time."

She sat in her octagonal study. She had pulled the blinds to shut out the greater part of the brilliant autumn sunshine, yet the room was warmly lighted and not gloomy. What was more, it was private, shut off from the view of neighbors and the street.

Lisa sat down on the couch. She fought back drowsiness.

"Well . . ." she said quietly. "Why can't I see you? Why can't you talk to me? Is it that you can't or that you won't? Should I be afraid of you? Why don't you tell me? Obviously

13

it makes no difference if I am afraid of you or not, since there is nothing I can do to stop your doing whatever it is you want to do. Why can't I be allowed to understand it?"

Silence. Motes of dust moved and gleamed in the beams of sunlight that streamed between the slats of the blinds, and for a moment she imagined she saw them begin to organize themselves into an image. Nothing. When people want desperately to see something, they can make themselves believe they see it; but a rational person will soon know the imagined is only the imagined.

"The crucifix is in the bedroom. The holy water is gone. I am not trying to keep you away from me. I am inviting you to appear and speak. I . . ."

She sighed loudly, conscious she was becoming languid. She would go to sleep. Only then would he come. In another dream.

She . . . She stood on Fourth Street, staring at the house. It was dusk. The house— It *was* the house, but something about it was very different. The trees were not the same, not placed the same, not the same size. And the light in front of the house had been moved. What was more, the gas mantle had apparently been broken, for instead of bright greenish light, a yellowish flame flickered behind the glass: a gas jet only, with no mantle. Similar warm yellowish light glowed from the first-floor windows, and as she watched, another room was lighted: her own bedroom.

A man walked along Fourth Street. He wore a beard and was dressed in black, with an exceptionally tall silk hat. As he passed Lisa, he swept the hat off and saluted her with it, and he bowed slightly.

"Good evening, Miss Tatum."

He turned in, unlatched a wrought-iron gate, and strode up the steps and along the walk to the second set of stone steps and the porch of the house.

The clop-clop of horses' hooves and the clatter of steel-tired wheels on the brick street filled the air. A carriage approached, carrying a man dressed much like the one who had just gone into the house, also a woman dressed in an elaborate dress with a bustle.

The man alighted and tied his horse's reins to the hitching post at the curb. Then he helped the woman down, and they walked to the gate. They noticed Lisa standing a little distance away, but they did not have to pass close to her and did not greet her—unless the man's brief nod in her direction was a greeting.

Obviously they saw nothing odd about her. She looked down at herself and found she was dressed like the woman who had just gone in. She touched her hair. It was ornately curled and held down by a bonnet.

The man she realized she was waiting for approached at last, walking briskly toward her on the brick sidewalk. "Good evening, Miss Tatum. I apologize abjectly for being late. My horse threw a shoe at the corner of Second and Putnam Streets, and I have had to walk from there."

"My father left me here ten minutes ago," Lisa heard herself saying in a voice sharpened by petulance. "He reminded me most emphatically that it is not correct for a young lady to loiter on the street. I forgive you in the circumstances, however."

The man was tall. He was in fact a fine figure of a man, probably ten years younger than she was, and handsome by anyone's standards: blond, wearing only a mustache and a scant beard along his jawline. His intent eyes were blue—a blue so pale it was all but unnatural. He, too, wore a tall silk hat, and the sort of old-fashioned necktie Lisa had seen in portraits of Abraham Lincoln, with a cardboard-stiff white shirtfront, fastened to his shirt by studs. His frock coat was not jet black but a dark gray, with black velvet inserts decorating his lapels.

She realized with a start that she knew his name. It was Roper. She did not know his first name.

He offered her his arm, and they walked into the house, where a score of people were mingling happily for some sort of party.

15

It was the same, her own home, yet so very different, its elegance eclipsed by florid ornamentation.

Gas jets lighted the rooms. Sometime later, some of the gas chandeliers had been fitted for electric light, and Lisa had kept them in the house, even against suggestions that they were not very good antiques and should be removed. She cherished some of them, particularly the ones of wrought iron, and here they were, burning gas as they had been designed to do, affording only dim, flickering light and staining the ceilings with greasy soot.

The pegged oak-plank floors she found so beautiful were all but hidden by an assortment of patterned rugs, each uglier than the other. The walls were covered with dark and ghastly silk and paper. The living room was crowded with chairs and settees, some upholstered in dark maroon plush, some in black horsehair. A piano dominated one side of the room, an organ the other. Every corner had a bric-a-brac shelf, half hidden by a potted palm.

"A charming home, is it not?" said Mr. Roper.

He was of a dream, so she dared speak under her breath, and say, "Hideous."

That he was of a dream was proved by his reaction. He smiled knowingly.

The elegantly mannered, sumptuously dressed people stank of sweat and worse odors, not overcome by copious quantities of artificial scents.

Mr. Roper and Miss Tatum were made welcome. Whoever she was, Lisa was known to these people, and her presence was no surprise. She detected, even so, a distancing of most of them from her. She was aware that something about her disturbed them.

She was aware, too, that none of them wished to offend her. Insincere though they were, they labored to make her feel welcome and one of them. They inquired of her family's health, and to her surprise she was able to answer, using names she had never heard before.

The party was unendurable. Although these people had supposedly assembled to enjoy themselves, a Methodist divine was called on to say a few words and to pray over them. He was conspicuously inarticulate, a fact that did not in the least detract from his pomposity. A woman who could not sing one individual note on tune sang nevertheless, accompanied by a man who caused the pump organ to bray like a jackass.

"Hideous," said Mr. Roper, whispering in her ear.

Lisa turned to him. She knew it was all hideous. Why did he and she alone know it?

"We need not stay," he said. "We have made a polite appearance. They don't like us, you know."

"Why?"

"They suspect."

"What do they suspect, Mr. Roper?"

She had not realized a simple smile could convey as much as did the smile she saw on his face. And so she knew. She had asked him to reveal himself, and he had.

"I do not understand," she said. They stood apart, where quiet conversation was possible, away from the sonorous voice of the Methodist preacher and the shrieks and groans from the woman and the organ. "Tell me what they suspect."

"That you and I are not of them."

"But I am. I was born and—"

Abruptly she realized she knew every one of these people. Suddenly her mind was flooded with what she did not need to know, did not want to know: who each one was, name and family and history. In an instant she was of this time and this place, and she was terrified she would not be able to escape from it.

He knew. "You are not of them, just the same," said Roper. "Any more than I am."

Jerked back into her dream, she said, "So . . . You are Mr. Roper. But how . . . ? Why? *Please!*"

He shook his head. Then he became indistinct. She was not sure if he walked away from her or if he faded into the air. But suddenly she was alone.

Alone . . . Yes, alone. Also, no longer in the house, no

longer at the party. Not in her study. In another house, in a room she had never seen before. She was wearing a floor-length skirt, not the elaborate one she had worn to the party but another one, simpler, drab in fact.

A stern, forbidding man stood before her. His anger flowed over her like a flood.

"Disgrace! Ignominy!" he barked.

"Father . . . ?"

"It is plain, of course, that you can never marry, Angelina. Not now. No decent man would accept you."

She was in a strange house, a strange room. A woman stood behind the man, weeping.

"Mr. Roper will marry me," she heard herself say.

"Mr. Roper has been driven from this town, with full understanding that if he ever dares return here he will suffer the penalties reserved for men of his character."

"I love him! He is the only man who ever loved me, and I love him!"

"You love the Devil!"

"He is not evil! I am carrying his child!"

The stern man, her father, did not slap her. He struck her with his fist. He broke a tooth, and she fell, and her mouth filled with blood.

Angelina shrieked. On the floor, on her hands and knees, she clutched her mouth, her jaw.

Lisa was alone. The setting sun shone through the slats of the blind. A car horn blared on the street below.

"My child, I have spoken with the Monsignor. He will speak with the Bishop."

"Father, I withdraw my request."

"You do not want the exorcism?"

"No. It was foolish of me to ask for it."

"What has changed your mind?"

"Father, the visions have ceased to come. My demon, if that was what he was, has abandoned me."

"That is very good news."

"I plead with you, Father, to forget the whole matter. I am

sure you have guessed who I am. I am sorry to have troubled you. Your concern has been of great value to me. I am sure, though, you can understand how difficult it would be for me to confess this experience to anyone but you. My husband must not know."

"I have not identified you to the Monsignor. Your confidence in me is the confidence of the confessional. Be careful. Do not hesitate to raise this subject again whenever you feel you should."

2

DREAMS. WHERE DO THEY BEGIN AND END? WHAT IS REAL?
Learned men have given much thought to questions like
this. When Freud interpreted dreams, what was he inter-
preting?

Interpret. When something is real, what is interpretation?

Lisa knew her dreams were much more than fantasies,
vapors of the imagination. She was left with two questions
greater than the other questions: Who was Mr. Roper? Why
did he come to *her?*

The next dream was horrible.

She was a witness; yet she was at the same time the person
whose tragedy she witnessed. She was two people, but she
was one person. She was an invisible presence, watching;
she was also the woman she was watching, since she knew
her thoughts and her feelings.

Angelina Tatum.

She was locked in a room on the third floor of a great brick
house. It was a servant's room, furnished only with a bed, a
nightstand with stoneware pitcher and basin, a chamber
pot, and a straight wooden chair. She sat on the chair. She
was modestly dressed in a black skirt and a plain white
shirtwaist. Her ankles were shackled by a short chain,

fastened on her with two heavy padlocks. She could wear no drawers, since they could not be changed without removing the chain, and no stockings, since the chain had torn the pair she was wearing when it was put on her. They had taken her shoes away from her, so her feet were bare.

Her father had done this to her. Her mother had consented. In fact, it was her mother who had knelt and locked the chain on her ankles while her father held her and stifled her hysterical cries with a hand over her mouth.

Angelina's powerful emotions in that dreadful moment of watching her own mother shackle her reached the dreaming witness Lisa, so that Lisa knew Angelina's every thought and feeling.

In that moment, that horrible moment, mother and daughter had communicated as they had never communicated before—or ever would again, as Lisa somehow was able to understand. Something passed between them, a silence in which the mother said, *I can help you, but I believe you know it is better that you help yourself,* and the daughter said, *I understand.* Lisa sensed, too, that both of them were surprised by this enigmatic exchange of understanding.

The moment ended when the locks were snapped shut and the chain was cruelly secure. Like an electromagnetic field that suddenly disintegrated when the current is interrupted, their understanding decayed and failed, and neither of them understood just what had happened.

So Angelina had sat down on her bed, staring unbelieving at the chain locked around her ankles, and then had closed her eyes against both parents as she wept. She had not opened her eyes until she heard the door closed and latched.

Looking around then, she had seen that she was alone, locked in and chained. Her tear-filled eyes had seen the room only as a blur. Yet—something had seized her attention. On the window sill. Lying there in the sunlight was the amulet! The heavy bronze amulet, maybe a talisman, was the image of a nude woman, probably a goddess, in the coils of a huge snake. The carving was so finely expressive that it could be seen that the woman was without fear, to the contrary accepted the embrace of the snake as though it shielded her, as it did indeed cover her most private part. The serpent's head was close to her face, as if it were adoring her. Jonathan Roper had worn it, on a bronze chain around his neck. She had seen it when he undressed to make love to her. And here it was! How? Oh, Lord, how? She had stumbled across the room, ankles jerking against her shackles, and seized it. An overpowering intuition had told her to hang the chain around her neck, letting the cool heavy amulet rest between her breasts.

Everyone condoned what her parents had done to her. The town condoned it, though it might not have if people had known she was shackled. The adulterer had been driven out of town, and the adulteress had been confined by her parents. It was the only thing to do.

She had been here three weeks.

Prayer had made her imprisonment easier. She thanked God for many things, most of all for her faith in Him and her confidence that He would make all things right. Her Father in Heaven had sustained her through worse things than being chained in a servant's room high up under the eaves of the house. He had sustained her through the shame of being . . . not left at the altar, really, but abandoned only two weeks before she was to have been married. He had helped her keep the secret of her sin with Caleb, who had begged her for her womanly favors before he went away to war, had taken them, had gone away and never written, and had died at Shiloh. If God had denied her anything, it was beauty. She was not drab but plain. That was the word she had always used for herself: plain. Being big and plain was, she was sure, God's test for her, against which she could testify to her faith or fail and suffer everlasting torment.

Her mother had brought her Testament to this room, though her father had ordered even that consolation withheld from her. It was through her mother's insistence, too, that the Reverend Dr. Agnew was allowed to visit her. It would be a sin, her mother had argued with her father, to deny Angelina the consolation of Holy Scripture and the ministrations of a man of God. Dr. Agnew sympathized with Angelina and promised to demand that her father remove the chain—in due time, when his wrath had cooled a bit. He reminded her, though, that she had committed mortal sin. Her punishment, though severe, was just.

She knew she had an extraordinary affiliation with God. He had given her strength sometimes to endure the unendurable—also insights that had enabled her even in these painful weeks to perceive the anguish behind her father's anger.

Above all, Her Father in Heaven had given her some quality she had never before possessed and did not understand. He had given a plain girl, beyond her best years, a means to attract the handsome young Jonathan Roper; and He had given her the courage to meet Jonathan's masculine demands long after she had come to believe she could never do that again. He had given her the will and vigor to commit carnal sin—and even to take joy from it. Above all, He had given her a child, which lived now inside her and would be born for some great purpose.

Angelina was at peace. Even the humiliation, the whole town knowing she was an adulteress confined to a room in her parents' home, did not torture her. (Dr. Agnew had assured her no one knew her ankles were chained; she was spared the shame of having that known.) She knew that somehow, even from all this, something good would come, for the Lord did nothing except for good.

And then the physician came to examine her, which was abhorrent. He told her father she really was pregnant, as she had said; it was not just hysteria.

If there was hysteria, it wasn't hers.

"No, no, no! No, you will not give birth to the bastard! It is not to be endured!"

"Will not? What do you mean to do, kill me?"

"Don't suppose I have not considered it. In a few minutes of selfish lust you destroyed what it took three generations to

23

build: name, reputation, the respect of the community. I am a ruined man, a laughingstock, the father of a slut who gave herself to . . . to a riverboat gambler."

"Mr. Roper is not a riverboat gambler."

"No? Then what is he? What is his calling? What was the source of his funds?"

"I don't know. He is from England."

"England! I will be surprised if he is from any farther place than Pittsburgh."

"He is not what you think."

"He is everything I think. The proof is in your belly."

"The child I am carrying—"

"You will not give birth to his bastard!"

"You can't prevent it. Nor could I, even if I wanted to. You can knock out my teeth. You can chain me in the servants' attic. But you can't stop the birth of a child. That is beyond your power."

"It is *not* beyond my power. There are ways."

"It would be a crime and a mortal sin!"

"You talk to *me* about sin?"

"What do you plan to do, pound my belly with your fists?"

"If necessary!"

She rose and walked across the room to the window, limited by her chain to short, awkward steps.

Her father spoke to her back in a low, sullen voice. "If Roper is not Satan, he is of Satan's legion. Bad enough it would be if every day of our lives we had to face your bastard, living in this house, as I suppose you would expect to do. Bad enough that the town would see it. But it would be a child of evil. *It must not be born!"*

She turned and faced him. She was alarmed by the cold anger in his voice.

He reached inside his coat and withdrew a small flask. "You will drink this," he said. "It will expel the evil thing from your belly. If it does not, then we will look to something else. But we will try this first. Drink it! All of it."

He thrust toward her the flask filled with ominous black fluid, something vile.

She shook her head.

"You . . . *will* . . . drink it," he growled. "If I have to, I will hold you down and force you."

She extended her hand, but instead of taking the flask she closed her hand around his wrist, astonishing herself as much as him by the brute power of her grip. Her father tried to jerk his arm back, but she was too strong for him. He roared and struggled. And then—

With a will she didn't know she had and with strength beyond imagining, she threw him. With one powerful sweep of her arm she threw him out the window. The sash and glass shattered as if from the force of an explosion, and glass, wood, and man plummeted to the ground.

She sat on a cot inside a pen—and a pen it was, made of heavy chain link stretched on a steel frame—in the county jail. Dr. Agnew stood outside. He wore black. So did she. Black had been forced on her. It was not what she had wanted to wear. She had faced this day with a white dress in mind: white, the color of innocence.

"Take comfort that the child—"

"Comfort! What is comfort, Doctor? What offers me comfort? My daughter will live in the custody of people who will hate my memory and teach the child to hate it, too. Is that supposed to bring me comfort?"

"My child, you murdered your own father! In a less just society you would be burned alive!"

The woman sitting on the cot in the pen was Angelina. She was Lisa, also. Lisa watched from outside the pen, as an invisible witness, but she was the woman inside the pen, too. She was a detached observer of her own ordeal. The distinction was not easy to maintain and understand.

The law . . . The law said that when a woman condemned to death proved to be pregnant with child, her execution would be postponed until the child was delivered, for the state would not take the life of the innocent baby with that of the guilty mother. After the baby was born, the woman would be executed as the law provided—grateful, it was supposed, for the suspension of sentence that allowed the child to be born.

This was the law that had been applied. Angelina had spent the past seven months in this pen. It was the women's quarters in the county jail. She had been convicted and sentenced and would have been hanged long ago but for her pregnancy and the mercy of the law. The baby had been delivered here by a doctor who had used chloroform to relieve her pain, for she was a little old to be giving birth for the first time. He had been assisted by the kindly wife of the sheriff.

Now, on the small green in front of the jail at Second and Putnam Streets in Marietta, a gallows had been erected.

It had been erected many times before, from the same parts, with the holes drilled and ready to receive the bolts that held it together. Executions were rare in a county of only a few more than thirty-nine thousand people, but they did take place, necessarily, two or three times a year.

"Do you accept Jesus Christ as your savior?"

Angelina voiced the dreadful conclusion to which she had come these past seven months. "I don't accept any god who would allow this to happen to me."

"Your defiance condemns you more than does your crime."

Suddenly she was outside the jail, in sunlight.

Lisa felt a reassuring hand gently tighten its grip on hers. Jonathan Roper had brought a surrey, and from their comfortable seat under its fringed canopy, he and Lisa could see the gallows. A few other citizens sat in carriages, too, but most of the people in the crowd—it was a mob, actually—shuffled their feet in the dust.

Suddenly the crowd moaned: an animal sound filled with so many different emotions that no one could be identified. That moan was their reaction to the sight of the woman now being led out of the jail by the sheriff and his loudly weeping wife.

She was dressed in black. Her hands were tied behind her. The rope circled her body as well, pinching her black dress tightly to her waist. She shuffled and stumbled, her head hung low, her eyes fixed on the ground.

Perhaps no one in the crowd noticed that the woman sitting beside the handsome blond man in the surrey might, except that she was taller and more full-figured, have been a twin of the woman being led to the gallows. Anyone who did notice undoubtedly dismissed the thought, for everyone knew that Miss Tatum was not a twin.

Lisa was prettily dressed. Her face was shaded by a ribboned bonnet. She did not want to watch what was about to happen. She did not like this dream. But she couldn't escape it. She could not even force herself to look away.

As she watched, the sheriff seized the woman under the arms and carried her up the traditional thirteen steps to the scaffold where the minister and a deputy waited. The deputy knelt and bound her ankles as she tottered and seemed about to fall.

The minister spoke to her and offered the Bible for her to kiss.

She shook her head!

A murmur rose from the crowd.

Now the sheriff lowered the noose over her head and drew it tight around her throat. He had to pull at the back of her hair to raise her chin so that the rope could go under it. Finally the sheriff covered her head with a black hood, which he secured with a string tied under her chin.

The minister stepped away from the woman. The sheriff stepped back and grabbed the lever that released the trap-door. With a dramatic movement of his arms and shoulders, he threw the lever.

The door slammed down with a great bang. The woman dropped.

Lisa spoke to Jonathan Roper in an awed, quiet voice. "Somehow I thought you'd save her."

"But of course I did," he said with an enigmatic smile.

The dreams became an obsession. Lisa pretended a new interest in the history of Marietta and troubled the librarians with requests for information.

The college library had files of old newspapers. They were not indexed but fortunately had been microfilmed. She spent two afternoons at the microfilm reader before she found what she wanted in the Marietta *Register* for Friday, November 6, 1868:

TRAGIC SCENE!

Public Hanging of Miss Tatum
Witnesses Weep
As Justice Is Done

As many as a thousand citizens of the vicinage, few of them dry-eyed, witnessed the dramatic public execution on Wednesday morning of Miss Angelina Tatum, condemned to die for the murder of her father, Colonel Josiah Tatum. Although the necessity of the hanging was denied by none, few could suppress painful feelings of sympathy for the condemned, and more than a few, including some men, fainted as Miss Tatum dropped to her untimely and disgraceful death at the end of a rope.

It may be hoped that the painful and shameful death of Miss Tatum will stand as a moral lesson to the younger citizens of the community, who should take note that her crime and punishment were the consequences of her infatuation and illicit connection with a traveling man, who, it should be emphasized, abandoned her to her fate and lifted not a finger to assist or comfort her in her travail. Let every young woman note the consequences of liaisons with the sort of men who come and go on the packets.

Miss Tatum caused the death of her father by pushing him from a high window. He plunged to his death on a flagstone walk between his handsome residence and his carriage house.

Colonel Josiah Tatum was one of the most respected and useful citizens of the community. A Methodist by faith, a Freemason for fellowship, a Republican for his politics, he was a veteran of the late War of the Rebellion, in which he served initially as a captain, before rising to the rank of colonel before the war ended. He saw action at such battles as Antietam Creek and Gettysburg.

Mrs. Tatum left this community for her home in Kentucky shortly after her husband's death and her daughter's incarceration. She has made no contact with anyone here since her departure.

The unhappy Miss Tatum gave birth to a love child three weeks before her execution, the hanging having been deferred so that the child might be born. The child, a female, is at present a resident of the Washington County Children's Home. It is hoped that some family will elect to adopt her.

Compulsorily dressed in black, Miss Tatum went to her death without visible tears. She is reported to have resisted the consolation of prayer. She is reported to have turned her head away from the Bible offered her to kiss just before the hood cut off her last view of the world.

Tightly bound with rope, she required assistance in climbing the steps to the gallows. As the Reverend Dr. Horace Agnew spoke to her, Miss Tatum glanced around and twice nodded, as if she had caught the eye of some friend in the crowd and was saying good-bye. When the trapdoor was sprung, she dropped to the end of the hangman's rope. The rope cracked loudly, nearby witnesses said. Miss Tatum was not heard to choke or offer the slightest sound. She did not kick or jerk around at the end of the rope, as some executed men have been known to do. The sheriff acknowledged later that he had been concerned that the slight woman's weight might not be sufficient to make a "clean" execution, and he had considered hanging a pair of sandbags around her waist to be sure. His decision not to do so was apparently correct.

Miss Angelina Tatum was just thirty-nine years old and had been a maiden until her unhappy connection with Mr. Jonathan Roper. It may be hoped that her death will serve to discourage other girls from risking the consequences of sin.

As we write, her body remains unclaimed. If it is not claimed today, it will be deposited in an unmarked grave, at the expense of the county.

As Lisa had dreamed it. In every detail, as she had dreamed it.

The next week's edition of the newspaper noted that no one had come forth to claim the body of Angelina Tatum and that it had been buried in an undisclosed location in a canvas bag, since the county had no funds for paupers' coffins.

Lisa knew the name of the family that had built the house: Warren. The lawyer who checked the title had given the Hamiltons an abstract of title, and it was easy to see that the house was built by another man with the title colonel: Colonel J. M. Warren.

She threaded back through the issues of the *Register* until she came to a social note:

The Fourth Street residence of Colonel and Mrs. Warren was the scene on Tuesday evening of a delightful party, much enjoyed by all the guests. Given in honor of the birthday of Miss Henrietta Warren, the party was attended by two score guests, many of them members of the younger set.

The Reverend Dr. Horace Agnew was present to offer

proper sentiments and to organize innocent games for the amusement of the guests.

Among the guests were Miss Dorothy Warren, escorted by Mr. Donald Gilchrist; Miss Judith Frazer, who came with her parents, Dr. and Mrs. Frazer; and Miss Angelina Tatum, who was escorted by Mr. Jonathan Roper, a guest in our city from London, England.

Lisa read quickly, scanning the names of the people she had seen in her dream of the party. And . . .

Jonathan. Jonathan Roper. It was he, of course, not poor Angelina Tatum, who had thrown Colonel Josiah Tatum from the third-floor window: he acting through the woman, for the moment given demonic strength.

Lisa thanked the librarian who had helped her locate the newspaper microfilms. She walked out onto the campus of Marietta College, into bright sunlight that seemed to cleanse her mind and body. She walked home and climbed to her study.

Why? Why had Roper come to her? Would he make her pregnant as he had made Angelina pregnant? Had he done it to Angelina in a dream? Why would he choose a thirty-nine-year-old woman to make pregnant? A forty-one-year-old woman to make love with? What did he want? What was his purpose?

More than that, why had he chosen to reveal so much of himself to her? What purpose did he fulfill by showing her what he had done to Angelina Tatum?

Roper . . . Tatum . . .

In a bottom drawer of her desk in her octagonal study lay a file, one she had not glanced at for years. It was an incomplete and amateurish collection of genealogical information. She had made a chart of Ben's family, so far as the Hamilton family knew it. Ben was descended from a Scots family that immigrated to Connecticut in the late eighteenth century, after the Revolution. Lisa glanced down the chart. There were no Ropers, no Tatums.

She turned to the chart of her own maternal family:

31

Elizabeth (Lisa) Catherine O'Neil (b. 1951, m. *Benjamin O. Hamilton*) is the daughter of . . .

Mary Kathleen Horan (b. 1925, m. *John C. O'Neil*) is the daughter of . . .

Elizabeth Catherine Kennedy (1899–1977, m. *Patrick Horan*) was the daughter of . . .

Elizabeth Mary Spencer (1868–1951, m. *Sean Kennedy*) was the daughter of . . .

Elizabeth Christina Dugan (1839–88, m. *Timothy Spencer*) was the daughter of . . .

Kathleen Mary Finn (1821–70, m. *Charles Dugan*) arrived in Philadelphia from Ireland, likely from County Cork, in 1834.

This was the main line of the chart, as it interested Lisa—and she had always been, for no reason she was conscious of, far more interested in her maternal descent than in her paternal ancestors. Obviously all the women had borne more children than just those eldest daughters. Lisa herself had two brothers and a sister. Sometimes she regretted that she'd had no daughter and so had allowed the mother-daughter line to run out after so many decades.

Anyway, among all those names there was no Tatum and no Roper.

She had added some notes to the chart, which she had made while her grandmother was still alive. The Sean Kennedy who married Elizabeth Mary Spencer was a lawyer in New York City. The Spencers were a Philadelphia family, and how Elizabeth Mary came to meet the New York lawyer was nowhere recorded. In any event, it was a brilliant marriage, according to family tradition. The Spencers were solid, prosperous people, but Kennedy, though remembered as a somewhat flashy character, made a great deal of money and moved in heady financial and social circles. The next generation, Elizabeth Catherine Kennedy, was sent to Smith College, which established a tradition followed by the following generations that the eldest daughters in the line would graduate from Smith.

Lisa stared at the chart and at her notes. There was no place on the chart for Jonathan Roper, none for Angelina Tatum, none in fact for anyone from Marietta, Ohio.

Even so, on impulse, she lifted her telephone and called her mother in Chappaqua, New York.

"Question," she said after a few minutes' chat. "Does the name Tatum mean anything to you?"

"No. I don't recall ever having heard that name."

"All right. What about the name Roper?"

Mary O'Neil was silent for a moment. Then she sighed. "I haven't heard that name in more than forty years."

"Well, who is it? Who was it?"

"You're too young to remember your Great-grandmother Kennedy, or your great-grandfather, either, for that matter. She was a magnificent old lady, lived into her eighties. It's too bad you couldn't have known her."

"I used to wonder if we were related to the Boston Kennedys."

"We talked about that. If there's a connection, it's very distant. My Grandfather Kennedy was fascinating, too: as Irish as any man could be. Red hair. A brogue."

"Mother . . . how does the name Roper come in?"

"I only heard the name one time, only once in my life—but in circumstances that made me remember it. Grandmother Kennedy was on her deathbed. It was tradition, you know, for the family to assemble. A ghastly tradition. Anyway, I was there. The priest was beside her. So was the doctor. She had been slipping in and out of consciousness for two days, but the periods of consciousness were becoming shorter, and her breathing became weaker. It was obvious that she was going. I was twenty-six. You were three months old and at home with your father. My mother was crying. So were the aunts and cousins. And just at the end Grandmother Kennedy opened her eyes and smiled, as if she had just recovered and might live ten more years. She spoke distinctly. And she said, 'Thank you, Mr. Roper. It has been wonderful.' Those were her last words. She closed her eyes again and died with a happy smile on her face."

Lisa shuddered. For an instant she had the impression that Roper was there in the room with her.

"Mother . . . Did anyone in the family ever mention the name Angelina?"

"No. No, I have never heard that name."

"I'm going to ask you another question. Please don't think I'm nuts. Please don't think the question is too personal. Have you ever dreamed that a strange man comes to you in the night and makes love to you?"

Lisa's mother laughed. She was known for, inter alia, a distinctive laugh, at once melodious and generous, yet a little out of tune, because behind it there was a distinct suggestion of scorn. It irritated people. She knew it did, and she tried not to laugh aloud. But now she did, and Lisa heard the discordant Mary O'Neil snicker.

"Well?"

"Lisa . . . Lisa honey, did any woman ever live who didn't have that dream?"

"Then you do have it?"

"Of course. And men have it. They dream they're making love to a strange woman. Why do you ask? Have you just experienced it for the first time at your age? If so, you must have had a supremely happy sex life with Ben."

"Does it happen to you often?"

"Not at my age, very often. It used to, occasionally."

"Could you ever recognize the man?"

"No. I never knew who he was."

"Did you ever have a sense that he was real, not just a dream?"

"I suppose that's always a part of it."

"But you never doubted it was a dream?"

"No. What's the matter, Lisa? Do you have a sense that you're committing adultery in your sleep?"

"So much so that I confessed it."

"And what did the priest say?"

"That it wasn't a sin and that I should see a shrink."

"Maybe you should."

"Maybe I will."

"Maybe you should come home and see one here. There's a woman over in Greenwich who's very good. She might understand you better than a man could."

"I'll think about it. There's not a shrink in this area that I'd want to talk with. I'll give it some real thought, Mother."

"All right. Don't let it bother you too much. It's perfectly normal."

"Thank you. I feel better for having talked with you."

"Any time, Lisa. Any time."

Lisa put the phone down. Normal? Normal to find ballpoint ink smeared over the skin of your bottom? Normal to dream about a hanging that occurred a century and a quarter ago and then find a newspaper account of that hanging, identical in every detail?

She found herself drenched with sweat, though the room was cool.

"Jonathan Roper . . ." she whispered wearily. "What do you want from me?"

Ben Hamilton had lost most of his hair before he was thirty. Other than for that, he was much the same man she had married: tall, muscular, slender, brown-eyed, purposeful, organized, effective. It was only after they had been married some years that she realized he was also literal, predictable, and unoriginal. Her mother's description of Ben was accompanied by the Mary O'Neil wicked laugh. "He is a *good* man. Too damned good."

He was a graduate of Groton, then of M.I.T. with a degree in chemical engineering, later of Harvard with an M.B.A.— these degrees honorably obtained but without any *laudes* attached. He had played lacrosse and had been disappointed that none of the towns where they had lived had afforded his son an opportunity to play. He didn't know what Lisa knew, because her son—typical son—confided in his mother more than he ever did in his father: that Benny would never have played lacrosse, which he considered muddy, sweaty, and apt to produce bruises. Had he not been so devoted to lacrosse, Ben would have played rugby, and he loved to quote a saw he had heard somewhere—he didn't know where—which went, "Rugby is a game for hoodlums played by gentlemen. Football is a game for gentlemen played by hoodlums. Hockey is a game for hoodlums played by hoodlums."

Ben was also a man who could go to Rotary meetings, talk and laugh with his table companions, listen to the speeches, and go back to his office with a self-congratulatory sense that he'd spent his lunchtime profitably. He was a man who listened attentively to sermons.

He was not the kind of man with whom you could discuss the invasion of your mind and body by . . . Well, by whatever Jonathan Roper was.

"Ben . . . Would you mind if I fly up to Chappaqua and spend a week, maybe ten days, with Mother?"

"Not at all. Uh . . . Is there any particular reason for going right now?"

She shrugged. "I don't know. I've been feeling uneasy . . . nervous. I thought maybe—"

"I've noticed you toss in the night. And mumble."

"Do I say anything?"

"You mention the name—or word—Roper." He lifted his chin. "I'll make a confession. I checked the telephone directories—Marietta, Parkersburg, Saint Marys—to see if I could find anyone named Roper."

"How trusting. So what did you find?"

"No Roper. When do you want to leave?"

"Not this week. Maybe the middle of next week."

"I wish I could go. But you know how it is. Always something."

"Sure. Always something. You're a good man, Ben. You don't neglect those somethings."

She returned to the college library. The woman who helped her there was curious about her by now and was inspired by her curiosity to be even more helpful.

"Colonel Josiah Tatum . . . Yes, yes, he was murdered. By

his own daughter, an old maid who lived with him. She was hanged in front of the jail, which is where the old First National Bank Building now stands, at Second and Putnam. Is that what you were looking at in the files of the *Register?* Interesting story, not much explored. The town didn't like it much, as you can imagine. For fifty years there were people who didn't want to talk about it. Josiah Tatum's younger brother lived on for many years after the colonel was killed. I'd guess people didn't talk much about the Tatum murder until old Harman Tatum died."

Lisa learned that in 1902 a history of Washington County had been published. The funding for this enterprise came chiefly from sponsors, whose biographical statements were published in the back of the book as "Representative Citizens." Among the representative citizens who lauded themselves there was Harman Tatum. Lisa read his statement:

Harman F. Tatum, a prosperous farmer and oil producer of Wolf Creek, Washington County, was born September 7, 1830, in Marietta, where his father, Josiah Tatum, Sr., operated a woolen manufactory.

The subject of this sketch was educated in the common schools and attended Marietta Academy for a term. He took employment in his father's business and continued there after the death of his father, when control of the business passed to his elder half brother, Josiah Tatum, Jr.

On the outbreak of the War of the Rebellion, both brothers volunteered for service in the Union Army. Harman Tatum enrolled as a second lieutenant, served in Company D, Sixty-third Regiment, and was mustered out early in 1863, having contracted a debilitating disease of the lungs. For reasons of health, he elected not to return to the family business or live in Marietta but purchased the 270-acre farm which has since been his residence and principal occupation.

He was united in marriage in 1867 to Miss Emeline Tupper, daughter of the distinguished Ohio family. They are the parents of twelve children.

His elder brother, Colonel Josiah Tatum, was the victim of murder in the year 1868. Colonel Tatum, who was born in 1809, had been united in marriage in 1824 to Miss Honor Trowbridge, a subject of the British monarchy, whose parents had brought her to this country only a year before. After the tragic death of Colonel Tatum, Mrs. Tatum repaired first to her parents' home in Lexington, Kentucky but eventually returned to London, England, where she died in 1899.

Harman Tatum is a Methodist by faith, an Oddfellow, and a devoted supporter of the principles of the Republican Party.

And so on. The autobiographer chose not to mention the fact that his niece killed his brother and was hanged for it, nor did he mention the child born to Angelina Tatum shortly before she was hanged.

The librarian—she had introduced herself as Miss Whitaker—could shed no light on the fate of the child. "That record would be in the files of the Probate Court. Even if it survives, it's a sealed record. You can't see it. Oh . . . There is one thing. The records of the old Children's Home . . . I have some of those records here."

A crumbling ledger book covering the years from the founding of the orphanage until 1875 produced a brief entry: "Baby Tatum. Received as infant girl, October 17, 1868. Given no name, pending claim by family or adoption. Adopted, discharged, January 11, 1869."

Miss Whitaker smiled and shook her head. "What wouldn't we give to know who adopted that little girl? But I don't think there's any way to find out."

3

THE HOUSE IN CHAPPAQUA WAS NOT LISA'S HOME. HER MOTHER called it home, but it wasn't hers either. Situated below the road in a grove of trees behind low stone walls, it was the house John C. O'Neil had decided he could afford in 1981, where he had moved a family that did not include his eldest daughter, because she was already a wife and mother. Lisa had been assigned a room in the house and called it hers, as her parents wanted her to do, but she had never thought of it as her home. Her home, if she'd really had one before she and Ben bought the Gothic Grotesque in Marietta, had been a house not nearly so grand in Greenwich, just across the state line in Connecticut. The O'Neils had been crowded there, but they had been a warm, supportive family.

Lisa's father was a bond trader. He made his money in mysterious ways she could never understand, no matter how many times he explained it. She and Ben had visited his desk on the bond-trading floor of Salomon Brothers, had listened to him shrieking expletives into the telephone and doing deals that . . .

Well, the best thing that ever happened to him, financially, as he said, was the Arab oil embargo. It had raised his income from about a quarter of a million a year to a million and a half. He had retired two years ago, a very wealthy man in spite of heavy losses on his own investments. What was more, not a speck of taint had ever adhered to him.

"Why steal," he had often said, "when they throw money at you in buckets?"

He'd had, it was said of him on Wall Street, what the Germans called *Fingerspitzengefühl,* a genius instinct in the tips of his fingers for feeling out strong points and weak points and deciding on the basis of a mystic intuition he could not explain.

Knowing that Lisa was coming, her mother had arranged an appointment for her with the psychiatrist she had mentioned on the telephone. That was tomorrow. They did not mention it to John O'Neil as they sat over dinner and were served by the houseman and his wife.

Late in life O'Neil had developed an interest in and a taste for good wine. There were two bottles on the candlelit table, and he examined his glass by holding it up and squinting at a candle flame through the wine.

Lisa interrupted his wine reverie. "Have you ever heard of a family named Tatum?" she asked.

Her father shook his head. "Hell, Liz," he said—he had always called her Liz, which he insisted was the proper nickname for Elizabeth—"in my line of business, you come across a hundred thousand names, I suppose, in the course of your life. I can't say I remember ever having heard the name Tatum."

"Trowbridge?" she asked, glancing at both her father and mother.

"Oh, sure. There are Trowbridges around. Can't put my finger on one."

"English family."

"I daresay."

The room her mother said was Lisa's could have been a room in a motel. She was pleased to retreat to it about ten o'clock, even so. She had flown a commuter plane to Pittsburgh, from there taken a flight to La Guardia, and then taken the limousine to White Plains, where her parents had met her and driven her the final ten miles to Chappaqua—a tough day's traveling.

She stretched out on the bed in her clothes, thinking she would work on the *New York Times* crossword puzzle, which she had saved for her nights in Chappaqua and had carried in her luggage. Maybe she would be awake long enough to watch the eleven o'clock news. Seeing the local evening news on WCBS, WNBC, or WABC was one of the few things she had missed since leaving the metropolitan area, now that she was so well settled into her Marietta life. She couldn't remember when she had last seen a live TV news story about a gang hit. She longed for another look at the craggy face of Jim Jensen.

Ten minutes after she lay down, she was asleep. And the dream came.

"Jonathan Roper, you might as well show yourself to me. I know who you are."

Once again she was a witness to herself, sitting apart, seeing herself lying on her own bed. But her view of herself was partially blocked by the naked body of the man who faced the Lisa on the bed. His back was to her, but this was the most vivid image she'd had of him during one of his carnal visits. She had seen him at the Henrietta Warren birthday party and at the hanging, but still when he came to her, he came obscure.

He turned and faced her—that is, he turned away from the Lisa on the bed and faced the witness Lisa. She looked down and could not see herself.

But she could see him. He was the handsome man at the party and in the carriage at the hanging. Only he was naked, wearing nothing but an odd, heavy bronze amulet on a chain around his neck. He was the ideal of an athletic young man. Athletic, yes, but not muscle-bound, not bulky. Lithe. Her eyes dropped to his loins. Yes. Like Michelangelo's *David.*

"My great-grandmother died with your name on her lips," she said.

He did not speak. He turned to the Lisa on the bed and gently, deftly stripped her of her clothes. Then he mounted her and drove his manly organ into her.

Her consciousness, if that was what it was, moved to the Lisa under the man. She was even aware that a vague image of herself was sitting across the room watching as she received the man and joined him in the act.

In a minute or so he was finished, and he moved aside and sat down on the bed. The witnessing Lisa came to life again, watching him caress the other Lisa's naked thighs and breasts.

"What do you want?" asked the witness Lisa.

He stood up, came to her in one quick stride, and embraced her. He kissed her lovingly on the mouth and on the throat. Then he lifted her and carried her to the bed. As he lowered her, she merged with the bed Lisa. He caressed her cheek and forehead for a brief moment and then was gone.

"Every bit of it, including the physical manifestations, could be mental," said Dr. Frances Gerard. "You understand that? They could be—"

"How can I have dreamed every detail of an execution that happened in 1868?"

Dr. Gerard shook her head. "Do you remember the book that got so much attention thirty-five years or so ago, *The Search for Bridey Murphy?* The woman, though she had no conscious memory of them, had heard as a child the stories that came back to her under hypnosis and made her believe she had lived in another incarnation. I don't say that explains your phenomenon, but it is possible that sometime in your life you read the account of a hanging on a town square somewhere. Now you live in Marietta, the town has made an impression on you, and you have subconsciously merged the two impressions. Is that impossible?"

"Why did my great-grandmother speak to Mr. Roper in the last moment of her life?"

"Someone told you that story when you were a small child. You had forgotten it, but it left an impression. So you have named this dream man Roper."

"And the ballpoint ink?"

"I don't know. But there could be a rational explanation. I would look for any explanation that is rational before I accepted the irrational."

Instead of meeting in her office, Lisa and Dr. Gerard were sitting over lunch at Bertrand's, a fine and expensive restaurant in Greenwich. That had been Dr. Gerard's suggestion.

Dr. Frances Gerard was Lisa's age, roughly. She was a tall woman without much figure—that is, without prominent breasts, which seemed to define "figure" for most people. She wore her mousy blonde hair in a style Lisa did not favor: stuck close to her head by a hairdresser who must have sprayed it heavily once a week. She was a graduate of Vassar, then of Harvard Medical.

"We are educated," said Dr. Gerard, "to seek rational explanations for the inexplicable. That is the definition of science, after all, is it not? Scientists look for facts and relate them by reason, to eliminate uncertainty. I do not say to you absolutely that you cannot be the victim of demonic possession."

"But why me?" Lisa asked. "If he is something beyond the realm of reason, what is there about me that brings Jonathan Roper to me—in my dreams, if that is all they are?"

"I would like to find an explanation for the inexplicable facts," said Dr. Gerard. "The dream of a hanging that actually happened. The ballpoint ink. If we can find the explanations of those, we can solve the mystery."

Lisa lowered her fork, putting back on her plate a morsel of succulent lobster. "He came to me last night," she said. "The usual way. Dually. I was both witness and participant. He made love to me. I sat apart and watched. At the same time, I did it. Exactly as it was when I was a witness to my own hanging. Do you understand, *I saw myself hanged!*"

Dr. Gerard glanced around, making it apparent that whether the subject was hanging or hangnails, she did not want to make a fuss in a Greenwich restaurant.

Lisa sighed. "I'm sorry. I'm not hysterical. I really am not. But I have to wonder if he's going to make me pregnant. He did that to Angelina Tatum. And he was supernatural then. He gave that little woman the strength to throw her father out the window. The town supposed she'd pushed him out, but I saw her *throw* him out. I saw it!"

Dr. Gerard glanced around the room, then frowned and leaned a little closer to Lisa, to ask a quiet question. "I'm sorry to have to ask this question, but . . . this man, Jonathan Roper. How does he feel?"

"What do you mean?"

"Well . . . Dammit. All right. What about his male organ? How does it *feel?*"

Lisa flushed. "It feels good," she whispered. "I mean . . . he does what he's supposed to do."

"What about its size?"

Lisa shrugged. "Ordinary. I don't have an extended frame of reference."

"Cold?"

"No. What are these questions?"

"Can you read French?"

"Yes. Haltingly."

"I'll lend you three books. Read in them and see what you think."

Not until late that evening did Lisa have time to examine the old books. The first—*Discours des Sorciers* by Henri Boguet—was an early nineteenth-century reprint of a book that had been originally published late in the sixteenth century. She sat on her bed, with a French dictionary from her parents' library to help her, and began to read the part Dr. Gerard had recommended to her. The antique French was difficult to translate:

*L'accouplement de Satan auce le Sorcier est réel et
non imaginaire. Les confessions des Sorciers que j'ay eu
en main, me font croire qu'il en est quelque chose.
L'autant qu'ils ont tout recogneu, qu'ils auoient esté
couplex auec le Diable, & que la semeuce qu'il iettoit
estait fort froide . . .*

"His semen is very cold . . ." Lisa saw the point behind
the psychiatrist's question.
She continued translating:

Iaquema Paget, who confessed to holding the demon's member in her hand many times, always recog-
nizing it for what it was, testified that the member was
cold as ice, about as long as a finger, and less thick than
that of a man: Tieuenne Paget and Antoine Tornier
testified also that the member of their Demons was as
long and thick as one of their fingers.

Another small book was in English translated from Latin.
Lisa read a passage from the *Praxis Confessariorum* by Saint
Alphonsus Liguori: "Some deny that there are evil spirits,
incubi and succubi, but writers of weight, eminence and
learning, for the most part lay down that such is verily the
case."

A passage from *De Demonialitate* by a Franciscan brother, Ludovico Maria Sinistrari, read:

It is undoubted by Theologians and philosophers
that carnal intercourse between mankind and the demon sometimes gives birth to human beings; and that
is how Antichrist is to be born, according to some
doctors. They further observe that, from a natural
cause, the children thus begotten by Incubi are tall,
very hardy and bloodily bold, arrogant beyond words,
and desperately wicked.

* * *

"You can call me Frankie," said Dr. Frances Gerard. "Friends do."

This time they were meeting in the psychiatrist's office in downtown Greenwich.

"There's no nickname for Lisa, I'm afraid. In fact, it *is* a nickname—for Elizabeth."

"Maybe you're lucky. Anyway, did the books help?"

"Yes, I suppose so."

"My idea was to let you read about the characteristics of the traditional incubus so you could compare him with your dream lover. He is not the same, is he?"

Lisa shook her head. "He's not cold. Not at all. And he's well enough hung."

"So he's a dream of a real man, then? So can we put aside, for now anyway, the idea that we're dealing with something supernatural?"

"But, Frankie, wait a minute. Suppose Jonathan Roper *is* a supernatural being . . . An incubus. Say even Satan himself. What does that make me?"

Dr. Gerard smiled. "The whole notion is beyond silly, isn't it?"

"It would make me what?" Lisa persisted. "A *sorcier!* Translate it, Frankie! That would make me—"

"A witch."

"Yes," said Lisa. "That's what the learned authors said, isn't it?"

"Lisa . . . Isn't it obvious to you that you're not a witch?"

Lisa forced out a discordant laugh. "If I were, I should have powers, shouldn't I? And I have none . . . that I know of. I mean, I've had hunches that turned out valid, and like that. Who hasn't? I remember having a frightening intuition about my son once. I was sure something had happened to him, that he was injured; and within minutes I got a call from the town emergency squad, saying he'd hit his head on a diving board and was being taken to the emergency room. Don't we all have those premonitions that sometimes turn out true? We remember the ones that turned out true and forget a thousand others that didn't. You don't need witch powers for that. I can't make cows give sour milk. I can't make hens lay sterile eggs. I can't forecast the weather any better than I get it on television." She paused and grinned. "Anyway, I don't think I can. I've never tried, come to think of it."

"I would like to turn the conversation away from myth and superstition," Dr. Gerard said firmly. "There is a rational explanation for your problem. You know that, and I know it. I wanted you to read a little from the old books to see how silly they are. Lisa, some very learned priests four hundred years ago justified their belief in incubi and succubi, witches, and children born of demonic unions by asking how else anyone could explain the birth of Martin Luther!"

"Who himself believed in witches," said Lisa. "As did Saint Augustine and Saint Thomas Aquinas."

"Are you suggesting you believe in witches?"

"No, but let me tell you something more I've learned. I asked my mother about my great-grandmother, the one who seemed to be speaking to Mr. Roper with her last breath. Maybe it means nothing—probably it means nothing—but my mother says my Great-grandmother Elizabeth Kennedy was a strapping big woman, tall and husky. She had a reputation for being outspoken. What did Sinistrari write? Remember? 'The children begotten by Incubi are tall, very hardy, and bloodily bold.'"

"I hope you're not suggesting your great-grandmother was a witch."

"No, of course not. But there is one more thing. Great-grandmother Kennedy was a blonde. Blondes are unusual in our family. But Roper is blond."

"Lisa, I'd rather be looking for the rational causes of your dreams."

"I want to eliminate these other possibilities. Eliminate the irrational before searching for the rational."

"All right," said Dr. Gerard, a faint hint of annoyance in her voice. "Is there anything else?"

"Well . . . Actually, for the moment, no."

"The name Roper. You've heard it in your dreams. As best you can remember, you never heard it awake until your mother told you your great-grandmother spoke it just before her death. Think about that. Explore your memory. Your mother was impressed by the mention of the mysterious name. Maybe she talked about it, maybe with your father, and you overheard."

"I was three months old."

"That doesn't necessarily mean you were unable to retain something of what may have been a somewhat emotional conversation. More likely you overheard your mother tell the story later, maybe when you were two or three years old. You don't remember. She doesn't remember mentioning it in front of you. But the fact that your great-grandmother mentioned Roper on her deathbed may have left an impression on you that you've retained subconsciously. Is that impossible?"

"I suppose it's not impossible."

"Erotic dreams are not at all unusual. Typically the dreamed sex partner is vague, and when you waken you can't remember what he looked like. That's how you said it was with Roper at first. But when these dreams continue, it is not unusual for a person to dredge a memory out of the subconscious and give the dream person the characteristics of someone forgotten."

It seemed to Lisa that Frankie Gerard was building a psychobabble structure hardly any better founded in reason than her own suspicion of supernatural intervention in her life. The doctor's determination to find explanations based on natural causes was hardly, if at all, more rational than the church fathers' determination to look for mystic causes. Science itself, she had read somewhere, is a religion.

"What's the origin of your own interest in incubi and succubi and witches and all the rest?" Lisa asked. "The books you lent me aren't usually found in a doctor's library."

"I've been practicing psychiatry for sixteen years. You are my eighth patient with a suspicion of demonic possession. Two of the others were very well versed in the mythology, and I found I couldn't deal with them unless I learned something about it, too."

"Did you cure them of the delusion?" Lisa asked.

Dr. Gerard's crisp little smile said she did not much care for the question. "No, as a matter of fact. Not those two. And not another one. The other four, yes."

"What became of those three?"

"One of them is in prison. She killed her husband. In fact, it was at the New York correctional facility for women at Bedford Hills that I first saw her. They called me in to try to cure her of the delusion and make her a more tractable inmate. It didn't work. She is still incorrigible."

"Her demon won't let go," said Lisa dryly.

"That's how she explains it. One of the others is dead. She died of natural causes at age seventy-eight, still believing she was a witch, still telling how she flew around the world at night. I've lost track of the third woman. She moved away."

"The other four were . . ."

"Psychiatric hypochondriacs. A large number of patients are cured simply by getting a sympathetic hearing. Their spouses or families won't listen to their hysterical maundering. The psychiatrist listens, gives them some kind of assurance, and they walk away happy. They come back six months later with a new delusion, like physical hypochondriacs, who are unhappiest when newly cured and are obsessed with finding a new disease, so they'll have something to talk about."

"To put things in perspective," said Lisa, "you are the first psychiatrist I have ever consulted. And probably the last."

"I'm the only one you'll ever meet who has a sense of humor."

Lisa grinned and chuckled. Then abruptly she turned serious. "Frankie . . . Who is Jonathan Roper? What does he mean?"

Dr. Gerard stared at her for a moment, then asked, "Would you submit to hypnosis as part of an effort to find out?"

Two days later Lisa lay on a comfortable couch. She had just come out of the hypnosis and was sipping a glass of cold ginger ale through a curved straw, and she was oddly exhausted, for no reason she could perceive. Dr. Gerard had rewound the tape she'd made of the session. Lisa had consented to hypnosis and to the recording on condition that she be allowed to hear the tape.

Her voice sounded thin, but she knew it was her own voice:

—This is what Freud objected to, what he called the hocus-pocus of it. But okay. I'll go along. I know it can't possibly work if I don't cooperate.

Frankie Gerard's voice sounded more nearly normal:

—That's right. So just watch the lights move. Don't think of what they're for. Just watch. Let yourself be entertained by them.
—Frankie . . .
—Umm?
—I'm afraid.
—Everyone is. And no one has ever been harmed by hypnosis. Can you see a pattern in the way the lights move and blink? Don't strain to see one. Just watch closely and see if you do.

Lisa recalled from a college psychology lecture that Freud had called hypnosis hocus-pocus. After an early fascination with it, he had concluded it was an ineffective diagnostic technique, because the patient under hypnosis was too susceptible to suggestion. Dr. Gerard had said that was a fault in Freud's technique, not in hypnosis. She had also said it would be more difficult to hypnotize a patient who knew this much. She would try to omit as much of the hocus-pocus as possible, she had promised, though she acknowledged that inducing the sleeplike state, the "trance," was difficult without some sort of mechanical aid.

The room was not dark, just dimly lit by a low sun shining between the slats of the venetian blinds. Lisa lay on a couch upholstered in nubby lemon-yellow fabric. The light machine consisted of red and green and blue lights that blinked and moved.

Lisa heard her voice on the tape:

—Lights . . . A banality to call them hypnotic.

—They make *me* sleepy, too. Just watch them, Lisa, and don't fight back drowsiness.

—Don't fight. You said that before. I'm still afraid.

—Don't be. Just relax.

—Yeah . . .

—Let go, Lisa. Let the tension run out. Forget about the mind. Let your body relax. Body. Focus on your body. Let your arms and legs go to sleep if they want to.

—Okay.

—Feel good?

—Yeah.

—Don't close your eyes. Watch the lights.

—Uh . . . I . . . Frankie?

—What?

—Are you my friend?

—Of course.

—You wouldn't send me to a . . . hospital?

—I wouldn't think of it.

—Frankie . . . *He's here.*

—Who is here?

—Jonathan . . . Jonathan is here.

—Jonathan Roper?

—Yes. He's here. Jonathan, why did you come here? You understand what I'm doing here, don't you? I'm trying to find out what you want with me, since you won't tell me.

—What does he look like, Lisa?

—Am I the only one who can see you? Will it always be that way? That makes me look like I'm nuts, you know. Frankie . . . Dr. Gerard . . . She doesn't believe you're real, and right this minute she believes I'm talking to myself. Or in my sleep.

—Show yourself to me, Jonathan Roper. I'm trying to help Lisa. I know you're real. Let me have a look at you.

—Or speak, Jonathan. For God's sake, say something!

—Describe him, Lisa. Is he standing, sitting? Where? What is he wearing?

—You saw the books, Jonathan. Well, all right. Are you what they talk about? Are you anything like that, Jonathan? For God's sake tell me you're not! I couldn't bear it! Not you!

—Lisa!

—Jon-a-than . . . No, I . . . No, I . . . Then what, Jonathan? Tell me.

—Is he touching you, Lisa?

—*Incubus! Ugly word!*

—Jonathan! Am I a witch?

—Lisa!

—*Malleus Maleficarum. Read and learn. Witchcraft requires three things: the Devil, a witch, and the permission of Almighty God! Which of those is missing? All three!*

—Lisa! Come out of it! Wake! Wake! Lisa. Jesus . . . Christ! Wake! Now!

Dr. Gerard slammed down the OFF switch on the tape player.

"If he spoke to us, Lisa," Frankie said, "he spoke through you. Your lips were moving."

"That voice . . ."

"It's your voice. It's distorted, but it's yours."

"The words. The Latin. What was it?"

"Malleus Maleficarum. It's the great encyclopedia of witchcraft, published in the fifteenth century. I've seen many references to it, but I've never seen a copy."

"I've never heard of it."

"Well . . . Lisa. Maybe. If you studied European history at all, you may have heard of it."

"And stored it in the card catalog of my subconscious," Lisa said bitterly. "Together with the three requirements for witchcraft. Those I can swear I never heard of!"

"Do you want to listen to the tape again? There's something I want to ask you about."

"No, I don't want to hear it again."

"Well, do you remember it? When you heard the tape just now, were you hearing the words for the first time or the second? I mean, did you hear him speak when you were under hypnosis?"

"The second. I heard him."

"You heard him speak?"

"Yes."

"That's the first time he's spoken to you in a contemporary manifestation, isn't it? I mean, he spoke in your dreams of times past, but he never before spoke to you when he was with you in the present. Right?"

"Right."

"What was going on when he spoke? Was he caressing you?"

"Yes."

"What did you mean when you said you couldn't bear it if he was an incubus?"

"I don't know."

"Do you love him, Lisa?"

Lisa flushed. "I . . . don't know."

"You can't say no?"

Lisa shook her head.

"There is a possibility," said Dr. Gerard hesitantly. "I don't want to do it right now. Not yet. But I want you to think about it. If what you are experiencing is mental, entirely mental, something terribly troubling emerging from your subconscious, there is a simple way to dispel it."

"Drugs," said Lisa.

Dr. Gerard nodded. "One of the tricyclic antidepressants. That would relieve the anxiety, at least. If what you are suffering is a hallucination, a drug like amitryptiline might well dispel it."

Lisa shook her head firmly. "No."

4

"To place our conversation in its proper context," said the white-haired priest, "do we agree that you have not come to seek absolution?"

"Yes, Father," said Lisa. "I confessed to my parish priest in Ohio, and he assured me I haven't sinned in this matter. Even so, if you advise me I have sinned, I'll confess to you and ask you for absolution."

Father William Longford had received Lisa Hamilton and Dr. Frances Gerard in his study in the rectory of the Church of the Holy Name of Jesus. Lisa saw him as an archetypal priest in an archetypal rectory. He was a man in his early sixties, white-haired, ruddy of complexion, tall and broad-shouldered and bulky. Lisa knew the type well and guessed he had made much of a point throughout his priesthood of being the big, jolly, athletic fellow, the kind of priest whose authoritarianism set well. He was also, Frankie assured her, knowledgeable and tolerant. Frankie had brought one of her demonic-possession patients to him before.

"Do you mind if I smoke?" he asked courteously, picking up a pipe from a big amber-colored ashtray on his desk. "It is an indulgence of mine, offensive to some people."

"Not at all," said Lisa, though in fact she regarded tobacco as a curse and wished no one smoked.

"Thank you. And do the same if you wish." He took the better part of a minute to complete the ritual of packing and lighting his pipe. "Now, I have listened to the tape that Dr. Gerard sent me. And she has told me a good deal on the telephone about what you have experienced. I want to ask you frankly, Mrs. Hamilton, just what you would like to achieve through Dr. Gerard's professional ministrations or through mine as a priest. Do you want to be rid of this dream or apparition?"

"I am not altogether certain, Father. I know I want to understand it."

"What if it is evil?"

"Then I would want to be rid of it."

The priest puffed thoughtfully for a moment, regarding Lisa from beneath thick white eyebrows. "You 'would want to be rid of it.' Unless I make too much of your choice of words, you are not convinced it is evil."

"Is it, Father?"

"I don't know. What do you think?"

"It seems to use me sexually. But maybe I only dream that, and everyone I've told says it is not unusual for a woman to have such dreams. On the other hand, it killed a man in 1868. Father, the man did die, by falling from a high window. I can't imagine how that little woman threw him out."

"How do you know she was little?"

"The newspaper account of her hanging said she was so slight that the sheriff considered tying sandbags to her when he hanged her, for fear her weight wouldn't break her neck."

Father William paused again. A pipe affords a man many opportunities to look thoughtful.

Lisa found the rectory and this priest familiar and comfortable. She liked the old stone church and the musty, dusty air of the rectory. She had dressed for this meeting in a belted white linen dress with a full pleated skirt, recalling her mother's insistence that a woman dressed *respectfully* to go to church, even for a call at the rectory. She was a little surprised at Frankie, who had worn soft, well-faded blue jeans and a sweatshirt, maybe because she was taking the afternoon off from her office and had suggested to Lisa that they might spend a little time in a shopping mall after this visit. Lisa was not yet sure whether or not Frankie was Catholic.

"Malleus Maleficarum," said Father William. "Your reference was correct. Unless you read Medieval Latin, I doubt you have read anything in it. You may well, on the other hand, have read *from* it. It is often cited, sometimes quoted, in translation. The allusion is interesting. For the practice of witchcraft to occur, three prerequisites must exist: the Devil, a witch, and the permission of Almighty God. Your voice said that none of those prerequisites has been present. That could be your subconscious protesting your innocence. Or it could be a supernatural manifestation of some sort, protesting that it is not of Satan."

"It could be either one lying," said Frankie.

"Father," said Lisa, "I cannot believe the words came from within me. I may have heard of this book sometime, somewhere, but I am sure I could not have remembered an idea from it."

"You would rather, then, believe you are being visited by something supernatural, which is protesting that it is not Satan or an incubus."

"Yes, I would rather believe that."

"Then you must beware of something."

"Yes?"

"If the thing is evil, it will lie. As Dr. Gerard suggests. So don't judge it by what it says."

They left the study, which after a time came to seem oppressive—Father William sensed it, too—and walked around the old church. Part of their walk took them through the church's burying ground, which was as peaceful and consoling a place as Lisa had ever known. It was redolent of fallen pine needles, the same sharp, pleasant odor she often smelled under the pines in front of her house in Marietta. There were no forbidding marble or granite markers, just old tombstones from the eighteenth and early nineteenth centuries, some of them leaning at crazy angles above their little mounds.

"My greatest fear," Lisa said again, "is that I will become pregnant. Angelina Tatum did."

"There could be many explanations for that young woman's pregnancy other than that she was made pregnant by . . . well, by whatever Jonathan may be," Father William said. "She was not, I believe you told me, chaste. Anyway, do you still have marital relations with your husband?"

"Yes. But I must confess to you, Father, that we have used contraceptives. In fact, I took the pill for many years. Lately we have used condoms."

"How many children do you have?"

"Just one. A son."

"Do you feel guilty that you have prevented the conception of others?"

"No, Father. I am sorry to have to tell you so, but I don't feel guilty. I feel my husband and I made a rational decision."

"Fear of pregnancy . . ." He puffed on his pipe and nodded. "Another interesting possibility."

"A great many problems of sexual dysfunction result from a subconscious fear of pregnancy," Frankie said. "It can generate strong emotions."

"Father . . . I came to you to talk about two possibilities. It seems to me that Jonathan Roper must be one of two things. Either he is something that is within me and has been within me for years, that now comes up from my subconscious, in which case help will come from Dr. Gerard, or Jonathan Roper is real and is something from the spiritual or supernatural, in which case I would like to turn to you for help."

"But you don't want to be rid of him, you said. You want to understand him, which implies you want him to continue to visit you. You think that will be all right so long as you understand him. It implies, too, a sympathetic relationship, at least an empathetic one. So what help can you receive from either Dr. Gerard or me? I believe Dr. Gerard will agree with me that all either of us can do is help you get rid of Jonathan Roper."

"Exorcism?"

"No, not formally. No. Spiritual exercise. The formation of an unambiguous determination to be rid of this thing. You . . . Hmm. Beginning to rain. Let us continue inside."

They had twenty yards to walk to reach the shelter of the church, and in the time it took them to cover that distance the rain began to fall in a steady torrent. By the time they reached cover, the three of them were drenched.

"Tomorrow?" the priest asked. "Would you like to continue this talk tomorrow?"

"Yes, Father. Thank you."

"I won't be able to join you," said Frankie Gerard, "but I think you will have made a very good start, Lisa, if you make the decision that Father William is suggesting."

"I will be ready to talk about it tomorrow," Lisa said to the priest.

"You always did enjoy a good brandy, didn't you, Liz?" her father said to Lisa as they sat at the table over coffee and cognac after dinner.

"Damnedest storm," said her mother. "We didn't get a drop of rain here."

"We got plenty where I was," said Lisa.

"Where were you, Liz?" her father asked.

"Oh, uh . . . Over toward the Hudson. Shopping."

They had not told her father Lisa was seeing a psychiatrist, much less an out-of-town priest.

"Well, have another dash of cognac," said her father. "You'll sleep well."

She wondered. She wondered if Jonathan would come to her in the night.

He didn't. She wished he had.

The dream—

A road. She trudged along an unpaved road. Part of the time it seemed she was invisible, for people did not glance at her. Others did look, and saw her. She saw herself. She was barefoot and dressed in torn and dirty clothes: an ankle-length brown skirt, a dark green laced bodice over a ragged white blouse. She was tired. She was hungry. And, as is often true when one walks a road in a dream, she walked and walked and covered no distance. Sharp stones hurt her feet. Her knees seemed not to work right, and sometimes she was sure she would fall.

It was an autumn day. Many red and yellow leaves clung to the trees. Other leaves flew on the wind: dry, tumbling, rustling. The weather was cool, not cold. The sky was obscured by thick gray clouds. Many others trudged the road as she did, most of them with downcast eyes. Few were dressed better than she was. From time to time everyone scattered to the sides of the road as one or two horsemen clattered by. No one looked at the horsemen. Men doffed their caps and tugged at their forelocks. Some people knelt. The horsemen ignored them.

Then she saw what almost certainly was the reason for the dream—for she never doubted, even *in* the dream, that it was a dream. She saw—

Stakes. Fires. *Holy Mother of God!* They were burning people!

Five of them. Six. Seven. Eight. In a line across a hillside. Eight stakes.

The apparition on the stake closest to her was long dead. A ghastly remnant of what had been human an hour before hung in the chains that bound it to the stake. The flesh was charred, yet oozing. The clothes were burned away. So was the hair. The wood beneath the body was almost all gone. The flames were low and blue, except when a globule of grease fell and sputtered into yellow flame.

Another horror, a short distance away, still jerked. It still felt pain.

Others—they writhed and shrieked. It was possible to see that they were women. One pleaded hysterically as her tormentors shoved torches into the wood heaped around her. The smoke and flame rose around her, and her skirt caught fire.

The rising flames had quickly burned away the placards nailed to the stakes above all but three. Those three could still be read. Two of them read:

HEXE

Witch.
The third read:

JUDEN

Wind carried the smoke to the road. Lisa was not the only person who gagged.

Other charred stakes covered the hillside, as if this were a burned wood. Scores of people had been burned here!

Oddly, Lisa knew where she was. The town ahead was Trier. The river was the Mosel.

In dreams, time and place swim. Now she was no longer a witness. As for a time she had been Angelina, now she was the suffering woman and not just an onlooker. Now she was a woman named Mathilde Seiler.

Now she was in a dungeon—in a torture chamber, actually—where other women lay around her on the stone floor. Heavy shackles riveted on her ankles were joined not to chains but to iron bars attached to an iron belt around her waist, utterly depriving her of any movement of her legs. She could not have walked even if she could have risen. She wore an iron collar, too. Ponderous chains ran from the collar to the manacles on her wrists. Besides all this, still another heavy chain was locked around her waist and snaked away across the stone floor to a ring, to which it was attached. She lay on the floor. The weight of so much iron was so great that she could hardly have moved even if the chains and bars had not so cruelly restricted her.

A torn skirt was all she was wearing. She was dirty and surrounded by her own filth.

Was she to witness her own burning, as she had witnessed her own hanging?

Or was she to experience it?

They had whipped her. A mass of swollen, festering welts covered her shoulders. Others, not so many, crisscrossed her back. The tongue of the whip had slashed around and split her right breast. But she had been surprised. The sight of the lash had paralyzed her with terror. Its bite had been nothing near as cruel as she had expected. It hurt. Oh, it *hurt,* yes! But it had not shifted her focus from her furious hatred of her tormentors to total occupation with her agony. She had discovered she could endure this torture. It had damaged her flesh more than her spirit.

They had poured brine on her raw welts—to stop the festering, they had said. She had shrieked, more in fury than in pain.

They had not yet done to her what she had watched them do to others. She had seen three women tortured on the rack, stretched until their joints separated with sickening audible cracks their screams did not overwhelm. The same women had been burned with hot irons and tongs.

They had tortured an old woman—very old, maybe as old as seventy—with the boot. That she was already so weak she could not carry her chains earned her no pity. They dragged her across the chamber and added more chains, to bind her to a heavy wooden chair. She babbled and slobbered as they clamped the iron boot on her leg and then slowly tightened it until the pressure crushed the bones of her leg and rendered her a cripple for whatever hours or days remained of her life—a torture said to be particularly excruciating. Her pathetic shrieks won her no mercy.

All these women confessed they were witches. All their confessions were virtually identical. They were simple country women of middle age and beyond, mothers and grandmothers. All of them had somehow offended their neighbors and were known as quarrelsome women at best, nags and termagants at worst.

The first confession Mathilde heard was typical of all the others she had heard during her three weeks chained in this place. The woman was forty years old and named Luise. She confessed on the rack.

Satan had come to her in the night: a huge man dressed in black and wearing a thick coal-black beard. He had seduced her with promises of great pleasure and great good fortune, and she had chosen to couple with him. Sexual contact with him had been no pleasure, for he was stone cold and his male organ was no bigger than her index finger, and so far good fortune had not come to her.

One night he had summoned her to come away with him. He had carried her through the air, a great distance, an exhausting journey. They had arrived at last at a meadow on a mountainside where many men and women were assembled: feasting, dancing, copulating. When Satan assumed the body of a huge bear, though retaining his human head, they had broken off their revels and groveled before him. He invited Luise to renounce the Christian religion. She did. He handed her a crucifix and demanded that she spit on it and trample it in the dirt. She did. The crowd cheered and returned to their joys. She joined them.

Since that night Luise had gone back to the witches' Sabbath—for that was what it was—many times. She could fly, riding astride a pole or a broomstick.

She was a witch, she solemnly confessed. She had made a young woman barren. She had taught a neighbor's pigs to escape their pens and ravage his garden. She had caused the death of a bull. She had caused women to drop whole baskets of eggs. She had caused lightning to strike and set a thatched roof on fire. She had caused a priest to stumble and spill the Holy Blood of Christ from the chalice.

Except for the details of their crimes, all these women had experienced exactly the same thing: the visit by the big man in black, the seduction, the unredeemed promises, the journeys to the witches' Sabbaths. Even their acts of witchcraft were much alike, most of them petty: the women caused cows to dry up, butter to turn rancid, pigs to invade kitchen gardens, neighbors to be annoyed by nighttime bumpings and thumpings, and so on. None of them ever caused illness or death. The roof fire Luise caused had been extinguished with a couple of buckets of water.

Mathilde was here because of the avowal of a neighbor that he had seen her pour poison into a public well. He had sworn he watched her weight a small leather bag with stones and drop it into a roadside well used by villagers and travelers.

What was more, only the day before she had been observed in derisive conversation with the Jew Elias, son of Samson, the two of them chatting and laughing. No one had seen Elias hand her the bag, but he confessed that he had and that the bag was in truth filled with the dried blood of poisonous snakes. He had in fact confessed twice, once under torture and again after he was relieved from torture. It was well known—had been known for centuries—that Jews poisoned the wells from which Christians drank. It was notorious that they formed alliances with others— madmen, lepers, and witches—who did their dirty work for them.

Obviously an honest Christian girl would not undertake a Jew's loathsome enterprise. But a witch . . .

Mathilde was very different from the others. She was only nineteen. She was an acknowledged beauty, not just in the village of Saarfeld, where she lived, but in the town of Trier as well. She was tall and blonde, and now that she was accused of being a witch it was said of her that she carried herself too rigidly erect, without the modesty befitting a Christian girl, and people said she boldly met their eyes with hers when she encountered them in the village or on the road to Trier.

She was different in other ways, too. Her family was foreign—Swiss, it was said—living in the archbishopric of

Trier by the favor of the prince-archbishop-elector. Her father was a wine merchant named Johann Seiler. Though he had a German name, he spoke with a French accent. He was mysterious about where he came from and why he had removed to Trier. Mathilde's mother, now a year dead of the flux, had borne a French name: Angélique. She had been a withdrawn, taciturn woman, and people had noted a strange, furtive sadness about her. Mathilde's brother, three years older, also had a French name: Philippe.

As a dealer in Rhenish wines, Johann Seiler traveled and was often gone from the family for weeks on end. No one ever saw any evidence of his business, except that he returned from his travels with money. The family lived modestly. Some said they wanted to keep their gold, especially its source, a secret.

They were faithful Catholics—almost, it might be said, too conspicuously devout. Switzerland, as was well known, was diseased with horrible heresies, and some people wondered if the Seiler family had not been contaminated with heresy. If so, they had come to the wrong place, for Johann von Schöneburg, the Archbishop-Elector, was devoted to the Jesuits and was piously determined to rid his extensive and prosperous archbishopric of all Protestants, Jews, and witches. If the Seilers were any of these, or infected by any of them, they should have fled before their daughter was observed in close and gladdening conversation with a Jew.

At first, pain and terror, helplessness and hopelessness, had been the whole focus of her existence in this place. Now the focus had changed. *Now she hated.*

Lying in chains on this cold floor at night, she dreamed. She dreamed of her father. She dreamed he had told her things years before. Or had he? Or was he appearing in her dreams and telling her now? Anyway, he told her to hate. It would be her defense, he said, and her victory.

Hate, Mathilde! And revenge. Concentrate on hate and revenge.

Once again time and place fused. Now Lisa—Mathilde—stood in a huge room, facing an immense table. Some of the people around her knelt, facing the table and the men seated behind it. She could not kneel. The thick iron bars between her shackles and her iron belt would not allow her to bend her knees. Indeed, they'd had to lift her from the floor and carry her to the table. To her left a fire roared and crackled in a fireplace. She wished she were closer to it, because she was cold.

"Mathilde Seiler!"

A man seated at the table spoke her name. She lifted her face and looked at him. She knew who he was. She had seen him in the dungeon many times. He was Peter Binsfeld, Suffragan Bishop to the Archbishop-Elector of Trier, Johann von Schöneburg, who sat next to him in a chair a little higher, a sort of throne.

"Mathilde, you have confessed that you are a witch."

The Suffragan Bishop spoke German. Lisa was surprised to find she understood it. She had studied German but had never become so fluent as to understand conversation readily, certainly not this oddly accented German.

"I was tortured," she heard herself say in German.

"You were not, but you will be if you abjure your confession."

"I was kept awake for eight days and nights."

"Tormentum insomniae," said the Suffragan Bishop. "A gentle form of persuasion. You've had a touch or two of the whip. You have not worn the boot. You have not sat in the witch chair. You haven't even seen the chair, with the red-hot spikes. In fact, you haven't felt hot iron. So without any of the more rigorous forms of persuasion, you put your name to the confession written for you by Brother Balthasar. Do you mean now to deny that you confessed?"

She shook her head. No, she had confessed. Her father had come to her in a dream and told her to.

"In any case, you bear on your body the grave *indicium,* the extra teat by which you suckled the Demon. It is irrefutable evidence."

She looked down. Mathilde had the same mark, in the

same place, as the real, living Lisa: a small, flat brown mole on her left breast, an inch or so from her nipple.

Unwiderlegbarlisch Beweis. Irrefutable evidence.

"You confessed that you attended the *Sabbat*. Recite for us what happened, what you have already confessed."

Lisa heard herself saying, "The Devil came . . . Satan. He was a big man, all dressed in black, with a big black beard. His eyes . . . gleamed. There was light in them, like the light from a fire, only more blue than red."

"And you gave yourself to him."

"Yes. I have confessed it."

"Tell us about that."

Suffragan Bishop Peter Binsfeld leaned forward over his crossed arms, which lay on the table. He all but licked his lips in anticipation of the words he was about to hear. The Archbishop-Elector sipped thoughtfully from a silver cup of wine. Both men were gaudily dressed in rich robes, the Archbishop-Elector's garb including a red velvet cape bordered with ermine. Both wore big gold pectoral crosses, and a large cross decorated the rich cloth that covered the table.

She said what the other women had said—what these men expected to hear. "He promised me a very long life and riches. He promised I would marry a rich man and be the mistress of a big house with many servants. He promised I would be happy and never suffer illness. He mounted me like a stallion, except that his part was tiny. He was cold, as cold as ice, and the little thing he shoved into me was colder still. I suffered. He had said I would feel great pleasure, but I didn't."

"He suckled you," said the Suffragan Bishop.

"Yes." She lifted a chained hand and touched the mole. "Here. He took milk from me."

"When did you last see him?"

"Last night. He comes to me here in prison."

"All this you freely confess."

"All this I confess."

"Then clearly you are a witch."

"But I have harmed no one. No one has come forward to accuse me of any harm. They say I put poison in the well, but no one has become sick from drinking the water."

"What harm is required?" asked the Suffragan Bishop. "That a witch exists is harm enough."

"Am I to be put to death for doing no harm?"

"Do you mean to deny the Word of God?" the Suffragan Bishop asked indignantly. "For does not Holy Writ emphatically tell us, 'Thou shalt not suffer a witch to live'?"

"If I've done no harm . . . ?"

"The word of God, Mathilde! The word of God will be obeyed!"

"My family knew nothing of this," she muttered, pursuing what she knew was a vain hope.

"They knew everything!" screamed the Suffragan. "And they escaped! But let them not suppose they will avoid the all-seeing eye of God. We will find them. They will be delivered to our justice!"

The hillside, the charred stakes. And it was as it had been at Second and Putnam Streets. Lisa stood in the frostbitten grass on another hillside across the road from the burning ground and watched the procession come out from the town.

In her persona as witness, her hair was bound inside a headdress of white linen, a cap to which flowing wings were attached and fell to her shoulders, all of stuff so finely woven that a single layer of it was transparent. Her neck was bare, showing a small jeweled crucifix that hung from a fine gold chain. Below, she wore a blue linen shift, the uppermost part of which showed under a blouse of the filmy white linen. Her dress was of maroon wool, straight and simple and cinched at the waist by an ornamented belt with a jeweled buckle. She kept her hands clasped before her as if she were praying.

The man standing beside her wore a long woolen robe, like a student's or a professor's gown. It was made of costly stuffs, in gray, with designs embroidered in gold and silver near his throat. He wore it open, displaying a silk shirt. He wore his blond hair long, letting strands of it fall carelessly over his forehead and his shoulders. His beard and mustache were more neatly trimmed but were thick and healthy.

She knew his name. It was Johann Seiler. And the woman to be burned was Mathilde Seiler. What relation he was to this Mathilde was not clear.

The procession approached. Mathilde, dressed in a black shift, rode in a cart, unchained but bound with rope. A placard above her on a stake read:

> **THIS IS MATHILDE**
> **WITCH SORCERESS IDOLATER**
> **BELOVED OF SATAN**
> **WHO HAS SUCKLED THE BEAST**
> **IN THE PRINCE'S JUSTICE CONDEMNED**

Around the stake where she was to burn, the executioners had built a platform, five feet above the ground, leaving room beneath for firewood. The wood had been carefully piled: pine, to burn quick and hot and send up the thick smoke that suffocated some victims and spared them the ultimate agonies, then hardwoods to keep the fire going until the witch was reduced to ashes, especially non-seasoned oak, which would be long catching fire but would glow with a fierce heat for hours after all other wood was gone.

A few yards from the stake stood another platform. There the Suffragan Bishop of Trier sat on a comfortable chair and waited for the witch to be brought. Facing his platform was still a third. There the condemned woman would stand and hear Peter Binsfeld's sermon on her death.

The soldier guards took Mathilde to this third platform. They held her facing the Suffragan Bishop and forced her to listen to his sermon.

He spoke for a long time. Lisa, standing by Johann Seiler, decided she hated Peter Binsfeld. She decided he was a sadist. She wished the Suffragan Bishop could be bound to the stake instead of Mathilde.

Finally he finished. The soldiers led Mathilde down from

the third platform and to the ladder to the high platform. Soldiers were waiting on that one, and as her guards pushed her up the ladder, the ones on top reached down and lifted her up. Because rope would burn, they bound her to the stake with chain. They tore away her clothes, so the charring of her flesh would be seen. Baring her upper body, they exposed a medal or amulet hanging on a chain around her neck. From the slope across the road, Lisa could not tell if it was the woman-snake amulet Jonathan wore, the one Angelina had found on the window sill.

So badly had Mathilde been abused that it was difficult to tell how she might have looked before she was chained in a dungeon and her back torn open with a lash. Her wrists and ankles carried masses of oozing scabs, from the chains that had only now been knocked off her. She was pallid and unnaturally thin. Her eyes were dark and hollow. Her lips were cracked. It was possible to see that she was blonde, though most of her hair had been torn or cut away. She jerked her head, shooting furious glances into the eyes of her tormentors, and they fell back and crossed themselves as if they felt fire from her eyes.

Few people watched. It was as though the town and neighborhood were sick from witch burnings. Some stopped on the road. Half a dozen monks watched pensively, standing not far from the stake, their hands clasped inside their long, full sleeves.

A wind had whipped up. All the people, Lisa included, folded their arms to hold their clothes closer.

The soldiers on the platform now came down the ladder and pulled it away. Four men with torches trotted forward and pushed their torches into the heaped firewood. The pine wood took fire immediately, and smoke began to rise.

Lisa wept. She spoke to Johann Seiler. "I thought you might save her."

"I need not," he said quietly. "This one can save herself."

The flames gleamed and grew, and the smoke thickened. But suddenly a thick bolt of blue-white lightning cracked across the leaden sky. The thunder seemed to have ruptured the heavens, for rain fell as though a bladder had burst above the overcast, releasing a deluge that fell like a waterfall.

People ran, some in terror, most just to escape, but many in fear of what had to be a supernatural event.

Only a few noticed that the torrent had put out the fire under Mathilde.

Few witnessed what happened next. Few would be able to testify to it. Lisa saw. Her eyes were fixed on the young woman chained to the stake, and they never left her.

The chains fell. The woman dropped away from the stake, and in dropping she metamorphosed into a great, lean gray wolf. In a bound she leaped from the platform and crossed the narrow ground toward the platform where Peter Binsfeld remained seated under a canopy that sheltered him from the downpour. The wolf leaped to the platform and lunged at the Suffragan Bishop.

Peter Binsfeld screamed.

The wolf did not rip his throat. Instead, with a furious snarl, it tore off his left ear. Carrying the ear in its mouth, it leaped from the platform and trotted up the burning hill, among the charred stakes. From time to time it turned and snarled. No one dared move. At the top of the low hill it stopped and let the ear fall into the mud. It lifted its head and emitted a terrifying, defiant howl.

For the next ten minutes no one felt free to pursue, as the howl was heard again and again, ever more distant.

"Johann von Schöneburg was indeed Archbishop-Elector of Trier, beginning about 1580. His Suffragan Bishop was Peter Binsfeld. They burned hundreds of witches. Hundreds, if not in fact thousands. I am not aware of anything in the history to the effect that Binsfeld ever lost an ear to a wolf. Are you certain you have never read a history of these things?"

"Father, I am like anyone else. I am aware of the history of witch burnings. In Salem—"

"No," Father William said firmly. "Witches were not

burned in England and Scotland or in New England. They were hanged. The burnings happened on the continent of Europe, in the Rhine Valley especially. Also in the mountains."

"You see? I know something of the general history, nothing of the details. I could not have named Trier as a place where witches were burned. I am certain I never read the names Johann von Schöneburg or Peter Binsfeld."

"Well, then, do you know the meaning of the German name Seiler?"

Lisa shook her head.

"It means rope maker. Or Roper," said Father William. "Of course, Johann and Jonathan are the same."

"Yes. He was the same man. I knew it."

"Curious variation in the story, though," said Father William after puffing for a moment on his pipe. "He let Angelina die, but he saved Mathilde. Have you any suggestion of a reason?"

"No. Except what he said. He said he *had* saved Angelina, even though he had just seen her die. Of Mathilde, he said he didn't need to save her; she could save herself."

"And she did—that is, if we may assume a creature who turns into an animal, attacks a man, and bounds off has been saved. Also, she suffered weeks of agony, lying chained in a dungeon, being deprived of sleep to elicit her confession. If she had the power to save herself, why didn't she do it sooner?"

"She said the Devil came to her in the dungeon. Maybe he gave her the power only at the end."

"Her confession is a typical witch confession. She said he coupled with her but that it gave her no pleasure."

"She confessed to whatever they demanded of her. It was plain, listening to her, that she would have confessed to riding around the world on a broomstick if that was what they demanded. Her inquisitors were the source of the fantasy."

"Your sympathies were with her entirely."

"Of course."

"But if the woman could call down a cloudburst, then turn herself into an animal, she *was* a witch."

"Do you believe in witches, Father?"

"The question is, do you?"

"I've seen only one shred of evidence to suggest that witches could exist, and that was in a dream. So I don't believe in them. Does the Church require me to believe in them?"

"The Church has historically accepted the possibility that witches do exist. God says nothing in vain, so why did He say to Moses, 'Thou shalt not suffer a witch to live'? It is possible that some people commune with Satan, or try to. It is possible some of them succeed. The Church does not ask you to accept as valid any particular manifestation alleged to be of witchcraft. Obviously the Church condemns the witch craze of the sixteenth and seventeenth centuries, when thousands of innocent people died horribly."

"If what I dreamed has any basis in fact, what they did to people was horrible beyond belief."

"If what Mathilde was able to do has any basis in fact, *that* was horrible beyond belief."

They were walking again in the pine-shaded churchyard, again through the old burying ground. It called to Lisa's mind the words of Gray's Elegy:

Beneath those rugged elms, that yew-tree's shade,
Where heaves the turf in many a moldering heap,
Each in his narrow cell for ever laid,
The rude forefathers of the hamlet sleep.

It was like the Mound Cemetery near her home in Marietta, and she decided now there was no hint or suspicion of the morbid in walking among the old headstones, reading the inscriptions, and wondering about the men and women who lay below. She had done that in the old cemetery a few blocks from her house, reading and pondering on what was carved on the stones of veterans of the Revolutionary War. She had climbed the Indian mound in the center and wondered about the graves far below.

Father William sensed her thoughts and said, "Not many of our faith lived out here when this little plot was filled with graves. This was thought to be enough land. No one has been buried here since 1814. The present church edifice was built in 1838."

"I'm sorry, Father. I should be concentrating on what I'm here to talk about. I'm taking advantage of your time."

"Not at all," he said as he stopped to knock his pipe on a molded-concrete fence post. "I've been a priest a long time, and I've never come upon a case quite like yours. If nothing else, talking with you has been a memorable experience for me."

"I'm grateful to you, Father."

"I'm retiring shortly. I'm glad to have a problem toward the end of my vocation that appears to be truly spiritual, not organizational and not—with due respect to Dr. Gerard— psychological."

"Do you think Jonathan made it rain yesterday afternoon, just when you and I had reached what may be the crux of . . ."

Father William chuckled. "That is an interesting possibility. Yes. I had just asked you if you'd reached an unambiguous decision that you wanted to be rid of Jonathan Roper. And you hadn't answered."

"I believe I said I didn't know."

"It is essential that you make up your mind about Jonathan. As long as you are ambivalent, you will never be rid of him, whether he is psychological or real."

"How do I declare my decision?"

"First, by telling me, firmly and without reservation, that you want never to see Jonathan Roper again. Then you tell Dr. Gerard the same. Then you pray; you tell God. When you tell God, you will be telling yourself, and you will be telling Jonathan. You pray before you go to sleep, pray that you will be spared dreams; tell God you do not want them;

ask to be protected from them. That is a spiritual commitment. It is also a psychological one. You must convince yourself, and God, and Jonathan."

Lisa nodded. "I . . . Father, I can't be unambivalent about it today. I cannot truthfully say what you want me to say, without reservation. I have to think about it a little more."

"Lisa," the priest said gently, "part of your problem is curiosity. I feel it, too. I, too, am not absolutely certain I want you to rid yourself of Jonathan. Our problem is that we live in a world that extols curiosity. We want to *know*. We want to discover everything. You are reluctant to be rid of Jonathan because you are not convinced he is evil. You wonder if knowing him might become the supreme experience of your life. Our ancestors would have had no trouble with this. They would have said, 'We already know all we want or need to know, and we want no contact with anything that calls into question the basic truths that are the foundation of our lives.' In our century the basic truth is that we must always pursue more truth."

"Yes. The secular, science-oriented frame of mind."

"Remember one thing, though, Lisa. This dream you are having, or this ghost you are seeing . . . It can be very dangerous."

5

"I'M NOT ASLEEP."

"No."

"I am not dreaming."

"You are not dreaming."

She had been asleep. Sometimes in dreams a person senses the presence of another person in the dark bedroom. It is perhaps the most horrible of all nightmares: to waken with a sure sense that another person is there, silent and menacing. The boundary between the nightmare and reality is all but impossible to discern. Cardiologists suspect that a few people found dead in their beds were literally frightened to death by this nightmare; sheer terror was so great it stopped their hearts. She had experienced that terrifying nightmare once, years ago, and had hoped never to experience it again.

But he was there. She sensed him. Then she felt his weight at the foot of the bed, on the left side, depressing the springs and mattress. She lay still for a full minute, fearful and indecisive, before she reached for the switch and abruptly lighted the bedside lamp.

He was stark naked, as he had been before when he came to her room. He looked down at her and smiled.

"Why? Why now? What do you want?"

"It is what *you* want that brought me. I am here because you called for me. This time. Before, I came of my own. This time you called me. I am grateful."

"I called for you?"

"Yes. You told the priest you could not unambivalently say you didn't want me. I was happy to hear you say that."

Lisa sat up, pulling up the sheet to cover her breasts. "What difference does it make whether I want you or not?" she asked sharply.

"A very great deal of difference, to me," he said. "You can't send me away, and I couldn't leave you even if I wanted to. To know you don't find me abhorrent, don't want to be rid of me at all costs, is very . . . gratifying. I have come to you for a reason, Lisa. It is a reason that involves everything . . . good and positive. I can't leave you, but to stay with you knowing you hate me would be onerous indeed."

"What if I prayed to God to send you away from me?"

He shrugged. "I am not sure what the Almighty would do. But I am confident you won't say that prayer. I don't think you will, Lisa. I fervently hope you won't."

He looked different, a little. At first she wasn't sure what was different. Then she realized he had no beard or mustache, and his hair was shorter. It was as if he had styled himself for the final decade of the twentieth century.

Otherwise he was as he had been. He was young: younger than she was. He had the body of an Olympic diver: an ideal of supple, youthful musculature, with prominent but not exaggerated male parts. His penis, now flaccid, hung like some kind of odd fruit or flower growing out of the lush foliage of his blond pubic hair. It extended just below his scrotum. The corona was prominently visible inside its fleshy covering, his pale, blue-veined foreskin.

"If simply I tell you to go away, that I want nothing more of you, nothing more of your dreams—"

He interrupted. "There will come a time when, if you say

that, I will go away. That time is not yet. I hope you will never say it."

"Why? Why should I not want to be rid of you? What is the meaning of the dreams you give me?"

"I am teaching you," he said simply. "It takes time."

"Whatever it is you want me to know, why can't I know it all at once?"

"It might drive you mad."

"Angelina . . . Mathilde . . . Who were they, Jonathan?"

"All will be made clear, in time."

Lisa dropped her chin. Her hair fell around her face and for the moment hid it from him. "Are you evil?" she whispered.

Jonathan Roper shrugged. "What is evil?" he asked blandly. "Who was evil, Mathilde or Binsfeld? Or von Schöneburg? Angelina Tatum or her father?"

"You killed Josiah Tatum."

"Yes. In a sense, anyway, I did. And in time you will know why. I have killed. Perhaps I will again. Killing is not the most evil thing in the world."

"You confess this?"

She looked up in time to see a tolerant little smile come to his face. "The word 'confess' has long since been lost to me."

Lisa sighed loudly and shook her head. "Jonathan, Jonathan—"

"The priest suggested that curiosity is your strongest motivation. If I should go away, you would never know the answers to all your questions. I am confident you won't even think of sending me away. I know you, Lisa. I know more about you than you dream. You will not tell me to go away."

"Even Father William would regret my losing you before learning who and what you are."

He extended his hand toward her. "Tell me, Lisa . . . Do you want me? I mean, physically and right now."

She reached out. Their hands met and clasped. His hand was warm.

"Satisfy a major element of your curiosity," he said,

nodding toward his crotch. "You should already know. But find out. Satisfy yourself."

He guided her hand down, then let go of it, so that she touched his penis of her own will. It was warm. It rose under her touch and was warm. She satisfied herself that she had not been deceived, that it really was warm. She closed her hand affectionately around it and felt it surge and throb. She took his wrinkled foreskin between her thumb and two fingers and pulled on it gently. It stretched, and his shaft swelled.

"A man . . ." she murmured.

Jonathan chuckled under his breath. "No incubus, hmm? *Malleus Maleficarum*. Did you know that Peter Binsfeld himself wrote a book of like ravings? You saw him. You saw him as he really was. Peter One-Ear, they called him later."

Lisa let go of his penis but kept her hand on his leg. "So what was Mathilde? How did she—"

"Lisa . . . Do you want me? I mean, do you want what you've been touching?"

She sucked in a deep breath, conscious that her heart had begun to pound unnaturally. "It's very different. . . . This. Very different from a dream. This is . . . When I dreamed you, I—"

"You were not committing adultery," Jonathan said.

"Yes. No. I wasn't."

He smiled. "And with a man who appears in your bedroom in the middle of the night and will soon disappear the way he came? What will Father Longford say? What will Dr. Frankie say? What am I?"

"Who commits adultery in his heart—"

"Yes, yes, of course," he interrupted impatiently. "We're not talking about your heart. Do you *want* me, Lisa?"

She lifted her chin high. "Not the way it has been," she said. "All you've ever done is . . . enter. You've satisfied yourself and then—"

"You told Frankie you took pleasure in it."

She tossed aside the sheet, revealing her naked self. She was uncomfortably conscious she was not a goddess to match the god he was. "Are you capable of love, Jonathan?" she asked.

"I am a man," he said simply.

Lisa moved back, to make room for him beside her, and Jonathan stretched out facing her. He put his left arm over her, and his left leg, and kissed her.

Shortly she knew he was indeed capable of love. Supremely capable. Was it but coincidence that when he kissed her breasts he seemed to concentrate on the small, dark, flat mole?

"I'm going home," Lisa said to Frankie Gerard over lunch at the Indian Harbor Yacht Club in Greenwich. She was comfortable in soft, faded old jeans, bare feet in Top-Siders—the Greenwich uniform, almost.

"Have you told Father William?"

"I would be grateful if *you* did. And incidentally, my mother will pay your bill for professional services. She insists. I would and can, but I'd just as soon not have to explain to my husband."

"What do I tell Father William?" Frankie asked. "What are you going to tell your husband?"

"I'll tell Ben nothing, at least for now. I'd appreciate your explaining to Father William that I'm just not yet ready to make a final decision."

"Jonathan has manifested himself to you again," said Dr. Gerard.

"Yes. Differently."

"Not a dream."

"Not a dream."

Frankie Gerard tipped her head back and closed her eyes for a moment. "Lisa, I have to tell you something," she said solemnly. "I'm not surprised. This may be the next stage of something that you are going to have to face sooner or later."

"That I'm losing my mind."

"Let's not talk that way. But, Lisa, when a schizophrenic

hears voices, he *hears voices*. Physiologically, not just psychologically, he hears voices. Under electroencephalographic examination, he generates the same electric waves when he says he hears voices as he does when we speak to him and he actually does hear voices. Do you understand?"

"I'm beginning to understand that if I were to continue as your patient you would probably want to institutionalize me," Lisa said coldly.

"The last thing in the world," said Dr. Gerard. "I simply want you to understand that dreams can become reality. They can be so real that they replace reality, and we don't always have the ability to distinguish."

Lisa put down the Beefeater martini she had just raised to her lips, without taking a sip. "What if I tell you I washed his semen off my legs early this morning, just after he left?"

Dr. Gerard nodded. "If it is still a dream, that is another part of it."

"Is it still a dream, Frankie?"

"There's a way to find out. Father William suggests you can rid yourself of Jonathan by spiritual discipline. You could also do it by undergoing analysis and therapy. Or, for a quick fix, I could prescribe the drug I mentioned. That would probably rid you of Jonathan."

"And fry my brains," said Lisa caustically.

Frankie Gerard reached for her Scotch and took a swallow. "You've turned hostile," she said.

"I'm sorry. But I want to cope with Jonathan, not drive him away with exorcism or burn him out with a chemical."

"I have one more question. Answer this honestly, Lisa, or don't answer it at all. Be honest with yourself as well as with me. You like Jonathan, don't you? Maybe you even more than like him. Maybe you love him?"

"Father William suggested to me yesterday that maybe I think knowing Jonathan will be the supreme experience of my life. He suggested I'm driven by curiosity, that I don't want to give Jonathan up until I know what he is and why he has appeared to me."

"You're skirting the question."

Lisa took a sip from her martini. "Do I like him? Yes. Yes, I like him."

"Are you in love with him?"

Lisa shook her head firmly. "No."

"Does it trouble you that whatever this man is, he is intruding on your marriage?"

Lisa sighed. "I'd like to laugh that question off by saying I can hardly violate my marriage vows by dreaming."

"We talked a little about your marriage. I gather you're not entirely happy with it."

Lisa shrugged. "How many people are happy with twenty-year-old marriages?"

"About the same number as are happy with seven-year-old cars," said Frankie. "The question is, are you ready to junk it?"

Lisa shook her head. "I suppose not," she said. "Not for a ghost, especially."

Lisa stayed in Chappaqua a few days less than the ten she had said she might stay. Mary O'Neil was sensitive to her daughter's moods and insisted on being told what was troubling her. That was one reason why Lisa left.

Her mother drove her to La Guardia. On the way in, Lisa asked her mother to tell her more about Great-grandmother Kennedy, the one who had spoken of Mr. Roper on her deathbed.

Mary laughed. "I can tell you one thing more. It was a mistake to play cards with her. She always won. Not only that, she won money betting on horses. The luck of the Irish, everyone said. Others said she cheated—though I promise you no one ever said anything of the kind in her presence. One old Irish maid who worked for her said Grandmother Kennedy had the evil eye and could put curses on people. Also, she could find lost things that nobody else could find."

"Like the silver thimble," said Lisa.

"You remember that story? Grandmother Kennedy's own mother was Elizabeth Christina Spencer, and she had lost a silver thimble—I mean, lost it weeks or months before. One day she happened to mention the subject in front of Grandmother Kennedy, who was only four years old at the time, and the child toddled off and came back in two minutes with the thimble in her little hand. She'd found it, but she couldn't tell her mother where. It was the right thimble, engraved with the initials E.C.S."

"You said she was a powerful personality."

"Everyone was in awe of her. Intelligent . . . Strong . . . Stubborn. A memorable woman."

"Do you have any sense that her descendants inherited any of that from her? Did you? Did I?"

Mary laughed again. "We don't look like her. You inherited something of her, I think. You don't seem to be aware of this, Lisa, but you are a natural leader. You've been a big duck in small ponds, and I've sometimes wondered if you wouldn't have been a big duck in a big pond."

"What do you mean?"

"People look to you for advice, suggestions. People trust you. They tend to do what you suggest. You've used your talent only in women's organizations and the like, and I've wondered if you wouldn't have gone far in business or politics."

"Let me tell you, if I'd graduated from college twenty years later, even fifteen, I'd have insisted on being something more than wife and mother. I like being wife and mother, but I'm like you in wondering if I couldn't have done other things, too. Not instead. In addition. I have a sort of sense of being Elizabeth Mary Kennedy's great-granddaughter. Sometimes I've thought I . . . heard from her. Sometimes I've thought she was watching over me."

Mary shook her head. "That's eerie, Lisa. She's been dead more than forty years."

Ben met Lisa at the airport. They ate out that night. When they went to bed, Ben said maybe they should have sex, since it had been two or three weeks since they'd done it. She agreed to it, and he rolled on a condom and performed stalwartly—never suspecting, of course, that she could not help comparing his performance to Jonathan's of two nights before. Ben wasn't as adept a lover as Jonathan was. He never had been.

He meant well. Ben always meant well. He made sure she was ready and was comfortable before he mounted her. She had realized a long time ago that he was in some sense in awe of her. He recognized her intelligence, and sometimes he glimpsed the busy imagination that supplemented intellect with insight. He contrasted all that with the prosaic turn of his own mind and found his wife fascinating and a little mysterious.

He had asked her once if when he was making love to her she didn't sometimes fantasize that he was someone else. She had answered by asking him if he didn't sometimes pretend he was making love *to* someone else. The answer was too clever, and she sensed he was not satisfied with it. But he dropped the subject and never asked again.

It was very well, maybe, for him to think she was cleverer than he was. It was also very well to know he loved her. It was very well to know that he regarded their marriage as successful—his word for it: successful. She suspected he used the word in a sense not very different from the way he used it with reference to a business venture. In business, a successful venture could be ignored. It was doing what it was supposed to do and need no longer be the center of attention.

Was that a cliché? Probably. Sure. The cliché was, "If it ain't broke, don't fix it."

Anyway, they did it, and deferential though he was about it, she was well and truly fucked; she went to sleep feeling a pleasant little defiance toward Jonathan, knowing he wasn't the only man who could satisfy her.

Not until morning, after Ben had gone to the plant, did Lisa open her accumulated mail. Among other things, she found a note signed "Dana Whitaker." She had to read the note before she realized it was from the college librarian, whom she had always called Miss Whitaker.

Dear Mrs. Hamilton,

Having learned that you are out of town for a week or so, I thought I would send you the enclosed, so it will be waiting for you when you return. In my spare time I have done a little research into the genealogy and history of the Tatum family. I hope the enclosed is interesting to you.

Dana Whitaker

The enclosure was a genealogical chart of the Tatum family:

ANGELINA TATUM (1829–68)

Colonel Josiah Tatum (1809–68) m. Honor Trowbridge (1810–99)

Rufus Tatum (1784–1848) m. (1) Martha Fearing (1792–1827) (2) Constance Trumbull (1812–83)

Andrew Tatum (1759–1812) m. Susan Mead (1764–1839)

Jacob Tatum (1709–84) m. (3) Abigail Worthington (1740–1809)

Samuel Tatum (16??–1731) m. Elizabeth (maiden name and dates?)

Notes: (1) Angelina Tatum was the only child of Josiah Tatum and Honor Trowbridge. (2) Harman Tatum was the son of Andrew Tatum's second marriage and was Josiah's half brother. (3) Samuel Tatum arrived in America through the Port of New York in 1699. (4) Andrew Tatum served under General Greene in the Revolutionary War and brought his family from White Plains, New York, to Marietta in 1791.

Lisa telephoned Dana Whitaker to thank her. She asked her if she had any further information about the women in the line, especially about Honor Trowbridge.

"I'm afraid we don't have anything more about Honor Trowbridge. It was Rufus Tatum who was interested in the family history and compiled what I sent you. Josiah and Harman were satisfied with what he had done and added nothing to it. As for the wives, I can tell you something about Martha Fearing. She was of a rather prominent local family. Susan Mead must have been born in the vicinity of White Plains, New York, where Andrew came from. There could be family records there. The same would be true of Abigail Worthington."

"I can't tell you, really, how much I appreciate the trouble you've taken."

"It's been no trouble, really. I'm afraid Angelina descended from a pretty ordinary lot of people. Of course, families conceal their scandals, but there's nothing in the old records here—that I've found, anyway—to indicate anything unusual. Until Angelina killed her father, the family history was prosaic."

Lisa placed a call to Father William Longford. He was out, but after about an hour he returned her call.

"I'm sorry to have fled back to Ohio without saying good-bye. Frankie may have told you I had another experience with Jonathan after our last talk. I think of you as my friend and mentor, Father. I'll keep in touch."

"Dr. Gerard did call. I understand from her that the last manifestation of Jonathan was the most vivid and powerful yet."

"Yes. It was, Father. It most certainly was. But when I returned to Ohio, I acquired some new information. I'd like to mention two names to you, to see if they mean anything."

"Of course."

"Among the ancestors of Angelina Tatum were Susan Mead and Abigail Worthington, from your part of the country. Do those names mean anything to you?"

"A Mead family has long been prominent in the Greenwich area. Worthington . . . ? I don't know that name."

"Is there anything odd about the Meads?"

"Oh, very definitely. They must surely be among the most boring people I have ever encountered."

"Father . . . I'm looking for evidence of witchcraft, as you must know."

"Look for it, Lisa, among people of wit and learning. The Meads have insufficient imagination to be witches."

"Did you know my great-grandmother Kennedy?"

"By name. I never met her."

"Could she have been a witch?"

"If *you* could, she could have. She was a woman of stature, a woman of presence and force—so I have been told."

"What was said of her?"

"Nothing but good. That she was exceptionally intelligent, exceptionally personable."

"What about my grandmother? My mother?"

"Lisa, I know nothing of them. I've heard nothing said of them. Your family is known in this area, of course. No scandal has ever been attached to them, to my knowledge. If I were you, I would regard your great-grandmother's reference to a Mr. Roper as coincidence, or as something you have long stored in your subconscious and are bringing up now."

"Again, I'm sorry I ducked out so unceremoniously, Father."

"Feel welcome to call me any time, Lisa. I am most interested in your experiences."

Jonathan did not come, either in her dreams or in person. She did not experience another spectacle of horror: no hangings, no burnings, no brutal torture.

Thanksgiving. The fraternity house was deserted, and Ben Junior—Benny—came home for a long weekend.

He had an announcement to make. He told his father and mother over dinner his first night home that he was no longer a Catholic. He said it modestly, hesitantly, and yet bluntly, with finality.

"So what are you, then?" Lisa asked.

"I'm not sure. I think I'm nothing. Not an atheist. An agnostic, I guess."

"Well . . . that's interesting," she said, trying to be gentle, not to sound derisive when her eighteen-year-old son made so profound an announcement. She knew that scorn would only harden his determination. "I think I'd be careful, Benny. Eighteen is an early age to be concluding you are wiser than the past hundred generations of mature men and women."

"Just because I'm young, I'm not necessarily wrong."

"True. But not necessarily right, either. Will you let me suggest to you that it's a bit early for you to be making decisions you may have to live with for the rest of your life? And maybe long beyond."

He was very much like his father: tall, brown-eyed, already beginning to lose his hair; and, far more importantly, he was dead-serious, unhappily lacking in perspective and a sense of humor. Ben had been like that when she met him—a little too sure and at the same time a little too unsure, too quick to decide, then too ready to back down in the face of scorn. Both men, the older and the younger, were to a large degree guileless. She had to wonder if her son did not proclaim himself an agnostic just because the last person who talked earnestly to him had claimed *he* was an agnostic.

She had worried about that with Ben. She had to think about it now with Benny.

Ben was like her own father: willing to leave this earnest conversation to those who were earnest on the subject.

"Okay, Mother . . . Do you believe in the doctrine of the Trinity?"

"Credo quia absurdum," she said.

"Lisa," Ben interjected, "we know you have a classical education that includes Latin, which I don't and Benny doesn't yet. So, what the hell does the Latin mean?"

" 'I believe it *because* it is absurd.' "

"Which makes no sense at all," said Benny.

She shrugged.

"Voltaire said he wondered what Christ would have thought of the idea of the Trinity," Benny said.

"Voltaire and I have that in common."

Ben Junior frowned over his plate of pasta, his glass of red wine. "Do you still confess? Do you believe the priest can absolve you of your sins?"

"I do confess occasionally," she said. "But I live such a dull life that I have few sins."

"But do you think the priest can really grant you absolution?"

"For two thousand years people have thought so," she said. "I'd have to hear some pretty convincing argument or evidence before I gave up the idea. That's all I ask of you, son. Don't be too facile in abandoning something you might long regret abandoning."

"Have you been forgiven for practicing birth control?" her son asked pointedly.

"Has the pope been forgiven for prohibiting it?"

Ben laughed. Benny laughed. Lisa grinned and poured wine.

"Ben," she said later, when Benny had left the table, "would you object if I spent a little money on a piece of genealogical research?"

He swirled the wine in his glass and stared into it. "I thought you had your family history pretty well established."

"This is something else. I've gotten interested in something and have been doing some reading in the college library. The man who built this house was named Warren— Colonel J. M. Warren. In 1868 he had a birthday party here for his daughter Henrietta. One of the guests was an unmarried woman named Angelina Tatum. She was escorted to the party by a man named Roper, a sort of mysterious figure who shortly disappeared. A few weeks after the party Angelina Tatum murdered her father. She was hanged at the corner of Second and Putnam. I am fascinated with her. One of the librarians has run the genealogy of the Tatums back to the seventeenth century. I'd like to know who her mother's family was. Angelina's mother came to the States from England, from London. I'd like to hire a London researcher to do just the minimum of research, to see if he can find out who Angelina's mother was."

"You going to write a book on this?" Ben asked.

Lisa nodded. "At least an article. I've been thinking about it. Was there something in Angelina's background that made a timid spinster commit murder?"

Ben grinned. "If you can limit the cost to three or four hundred dollars . . . what the hell? My wife the biographer."

"I'm not sure the town is going to like it much. It's a scandal that has been hushed up for more than a century."

Ben sipped wine. "I don't know about you," he said, "but I've always found this town spooky. I mean, look at those huge Indian burial mounds. And some of the old houses. Including this one. There's a story that one of the old Victorian houses over beyond Seventh Street was the home of a man who dressed in nineteenth-century clothes until he died in the 1950s, and his elderly sister banged ghostly tunes out of a big organ for ten years more. One of the old houses was a station on the Underground Railroad."

"The town has atmosphere," she said. "It lives with its history."

"If you want to spend a reasonable amount of money running down this . . . What was her name?"

"Honor Trowbridge."

"Honor Trowbridge. Do it. Run her down. But I want to know all about this. I want to know what you're finding out."

One of the differences between Chappaqua and Marietta was that the people of Chappaqua drove more imported cars—Mercedes, BMW, Saab, Volvo, Honda, Toyota,

Mazda, Lexus. In Marietta, people drove Chevrolets, Fords, and Buicks, mostly. It was not easy to get all the foreign makes serviced in the Ohio Valley. So Lisa drove a Ford Probe and hated it.

She drove it on Wednesday to a bridge party in a suburb called Devola. It was Marietta custom to serve drinks at bridge parties, even in the afternoon, so when she drove back to town about four o'clock she was comfortably impassive: the effect of two martinis. On the way home she stopped at the Kroger Supermart to pick up a small beef roast for dinner.

To pick up her roast, ordered by telephone earlier, she did not need a cart. She walked through the store, wearing blue jeans and a sweatshirt, with Top-Siders—as common in this river town as in New England—toward the butcher shop in the rear of the store.

He was there!

He stood at the produce counter examining one tomato after another, as if he had never seen tomatoes before—or as if he found them extraordinarily expensive and was determined to buy only tomatoes that were absolutely unblemished. He wore khaki pants, a white dress shirt, open at the collar, and looked like an instructor from the college.

But he was Jonathan Roper! She had never before seen him, never imagined him, in the cold glare of fluorescent light.

She stepped up beside him. "Here?"

"Why not? You are here."

"In daylight, in public? In my dreams, yes. Never—"

"Why not?"

"My God, what are we, Jonathan?"

"You still don't know?"

"No!"

"Lovers," he said. "That's what we are."

Lisa glanced around the busy supermarket. "The question," she said, "is not what *we* are but what *you* are."

"And that, too, my darling, I think you must understand by now."

"Are you telling me I was Mathilde? Angelina?"

"No. Oh, no. Not at all. Of course not."

"Then . . . ?"

"Do not ask to know too much, before the time."

"Before what time?"

"Trust me, Lisa."

"Have I any choice? You come. You go. Am I to see you always now: in the grocery store, on the streets?"

"You called me, Lisa. I was on your mind."

"You are always on my mind, Jonathan. How could it be otherwise?"

He smiled. "You are always on mine, my darling. I think of little else."

"So what happens now? Do you disappear? Do you fade away? Do others see you, or do I look to them like an idiot, standing here holding a conversation with the air?"

Jonathan laughed. "Excuse me," he said to a woman walking by. "Is that your pen on the floor? Did you drop it?"

The woman glanced at the ballpoint pen lying at her feet, then at Jonathan. She smiled. "No. I didn't drop it, but thanks anyway."

He nodded and smiled. "Whoever lost it didn't lose much, hmm?"

She glanced at the pen again. "No. Whoever lost that didn't lose much. So thanks."

He looked at Lisa and shrugged. "Yes. Others do see me. I am very real, Lisa."

"When you choose to be," she said.

6

THE NEXT DREAM WAS IN SOME WAYS THE STRANGEST OF ALL. IN IT she was a witness to a conversation between Father William Longford and Dr. Frances Gerard.

They sat in his study in the rectory of the Church of the Holy Name of Jesus, sharing a pot of tea and some cookies. The priest's pipe lay aside in his ashtray.

"Both of us have the same problem," said Father William. "Lisa Hamilton is no longer your patient. She never was my parishioner. If we do anything now, we are nothing but officious intermeddlers. I am deeply concerned that she must now be trying to cope with this thing without our assistance, but I cannot find a way in which we can intervene—particularly, of course, since she has gone back to Ohio."

"I've thought of speaking to her mother," said Dr. Gerard. "It was her mother who referred her to me in the first place. But it would be questionable medical ethics, if not an outright violation. My patient spoke to me in confidence."

"If she were my parishioner, I might feel I could talk to her family. As it is, she is only a troubled woman who came to me for counseling, and I cannot violate her confidence."

"The basic problem is that she does not *want* to be rid of Jonathan. I asked her if she was in love with him, and she said she wasn't, but she would not deny she likes him."

"Dr. Gerard . . . is it your professional judgment that all this is in Lisa's mind? What does the medical literature say? How can we explain her dreaming exact details of things she is most unlikely to have read?"

"In the course of a good college education, a person is exposed to many things that do not remain in conscious memory. Lisa could have read accounts of witchcraft trials and burnings, and not specifically remember the details. In fact, maybe she was so horrified by what she read that she put it out of her consciousness. But it has been tucked away somewhere in her mind and begins to come out now. I say, Father, that this is possible. I don't say that is the answer; I say it is possible."

"Let us consider an alternative," said Father William. "If her Jonathan is real, some kind of supernatural manifestation, then could he be guiding her to turn away from us—away, that is, from anyone who might show her how to be free of him?"

Dr. Gerard put her teacup back in its saucer. Lisa read in Frankie's mind the wish that the priest would offer her a Scotch. "I don't think of that suggestion as an alternative, Father. I mean, it is not outside the realm of natural phenomena that her self-created Jonathan guides her to keep him close. He doesn't have to be supernatural to do that."

"You mean he may be a separate personality within Lisa's mind?"

"That's as good a way to put it as any. In fact, I rather like that way of analyzing it."

"In which case he is a manifestation of some deep-seated psychological problem of hers."

"Exactly. And of course he's defensive. The Jonathan personality does not want to be destroyed, so he introduces into her Lisa personality a strong affection for himself. Also, Jonathan-Lisa inspires in Lisa-Lisa an intense curiosity about himself. So he struggles for his survival on two fronts: in her emotions and in her intellect."

"But he is only Lisa."

"Yes. Only a part of her. I am interested in how much he is her opposite. She's female; he's male. She's dark; he's blond. She is introspective and not entirely self-confident; he is extroverted and satisfied with himself. In a sense, Jonathan is what Lisa wishes she had been."

"Are you prepared to say Lisa's dilemma is so assuredly self-contained that it is outside my realm?"

"Not at all, Father. It may well be that Jonathan is more within your competence than mine. A healthy mind is not exclusively a natural phenomenon, nor is a sick mind. Both have spiritual aspects. I wish Lisa would come back. I think we could, working together, rid her of Jonathan. Your contribution would be very important."

"What if he exists independently of her mind?"

"Then Lisa is in mortal danger," said Dr. Gerard solemnly. "I am not so committed a rationalist, Father, as to reject the *possibility* of demonic possession."

In the morning Lisa telephoned Frankie Gerard.

"I have one quick simple question for you, Frankie."

"Well, I'm glad to hear from you, Lisa, and will be glad to answer any question I can."

"Did you go to see Father William yesterday afternoon, have tea with him, and discuss me?"

"As a matter of fact— My God, Lisa! I did, but how do you know?"

"I think you had better ask Father William. There may be more to Jonathan than something in my mind. Right now you are talking to Lisa-Lisa, not Jonathan-Lisa."

"My God, Lisa!"

Dana Whitaker helped Lisa locate the name of a genealogical researcher in London. The library had a directory of ethical genealogical researchers. Lisa telephoned him. Yes, yes, he said, he could check the records for a Miss Honor

Trowbridge, who emigrated in 1823. She was interested in Honor Trowbridge's maternal descent. Yes, he could charge his services to an American Express number. And yes, he could transmit his findings to the American Cyanamid fax machine in West Virginia. Lisa told him the maximum fee she was willing to pay, which he did not find unusual; and he said in a matter of days he would report on all the work that much money would allow.

Jonathan, she discovered, had taken a room in the Ramada Inn, just outside town, and was living there, taking his meals in the restaurant, and driving around town in a BMW. He came to her at night, but only in dreams, never in his physical manifestation, because he could not be physically present in her bed when her husband was asleep beside her. After the occasion in the supermarket, he did not approach her in her waking hours. She saw him. He smiled at her. He made no contact.

She was annoyed.

Another dungeon. A woman—a girl, actually, certainly not yet twenty years old—lay in chains on a stone floor. This dream was worse than the dream of Trier. In the Trier dungeon Mathilde had not been tortured, except for whipping, only kept awake until she signed a confession. This girl had been burned with hot irons, her flesh pinched with red-hot pincers, and worse. Worse. Her right leg was broken in three or four places. Even so, the swollen, suppurating leg was tightly squeezed by an iron shackle.

Lisa did not enter the body of this tortured girl. To this agony she was only a witness. It was apparent to her that the girl lying on the stones was dying. Lisa was that girl, but she was not within her. She was disembodied and hovered in the air, watching.

A man lay a few yards away. He was chained as the girl was. His body was broken. The bones of both legs were shattered. Bone fragments showed through his flesh. His hands were bloody, mangled things, hardly recognizable as hands. His genitals had received the attention of his tormentors and were bloody and swollen. To Lisa, it was apparent that he, too, was dying.

He was Jonathan Roper! Even as he was, she could recognize him. She realized he *wanted* her to see this, that it was to be a part of her understanding.

He raised his eyes toward Lisa, the invisible witness, and she saw in his eyes—heard, more likely, a cry from his spirit—an appeal that she see and understand.

Now she was no longer a witness but was the girl. Thank God she was not yet dying on that dungeon floor but was a young mother, sitting on a stool in the doorway of a small house on a cobblestone street, nursing her child. Her daughter.

She sang to the baby as it suckled: an old song in a French dialect of which Lisa could understand but a few words. In the dream she could sing words she could not understand, and it made no difference that she had never heard them before. She stared down at the infant at her breast. She noticed that this girl—and she was a girl, barely eighteen years old—had no mole beside the nipple of her left breast.

She was a tiny girl, barely five feet tall, with very fine shoulder-length blonde hair admired by everyone who saw her. She wore a brown wool skirt and a white linen blouse, both clean and well fitted to her plump little figure.

So far had Jonathan drawn Lisa within this girl that she knew not only the song the child-mother was singing but who she was and where she was and when it was. She was Jacqueline Cordier, the wife of Jean Cordier, this city was Geneva, and this was the Year of Our Lord 1559.

Jean Cordier's grandfather had been a rope maker—hence the name. But Jean was not, nor had his father been, a rope maker. Jean's father, as a boy, had been apprenticed to a silversmith and had learned to fashion marvelous silver cups and bowls and trays. Jean himself was an engraver, who worked elaborate and delicate patterns into the metal and created objects of fabulous beauty, which Cordier et Fils sent to clients all over Europe.

Jacqueline d'Alembert was the daughter of a clothing merchant who sold the work of two dozen tailors. The two fathers had arranged the marriage of Jean and Jacqueline, and both were pleased, particularly when Jacqueline conceived within three months of the wedding. Their satisfaction could have been greater only if the child had been a son. But there was time for that. Jacqueline had conceived when she was sixteen, had borne the child when she was seventeen, and would undoubtedly go on bearing until there was not just one son but two or three or four.

Jacqueline was happy. Her baby was healthy. Jean did not beat her. Her father beat her mother; her sisters' husbands beat her sisters; but Jean had never used his fists or a cane on Jacqueline, and she had begun to doubt he ever would. Both families' businesses prospered.

Jean had spent months engraving a huge silver tray for an infidel king whose name and title she did not understand: the Sultan of Algiers. The god of these infidels condemned the representation of any person or thing in art, even a flower or a leaf; and the great silver tray was engraved in elaborate and curious patterns that looked like nothing that lived or ever had lived, man, beast, fish, or fowl. The payment for this tray was in gold and would sustain the Cordiers for years, if they did nothing else. So far had the family reputation extended.

The clothing merchants, the d'Alemberts, prospered as well, though they had experienced difficulties for a while. Under the laws of the new government of Geneva, men and women were forbidden to dress in the cheerful colors and flamboyant styles they loved but were required instead to go about in sobersided black and brown and gray. At first it had seemed this would ruin the business. Then the family had discovered that the Genevans, though forbidden to compete in gaudy adornment, did compete in the quality of the stuffs and the excellence of the tailoring that went into their drab clothes. The rich wore better clothing, as always. So . . . what difference? In terms of profit, what difference? The d'Alemberts who had imported from Venice now imported from Brussels, whence came the sturdy English wool.

Far more than clothing was governed by the ordinances of the city of Geneva. In the very year of Angélique's birth, the city had fallen under the dictatorship of the heretic fanatic Jean Chauvin, and since then everything in life had been regulated by his laws. How many dishes could be served at a meal was regulated by law. How a woman's hair could be styled was prescribed by ordinance, and only last year a woman had been taken to jail and locked up for several days because her hair was arranged "immorally." The theaters were closed. Dancing was forbidden. So was card playing. So was profanity.

What was more, it was a serious crime to criticize any of these laws or to speak disrespectfully of Jean Chauvin and his fellow ministers.

The worst was that Chauvin was a heretic. Not only that, he demanded that every man, woman, and child in Geneva become a heretic, too. Attendance at Protestant preaching was required, except for small children and the woman who stayed at home to care for them. The birth of her baby had relieved Jacqueline of the onerous burden of having to sit through four or five repugnant sermons a week, some of them by Jean Chauvin himself.

Only six times in her life had Jacqueline been privileged to attend Mass—when a brave Jesuit said it in secret, in the cellar or attic of a home or shop. Officially her daughter was Rebekah. Chauvin's law demanded that children be named for characters in the Old Testament, and an odious Protestant preacher had baptized the child Rebekah—never guessing that the child had already been baptized, by a Jesuit. Her name was Angélique.

Happily, the Jesuit had heard Jacqueline's confession, and Jean's, and granted them absolution during that same visit. She yearned for that, for the solace that came only from the Church and not from these haughty Protestant scolds by whom everyone was plagued day and night.

For a long time the Cordier and d'Alembert families had kept alive the hope that the people of Geneva would become exasperated with the despotic Chauvin and his heretic clique, banish them again as they had once been banished from Geneva, and welcome the return of the holy bishop and the priests. The hope dimmed as years passed and the population sank deeper into the Chauvin heresy. There had been hope, too, that Chauvin would relax his rules, since no one could really live with them. Instead, he and his gang became even more intrusive.

You could live happily in Geneva if you kept to yourself, said nothing, conformed outwardly in dress and speech, and focused your life on your home and family. To receive the consolation of true religion from time to time was to take a dangerous risk. For Jacqueline, the risk was welcome, the danger not fearful; she accepted them for the sake of her soul. Risk and danger even added a certain spice to life; if you were young and confident you would avoid denunciation.

The priest was in town. Father Vincente, a French Jesuit, was in the city in the guise of a wool merchant from Flanders and was saying Mass in the attic above the d'Alembert shop. Tonight Jacqueline would hear Mass. Tomorrow she would confess and, she hoped, receive absolution.

A black-gowned Protestant preacher strode through the street. As he passed, he glared at Jacqueline. He deplored her bare breast, even though she had an infant at it. He said nothing, but she sensed his thought, amplified as it was by his annoyance. Sometimes she could tell what people were thinking, particularly if they were emotional. Jacqueline sighed and tucked her breast back inside her bodice. Angélique was satisfied anyway.

Jean would come home for their midday meal. It was time for her to begin to prepare it. She took the baby inside, put her in her cradle in the kitchen, and knelt to shove sticks of wood onto the coals in the fireplace. She was annoyed with herself that she had let the fire so nearly go out. She had to lean forward and blow on the coals. She held the thinnest of the sticks against a faintly glowing coal, blew as hard as she could, and was thankful that the coal gleamed red and produced a small flame on the stick. Blowing and adding more sticks, she generated a healthy little fire. She swung the pot around over the flames.

As she rose and turned, she was horriied to discover she was not alone in the kitchen. A man had come in! He was a big man, tall, with an angry-looking face, dressed in black.

Jacqueline opened her mouth. He shook his head. He continued to shake it. He stood in the doorway and made no move to come closer to her.

"Who are you?"

"Who are you?" he asked.

"I am Jacqueline. This is my house, and my husband's. Why have you—"

"My child, I am Father Vincente. I have terrible news. We have been discovered. The watchmen have invaded our homes and businesses. Your family has been taken. The Cordiers, too. I have no doubt the watchmen are on their way here, to take you."

"How did *you* escape, Father?" she whispered. "God be praised that you did. But how?"

"One of the watch remains faithful and ran ahead to warn me. He warned your father, but there was no place for him to go. My face is not known on the streets. I hurried to the Cordier home, but I was too late. It may be that you can escape with me. But we must go now."

"No. I will be recognized. I'll try, but— Father, take my baby! Go alone, without me. I will try to escape. But my baby has a far better chance with you. Please, Father! Please!"

The tortured woman, Lisa now noticed, lay with her head turned toward the man. She was watching him. He stared at the ceiling. They were beyond speaking to each other, and he was beyond responding to her gaze, if he was aware of it.

"Jonathan!" cried the disembodied Lisa, her cry unsounded. "Spare me this!"

The man on the floor neither heard nor responded. No other Jonathan appeared at her side.

"Jonathan, I don't want to see this! I don't need to see this! I believe whatever you want me to believe! Don't make me—"

With a rasp like an anguished shriek, a door opened. Four men entered the dungeon chamber. All looked alike. All wore long black woolen gowns and flat-topped headdresses that covered their heads and necks but left their ears exposed. One wore a long thin beard, extending halfway to his waist.

The one with the exceptionally long beard stepped forward. The others stood back, respectfully.

"Jean Cordier," he said sepulchrally to the man on the floor, "do you remain obstinate?" He spoke oddly accented French, but Lisa understood him.

The man did not answer.

The bearded man turned to the woman. "Jacqueline d'Alembert, do you remain obstinate?"

The woman did not answer.

"This is your last chance to earn our mercy. No further opportunity will come. Have you no concern for your souls? Eternity is long. Have you no concern for where you will be for all eternity? For all eternity!"

The dying man and woman remained silent. The woman's eyes were fixed devotedly on the man. He turned his head now and looked at her.

"Recite the charges against them," the bearded man said to one of the respectful ones hanging back.

"Witchcraft," intoned the man. "In that both of them, in violation of God's holy laws and ordinances and the laws and ordinances of the city of Geneva, did, not once but repeatedly, attend and participate in the ritual of the AntiChrist commonly called the Mass, did repeatedly express their devotion to the Church of Satan, commonly called the Church of Rome, did promise obedience to Satan's chief servant, commonly called the Bishop of Rome or, worse, Pope, and did participate in a mockery of holy marriage by allowing themselves to be the subjects of an unclean ritual called a marriage, performed over them by a servant of Satan—the worst kind of such servant, a Jesuit. Contumaciousness. In that both have wickedly and defiantly refused to name other participants in these vile and unholy Satanic rites. Defiance. In that the woman malevolently caused the child she sinfully conceived to be taken away, probably from the city, and has insolently refused to reveal the whereabouts of this child."

"Jean Cordier," intoned the one with the long beard, "do you persist in denying that the so-called Mass is witchcraft at its unclean worst?"

The man said nothing.

"We are under severe obligation to save the souls of the world, so long squandered by Satan in his popish manifestation. Were we to grant mercy to you, we would imperil our own souls and countless other souls. The two of you are a threat to man's salvation! Even so, we suppose no soul is beyond redemption. Confess your guilt! Embrace true religion! And I will instruct the executioner to strangle you before the fire rises around you."

Neither of the dying couple so much as shifted an eye toward the man. They gave no sign that they had heard him.

"The penalty will be imposed," said the bearded man. He stepped nearer the woman. "Jacqueline d'Alembert, you will be taken to the execution square and there chained to the stake. Before your fire is lighted, your teats will be ripped from your body by glowing pincers. Hot iron will be inserted where you received the organ of the AntiChrist. And only then will you be burned."

The woman sighed. The man did not know what Lisa immediately knew: that Jacqueline had just died.

The bearded man turned to Jean Cordier. "Before your fire is lighted, the tongue you have used to speak false doctrine will be ripped from you. You will be blinded. Your sinful parts will be torn off. Only then will you have the mercy of the fire."

Jean Cordier spoke. "May the ever living God impose an eternal curse on you, Johannes Calvinus," he muttered. "Jean Chauvin. The true AntiChrist. Idolater. Chief worshiper at the shit-fouled idol of . . . of *himself!*"

John Calvin spat on the man. "God does not hear the prayer of a Catholic," he said.

"No. I should judge He has not heard mine," gasped Jean Cordier. "If He had, you would be shriveled by loathsome disease. He has not heard my wife and me. He has given us no mercy. He has allowed us to be destroyed by the abhorrent heretic who has seized our city and destroyed true faith here."

"Does it occur to you that all you say proves you are wrong?" asked John Calvin.

"It proves that God is wrong!" screamed Jean Cordier.

Calvin recoiled in horror, throwing his arm before his face as if to protect himself.

"I curse the God who has allowed us to die this way!" Cordier yelled. "For Him! It was our sacrifice for Him! And out of His mercy and His gratitude for our sacrifice, He has ordained that you should live to gloat and we should die in agony! *Satan! You* hear me! I call you! I will worship you! I will serve you! *Satan!*"

John Calvin backed toward the door. *"Silence him!"* he roared.

Lisa stood in the crowd. All were silent. No one dared speak a word.

Carried out from the dungeon— Not Jean and Jacqueline. Not even their corpses. Effigies. As the people stared and gaped, straw-stuffed dummies of a man and a woman were carried to the stakes.

The sentence was carried out as John Calvin had pronounced it, as near as the executioner could do it. He used glowing pincers to tear away some of the cloth and stuffing from the effigy of the woman, where her breasts might have been. The effigy caught fire, and an attendant threw water on it. The executioner shoved a red-hot iron rod between the legs of the dummy. Again it caught fire, and again water was used to put out the fire.

The laboring executioner did as much as he could to carry out the sentence on the effigy of Jean Cordier.

Finally, huge fires were lighted under the two effigies. In minutes the dummies were consumed, but the fires burned for hours, as if real people had been burned.

Lisa left the bed. Ben didn't notice. She climbed the stairs to her octagonal study in the tower, closed the blinds, and switched on the lights.

"All right, Jonathan," she said in a low voice.

And he was there.

This time he was not naked. He was dressed in gray flannel slacks, a white shirt open at the collar, and a dark-blue cashmere sweater. He was sitting in the chair at her desk.

She sat down on the couch, wearing a thin but not sheer white nightgown.

"Your husband?"

"He won't waken," she said. She was not certain how she could be so confident of that, but she was. She shrugged. "I know he won't. I . . . I somehow know."

Jonathan smiled.

"As Jean Cordier you called on Satan," she said dejectedly. "And I suppose he—"

"Helped Jean Cordier? Not for the moment, anyway. Jean Cordier died. Calvin ordered them to silence Jean, and they did. They did not understand the mercy of the blow that smashed my skull."

"And then they performed an obscene ritual on the square."

"Yes. I wanted you to see what the great Jean Chauvin, Johannes Calvinus himself, was capable of doing, lest you think it was only the fiendish Dominicans and other brutal

Roman inquisitors who tortured and burned. It went on for well over a century, Lisa, and tens of thousands of innocent women, plus other thousands of innocent men, were put through torments that Satan himself never ordained in Hell."

"Who are you, Jonathan? Are you Satan?"

"No."

"But Satan lies."

He smiled again. "Yes. When it suits him. And I do when it suits me. As you do, too—not often enough, but as you may learn to do."

"What do you want of me?"

"It will be revealed in time."

"Was Mathilde a witch?"

"Yes."

"Then there are such things as witches? Witchcraft is not a fable."

"Remember *Malleus Maleficarum*, the Hammer of Witches. An encyclopedia of insanity, written by two deranged men. But it contains some truths, perhaps specially revealed to those two crank Dominicans, Heinrich Krämer and Jakob Sprenger. Recall what they wrote: for witchcraft to be practiced, three prerequisites are necessary—the presence of the Devil, the presence of a witch, and the permission of Almighty God."

"How could God permit—"

"The Almighty never did, until the witchcraft craze threatened to depopulate Christendom. Even Augustine and Aquinas, wise men in most respects, were deluded on the subject of witchcraft. As were thousands of others throughout the Middle Ages. But *their* delusions did not lead to mass murder. That remained for—"

"You say 'mass murder'? Surely—"

"Lisa! Do you realize there was a town in Germany where *only one woman survived the burnings?* Many towns lost half their women, and by no means were most of them pitiful old women; healthy, lusty girls and women of childbearing age were burned. Others were hanged. Many died under the torture, or from the cold and damp of dungeons. There was something entirely new in these persecutions. For centuries witches had occasionally been burned, but only if some offense could be proved against them. Mathilde pleaded she had done no one wrong. Binsfeld told her that made no difference. I need hardly tell you what little evidence was sometimes required to prove a supposed witch had harmed someone, but at least someone had to *be* harmed. That was limiting. Without that limit, the witch burners could kill anyone they chose. And the numbers were growing."

"But God's *permission*—"

"The Almighty *gave* permission! I say to you, Lisa, that the Almighty was so disgusted with the world that He gave careful consideration to destroying it again, as he did in the great flood. Instead, the Almighty gave permission for . . . He made witches, and there have been witches ever since. The poor women needed powers to save themselves. You saw Mathilde save herself. And the witch burners had to be punished. You saw her punish Binsfeld."

"I cannot believe God would intentionally unleash evil on the world."

"Who says witches are evil? The only evil ones are those who have persecuted them mercilessly and have needed to justify themselves."

"Isn't Satan evil?"

"Satan is a lesser god. If you want to be strictly monotheistic, then he is not actually a god but is an angel of the highest order: a seraph. The Almighty is greater and could destroy Satan. Have you never wondered why Satan lives? Why does the Almighty not just sweep Satan away? A sea of ink has been spilled in trying to explain that. But the Almighty has a purpose in keeping Satan alive, and that is why Satan lives."

"That is a gross heresy."

"The Almighty has a purpose for heresy, too."

"Are there many witches?"

"Not many. I suspect that the Almighty would withdraw permission if there were too many."

"Was Angelina a witch?"

"Yes, but only a minor one. She didn't know her powers."

"Are you telling me that she herself, by her own strength, killed her father?"

"Forming the will was more difficult than finding the strength."

"Then why didn't she save herself from hanging? You . . . You said you saved her."

"Angelina was strongly faithful. Faith had been so thoroughly inculcated in her—as it had in her mother, who was the mistress of her education and of her mind—that Angelina did not want any more of this life. She wanted martyrdom."

"But she rejected God, at the end."

Jonathan smiled. *"'Eli, Eli, lama sabachthani?'* My God, my God, why has Thou forsaken me? Part of the drama of martyrdom. If Christ could accuse God of forsaking him, why couldn't Angelina?" He sighed. "Anyway, she didn't know her powers. Nor did her mother. And neither of them called for help. Angelina wanted to move on. She did. She wanted to see the face of the Almighty. She does. Or—Well . . . she thinks she does."

"What became of her daughter?"

"She died."

"She was adopted."

"She died later."

"You were the father of that child."

"Yes."

"Then you can impregnate a woman."

"Yes."

"Jonathan . . . Have you impregnated me?"

He reached for her hand, took it, and pressed it to his mouth. "Yes, Lisa. You are going to bear my child."

The gynecologist confirmed it. She was pregnant.

"So how do you explain *that,* Frankie?" She had telephoned Dr. Gerard as soon as she reached home again. "How can I be *pregnant?*"

"Lisa! You still have relations with your husband. You told me that."

"We've had no broken condoms. Do you want to tell me they leak?"

"You're an intelligent and educated woman, Lisa. You know as well as I do that there could be a hundred rational explanations for your pregnancy."

"Have you and Father William found an explanation for my knowing that you met and discussed me?"

"No."

"Maybe I am beginning to develop second sight."

Frankie Gerard was silent for a moment, then said, "Can you come back here?"

"I have to celebrate Christmas in this house shortly. That's a big deal for this family. No, I can't leave town again and stay away a week."

"Have you told your husband you're pregnant?"

"I've only known it an hour."

"May I assume you are going to tell him?"

"Of course I'm going to tell him."

"When is the baby due?"

"August."

"Will he think it's his?"

"I can only hope so."

"I'll talk to Father William. Do you want us to keep away from your mother?"

"Absolutely."

"We'll follow your wishes."

"Please."

"Is Jonathan there?"

"Yes. In a corporeal manifestation. He lives in a motel, drives a car."

"I'll tell Father William."

She did not tell Ben she was pregnant. Not that evening. The next day she telephoned her mother and told her. Her mother said a pregnancy at her age could be dangerous and that she must care for herself.

The next evening Ben brought a fax from London. It was the report of the genealogist. It included a chart.

HONOR TROWBRIDGE (1810–99)

John Trowbridge (1781–1858) m. Honor Osborne (1781–1826)

Samuel Osborne (1760–1819) m. Moll Douglas (1763–1821)

Sir William Douglas (1721–94) m. Amelia McClintock (1724–1790)

George McClintock (1698–1749) m. Katherine McNeill (1705–68)

Notes accompanied the chart:

John Trowbridge was a London merchant, a dealer in ships' stores. His family home was a handsome house facing on Lincoln's Inn Fields. Having accumulated a respectable fortune, he removed to America in 1823.

Samuel Osborne was a merchant banker in London. His countinghouse was in Chancery Lane.

Sir William Douglas lived on a substantial estate in Bucks, granted to him by King George II as a reward for his adhering to the King's cause and leading his Scots clan against the army of Bonnie Prince Charlie, which was also the origin of his knighthood.

George McClintock was a solicitor in Edinburgh.

This is as far back as I can go for the fee agreed to. Further researches would have to be undertaken in Edinburgh, for which you would incur substantially greater expense.

Ben was a competent, successful man who had done well in his company. Even though he was the manager of the Waverly plant, he was plagued, as every manager is, by the tensions of hierarchy—layers above and layers below—and it was not unusual for him to come home angry or worried. He rarely tried to explain to Lisa the source of his stress. To do that only meant that he would have to rehearse the whole thing. Not knowing the personalities, not knowing the policies and procedures of the company, she found the explanations difficult to understand, and they were boring to both of them.

Very often he settled down after dinner and stared at television for two hours. When there were no ball games to watch, he would watch "L.A. Law," "Heat of the Night," "Roseanne," "Knots Landing," or even "Grandma's Family"—anything for diversion. Distraction restored him. He was a more forthcoming man starting about ten o'clock.

This evening, while he was watching television, Lisa went to their bedroom. In the nightstand on his side of the bed he kept his packages of condoms. A box of Ramses. Two left. She tore open one package and left the torn package in the box. She flushed the condom down the toilet. The remaining one she carried up to her study and dropped in a drawer.

At ten he switched off the television set.

"Know what I'd like?" she asked. "I'd like to go for a little drive. I'll drive if you're tired. Just half an hour. No more. Game?"

She could read him. Plainly he didn't want to go, but plainly also he did not want to refuse to follow her little whim. He knew she thought him prosaic.

"If you don't mind driving," he said.

She had nowhere in particular in mind. Ten minutes out of town in any direction you could find yourself in silent woods, on a gravel road, climbing a hill, descending into a creek valley where the water rushed alongside the road. She drove. She didn't know the names of the roads or villages of the county. She wasn't even entirely confident of the way. But she had a general idea of it, and she drove into the farmland, then up onto a high ridge where a primitive road kept to the highest ground.

She recognized a tiny cemetery they passed—an old

family cemetery where the weeds were rarely cut, where only fragments remained of a wrought-iron fence. There were no more than twenty graves, and no one had been buried there since 1921. A professor from the college had scandalized the town last year by bringing a young woman, a college senior so thin she was all but gaunt, up here on an autumn afternoon when the low sun and the turning foliage created a brilliant yellow-white light, altogether unique, and having her pose in the nude among the flaking old gravestones. Everyone was more surprised, and many were more distressed, when the photographs were exhibited, first in the college arts center, then in Pittsburgh and Cleveland, and finally in Washington, won awards, and sold for hundreds of dollars per print.

Ben relaxed during the drive. He did not go to sleep, but he said almost nothing the whole time, and she doubted he saw much.

Back home, she asked, "Coffee? Tea? One light Scotch?"

"One light Scotch," he said.

"I'll bring them to the bedroom," she said. "You go on up."

They looked at the top stories of the news on the bedroom television set while they sipped Scotches that were truly light. They switched the set off.

"Ben . . ."

"Honey?"

"Guess what I want."

"Well, I . . . I guess I do, too."

She jerked her nightgown over her head. Ben slept in pajamas, and he needed only a moment to be rid of them.

"C'mere," she grunted as she stretched out on the bed.

Time was, she had admired his masculinity. Hell, she still did. It was foolish to suppose she didn't. He didn't lack anything . . . except maybe imagination, except maybe commitment. If their erotic partnership had not been all it might have been, she accepted half the responsibility. Maybe more. She could have demanded more. He would have given it.

It was comfortable to lie in his arms. He was like Mister Blanket: a comfortable habit you couldn't give up without an awful wrench, yet one you *could* give up, and you *would* survive the wrench.

He kissed her. He fondled her breasts and belly: the warm, familiar fondling. He kissed her nipples. For an instant she tensed as he kissed around her breast and his lips touched the tiny mole that Jonathan seemed to concentrate on. But Ben moved on, as she had known he would; she knew exactly when he would move to the next step.

"Ready, hon?"

Lisa nodded.

He rolled over and opened the drawer. "Oh, damn!" he muttered as he checked the box of Ramses.

"Damn what?"

"We're out of cockrubbers. I could have sworn . . . You suppose Benny—"

"You should keep better track. I mean, it's embarrassing for me to buy condoms."

"Well, I guess we'll have to wait until tomorrow night."

"Oh, no, my friend! Wait hell! Not now, we're not backing away. C'mon!"

"It's a risk," he said solemnly.

"Everything good is a risk. C'mon, Ben. You're not gonna get me feeling like this and back off. C'mon! Climb aboard. C'mon. That's it . . . Uhmm. The bare one always feels better. There's no substitute for the real thing."

As Ben labored and she closed her eyes, she heard something he did not hear. Laughter . . . All right, Jonathan, you son of a bitch! You don't have to watch. Go 'way! Go 'way, dammit!

7

THE HOUSE LENT ITSELF BEAUTIFULLY TO CHRISTMAS DEC-
orating, and every year the Hamiltons gave a large party to
which they invited friends, neighbors, townspeople, and
some of the staff from American Cyanamid. The two Bens,
father and son, took a special pride in the lights they hung in
the trees in front of the house, describing them as "Christmas maudlin." They were in fact tasteful, not gaudy. Lisa
decorated inside, climbing a ladder to put lights and orna-
ments on the huge tree the high-ceilinged house could
accommodate. The Hamiltons' Christmas decorations and
party had already become a town tradition.

Marietta did not have a catering service as such, but one
of the town's few black families accepted engagements to
cook and serve and clean up after large parties; and ever
since the Hamiltons' second year there, this family had
worked with Lisa to choose a menu and spend all day and all
evening—indeed until well after midnight after the party—
working until the house the next morning looked as if a
party had not been held there.

Lisa worked with these people until an hour before the
guests were to arrive, though she really didn't have to. About
the time she abandoned them to go up to dress, they took

twenty minutes off to go to a third-floor room and change out of their jeans and sweatshirts and into the garb of butler, houseboy, and maids. After the guests were gone, they would change back again.

Each year Lisa bought a dress for this party. This year it was red, with a stylishly short skirt and bold décolletage. The men did not dress for dinner. In fact, dinner was a buffet. Ben wore a double-breasted blue blazer.

"Lisa, you are simply gorgeous," he said to her as she showed him her dress in the bedroom just before they went downstairs. "That dress is just wonderful."

In years past she had prompted him to find words better than "gorgeous" and "wonderful" to praise something she had spent hours shopping for. Now she was pleased with "gorgeous" and "wonderful."

"Ben . . . I'm glad you think so. I have to tell you something. Maybe this is the best time, just before a happy evening."

"Lisa . . . ?"

She smiled. "Remember the night we took the chance? Well . . . It was good luck or bad luck, depending on how you look at it. Ben . . . I'm pregnant."

"Lisa . . . Well, that's wonderful!"

He took her in his arms and kissed her. Even so, he was not glad. She could tell. He would lie. He would lie about it forever. But he couldn't conceal his dismay. At his age he did not want to start parenting again.

"My mother knows," she said. "No one else knows it but the doctor."

"Do you want to announce it?"

"No. At the right time."

He kissed her again. "I'm glad, Lisa. I'm really glad. Maybe it will be a little girl."

"You'd like that?"

"Yes."

Lisa turned to the mirror. Ben had always been transparent to her. She had never needed any special power, given maybe by Jonathan, to look into Ben's mind, or Benny's, and see what either of them was trying to conceal. Tonight, though, she could *feel* Ben's despair. He felt trapped in a calamity and wondered if there were any escape.

Typical Ben. He had planned his life. He expected two more promotions from American Cyanamid, the last one to an office in the corporate headquarters in New Jersey, followed by retirement at sixty-five. He had already looked at Florida condos, priced them. (He had not read *Rabbit at Rest*, as Lisa had.) Ben had always known who he was and where he was going. She had once suggested he could take early retirement when Benny was out of college. There were a thousand alternatives to the life they lived, she had reminded him. His total response had been a quick shake of his head. Similarly, there was nothing in his plan about another child when he was forty-three.

Lisa's mother and father usually came to Marietta for the annual party. They had come downstairs ahead of her and were in the living room.

"You are a beautiful woman, Lisa," said Mary O'Neil, taking her by both hands. "Take very good care of yourself these coming months."

"I will, of course."

Her mother clung to her hands, smiling at her, admiring her—still, unable to conceal her concern for a daughter pregnant at forty-one.

Lisa looked at herself in the tall mirror across the room. She *was* beautiful. Hers was an unconventional beauty, but it was real. People *did* admire her. The scarlet dress set off her dark brown hair and her skin, which remained faintly golden, though the tawniness of summer was gone now. The full skirt that ended two inches above her knees set off her handsome legs in their dark stockings. All evening men would be glancing into her décolletage, hoping for a glimpse of a full, shiny nipple; and maybe one or two of them would be fortunate enough to see it. She had chosen this dress to flaunt herself. Maybe this was the last holiday party when she could be so audacious.

The president of Marietta College and his wife were among the first guests to arrive, followed by the president of the Rotary Club and his wife, followed by Pat and Richard Irving—Pat was a member of Lisa's bridge club. Shortly the house was filled with people, circulating through all the downstairs rooms and some going even to the octagonal tower, having heard of Lisa's study and curious to look into it. They found the door locked.

Lisa did not know everyone, not for certain. It made no difference. They knew who *she* was, that she was the hostess.

Ben Junior brought a date: a tiny, bespectacled, obsessively fussy young woman from the college, who seemed clingingly determined that not a speck of lint should remain on Ben's jacket, not a hair on his head should be a quarter of an inch out of place. She clung to him and picked at him and seemed hardly to notice that anyone else was at the party. Benny was beguiled by this treatment and accepted it as if it were an honor—indeed, as though it were his due.

Her name was Anne Merck. She mumbled to Lisa that this was a beautiful house and she just loved it, then returned her attention to Benny.

"Lisa, have you met this gentleman?"

She turned and saw her husband leading Jonathan toward her, his hand on Jonathan's elbow.

"This is Mr. Jonathan Roper, from London. He's spending a few days in town, and the Robertsons suggested he come along this evening."

"I am afraid I am intruding," Jonathan said suavely. He wore a modern version of the suit he had worn to Henrietta Warren's birthday party, in this same house, this same room, in 1868—a dark gray jacket with black velvet inserts on the lapels, a ruffled white shirt with broad black bow tie, black trousers, black Gucci loafers. "Ted Robertson assured me—"

"Not at all, Mr. Roper," said Lisa.

"I told him we're very happy to have him."

"We are, of course," Lisa said.

"I thought it might be appropriate to bring a small gift," said Jonathan. He handed her a foil bag that obviously contained a bottle of wine.

"Oh, open it, Lisa," Ben said with enthusiastic curiosity. "I want to see."

She did: Château Lafite-Rothschild, 1976.

"My God!"

"Mr. Roper, you shouldn't have," said Ben. "We are grateful, of course, but—"

"My pleasure. I hope you enjoy it."

Lisa signaled the man acting as butler. "Paul," she said to him. "Put this away somewhere safe and out of sight. It's not to be served tonight."

Ben spotted a man and wife from Cyanamid, looking lost. "Excuse me," he said and hurried toward those two.

"Mr. Roper from London," said Lisa. "I'm not sorry to see you here, but—"

"You are lovely this evening, Lisa. I have never seen you so entrancing. You fairly glow. Do you know that? You are great good fortune for me. I respectfully hope you will decide that I am the same for you. And, incidentally, the house is no longer hideous. You have exquisite taste."

"I'll say it more directly, Jonathan. I am glad to see you. But there are two people you must avoid. One, my mother, who remembers her grandmother calling out to Mr. Roper as her last words. Second, a woman named Dana Whitaker, a librarian at Marietta College. She has read the story of the murder of Josiah Tatum and the hanging of Angelina, and she knows the name Jonathan Roper. Ben should remember it, too, since I mentioned it to him when I told him I wanted to do some genealogical research on the Tatums. So far he seems not to have made the connection, but—"

"Which ones are your mother and the librarian?" he asked. "Point these two people out to me."

"You know which ones they are, Jonathan," Lisa said firmly. "I don't have to point them out. You know."

"You're a clever woman, Lisa. That's an impediment in

some ways. But in more important ways, it's most valuable. In fact, it is essential."

"I must speak with other guests. Thank you for the wine. You realize, of course, that you made yourself unforgettable to my husband."

"He and I should try to be friends."

She could not help but smile. "Is there no limit to your chutzpah?"

Jonathan glanced around to be certain no one could hear, then said, "I love you, Lisa."

Within ten minutes he had talked both to Lisa's mother and to Dana Whitaker.

"Charming man, your friend Mr. Roper," her mother said. "I mentioned how my grandmother called out the name Roper at the end. He found that fascinating, but he said his own family had always lived in England so Grandmother Kennedy and his own grandfather or great-grandfather could not possibly have met. In fact, he said, his English family in past generations had entertained a prejudice against the Irish."

"But he does not?" asked Lisa.

Mary laughed. "He assured me."

He had dealt equally smoothly with Dana Whitaker.

"He told me you had spoken to him about the Jonathan Roper who was here in 1868," she said to Lisa. "He is sure, he says, that he's the first of his family ever to visit America. Roper is a common name in England, he reminded me. So is Jonathan. Even so, he thinks he's the first in his family to be called Jonathan. An engaging man, isn't he? What an interesting coincidence!"

A few minutes later he spoke to Lisa, who asked for an explanation. He shrugged and smiled and said, "I can't have people in town that I have to avoid."

"I hope you don't mind my bringing Roper to the party," said Ted Robertson. "He's a client, all the way from

London. He's alone in town. Nice sort of fellow, don't you think?"

"Yes, he seems to be a nice fellow."

"He *is* a nice fellow, I can tell you. He gave some people here a bit of a scare. Could have made a lot of trouble for them, and didn't."

"How's that?"

"Well, I guess I can tell you without violating lawyer-client confidentiality. When he came here and retained me as a lawyer, he showed me papers from British records proving that he is a descendant of a woman named Abigail Trowbridge Kinney. The family tradition was that Abigail should have inherited a substantial amount of property here in Washington County, and didn't. He came to check on the claim. I researched the old land titles in the courthouse, and by golly, he was right! His claim would have raised complex questions of law, but he was right: he did have a claim to land in Washington County."

"How? What property?"

"Well, a man named Josiah Tatum died here in 1868. He was murdered, as a matter of fact, by his own spinster daughter, who was hanged for it. Under his will, his wife, whose name was Trowbridge, should have inherited half his estate. But she had disappeared. In fact, she had gone back to England. Josiah Tatum's half brother, Harman Tatum, claimed the estate and took it. Things were done informally in those days. Harman was an aggressive fellow, probably, and prominent, so when he demanded the estate, the probate judge approved transfer of the property to him. Anyway, Honor Trowbridge Tatum never remarried and died leaving no will. Her rights passed to her sister's descendants—that is to say, the descendants of Abigail. So . . . Jonathan Roper has a claim to some valuable property. Some of it had been sold off, but there's enough left in the hands of the descendants of Harman Tatum to meet his claim."

"So what makes him a nice fellow?"

"Having established his claim, he said he didn't want it,

only came here out of curiosity, to check on it. The Tatums offered him ten thousand dollars for a quitclaim deed. He wouldn't accept it. And he signed the deed anyway. He told them not to worry about it; he hadn't come to claim their property."

"That should make him a popular fellow, at least with the Tatum heirs. Will he be going back to England now?"

"Maybe not. He's thinking of buying a home here. He has a realtor looking for a small house for him. He admires your house and is looking for something old—of course not so grand."

"Jonathan, for Christ's sake!" she hissed at him. "What the *hell* are you doing?"

He smiled insouciantly. "I established a reason for being here, so my presence in the town won't become the subject of damaging curiosity."

"Are you really a descendant of Abigail Trowbridge?"

"No."

"But Ted says you have papers—"

"Forgeries. Ted Robertson is no dummy. He would have discovered they are forgeries, if I'd pressed a claim. By establishing the appearance of a claim and then abandoning it, I won myself some friends in Marietta."

"Are you really going to buy a house here?"

"I may do that."

"Then you plan to stay here. How long will I have you around, Jonathan?"

"Till our child is born. And after. I want to see how she is reared."

"'She.' You are satisfied it will be a daughter?"

"I believe so."

"And she will be a witch?"

"Yes."

"Have I anything to say about this? What if I decide to have an abortion?"

"You wouldn't do that. That's a mortal sin. I am confident you won't do it. Anyway, you should be very pleased. You are going to have a daughter who will be an exceptional person."

"A witch!"

"You don't like the word 'witch.' It's ugly. Very well. The Romans called a supposed witch a *saga.* It means diviner, one who can see the future. The English word 'sagacious' comes from the same root. Maybe you prefer the French word, *sorcière,* or the Italian, *maga.* A witch, Lisa, is a woman with exceptional wisdom, wisdom denied to others. Lisa *saga.* A woman to whom special knowledge has been vouchsafed."

"The knowledge of good and evil," she said. "The forbidden fruit."

Jonathan laughed. "Our daughter will have the knowledge of good and evil," he said. "It will not be denied to her, not forbidden to her; she will have it with the permission of the Almighty."

"What if my child is a son?"

"It will be Ben's. And you and I will try again."

"What if I don't want to?"

"I will talk to you about that sometime. This is hardly the occasion for it, do you think?"

"Benny . . . I had not at all meant to do this. Anything like this."

Anne Merck was naked. Her party dress lay across the straight wooden chair at Ben Junior's study desk—together with her brassiere, a pair of panties, her garter belt, and her stockings. She lay on his bed and waited as he tossed his clothes on the floor.

"Neither had I, Annie," he said. "I hadn't really thought of it at all. Not for tonight. But suddenly . . . God, it came on me! I want you so much!"

"I want you, too, Benny," she whispered. "Can two glasses of champagne make us—"

He checked the door. It was double-locked. The young man strode to the bed. Without a moment of foreplay he straddled the girl and entered her—bare, with no precaution. She wanted nothing else. She rose up to meet his downward thrusts, bringing to the moment the earthy ardor of a virgin who had known nothing of the like before but instinctively knew what to do, as an unafraid woman intuitively does.

"Benny! Benny! *Yes, yes, yes, yes!*"

His fervor was not so intense as to drive from his mind the momentary thought that she had said no, no, no, no, only three evenings ago.

"Oh, Jesus Christ Almighty! Ben . . . *ny!* But . . . but, honey . . . Who's laughing? Who's laughing? *Benny?*"

"I don't hear anybody laughing."

"I do. But . . . God, don't *stop!* For Christ's sake, you can't *stop!* Whoever's laughing can go fuck himself. . . . We'll figure him out later."

Lisa broke away from the party. Inside her bedroom she locked the door, even though the bed was heaped with guests' coats. She went into the bathroom and locked the bathroom door as well. She had begun to suffer a vision.

My God! How much could she assimilate in one night?

Benny . . . Benny . . . Oh, Christ, Benny! Astride the strange little girl! The girl cried out! God, was he raping her? No . . . No. The whimper from that girl was no cry of protest. Lisa could see her. Her legs encircled Benny. She wanted all she was getting.

Christ! I don't want to know this! Why do I know? *How* do I know? She had known things about her son before, had sensed some of his moments of intense emotion, and had always attributed her knowledge to a mother's intuition, to that special inspiration nearly every mother claimed she had about things that happened to her children. But this . . . This image was not just vivid but explicit! Too damned explicit. It was one thing to sense that her son was having sex with a girl, quite another to hear her little ecstatic cries and see an image of her ankles crossed on Benny's back!

Did Jonathan have anything to do with this? He had projected visions into her mind, nightmares of hanging and torture. Could he have witnessed Benny with that girl and projected the image to her? If so, *why?*

Benny had always confided in her, had told her things he never told his father. Would he tell her this, that he took that girl to bed during the party?

Pat Irving, the member of Lisa's bridge group that played at the Betsy Mills Club, balanced a plate of food on her knee and somehow managed to eat and sip champagne without spilling anything. She was a heavy woman, always wore more makeup than Lisa thought she should, and had her hair done and sprayed every week. So her hair stood on end—spiked, they called it—and her mouth was a red slash across her face.

"I knew if there was somebody new and interesting in town, you'd have him here," she gushed at Lisa.

"I had nothing to do with Mr. Roper's being here," said Lisa. "He's a client of Ted Robertson, and Ted brought him."

"You never met him before tonight?"

"Well . . . I have met him. Once."

Pat grinned. "Lisa, if you want to keep a secret, be careful how you look at the guy—and tell him to be careful how he looks at you."

"No, Pat."

"Hey . . . I should be so goddam lucky."

"No, Pat. No. Really."

"Then give me a chance, baby. Hey, if you don't want the guy, I sure am interested. Introduce me."

"I'll be glad to. Come on."

Her mother confronted Lisa on the back porch. Lisa had gone to the kitchen to check with the servers. Her mother had followed and insisted she had to talk to her, so Lisa had led her out to the back porch. Mary lit a cigarette and blew the smoke upward, toward the starlit night.

"You are not subtle, Lisa," her mother said.

"Be specific, Mother," said Lisa coldly. "Please. No subtleties tonight. Be entirely specific."

"Jonathan Roper. It's plain on both your faces, Lisa. It's obvious every time you step aside with him and have such intense little conversations. He's no casual acquaintance you only met this evening."

Lisa glanced through the kitchen window. "We can't stay out here," she said, shaking her head. "We'll have to talk about this later, or tomorrow."

"We have an excuse. I'm finishing my cigarette. This man is why you came home and consulted a psychiatrist, isn't he?"

"Yes."

"Are you in love with him?"

"I don't know. I'm not sure. There is a great deal more to it than you know."

"Oh, I think I *do* know. He's the father of the baby you're carrying. Isn't he?"

"I'm not sure."

"But it's possible?"

"More than possible. Probable."

"I suppose Ben thinks it's his."

"Yes."

"But you know it isn't."

"I know it isn't. Jonathan knows it isn't. And now you know. It's a secret that has to be kept."

"That's the way you plan to work it?"

"I don't know for sure."

Lisa was struggling to hold back tears. At the same time she was a little relieved to have been able to confide in someone. She made herself rigid. She had to return to her party.

Her mother touched her shoulder. "I hope I don't have to tell you that I'm on *your* side, whatever you decide to do, however it works out."

Lisa sighed. "Mother, is it all so obvious? One of my friends said a while ago that obviously I was having an affair with Jonathan. I thought I'd been . . . more clever than that."

"Your friend is a tease and a gossip," said Mary. "No one but me has really guessed, I don't think."

"A mother's instinct, huh?"

"Well . . . Something like that. I've always had an instinct about things happening to members of my family. Especially you, Lisa. I . . . I will confess something to you. I'm not really sorry that you're pregnant, even if it is by Jonathan. I've always wanted you to have a daughter. We've talked about our long mother-to-daughter line of descent coming to an end. I didn't want to trouble you by emphasizing it too much, but I was disappointed that you didn't have a daughter."

"You were terribly disappointed," Lisa said. "Not just a little. I've always known."

"It has troubled me."

"What if this baby is a boy?"

"I don't think it is," her mother said. "I don't know why, but I don't think so."

"I can find out, you know."

"I think you can be confident of it."

"Mother, you and I are going to have to have a long talk. Later."

And they did, after everything was cleaned up and the serving people had left the house. Ben was asleep. Benny had returned after taking Anne to her dormitory, and he was in his room, if not asleep. Lisa had changed into a night-gown and robe. She had checked her parents' bedroom and found her mother awake, apparently waiting for her. They returned to the living room, where coals glowed in the fireplace, and Lisa tossed in two pieces of wood. Her mother poured herself some brandy.

"Do you have any sense at all of who Jonathan is?" Lisa asked. "What he is?"

Mary shook her head. "No. He's a charming young man.

He seems intelligent, too. If you had to have a child by another man, I suppose he's a good choice."

"Mother, I didn't *have* to have a child by another man. Ben is entirely capable of making babies. We had decided we didn't want any more. Benny wasn't easy. I had a difficult birth, as you well remember. I just didn't want to go through it again. Doctors couldn't assure me I wouldn't have a tough time again. In fact, one doctor said it might kill me. I didn't want to risk it. Neither did Ben. That's why you didn't get your granddaughter."

"Then why . . ."

"Jonathan seduced me. I might almost say he forced me. Well . . . Not that, exactly. But, Mother, there is a great deal to this that I don't think I can tell you."

"I guessed that."

"All right. You guessed it. Let me ask you something. Do you ever sense that you know things . . . that you have knowledge that comes to you in some extraordinary way?"

"Yes. So much so that I got from the library two books on parapsychology. Have you ever heard of Dr. Rhine? At Duke University?"

"Yes. J. B. Rhine. I looked into that, too, Mother. Parapsychology. Extrasensory perception. I took the test with the cards when I was at Smith. You know, the cards with the circles, squares, triangles, and wavy lines."

"Cards . . ."

"You know how they do it. You sit at a table with a barrier in the middle. You can't see the cards. Someone turns them over one by one on the opposite side of the barrier and tries to communicate with you by concentrating, by thought transference, without signaling in any other way. You're supposed to detect the thought and say, 'Triangle. Wavy line. Square.' And so on. It was eerie. I guessed right far too many times. I confounded their statistical mathematics."

Her mother nodded. "One theory is that the ability runs in families. I can do it, too. I wonder if that's not why my grandmother Kennedy always won at cards. She could see what other players held. Or could sense it often enough to break the odds."

"There was more to it than that. Wasn't there?"

Lisa's mother tipped her glass and finished her brandy in one great swallow. She was an unusually tall woman, her hair, once reddish, was now a gleaming silver. She was considered a woman of great dignity, supported by calm self-confidence. One of her friends had said of her enviously that nothing bad ever happened to Mary O'Neil.

"When I was born, your great-grandmother was in her late fifties. Your great-grandfather Sean Kennedy was an imposing man: a big, ruddy Irish lawyer. But she was the head of the family. People went to her for advice."

"Her family were the Spencers, right? Philadelphia."

"Yes. Her father was Timothy Spencer. Her mother was Elizabeth Dugan. Elizabeth Dugan was the daughter of Kathleen Finn, who arrived from Ireland in 1834."

"Do all the women in the family have . . . special insights?" Lisa asked.

Mary shook her head. "Your sister has none. At least, she's never mentioned to me that she does. My mother did. My aunts did not."

"The men?"

Mary grinned. "We've married strong men. I don't exclude your Ben from that, though I find him too good. Strong men. But . . . maybe too practical for insights. Maybe they have them but ignore them because they can't find rational explanations for them. I told your father about some insights I had about the stock market. I don't know what he did about them. But shortly after that, he made his fortune."

Lisa drew a deep breath and held it for a moment. "I'm going to ask you a question. Don't think I've lost my mind. But did it ever occur to you that we might be witches?"

Her mother frowned, then grinned. "Lisa . . . Do I look like a witch? Do you?"

"Be serious," said Lisa. "Special insightfulness that

passes from daughter to daughter—from eldest daughter to eldest daughter, actually. What does it mean?"

Mary's grin diminished to a smile, which remained, communicating skepticism and even a touch of scorn. "I have never been visited by the Devil," she said crisply.

"No. Well, maybe I have. And maybe my great-grandmother was."

"Jonathan Roper?"

Lisa nodded. "I first experienced him in dreams, the dreams I told you about. Then he became a man, in the flesh."

"Did you discuss this with Dr. Gerard?"

"And with Father William Longford at the Church of the Holy Name. They can't assure me. Not to my satisfaction, anyway."

"Are you trying to get rid of him?"

"You mean Jonathan? I tried at first, yes. But no longer. I'm carrying his child."

Lisa's mother closed her eyes. *My God!* Is your baby something . . . ? How do I ask it?"

"Is my baby something supernatural?"

Mary winced. "God forbid!"

"There's something about us, isn't there, Mother? We're different."

"I don't want to be different. I never wanted to be. I know it's there . . . something. I've rejected it. All my life, I've turned my face away from it. Yet it was there, always: something I couldn't define but knew I didn't want. And I'm afraid that in Jonathan it has come to you incarnate. Maybe that's why it has so forcefully imposed itself on you."

It was three o'clock before Lisa went to bed. Ben was snoring, unaware she had not been beside him for an hour or more. Just before coming to bed, she had gone up to her study to see if Jonathan would appear, but he didn't.

She dreamed. . . .

No dungeon. No prison. And this time she was not a witness. She *was* the woman. For sure.

She sat in the tiny, low-ceilinged parlor of a modest country home. Because the country woman was not thinking her name or the name of the place where she was, Lisa did not know. She was plainly dressed, in a gray woolen dress and white linen apron, her hair covered by a white linen cap. She sat on a sturdy wooden chair. A basket filled with colorful squares of fabric sat beside her, and she was sewing the patches together in a random pattern. When she had sewn a score or so of patches together, she would sew them to the lining stretched on a frame in a corner of the room, stuffing goose down between the lining and the patches and stitching it in place. She was making a goose-down quilt.

She was a placid woman, as Lisa sensed it. At peace, yet not stupidly at peace, she was serene because she chose to be serene, not because she wasn't alert and knowledgeable. Lisa was a party to her consciousness if not to her memory store but she could sense this woman had much in that store.

A man came in. "Brown-Spot has dried up," he said.

He was a robust young man, dressed in brown wool breeches, a white linen shirt, and a well-worn but well-cared-for leather jerkin. He wore cotton stockings and bulky shoes.

"She'll need'st be bred again," Lisa heard herself say. She spoke English, heavily accented but entirely understandable —but then, the German Lisa had heard in Trier and the French of Geneva had also been understandable. "God willing, she'll calve and give good milk another two years."

"A bit old," said the man.

"I hope you don't think of—"

"I have to think of it."

She nodded. Of course, they had to think of it. Beasts were given them by God to be of service. When they could no longer be of service, it was necessary to end their lives. Thus it was ordained, by God's law and by necessity.

"You will do what is right," she said calmly.

"What we agree is right," he said.

"Yes, I—"

"Maaa! Mama! Papa! Patience is— *Maaa!"*

"Patience is what, child? Patience is where?" The husband-father snatched the screaming little boy up from the floor.

"Patience . . . down the *well!"*

It was true. The woman ran to the well behind the house, reaching it before her husband. From the echoing noise of frantic splashes, screams, and choking, it was apparent that the little boy had spoken true—his sister was in the well, twenty feet down, drowning in the cold water.

"We need help!" the husband-father yelled. "I'll get Oliver! He can let me down on the rope. He has the strength."

Before she could object that her man could lower *her* into the well, he had dashed away, vaulted a low stone wall, running to fetch a neighbor.

The sounds from below grew weaker. It was dark twenty feet down. Rarely could they see a reflection of the sky on the water. She heard her daughter choking.

"Mathilde!"

The woman clutched the aboveground stonework and peered down.

She raised her face. *"Mathilde!"* she shrieked. Then . . . Then she did something incredible. She uttered a snarl. A snarl. The deep, wrathful growl of some kind of animal.

"Nein! Nein, meine Kinde!" Lisa understood the German. She had heard this dialect before. The words roared, as if on the wind. "Do what you can do! You know what you are!"

Lisa felt the panic and anguish subside in the woman. Then abruptly she was aware that the woman was no longer afraid, no longer tormented.

To the extent that Lisa shared the experience—and she was not at all certain to what extent that was—the woman seemed to have turned to stone. Or iron. She stared into the well. She extended her hands above it.

And suddenly . . . the child rose from the depths of the well. Spluttering, blowing out water, the little girl rose, as if she were a disembodied spirit. For a moment she hung at the surface. Then she extended her arms toward her mother, and Lisa felt her come into her embrace.

The goodman and the neighbors stood back. They had not seen the child rise from the water, but they were frightened.

"It is simple," Lisa heard herself say. "I let the bucket down, Patience seized it, and I lifted her up."

The neighbors edged back. They did not believe her.

"God saved her," Lisa said to them. "In His infinite goodness, which it is for us now to praise. Who will lead a prayer of thanksgiving?"

None would. They kept edging back. Lisa herself knelt, clasped her child to herself, and lifted her tearful face to speak her prayer.

"It is as well you *don't* hear my prayer, good people," she murmured to herself. Clasping her hands between her breasts, she squeezed the amulet that hung from the chain around her neck.

8

"MAY I TALK TO DR. GERARD AND FATHER LONGFORD?" LISA'S mother asked. She was packing for her return flight to New York. "I think you need help in coping with this thing. You can't get it here, I imagine."

"Here in Marietta I spoke with the priest in the confessional about having an exorcism performed. He said he'd try to get permission, but later I told him I didn't want an exorcism."

"He knew who you were, of course."

"I suppose so. Anyway, I feel more confident of Father William Longford. He's older. He understands more, I think."

"What of Dr. Gerard? How do you feel about her?"

"She's quite convinced I'm suffering from a delusion. Oddly, she's had several other patients who thought they were victims of demonic possession. She lent me books on witchcraft. Damnedest foolishness I ever read. Only . . ."

"So I return to the question. Do you mind if I talk to these two people?"

"I have no objection to that. Obviously I don't want the story going any further."

"Meaning, of course, don't tell your father."

"Meaning, don't tell anybody."

After returning from the airport, where she had watched her parents board a commuter flight to Washington to catch the shuttle for La Guardia, Lisa went up to her tower-room study and sat down, suddenly tired and wondering if her pregnancy was the cause of it.

She sat staring at her belly and trying to remember how far along she had been in her first pregnancy when she began to feel the presence of the baby boy. She wondered if this child would come any more easily than Benny had come. The story was that at her age childbirth was often difficult. Birthing was for the young.

For the young . . . My God! Anne Merck was pregnant by Benny!

Lisa was sure of it. How could she know? The girl herself didn't know!

Roper . . . Jonathan . . .

He was there. She turned away from her desk. He was sitting on the couch.

"Jonathan, what is happening to me? What are you doing to me? What are you making of me?"

He was wearing his dark-blue cashmere sweater, a white shirt and gray slacks, and he looked confident and comfortable. He smiled. "It happens, you know," he said blandly.

"What happens?"

"How shall I put it? Let us say you have begun to realize your potential. You had hints of it before and didn't take it seriously. Now you begin to know."

" 'Potential.' You mean I have powers. New powers. I can see things."

"Yes. And there is more. You can influence things."

"What if I don't want to influence anything?"

He shrugged. "Then don't," he said scornfully. "It isn't necessary."

"Could I pull a drowning child from a well?"

"No. You are not that powerful. Anyway, I don't think you are."

"Who was she?"

"Her name was Charity."

"Did she really do what I saw? I mean, did she really raise her child from the well?"

"Yes, she did. Charity McDougal Hollister was one of the four powerful witches."

"What four powerful witches? What does that mean, Jonathan?"

"In the line, there have been four powerful witches and twelve witches whose power varied but was nothing so great as the power of the four."

Lisa stood and looked out the window, down across the town to the confluence of the two rivers: the Muskingum and the Ohio. Although a resident could, with some imagination, call Marietta faintly romantic, her view of the town reminded her of reality, prosaic reality. A small town that had seen better days was a powerful prescription for dragging a person back into reality. It was a prescription she needed, in the middle of this talk of witchcraft and "powers."

"In *what* line?" she asked. *"Whose* line?"

"Our line."

"Your line."

"Our line," he insisted.

"Do you mean Charity was an ancestor of mine?"

"You are the seventeenth. They are all your ancestors. Sixteen of them."

"Mathilde. She turned herself into a wolf. Are you telling me I have an ancestor who could—"

"She was the most powerful of them all."

"Jacqueline . . . ?"

Jonathan shook his head sadly. "Poor Jacqueline was no witch. Would that she had been."

"Am I descended from her, too?"

"Yes, through her daughter. Jean Chauvin never found the child. That child was the mother of Mathilde."

"Angélique."

"Yes," he said. "Angélique."

"You mean, then, Jacqueline was no witch, but all her descendants are witches," said Lisa.

"Only the eldest daughters."

"It was you who cried out to Satan," said Lisa. "Not Jacqueline. And the priest had carried the infant Angélique away from Geneva. Do you mean to say that Satan made Angélique a witch because you had committed *yourself*—"

"Angélique was given power, enough power to defend herself and her daughter. But she never had to use her power and died without knowing she had it. A year before Mathilde was denounced, Angélique died of the bloody flux, as we called it: typhoid fever I suppose it was. She was thirty-seven."

"Couldn't you have saved her?"

"You have much to learn, Lisa—about the powers and about much else. Why does *anything* happen that we who have powers don't want? We don't govern the world."

"Did Angélique have the mark?" Lisa asked, touching her left breast.

"No. She was born of ordinary parents, mortal parents."

"Meaning that my mother—"

"Yes. Your mother. She has almost never needed her powers, doesn't want them, in fact, and almost never uses them. But she cannot deny her place in the line."

"But Mathilde . . . Who was Mathilde's father?"

Jonathan stood and came to stand beside her, looking down over the town and the rivers. "I was. I was her father and her grandfather," said Jonathan.

"Her father and her grandfather? You . . . Your own *daughter,* Jonathan?"

He nodded. "Father Vincente reared Angélique and married her when she was fifteen to a devout and prosperous old widower named Philippe Robeus, a money changer in Strasbourg, which was Father Vincente's ancestral home. He knew the family and was proud to present Angélique to them. He'd had her educated in convent schools, including one in Paris, and she was a quiet, devout, literate girl. She knew nothing of her mother or of me. Robeus was very fond of her, apparently. They had a son, also named Philippe. Then Robeus died. The Robeus family wanted Angélique to enter a convent. I couldn't allow that. She had to bear a daughter, or there would have been no line of witches. I—"

"Why not? What do you mean you couldn't allow it? Why couldn't you?"

"It was required of me. The Almighty didn't spare me without a reason. My Master required it, too."

"Satan."

"My Master."

"So you are the father of Mathilde."

"And her grandfather. I came to Strasbourg in the guise of a wine merchant and courted the young widow. I appeared to be a man not much older than she was, and of course she had no idea that I was her father and that I was . . ."

Lisa sighed heavily and shook her head. "Fifteen or sixteen years dead. You died in that dungeon in Geneva. You told me. They smashed your skull. I saw them burn a straw-filled effigy of you."

Jonathan nodded. "The Master came. He picked up Jacqueline's body and beckoned me to rise and walk. I didn't know who he was. I got up and walked toward him. Staggered toward him. At that moment I imagined I had somehow survived. But then my chains dropped off, and I knew. I knew I was dead, and I knew who my Master was. I was terrified. I had called for Satan, and this *was* Satan. I was dead, yet I was walking. Not only that. We walked through the stone walls. I realized I was not a man anymore. The man was dead. I was . . . I was a *soul,* Lisa, and Satan had claimed me. And Jacqueline. I couldn't understand what she was. He carried her body through the walls and out into the streets. I wondered if he had claimed her, too. I wasn't certain she was dead."

"She was dead," said Lisa. "Had been for some time. I knew when she died."

"The Master explained to me a little later that he couldn't

revive her. She had not called on him, and he couldn't take her. But he could carry her body away, even through the walls. We left the dungeon. We left Geneva. When"— Jonathan paused and smiled—"when the executioner came to take us out to the stakes, we were gone, and he had to burn effigies. Jean Chauvin insisted he do that. Chauvin was furious. He had the dungeon keepers tortured. To the day he died he believed that Catholics had rescued us, with the connivance of secret Catholics among the dungeon guards. He believed we were alive somewhere, and he never ceased to look for us."

"From that day you were what you are now?"

"In a sense. I was terrified for a long time. All my life I had been a devout Christian, and at the end I had cried out to Satan and given my soul to him. He gave me back my body and allowed me to live again. And he gave me powers. He laughed at me when he sensed my fear of him. He told me I had been saved for a purpose and that in time I would learn what the purpose was. I supposed there would come a day when I had served his purpose and then he would claim my soul and cast it into eternal torment. He sensed my thoughts, and laughed again. He said I believed too many myths. He commanded me to learn. I did. I did the best I could to understand what I was and why. Years passed before I finally understood that I had much to regret but little to fear."

"Anyway, you found Angélique. How did you know where to look?"

"I, too, have powers, as you have seen. At first Father Vincente had taken her only across the border, into Franche-Comté. But he was a Jesuit, called to various posts, and he put Angélique into convent schools, as I have said, and he took her eventually to Strasbourg."

"And you married her, Jonathan. And you fathered a child by her."

"I have been the father of other daughters in the line."

Lisa sighed and nodded. "Yes," she said mordantly.

"I did not want to remain in Strasbourg, to be subservient

to the Robeus family, so I moved our little family to Triers. The Archbishop-Elector gave us permission, as foreigners, to live in a village outside the town. You understand, of course, that the Archbishop-Elector was not just a church official but was the secular ruler of the Electorate of Trier. How could I have guessed that in 1581 the savage Johann von Schöneburg would inherit the title? I have always been grateful that Angélique did not live to see her daughter seized as a witch."

"Angélique died without knowing she was a witch," said Lisa, nodding thoughtfully. "Maybe that was fortunate for her. But Mathilde—"

"Eventually Mathilde knew everything and used every power," said Jonathan. "Including much that I didn't teach her. She knew who I was. I didn't tell her. She sensed it. Maybe the peculiarity that I occurred twice in her immediate ancestry concentrated our powers in her. From the time she was a little girl she sensed that she was different, more powerful, than other people. She killed a cat one day. She just stared at it, and it fell over and died. She was five years old. I was appalled."

"You wondered if you'd created a monster," Lisa suggested.

"I had created no monster," said Jonathan. "The Almighty had created her and me, for His own purposes, in a world in which He judged we were needed. The poison mixed by Jean Chauvin was spreading, even to England, from which it would spread to New England. Witches are God's creatures. I have no doubt of it. Maybe Mathilde had the greatest powers because she lived at hazard from the greatest wickedness."

"If she had such power," said Lisa, "why did she allow herself to be chained and tortured?"

Jonathan smiled tolerantly. "You have much to learn, Lisa. Don't press too hard."

"And the others?"

"The others had their powers for the same reason, really: to defend themselves and the line."

"What if the line fails?"

"It hasn't yet, in seventeen generations, through four and a half centuries."

"Are we of this line the only witches that exist?"

"I believe there are others, though I have never encountered any, not with certainty anyway. For every witch who has ever lived there have been a thousand women who called themselves witches or who thought they were witches. For every witch ever put to death, ten thousand women were put to death who were not witches, because real witches can usually defend themselves, as Mathilde did. As Charity did."

"And Angelina Tatum could not," Lisa interjected. "So . . . So Angelina was *not* a witch, not in the line? You showed her to me for another reason? Anyway, I know my ancestry back to 1834 when Kathleen Finn came over from Ireland. Or— Or am I wrong? My God, Jonathan! Am I descended from Angelina, too?"

"Let's leave Angelina for later," he said. "She was how I introduced myself to you. You dreamed something, and then you found out it was true."

"You say Charity had to defend herself? I remember dreaming what hostility those people felt toward her. It was . . . actually murderous."

Jonathan nodded. "Murderous hostility? Yes, precisely. And fear. But not of her. It was the child they feared. The child named Patience. You see, the old wisdom was that a witch could not drown, that the water would reject her. So when Patience did not drown, they took *her* for a witch, not her mother. They didn't believe Charity's story that she'd lowered the bucket. In fact, they saw that the bucket was dry. So they assumed Patience had flown up from the well. Everyone knew that witches could fly."

"What happened?" Lisa asked.

"They went to the kirk. The church. It was in Scotland, you know."

"I didn't know."

"The Kirk of Scotland was Calvinist, poisoned with the malevolent venom of Jean Chauvin. He is the ancient enemy of our line. Charity's mother had married a Scot and removed from the Continent to Scotland, thinking in her ignorance to escape the toxic influence of Calvinism, which did plague the Continent but was tolerant and kindly there, compared to what it was in Scotland."

"I'm glad I'm a Catholic," said Lisa.

"So am I, but don't forget the brutes of Trier. Anyway . . . the goodman, Charity's husband, begged his neighbors not to inform against his little daughter; but they were frightened, not to mention ignorant, and they went to the kirk and roused the preacher, a man named Callander. He ranted and raved, saying he had been warning the congregation for months that the Devil was at work in the neighborhood and here was proof."

"Proof . . ." said Lisa scornfully.

"Actually he wanted more proof. He said they would first strip the child and look for the Devil's marks on her. Especially they would look for a mole, like the one you have on your breast. Where the Devil suckles."

"A *little girl?*"

"We are not talking about a rational man. Or a rational mob. If they found a mark, any mark, they could call it the mark of the Devil, and then they would put the child to another test. They would throw her in the mill pond. If she floated—that is, if the water rejected her—then she was surely a witch."

"And if she drowned, she was not."

"Yes. Charity, I may tell you, had second sight. You are allowing yours to develop and give you clearer insights. Hers was far more powerful than yours. She heard every word Callander spoke. She saw him. She was a mile from the kirk, but she saw and heard as if she had been there. And . . . she knew the child had the mark. She had the mole already, which later would be on her left breast. Charity had it—"

"Mathilde had it," Lisa interrupted.

Jonathan smiled and nodded. "And you have it."

"My mother has it."

"Of course. I've never seen that one, but I know it's there. All of you have it."

"Not my sister."

"Of course not."

"Oh— All right, I see. So . . . they were going to drown the child."

"A few honest citizens dissented. But the Reverend Mr. Callander carried the day. He shouted the dissenters down, saying it was every man and woman's duty to save the village from the machinations of the Evil One. And so on."

"What was the husband, the goodman, doing all this time?" Lisa asked.

"Charity's husband was named William Hollister. Some feared he would resist the mob. And he would have, too. He was a rational man. So the mob set out to arm itself, some with agricultural implements, two or three with firearms. They took a lot of time blustering and bellowing, getting up their courage."

"I imagine they would need it."

"They would need it," Jonathan agreed. "Of the four powerful witches, only two ever knew each other. Mathilde, who had come to Scotland with the family, lived to be almost a hundred years old, so she lived to see and know her great-great-granddaughter. In fact, Charity was twenty-five years old before Mathilde died. Charity knew the story of how Mathilde bit the ear off Binsfeld. Great-great-grandmother Mathilde had told her all about it personally. Charity was inspired with the spirit of Mathilde, and Mathilde was a ruthless, ferocious witch. She took her revenge. Binsfeld's troubles did not end when he lost his ear."

"Are you saying Mathilde taught Charity?"

"Yes. Few of the seventeen have realized what they were. Some of them hardly even recognized that they had special insights, possessed a special ability to influence others, and were somehow different. Your mother, for example. Your grandmother, for another. They never had any special need to use their powers, so they never guessed they had them. And there have been others, in the last century particularly. We live in an age of reason, do we not? We don't look for extra-natural abilities in ourselves. Some did not even find their powers when they needed them. The need for them is a quick and powerful teacher. But none ever understood fully unless they were taught, unless I came to teach them."

"Or Mathilde did," said Lisa.

He nodded. "What of you? You didn't guess until I came to teach you. But you have always known you were different. Your mother knows. All of you have had insight. All of you have had powers that only a few of you have ever realized and ever used. Your great-grandmother knew who she was, what she was."

"She never told my mother," said Lisa. "Or my grand-mother either, as I understand."

Jonathan shrugged. "They didn't need their powers. If they had needed them, they would have discovered them."

"Do I need them? If so, why?"

"Never mind that for now. Mathilde encouraged Charity to make every use of her very considerable powers. Until the day she saved her daughter from the well, Charity didn't really need them. But she knew she had them. Mathilde, who was the most powerful of all, taught Charity what she could do. When the old woman was ninety-five years old, she and the girl terrified Selkirk by running through the fields at night as a pair of wolves. They killed no sheep, which for the neighborhood was worse than if they had. Wolves that did not kill sheep had to be supernatural— which of course they were. Mathilde showed Charity that she could change herself into a venomous toad when it suited her purposes. Or a black goat. Mathilde amused herself with this kind of thing. Witches were reputed to do things like this, so why not do them?"

"She had good reason to be vengeful," said Lisa.

"She killed. She took her vengeance. She used her powers constantly. Mathilde reveled in being a witch."

"So what did Charity do to Callander and his mob?"

"The mob had scattered to collect weapons. They were to reassemble at the kirk, then march to the Hollister farmstead. When they came back, they found their preacher quite naked, crawling around on the floor of the kirk, howling and shrieking. To use a phrase that might be used today, Charity had fried his brains. She had come as a wolf, entered his church, and before his eyes changed back into a woman. That might have been enough. But she was furious with him for organizing a mob to drown her little girl, and she struck his mind with her destructive power. He lived another ten years, a drooling idiot.

"That was the end for the mob. Some thought God had struck Callander. Some, the Devil. Some, the witch— meaning little Patience. They wandered away, disagreed as to what had happened and what they could do about it."

"So what happened?"

"Charity wasn't finished with them. That night she set their church on fire. It burned to the ground. That made them decide that what had happened had been the work of God, for obviously God would not allow the Devil or a witch to destroy one of His churches."

"Were they left in peace then?"

"Yes, but peace in a community that was afraid of the family and kept its distance from them. Charity encouraged her husband, William Hollister, to remove to Edinburgh, where they could live where people knew nothing of this history. The neighbors paid twice the value of his farmstead, whether just to be rid of the family or because Charity burned that idea into their brains, I have never been quite sure. Charity lived to be ninety-six years old. But the next powerful witch wasn't born until sixteen years after she died."

"The next powerful witch had to learn her trade," said Lisa sarcastically.

"Yes. As did the next. As will the one yet to come."

"They are to be feared," said Lisa. "They take a horrible vengeance."

"A just vengeance," said Jonathan.

"Except on the ancient and original enemy," said Lisa. "John Calvin seems to have escaped."

Jonathan laughed. His laugh was heavy with derision and triumph: a truly malevolent laugh. "Well," he said, grinning, "he murdered poor little Jacqueline in 1559, only five years before his own death. Mathilde wasn't born until 1578, and she was the first with enough power to take vengeance. But it wasn't necessary. It really wasn't necessary." He laughed again.

"Necessary? Why wasn't it necessary?"

"Remember what the good sisters taught you. All men and women partake of the Sin of Adam; all are doomed to everlasting torment. Christ died for mankind, however, and whosoever liveth and believeth on Him is saved! You can, by following the way of Christ—the way of the Church—avoid perdition and attain the Kingdom of Heaven."

Lisa nodded.

"Calvin taught otherwise," Jonathan continued grimly. "According to the righteous Jean Chauvin, when the Almighty created the world, He created its future, too, all at once; and therefore He knew, from the moment of Creation, everything that would happen—including who would be saved and who would not. Whatever God knew from that moment must happen. God's knowledge cannot be wrong. Therefore, the eternal fate of every man and woman is preordained. It was ordained at the beginning, and nothing can be done to change it. No matter what you do, you cannot achieve a salvation that was not preordained for you, not even with the help of Christ."

"What a cold, cruel theology," said Lisa. "It has made me shudder from the first time I heard of it."

"Jean Chauvin was obsessed with a text from Paul's Epistle to the Romans. As Saint Paul reminded the Romans, God said to Moses, 'I will have mercy on whom I will have mercy, and I will have compassion on whom I will have compassion.' Preaching on that text, Chauvin wrote, 'We affirm that this counsel, as far as concerns the elect, is founded on His gratuitous mercy, totally irrespective of human merit; but that to those whom He devotes to condemnation, the gate of life is closed by a just and irreprehensible, but incomprehensible, judgment.' He taught that the vast majority of mankind is doomed. Only a few can be saved. Only a few are of the elect."

"To believe that, he had to believe *he* was of the elect," Lisa sneered.

Jonathan guffawed. "Exactly!" he roared. "He believed he was of the elect, foreordained to attain the Kingdom of Heaven. But he wasn't! *He wasn't!* He was a sinful man. My Jacqueline was not the only innocent person he tormented to death. But maybe the intolerable sin was his overweening pride. Anyway, he has burned for four hundred years, so far. Jacqueline is avenged."

"You still have not answered the question that troubles me most."

"Ah. And what is that?"

"Who are you? What are you? You were Jean Cordier, weren't you? Cordier . . . Roper, in English."

Jonathan smiled lazily. "We have talked long," he said. "Think on what you have learned today. Then I'll reveal more. Right now it would be pleasant to make love with you."

"There's little point in denying you now," she said.

"The fetus is normal," Lisa said to Ben as they dressed for a New Year's Eve party at the country club. "It's a girl."

"It's amazing how that can be determined so early in a pregnancy," said Ben.

"You said you wanted a girl."

He nodded. "I'd rather, yes."

"The truth is, you don't want a baby at all."

"We'd agreed not to."

"Well, there's not much I can do about it, is there?"

"Actually, of course, there is."

"Abortion."

He did not turn away from the mirror, where he was struggling with his black bow tie. "I'm not suggesting that," he said. "I'd like to think, though, that we *decided* to have this baby. I'd like to think a husband and wife, two rational and intelligent people, weighed their alternatives and reached a decision."

"What of the Church?"

"Does anyone in the Church know you're pregnant? What the holy fathers don't know they can't condemn."

"Besides you, only my mother and the doctor know."

"So. What the Pope doesn't know won't hurt him."

Lisa would wear that night the same red dress she had worn for her Christmas party. At the moment, she was brushing her hair, wearing her bra and panty hose and her red high-heeled shoes. She was angry with Ben and withdrew from the conversation. That he could even mention abortion, much less scorn the teaching of the Church about it, dismayed her.

"All I'm saying, Lisa," Ben went on, "is that we should put any options we have on the table and make an intelligent choice." He frowned. "Maybe we don't have any options."

"Abortion is not one of them," she said sternly.

"Just remember, Lisa, that you will be sixty-four years old when this little girl graduates from college. Sixty . . . four . . . years . . . old. And I'll be sixty-six. If we wanted a second child, we should have had it fifteen years ago."

"You don't want the baby."

"I didn't say that. I'll be a good father to her, to the best of my ability. It's just that she's a very big change in our lives, and I wish we had made that change on the basis of a *decision.*"

Her gut reaction was to be angry with him for even talking to her this way. *How could he?* She was pregnant! She was carrying— But it wasn't his child. The birth of the baby would change his life. And the baby wasn't his. Damn

Jonathan! He wasn't just meddling in *her* life; he was meddling in Ben's.

Presumably . . . Presumably the birth of the baby would change everything. Because both of them would love her. Watching her grow up might be better than anything else either one of them could do. That was how couples talked who had accidental pregnancies too late in life.

But what would the little girl be like? Would she be so conspicuously unlike Ben that he would suspect? She would have the mark. She would be born with it. And she would have . . . powers? Ben might not see her powers, but if he did, how would he cope with the discovery?

Damn Jonathan! *Damn* Jonathan!

Of course, there was no point in damning Jonathan. If he spoke the truth—and she sensed that he did, more and more—he was the servant of an inexorable fate, which she shared, apparently, whether she liked it or not.

Country clubs were a corporate obligation. Like Rotary or Kiwanis. Absent the corporate affiliation, neither Ben nor Lisa would ever have had the least inclination to join a country club. Country club life, dominated by social climbers and would-have-been athletes, bored both of them. Ben could stand it better than Lisa could and even shot a round of golf two or three times a summer, just to establish himself as an all-round good fellow, at home in the camaraderie of the locker room and men's bar.

Not so for Pat and Richard Irving. Pat, the heavy bridge player of the spiked hair and emphatic makeup, didn't wait for Lisa to approach the bar but rushed across the room carrying a martini for her. Lisa, who meant to ease off on alcohol during her pregnancy—but couldn't yet explain that to Pat—accepted the drink and toasted the evening with it, taking a small sip.

"Look who's here," said Pat. "Tell *me* he's not a close friend of yours."

Jonathan. Of course. Jonathan, wearing a tuxedo like the

rest of the men but wearing it with a special flair none of them even approached. It was double-breasted, so closely fitted to his trim body that it had to have been done by an expensive tailor, almost certainly in London. His bow tie was black satin. He wore a white rosebud in his buttonhole. His cummerbund was gray, and one had to bend over to see that the dots that formed its pattern were in fact tiny black crowns.

"Who is he *not* a close friend of?" Lisa asked, trying to avoid sounding defensive.

"Well, not of mine," said Pat. "I'd give anything to get to know him better."

"I wonder if he ever goes home," said Lisa.

She had thought about that. Where had he come from when he came here? Where did he go? How did he travel? What was the source of his money? She wondered if he had a passport.

Pat began to shake her head. Her smile broadened gradually and remained gentle. "The way you look at him!" she said quietly. "Lisa, you're damned lucky. And you can count on me not to say a word to anybody. I swear."

"Pat, please—"

"Hey! You've got a friend. I think it's great. It's wonderful! And listen . . . If you need someplace where you can meet him in private . . . My house. I'll go out."

"Pat!"

"Sorry. Intruding."

Lisa touched the arm of the crestfallen woman. "No. Friendship. Just don't assume too much. And hang in there. I may need a friend."

"Lisa. I've always thought of you as not the ordinary business wife. I try not to be that myself, but I'm not as successful as you are at avoiding it. I mean, you're the type that does the *New York Times* crossword puzzle in ink. I bet you actually did read *Harlot's Ghost.* I'll wait for the film. I aspire to being your type by calling it a 'film' and not a 'movie.' But, babe, you could be heading toward calamity.

That's something I may know a little more about than you do. I've been there, Lisa. Things rarely end the way you expect, and it leaves a sour taste you can never get rid of."

Lisa could only nod. Some kind of confession might be coming here, and she didn't want to hear it.

"He is so *goddam* handsome and personable. And he's looking at you."

Lisa glanced at Jonathan. She had begun to suppose her mother had noticed because her mother had the family second sight. Certainly Pat didn't. And if Pat noticed—

Pat continued, "I don't know who he is, Lisa, or where he comes from or why he's here; but one thing is obvious: he dotes on you. He's no arrogant stud. He wants you. He needs you. Just look at him. He's not subtle, Lisa. You must teach him to be subtle."

"I'll try to. Right now. Thanks, Pat. Talk to you later. I'll go give him a lesson in cunning."

She walked across the room to Jonathan.

"You are the most beautiful woman here," he said.

"And you are the most handsome man. Maybe some people will be deceived into thinking that's why you cast me significant glances. People are *guessing* about us, Jonathan! For God's sake, be more subtle!"

"There is one thing about which I am not going to be subtle," Jonathan said.

She had not heard anger in his voice before—except in her dreams. It was chilling.

"What is that one thing?" she asked.

"If your husband continues to urge you to destroy our child, he will make himself my *enemy!*"

"That's a threat."

"Yes."

Her face was rigid. "There will be no abortion, Jonathan. No matter what he says. But remember: *his* wife is carrying *your* child. That he must never know. And if you heard the rest of it, you heard him say he will rear the child as a loving father. So don't threaten him. If you harm Ben, I will have the abortion. Can you stop me? I've begun to understand you, and I doubt it. There are limits to your powers, Jonathan. You wield them with the permission of the Almighty, so they are not infinite. Far less than infinite, I suspect. You need *us* to wield power. I've guessed that. You need the witches."

Jonathan stared at her, a spectrum of emotions running over his face.

Outside the country club the sky flashed blue-white, and the building shook with thunder.

"My God!" someone cried. "On New Year's Eve?"

Lisa stared at Jonathan calmly. Then she shrugged. "Not even any rain," she said. "Spectacular, but only a show."

"Whence comes your defiance?" he asked.

She shrugged. "Oh, I don't know. I have to defend myself and mine. This baby is important to you. And it will need a father after it is born, which *you* won't be. I don't think you'll destroy what you need."

"You are a fool, Lisa."

"I will meet you day after tomorrow in an isolated place. I want to see you turn yourself into a wolf, Jonathan, the way Mathilde could do. Or into a toad, whichever you please."

"You have much to learn. We *will* meet."

9

"REMOVE YOUR CLOTHES, LISA."

"Here? In full daylight? What if someone comes along? Anyway, it's cold."

"What you challenged me to show you is far more important than what anyone sees or whether or not it is cold," Jonathan said vehemently.

It was five in the afternoon. The sun was setting. They had met at the old cemetery on the gravel-road ridge some six or eight miles out of Marietta. It was the family graveyard where the professor had posed his model, and since then the locals had made a point of driving by from time to time to see if they could spot another naked girl among the gravestones.

"Jonathan . . . ?"

"You have *powers*, Lisa. They have been given to you. I don't know how powerful you are, but I am beginning to suspect you have more power than almost any other descendant of Jacqueline, except the four most powerful witches. *Do as I tell you!*"

They stood between his BMW and her Ford. She stared all around, in every direction, then opened her camel-hair coat and tossed it on the passenger seat of her car. A minute later she was naked, shivering in the cold of a January evening on a windswept hill as the sun set and frost began to form on the higher branches of the bare trees.

"So . . ."

"So now. If you did what you saw Mathilde do, with clothes on your body, your clothes might be destroyed in the process and you might have to go home naked. So—"

"Do what Mathilde did? Jonathan, my God!"

His eyes, fixed on hers, were like two cold marbles: dead and unmoving.

"You . . . can . . . do . . . it . . . Lisa. I can't, as you suggested, but you *can.* So . . . show me that power wherein you are my superior! It is a matter of will, Lisa. *Will it!"*

"No . . ."

"Will it!"

The whole scene . . . Naked. Naked at the edge of a country burying ground on a frigid January evening. Nothing could have been more unreal than the scene in which she found herself. She drew breath and willed.

But how do you *will?* What do you do to summon up power to overcome every law of nature? What does it amount to? Closing your eyes? Gritting your teeth? Holding your breath? Making your body rigid?

Lisa kept her eyes open. She stared, first at the face of Jonathan, then at the setting sun, and she exerted a force within her that she had never exercised before. She willed, and her will ignited a fire within her. For a moment she thought she was exploding inside, dying; she felt her heart bursting, her lungs filling with heat, her stomach spilling; and, worst of all, she felt her mind blazing. It was like what she had read that people being electrocuted must experience.

She opened her mouth to scream. And she did scream. But it was not a scream. It was the brutish snarl of the wolf she had become.

Wolf! My God! She *was* a wolf. Not some kind of half-wolf creature but a real wolf: lean and sleek, with rippling muscles and a bristling gray coat. Growling a warning, she tossed her head and looked around her. My God, she had the senses of a wolf! She could hear sounds she had not heard before: the skittering of little animals, the beat of birds' wings, the rustling of leaves, the piping screech of some tiny creature. She smelled what she could not have smelled before, especially the strong odor of the human, Jonathan. The old story that humans stank was true! He did, though she knew his body and clothes were clean.

She fixed yellow eyes on Jonathan. He was above her, taller, standing on two legs while she was on four. He was bigger, but he was afraid.

She snarled again. This time she meant it as a snarl, and she showed her fangs. And Jonathan . . . She saw that Jonathan was afraid. Saw? No, she smelled it. The stench of fear came from his pores. In a sense he had created her as what she was, but he was afraid. And she knew . . .

She knew he could not control her. She was not sure what would happen if she leaped on him and tore out his throat. She wouldn't. She didn't hate him. Besides, maybe he held the key to her returning from wolf to woman. But she understood, suddenly, that she was more powerful than he was.

She always had been. The potential had always been within her. Jonathan had brought her to knowledge. Perhaps she could have willed this metamorphosis any time in her life, if only she had known. That was Jonathan's purpose, apparently: to carry the knowledge.

She trotted into the little burying ground, turning her head around, scanning everything with malevolent eyes. She growled. She trotted to the falling remnants of the wrought-iron fence and leaped easily over it. She trotted up a slope to the highest ground on the ridge.

There she stood and stared at the setting sun, now deep red and falling beneath the nearest western hill. She snarled and barked. She looked back at Jonathan and defied him to come up here after her. She liked it that he was afraid of her. She was proud of herself as wolf. What had he said . . . ? That Mathilde reveled in being a witch. No wonder.

Or maybe— Maybe this thing was horribly flawed. Well
. . . She would have time later to think about that.

She swung her head from side to side. The wood was full
of terrified creatures, large and small—foxes, squirrels,
raccoons, skunks, groundhogs, chipmunks—that had never
sensed the presence of a wolf before. They were retreating in
panic. She snarled. Yes. Let them vacate the hillside, leave it
to their queen.

Quietly growling, she circled the little cemetery, pausing
here and there to spray her urine, marking the territory as
hers, not to be violated. But wait— Spraying was the
passion of the male wolf. That she trotted around spraying
meant . . . She was male, and female too. Of course. Just as
she was human, and wolf too.

Whatever she was, it was *glorious!*

She looked back at Jonathan. He was leaning against his
BMW now, smoking a cigarette. She bared her fangs. He
regarded her with caution but no longer with fear.

She decided to test her powers. She bolted along the ridge,
running faster than any man or woman could ever run,
slinking through heavy brush, terrifying a hundred creatures. Reaching an elevated point, she ventured out onto a
break in the wood and brush. She stood high, above all the
world within her ken. And there she raised her head and sent
out over that little world the howl that announced her
dominion over everything within her sight and hearing and
smell.

No one . . . nothing . . . challenged.

So . . . Such were her powers. She trotted back to where
Jonathan waited, and as she did so, she took pleasure in the
fluid ripple of her muscles. By an easier exertion of will, she
turned herself back into Lisa and stood stark naked between
the two cars. She threw back her head and drew a deep
breath. She was conscious that something cool and hard lay
on her chest. She looked down. The amulet hung between
her breasts. Jonathan's heavy bronze amulet. The woman
and the snake are ancient symbols of fertility and of
rejuvenation.

She lifted it to her fingers. "Why?" she asked.

"It is yours," he simply said.

Lisa sighed. "I'm not at all sure I like this thing you've shown me I can do," she said somberly.

"I wasn't sure you could do it," he said quietly.

She began to dress. "Could my mother do it?"

"I doubt it. The special relationship between you and me has given you this power, plus others. I am not entirely sure what powers you have."

"Why should I have powers my mother doesn't have?"

"You have powers you didn't have three months ago," he said. "I transmitted them to you when I entered you."

"Did you intend to?"

"I knew you would gain powers. Others have."

"Do you control what powers I have?"

"Not entirely. In fact . . . not very much at all. I had no control at all over Mathilde."

"Am I independent of you?"

"Even Mathilde was not independent of me. Don't think of denying me, Lisa. You can do things I can't do. I can do things you can't do. In any event, it is impossible for us to be enemies. We share a purpose. We will achieve our purpose."

She tugged her clothes on and reached for her coat. The sun had set, and it was almost dark. "What is our purpose, Jonathan?"

"You have learned much today," he said. "Absorb it."

He kissed her lightly on the cheek, moved fluidly to open the door of his car, got in and started it, and sped away.

Reaching home by six-thirty, she found two messages on her answering machine. One was from Ben, saying he would be half an hour late. The second was from her mother, asking Lisa to call.

She did.

"I've spoken with Father William Longford and Dr. Gerard," Mary said. "They want to know when you can come back here for more consultation."

Lisa had been standing at her desk, scanning the local

evening newspaper as she dialed and as the phone rang, but now she sat down.

"Mother," she said, "it's gone too far now. There is nothing those two well-meaning people can do. I can't confide in them now. If I told them what happened to me this afternoon, they'd want to institutionalize me."

She had thought this through on the way home.

She knew she was not deluded. What she was experiencing was far beyond the realm of psychiatry. Frankie Gerard, with her insistence that everything was in her mind, was irrelevant now. She did not want to see the psychiatrist again. Or any other shrink. Their facile rationalizations and their chemicals could never be anything but an intrusion.

Father William . . . This was within his scope. The wise old priest could help her if anyone could. The question was, did she want help? He had been discerning enough to see she was reluctant to give up Jonathan and the adventure he represented, even two months ago. Why should she want to give it up now?

Besides, she much doubted that Father William could exorcise Jonathan. He was too powerful. He *was* the servant of his master, and that master was no minor demon to be exorcised with holy water and prayer.

She sensed that a part of Jonathan's power emanated from her own reluctance to try to banish him. Probably he had implanted his own defense in her: an irresistible curiosity about all that he represented. Who could be exposed to that sphere and just reject it? Who could experience what she had experienced tonight and rebuff it out of hand?

Even if—bow to Frankie Gerard—it *had* been a wild delusion, she wanted to follow it at least a little further. How could she not want an explanation?

"My God, Lisa! What happened?"

"I can't tell you, Mother. I just can't tell you. I've been tested. The fetus is normal, and it is a girl. But . . . Ben doesn't want it. He wants me to consider having an abortion."

157

"To hell with that son of a bitch!"

"Mother!"

"He doesn't know the baby isn't his, does he?"

"No. I'm quite sure he doesn't even suspect it."

"Then he wants to kill— No, *God damn him!*"

"Mother . . . I could damn him, too. More emphatically than you can. Except that you and I know an essential fact that he doesn't know. He says he'll be a good father. He just reminds me that we will be well into our sixties before we get this little girl through college."

Lisa heard her mother's voice break as she said, "Oh, Lisa! I probably won't live to see her graduate from college. But I couldn't think of—"

"And neither could I, so don't worry about it," Lisa said resolutely. "It is not going to happen."

"You must tell me what happened to you this afternoon."

"I can't."

"You must. There's no one else you can confide in. No one else can possibly understand."

"Even you will think I've lost my mind. It's beyond anything my great-grandmother did."

"No one else will understand," Mary persisted.

"I can't tell you on the phone."

"Then come home again. Make up some excuse. Tell Ben I'm ill."

"I'll see what I can do."

"If you absolutely cannot come, I'll come to you. We *must* talk. I may be the only living person who can understand what you're experiencing."

"I don't want to raise emotions," Ben said over dinner. "But I want to know if you've given any more thought to the alternatives we may have about the baby."

"You don't want to raise emotions, and yet you suggest not only that I consider destroying the life that's inside me but also that I commit a mortal sin. It is not an alternative, Ben. Abortion is not an alternative."

"Maybe there are others."

"What others?"

"Suppose you went home to Chappaqua, left before anyone here but the doctor knew you were pregnant, and suppose you had the baby there and offered it for adoption. That's not destroying a life."

Lisa stared at her plate. In one day—within the past few hours—she had undergone the torment of feeling her body metamorphose from woman to wolf and back again, and now she felt another torment: the beginning of an evolution in her feelings toward her husband and the father of her son. How could the man be so cruel? So selfish . . .

And he *was* being cruel and selfish. He didn't know the baby girl was Jonathan's. He thought it was his, and still—

"Lisa . . ."

"No, Ben. No. Absolutely not. How can you ask me to do a thing like that?"

"It's no sin to place a child for adoption, if it's done ethically. We can retain a lawyer to handle it. We can see to it that the baby is placed in a proper home, a stable home, with resources. We won't want to meet the people, probably, but we can get all the assurance we need about the quality of the family. We can insist the adoptive parents be Catholic."

"Ben . . . *please!*"

"Well, I thought having children was a partnership thing. I thought I had some say in it."

"You had your say the night we made this baby."

"Hey, lady, you were horny! I said we couldn't do it, 'cause we didn't have any condoms, and you said you always liked the feel of a bare one better anyway, and you said the risk was worth it. Remember?"

"And you, of course—you with the erection like a utility pole—weren't horny. Sure, I could have said no. *You* could have said no, Ben! But neither one of us did. That was when we had our say."

"Think about the adoption idea. Just think about it. That's all I ask."

"Sure. Sure . . ." But— She wondered if her eyes narrowed. "Uh. Chappaqua. Go home and live with my parents until— Actually, Mother isn't too well. She's probably going to have to go into the hospital. . . ."

Lies flowed out of her with a new smoothness. Damn! She *was* a witch!

"Does she need you?" he asked. "Go home. Maybe you can help. And while you're there, you can at least investigate the possibility of placing the child. You don't have to make a commitment. Just find out what can be done. Lisa, we have the right to live the next two decades of our lives without—"

"All right, Ben. All right. Maybe. I'll think about going. I know this household can function well enough without me."

A dream . . .

"Don't suppose your powers are unlimited, and don't suppose you can invoke them whenever you want. The source of your powers is mercurial and arbitrary."

They sat on a moss-covered log in a forest, God knew where. Two women. One was Lisa. Or maybe it was someone else; it was in any event a woman in whom she lived. The other was her own age, forty or so, and a tall, slender, graceful blonde. Both were quite naked. Both were winded and exhilarated, apparently from some exertion they had enjoyed. Both wore the amulet.

Abruptly Lisa understood that they were tired from a long run through the woods—*a run as two wolves!*

She glanced at the other's left breast and saw the mole.

"You must bear a daughter, as I have done," the woman told Lisa. "Remember: the eldest daughter must bear a daughter. You are invaluable until you do that. Afterward, you are not. Then you may need your powers to save yourself. And they will not be withheld from you if you do. Their source is fickle and arbitrary but not ungrateful. We are his. He will not allow us to be betrayed."

Lisa stared at the face of this woman. She saw strength, confidence. Her eyes spoke wisdom. She was beautiful.

Where had Lisa seen her before? She would not have remembered, but she was struck with inspiration. This woman was Mathilde!

"Do not fear my father," Mathilde said. "The one who calls himself Jonathan. He is essential to us. Without him, we would not exist. But he is too human. He does not control his humanity. Do not let him deny how much he needs you."

"He told me he was your father," said Lisa. "He said he was the father of others, too."

"He was the father of Charity. My great-granddaughter Anna married a Scotsman named Angus McDougal, who proved sterile. My father went to her and remedied that."

"What happened to you after . . . after they failed to burn you? Where did you go?"

"My father had taken my half brother to Luxembourg. I joined them there. And not long after that, we moved to Amsterdam, where my father believed we could escape the witch burners."

"He says you always knew, from your earliest childhood, what you were and what you could do."

Mathilde nodded. "I always knew. I couldn't give it the right words at first. I didn't think of myself as a witch. But I knew I had insights and powers that other people didn't have."

"Why did you kill the cat?"

"Because it had scratched me. I was angry, and I was a child and didn't know how to restrain myself. My father didn't know the cat had scratched me because I had healed myself. I put my hand to my mouth in a childish effort to stop the pain, and I healed myself. I hadn't known I could."

Lisa raised her head and looked for the sun, where it shone down through the thick cover of leaves. Its heat came on the wind and warmed her naked skin. "Amsterdam . . ."

"We lived there for the rest of my father's life. He died there—that is, he died again. He aged in the natural way and died. I knew, of course, he wasn't dead; but he was gone.

I knew he could return. But he didn't, for a long time. He never appeared to my daughter or my granddaughter because they didn't need him."

"You didn't need him again in any way?"

"I married Henricus van Wildbad and lived the life of a rich woman." She smiled slyly. "My husband was extremely fortunate in business. He never invested in a ship that sank. My eldest daughter married well. Her name was Eva. Her eldest daughter was Anje. Anje married happily. Neither of those two ever used their powers. They had only a vague idea that they possessed any. All they ever did was experience insights. They were clairvoyant, but they never had the good sense to use that advantage to guide their husbands' business judgments."

"Why did you leave Amsterdam?"

"It was my decision. My husband died. I had continued to do what he had done—that is, to invest in merchant voyages. Ships I invested in never sank, never came home empty. I should have been more subtle and invested in a few ventures that failed. Ultimately, other investors began to mutter that I was using supernatural powers. They were infected, you see, with the theology of Jean Chauvin. Almost sixty years after I had been condemned to burn for poisoning a well, it began to appear as if I might be denounced again. Dutch Calvinism was not the vicious creed of the founder, but I was in danger. What irony it would have been, to be denounced for using insight and to return to the chains and the dungeon."

"You didn't poison the well, of course," said Lisa.

Mathilde sneered. "If I had, everyone who drank from it would have died."

"Couldn't you have somehow stopped the muttering against you?"

"Yes. But that would have caused worse suspicions. Anyway, the Scotsman, Angus McDougal, had petitioned for the hand of Anna, my great-granddaughter. I decided we had lived long enough in Amsterdam, had generated too much reputation there. Our kind have two choices: to bow and smile and conceal our gifts and live like the worst of our neighbors, or to use our powers and generate suspicion. We had stayed too long in Amsterdam. I was materfamilias. I granted the Scotsman's petition, on condition that we all emigrate to Edinburgh. We would not live grandly there. Maybe we could escape notice. I was a fool. I didn't know that the Calvinist poison was more virulent in Edinburgh than it was in Amsterdam, worse by then than it was in Geneva itself."

"How did Jonathan come to be the father of Charity?"

"Edinburgh . . ." Mathilde sneered. "It was sterile, and Angus McDougal was sterile. I willed my great-grand-daughter to become pregnant, but my powers were not so great as that. So *he* appeared. Jonathan, as you call him—as he has called himself the past three hundred years. He did it just as he did it with you. Anna thought she was dreaming, as you thought you were."

"Did Charity know Jonathan was her father?"

"Not immediately. I told her. I taught her. I knew I'd made a gross mistake in bringing us to Scotland, and I decided it was my duty to be certain she knew what she was. I was by then a very old woman. Charity was my descendant *and* my father's daughter. It was likely she would have great powers. It was likely she would need them. We were foreigners in Scotland: the very first people the Scots were likely to suspect of witchcraft. I feared she would have to defend our line, sooner or later."

"And she did," said Lisa.

"And she did," Mathilde agreed. "When William Hollister proposed that Charity should marry him and live a quiet, modest life in the country, I agreed to that. We had lived in cities. Maybe it was safer in the country. Again, I was wrong. I moved with them. So they had a very old woman in their house. I think that made their neighbors suspicious of Charity and her husband, from the beginning."

"Jonathan says you and Charity terrified the countryside by transforming yourselves into wolves."

"They were terrified, yes. But they didn't know it was

Mathilde van Wildbad teaching Charity Hollister to use her powers. If they had known what I could do—and was willing to do—they would not have dared come near us."

"Where were you when Patience fell down the well?"

"Four months dead. We are not immortal, Lisa. I can visit your dreams, but I am not real. Only my father returns corporeally."

"Why? Why he alone?"

Mathilde smiled. "The Master wishes it. The Almighty consents."

"I would like to see the Master."

"Really? Then call him. He may grant your wish."

Now the dream Lisa fused with the living Lisa. For a moment the woodland faded into the winter landscape below her tower study. She was surrounded with the warm comfort of an old flannel robe. Then the black and white of the leafless trees shimmered and returned to the lush green of the sun-dappled clearing where she sat naked with Mathilde.

A man on horseback rode toward them out of the depths of the cool, damp, green forest. He was a knight, dressed in full armor. He reined his big black stallion to a stop a short distance from the two naked women. Lisa stared at him. His armor was gilded and embossed in intricate patterns. The heads of cats were embossed on the knee guards, that of a wolf on the breastplate. Sunlight glinted off the steel. His horse snorted, pawed the ground, and tossed its head.

He was looking at Mathilde and Lisa through the slit in his helmet. He could see them, but they could not see his face. For a full minute he sat unmoving, with majestic dignity. Then with both hands he lifted off his helmet and shoved it into the crook of his left arm.

Lisa searched her memory for a hint of where she had seen this face before. Then she knew. His face was much like that of Michelangelo's *Moses*. He did not have the horns that Michelangelo had placed on the head of Moses in deference to Medieval tradition, and his beard was not the huge mass of hair the great artist had given Moses; but in his deeply furrowed brow and powerful lined face, in the imperious lift of his chin, and in the commanding gaze from his eyes, he was the *Moses*.

With his left hand he drew the gauntlet from his right. He extended the right hand toward the ground.

Mathilde sprang from the log, changing into a wolf as she moved; and she trotted to the man and began to fawn. She crept around his horse, very low on all four legs. He beckoned, and she stretched up and licked his hand, wagging her tail.

Lisa followed her lead. When the big man extended his hand toward her, she was there and ready and raised her head to lick his hand. He scratched her behind the ears. The pleasure was immense. His touch filled her with an exquisite sense of well-being: something more than euphoria.

And that was the end of the dream. She woke, conscious that the rapture of the dream was quickly diminishing and that she could not recover it.

What did it mean? Such dreams came from Jonathan. What did he mean to teach her by this one?

She decided to drive to Chappaqua. That way she would not be dependent on her mother's car while she was there. She decided, too, that she would wait a couple weeks before she left.

Jonathan bought a house. He managed to find an old house, brick painted buff, built before the Civil War; and the town gushed with gratitude for the way he began to restore it. He had the old plank floors stripped of accumulated dark varnish and refinished so the color of the original wood showed. A few planks had been broken, and he replaced them with lengths of oak cut to what was to today's lumberyards a nonstandard width. He spent the money to have seasoned oak cut to the old standard and fitted in. Outside town he found a nineteenth-century brick walk running across what had long ago been a farmhouse yard, and he bought that walk and had the old bricks brought into town to replace the concrete walk someone had laid from the street to the moss-green sandstone steps to his front door.

It was unusual for Benny to come up to the octagonal tower and visit with Lisa in her study. It was unusual for his father to come. They understood that Lisa valued the privacy of her study. She was surprised when Benny knocked on her door and asked if he could come in and talk to her.

She knew what he wanted to talk about. But she didn't want him to know she knew, or could know, so she told him to sit down on the couch, and she turned her chair and smiled at him, inviting him to talk.

"I've got an awful problem," he said. "To say it straight out: Anne is pregnant."

"By you?"

"Yes."

"Does her family know?"

"Nobody knows but the two of us. And the doctor. And now you."

"What are you going to do about it?"

"She's going to have an abortion. I have to ask Dad for the money."

Lisa closed her eyes for a moment. "You know I can't approve of that."

"I know. But it's Anne's decision. She's not Catholic; she's Jewish. She's old enough to decide for herself, and she has decided."

"Did she consult with you? You do have something to say about it, you know."

"Yes. I don't disagree. I can't support a family. I have to finish college. *She* has to finish college. She's very rational about it, not emotional."

"Do you love her?"

"Yes. I think so. She loves me, though. For sure. Anyway—"

"I can't like it, Benny. I believe it is morally wrong. I also think it's wrong not to tell her parents. Since you say no one

166

but you two and the doctor know she's pregnant, obviously you've had no counseling. Who is the doctor?"

"I drove her down to Parkersburg to see a doctor. He's a good doctor, no sleaze. And we did have some counseling. He talked to us. He understands the situation. He talked about alternatives, like having the baby and putting it up for adoption. And so on. Anne wants the abortion. She's thought the question through very carefully, and she wants it. The sooner the better."

"What will this doctor charge you?"

"Three hundred dollars. He won't do it before Friday. He says we have to think it over until then. But Anne has made up her mind. Look, I . . . I don't want you to think she's coldhearted about it. I mean, she cried about it and all. But she's made up her mind."

"How did you get her pregnant? Didn't you know how to prevent it?"

"It happened on an impulse. The night of the Christmas party. In my room. We all of a sudden wanted each other so much we just couldn't stop."

"You mean you've just had sex with her once?"

"No. We've done it lots of times since. But I bought the necessaries. And the doctor is going to give her a prescription for the pill."

Lisa frowned. "I could give you the money," she said. "But I won't. I can't be a party to what you're going to do. You'll have to talk to your father. I'm sure he'll give it to you. You'll probably have to listen to a lecture, but you'll get the money."

"I'll ask him."

"One thing more. When you go to Parkersburg on Friday, I'll go with you. Anne should have a woman with her. I'll hate what you're doing, but I'll be emotionally supportive."

Lisa drove her son and the pregnant girl the twelve miles to Parkersburg.

She had spoken the truth when she said she'd be emotionally supportive. She thought the two kids would need that from her. She didn't like what they were going to do—what Anne was going to do—but since she could not stop them, she would stand by them through what she was sure would be a draining ordeal.

She was Benny's mother, after all; and Anne's mother would not be here. The kids were very young. She doubted they understood the enormity of what they were doing.

"I hope you've thought this through carefully, Anne," she said. "I haven't talked to you about your decision, though I've expressed myself to Benny, and I suppose you know how I feel. You've made a very big decision. It's one you could come to regret for the rest of your life. I do want you to know that Benny's father and I will help you all we can if you decide to have the baby. We'll help you financially and otherwise."

"I think it would be irresponsible to have it," said Anne simply, and that was all she said.

The doctor was a young man with an air of cool efficiency. He thanked Lisa for coming. Benny could not be with Anne during the procedure, he said. Neither could Lisa unless Anne asked her to, which she didn't. They waited in the reception room. Benny glanced through two or three magazines, nervous but not distraught.

When Anne came out after about twenty minutes, she was a little pale and seemed slightly unsteady on her feet, but if she felt deep emotion she concealed it. She was in fact a little like the doctor: almost detached from what she had done.

That evening Anne had dinner with the Hamiltons, and she slept with Benny in his room. She wanted his arms around her all night, she said with quiet, unembarrassed composure.

The kids had not needed emotional support, nor had they sought approval. Only money.

Even so, Lisa decided she could not leave Marietta until she could be confident the emotions generated by the abortion were under control. There *had* to be emotions, didn't there? She was surprised at how comfortably the two young people seemed to live with what they had done. She was a little less surprised, but dismayed anyway, at how calmly Ben accepted the pregnancy and abortion. She seemed to be the only person distressed. She felt estranged from the other three. Even so, she felt her responsibility to her son required her to be around for a week or so more before she drove to Chappaqua.

It was the middle of February before she packed enough things for a long stay and set out for New York.

Days were short at that time of year, so she left at dawn. Her route was north on Interstate 77, which passes through Marietta, then east on Interstate 70 to the Pennsylvania Turnpike, to Harrisburg, then northeast on Interstates 81, 78 and 95 to the George Washington Bridge, and Interstate 95 to the Hutchinson River Parkway and so on to Chappaqua.

It was a twelve-hour drive at very best, more likely thirteen or fourteen. She wore faded old jeans and a sweatshirt, to be as comfortable as possible, and settled grimly behind the wheel, with no expectation of a pleasant drive.

The trip went well for only a short time. Near a Pennsylvania town called Claysville, not even ten miles from the Ohio-Pennsylvania line, the Ford began to show a red light, indicating engine overheating. She turned back and limped into Elm Grove, West Virginia, a Wheeling suburb, where the Ford agency mechanics diagnosed the trouble as a worn-out water pump, which would take an hour or so to replace. She told them to go ahead and replace it. Two hours and fifteen minutes later she drove out and continued northeast, having declared to the Ford agency that this was the worst car, bar none, she had ever driven.

Annoyed and concerned that she would not reach New York until well after dark, she pressed hard as she crossed the Turnpike.

The sun set as she crossed the Susquehanna River north of Harrisburg. The highway to Allentown and New Jersey passed through mountainous country. Shortly she was moving through the tunnel of light created by her headlamps and was glad for the red taillights she saw ahead of her, evidence that she was not alone in this great dark countryside.

Then the tire blew.

Barely managing to keep control, she drifted off on the berm and climbed out to stare at the shredded right front tire. She stood there for a minute, wondering if she could change a tire, or how long it would be before the state police might come along, when a pickup truck sitting on a high suspension pulled to the side and came to a stop a few yards behind her.

Two men climbed down. Both were obese. Both were bearded. Both wore caps and wool shirts and dirty quilted jackets. The name Rob was sewn in script on the jacket worn by the bigger of the two, the one with a full dark beard and long hair that curled up from under his plastic baseball cap. The other man was blond and was bearded only in the sense that he hadn't shaved for a week.

"Need some help, looks like," Rob said.

The other one stared at the tire. "Out of alignment," he said. "Wheel wobbles. She wouldn't do that to a tar if she was in alignment."

The first man nodded. "Yeah. Figure that's right, Gene. Anyways, you got a spare?"

"Whatever's in the trunk," said Lisa. She moved to the rear and used her key to open the trunk of the Ford.

The two men set to work. It was work they knew how to do, and they were strong and fast. Rob loosened the wheel lugs while Gene set the jack in place. He used the wrench as a jack handle and quickly raised the Ford. Within minutes the two men had the little solid-rubber spare in place.

"Listen, I'll be glad to pay you," Lisa said.

Rob grinned. "That ain't zactly what we had in mind, Gene an' me. We figure what we oughta do is hop over the guardrail and go down there in the woods an' have a little fun. Then we'll call it square."

Lisa shook her head. *"Oh, no . . . No!* I . . . No. I'll pay you. I don't . . . No!"

Rob grabbed her arm.

She stiffened in terror. "Please! Please, no!" she cried.

"It's only fair," Rob said, shoving her toward the guard-rail. "C'mon, now. It's only fair."

Lisa screamed. *"You'll kill my baby! I'm pregnant!"*

"Fer Christ sake, lady!" Rob growled. "I mean, we ain't gonna *rape* y' or nothin' like that. Gene an' me's nice fellas. You c'n jist go down on us guys. Nothin' rough. You don't even have to take yer clothes off, seein' it's so cold. Won't even take y' long."

Lisa stared past the big man, at the highway. Cars were speeding by. No one was paying any attention. Within sight of scores of people, she was alone, utterly alone. She wondered if even a state police car would stop, or would the troopers just see that a car was stopped with a flat and a couple of locals were changing it? Maybe that was why they had left her trunk open: to make it look that way.

She began to sob. *"Please!* Just go away and leave me alone. I'll give you money! Just . . . *just leave me alone!"*

Rob held her arm in a tight grip and led her toward the guardrail, where Gene grabbed her around the waist and lifted her over.

She screamed again. Rob clapped his hand over her mouth.

"Hey! Enough's enough, dammit. We ain' gonna hurt ya. Me an' Gene's *hung*. You gonna have a *good* time."

She stumbled, and they half carried her ten yards back into a tangle of frostbitten brush.

"Good place as any. Me first," said Rob.

He forced her down on her knees. As she moaned and trembled, Rob unzipped his jeans and pulled out his penis. In the light of headlights rushing past on the highway above, she could see what he now shoved toward her face. It was wet.

Lisa didn't will what happened next. Will was not the only catalyst for the metamorphosis, apparently. Terror was another.

She shook her head violently, and a threatening snarl

issued from her throat. Rob screamed. Lisa leaped for his throat. She tore it out with one vicious wrench of her powerful fangs, throwing blood and flesh. A flash of light showed her Gene, his eyes wide, his face distorted. She saw, too, that he had jerked a hunting knife from his belt. He slashed at her. She snarled and leaped and tore his throat. He stabbed her between two ribs as he fell.

The knife wound hurt. She slinked away from the light and put her muzzle to it. She licked it and tasted her own blood. Even so, she raised her head and claimed the land with one great, piercing howl.

Then abruptly she was a woman again. She was naked. As Jonathan had warned her, the change from woman to wolf had destroyed her clothes. They lay in tatters on the ground. The stab wound bled. She was not invulnerable. She was a naked woman, bleeding from a deep wound, alone in the cold.

Mathilde had said— She had said she healed the cat scratches. Lisa put her fingertips to her wound. She felt blood, too much blood, running down her side. But as she pressed her hand to the wound the blood ceased to flow. The wound closed.

She looked up at the sky and filled her lungs with cold air. She glanced at the bodies of Rob and Gene. She tried to find regret in herself, and couldn't.

Lisa gathered the tatters of her clothes and trotted in a crouch to the guardrail. She waited for a break in the stream of passing cars, and when no headlight shone on the Ford she snatched her suitcase from it, hurried into the car, and pulled on just a sweatshirt. She would drive away from here and stop a few miles farther on to put on more clothes.

My God! What power . . . But she knew it was not just for her. It had been given to her to save the child, the daughter, the eighteenth generation.

10

"FATHER, WILL YOU PLEASE REGARD THIS CONVERSATION AS A confession? I am asking for your assurance that whatever I tell you will be considered a confession and subject to your vocational obligation to hold it in absolute and strictest confidence."

They sat in his study in the rectory at the Church of the Holy Name of Jesus, and Lisa was surprised at what comfort she found in sitting over a cup of tea in this musty old room.

"There is no reason why confessions have to be heard only in the confessional," said Father William Longford. He laid his pipe aside, as if he thought it inappropriate for a priest hearing confession. "Yes. I will regard our conversation as subject to my obligation."

"Father, forgive me, for I have sinned."

"Tell me, my child."

Lisa drew as deep a breath as her lungs could hold. "Father . . . You must excuse what I am going to do. Please forgive it. I don't know any other way to make it clear that my problem is something Frankie Gerard can't deal with. I am going to show you something. I think you can stand it. I am not sure it would not drive Frankie out of her mind."

"Surely, Lisa—"

"Father . . . before I show you, I must take off my clothes. You can turn away and not look if you wish, but—"

"Lisa, please don't do that."

"Father, I know that hysterical women must have done this to you before. Please understand. If you don't see what I am about to show you, you can't help me."

"Lisa, I can't see how your taking off your clothes could possibly serve any purpose."

"I will leave my underclothes on. Father, I am not doing this for a thrill. It is a part of my confession."

"I could ask you to leave."

"If you do, then I will leave," she said humbly. "No hysteria. I will just leave—and try to cope with my spiritual problem without help."

He picked up his pipe, frowned over it, and sucked on the stem to see if any fire remained. Some did. He drew smoke. He nodded at Lisa, and while she undressed he poked tobacco into the bowl and got it lighted.

She had come in jeans and a sweatshirt, to make it easy to undress. She lifted the sweatshirt over her head, dropped the jeans and stepped out of them, and kicked off her shoes. Her white bra and panties remained.

"Now, Father," she said solemnly. "Don't be afraid. But watch. And please understand that what you see is real, not a delusion."

He nodded.

The effort of will was more difficult this time, as if she had to insist on the metamorphosis, against resistance from some vague source. But her will prevailed.

Once again the change destroyed her clothes. Her bra and panties simply dissolved in tatters and fell to the floor.

Father William gaped. He dropped his pipe into the big glass ashtray and sat ashen and trembling.

Lisa, as a wolf, walked around the study, sniffing, examining, looking for danger. She found none. She walked back to the chair where she had been sitting and regarded the priest with her yellow eyes. She did not snarl. She did not howl. She barked once, to let him hear.

Then she willed return, and in an instant she stood before him stark naked. She hurried to pull on her jeans and sweatshirt.

"Now do you believe?"

"I have suddenly begun to wonder just what I do believe," said the priest.

"What you believe is the truth, Father," she said respectfully. "I have no doubt of it. I think I have seen Satan himself, and he is not Jonathan. What you have just seen is the truth and becomes a part of your truth."

"I see why you don't want Dr. Gerard to witness this."

"She would have to believe it could be overwhelmed by prescription chemicals."

"It is not a matter of chemicals, is it?"

"No, Father. It's much more than that. Now I want you to read a newspaper clipping."

The clipping was from the Philadelphia *Inquirer:*

MYSTERIOUS HIGHWAY DEATHS

Men Killed by Beast, Apparently

The State Police barracks at Reading can offer no plausible explanation for the deaths of two men on Interstate Highway 78, a few miles from Shartlesville. Found dead in a patch of woods only a few yards off the highway late Thursday evening were Robert Murphy, 38, and Eugene Pfilzer, 36, both of Mount Aetna. Both men had bled to death as the result of their throats being ripped open, apparently by the fangs of a wild animal.

A pickup truck owned by Murphy was parked beside the highway, its lights still burning faintly as the battery ran down. The two men are known to have frequented certain bars in Reading, and their families speculate they may have been on their way there when they were overtaken by death. Admitting they have no idea what happened to the two men, police speculate that they may have left their truck and wandered into the woods to urinate when they were attacked. Police speculate further that the creature that killed them must have been a bear, perhaps a female protecting newborn cubs nearby. They admit that is a farfetched theory, since normally cubs are not born at this time of year.

Groups of hunters have formed to track down the killer animal. So far, they have found nothing. Dogs have picked up no scent that has led to anything. The exact cause of these two deaths remains a mystery.

"You, Lisa?" the priest asked. "Was it you? If so, why? Why, Lisa?"

"Rapists," she said. "I had a flat tire. They stopped and fixed it and then demanded I go into the woods and give them sex. They made it clear I had no choice. I went into the woods and— Well . . . you saw me."

"You had no choice but to kill them?"

Lisa shrugged. "Father, I was not conscious of making any decision. All I remember is stark terror and fear for my baby. I didn't even will the metamorphosis, which ordinarily I have to do."

"Could you have fled?"

She nodded. "As the wolf I could have, yes. But the wolf didn't want to. Father, I confess the wolf took *satisfaction* in killing those two animals! *I* wasn't the animal there. They were."

"A judgment you are not entitled to make," Father William said. "But let us call it self-defense. You have confessed it. Do you mean to say you have undergone this change many times? You will it, and it happens?"

"Jonathan showed me I could do it. I have done it a few times, not many. And I have other powers, Father. I have second sight. And who knows what besides?"

"Might we not suppose, Lisa, that these powers were given you to do good, not evil?"

"Jonathan says the witches in my ancestry did not kill, except in self-defense and in other circumstances that might have justified them."

"Lisa . . . I have made it a point to learn as much as I can about witches since we met; and I was already convinced you were not just an hysterical woman. The Halloween image of the grotesque hag with a pointed chin and no teeth and hairs growing from a mole, wearing a threatening black gown and a conical black hat . . . all that is in complete contradiction to what the record tells. I say 'record,' but there is nothing reliable, really. Such evidence as there is tells of young women as well as old, beautiful as well as ugly, benign as well as malign. You—"

Lisa interrupted. "God said to Moses, 'Thou shalt not suffer a witch to live.'"

"I am afraid, Lisa, that God said many things to Moses." The priest reached for a Bible, thumbed its pages, and found a passage he wanted to read. "Listen to what God promises to people who set up idols:

"And if ye will not for all this hearken unto me and walk contrary unto me;
"Then I will walk contrary unto you also in fury; and I, even I, will chastise you seven times for your sins.
"And ye shall eat the flesh of your sons, and the flesh of your daughters shall ye eat."

Father William laughed. "The things that you're liable to read in the Bible, they ain't necessarily so. That's one of the passages I sometimes read to people who insist on too literal an interpretation of the Word of God."

"So what becomes of me, Father?"

"Your concern is—"

"My immortal soul. What am I doing, Father? I won't deny that I *like* being a wolf. I feel . . . triumphant when I'm a wolf. I don't lose my identity entirely. I have human feelings, but I have animal feelings, too, all mixed together. Something else . . . I think a man I saw in a dream was Satan himself. I did not reject him. I changed to a wolf and fawned over him, like a dog over its master. Is Satan my master, Father?"

177

"I cannot imagine your coming here, confessing, and seeking absolution if Satan is your master."

"Can you grant me absolution?"

"I am troubled by one thing only. That is the element of will. I am prepared to believe that you did not wish, maybe did not even mean, to kill those two men. You acted in self-defense, in terror. Your will was not necessarily involved. But you do not wish to be rid of Jonathan. I doubt you wish to give back the powers you now have. Can you resolve that doubt for me? Do you want to be rid of Jonathan and everything associated with him? Truly?"

Lisa touched her belly. "What about the baby I'm carrying? It is Jonathan's, and I don't want to be rid of it."

"It really could be your husband's. Dr. Gerard told me you still have marital relations with him."

"My husband wants me to get rid of the baby. He wants me to have an abortion. If I won't do that, he wants me to offer it for adoption. That's why I'm in New York, supposedly: to investigate ways of placing the child for adoption."

"If you elect that alternative, I can help you."

"I don't think I'll elect it."

"If you could reject, put aside, put away your second sight, the power to turn into a wolf, and whatever other supernatural powers you may have, would you do it?"

"I don't know, Father."

"I can't give you absolution until you do."

"I'm not sure I can."

"You can try."

Lisa sighed heavily. "If I hadn't had the power to become a wolf, those two men might have killed my baby. They might have killed me. Maybe I was given the power so I can protect my daughter. I *am* a witch, Father. I can't doubt it. But I am a witch only with the permission of the Almighty."

"Well . . . so said the authors of *Malleus Maleficarum*. It's not Scripture."

"Nevertheless, is it not true that nothing exists without the permission of God?"

"Yes, but God has given us free will, Lisa," the priest said gravely.

"Father, I did not choose to be a witch. It is not of my free will."

"But perhaps by free will you can cease to be one."

"How would I do that?"

"Pray for it, Lisa. Ask God to release you from what is, after all, a curse. Ask to be relieved of the burden. Ask to be cleansed."

"Cleansed . . ."

"Do not be offended, but what you are is an unclean thing. Incidentally, have you taken Communion lately?"

She stiffened. "No."

"Not since Jonathan appeared?"

"Not since he appeared corporeally. When he was only appearing in dreams, I didn't feel . . . unclean."

"Have you shut God out of your life?"

"No, Father. No."

"You must pray, Lisa. And I hope I will see you in the congregation Sunday."

"You will . . . You *will*, Father."

After leaving the priest in his study, Lisa decided to enter the church before she left for home. Maybe she could pray there.

The old stone edifice had been built as a country church. It was very beautiful. The air inside was heavy with mixed odors: of the redolent oil used to polish the floors and woodwork, of dust and dampness, and of smoky candles. The floor creaked as she walked forward. She stopped at a pew, genuflected, entered the pew, and knelt.

An elderly woman at the front knelt and clutched her rosary and prayed audibly. On the opposite side of the church, a man sat and stared at the altar. The man—

Jonathan!

He turned and smiled at her, then turned back toward the sanctuary.

Lisa tried to pray. Appropriate words would not come. She remained kneeling, closed her eyes, and felt immersed in a smothering sense of helplessness.

She heard the floor creak. She looked around. Jonathan was leaving the church, going along the side aisle.

Lisa clasped her hands and pinched her eyes tight shut. She drew breath.

"Merciful God," she whispered. "Help me! I fear for my soul. Help me!"

It was all she could say. She stayed on her knees for a few more minutes, then rose and left the church.

Jonathan was waiting in her car.

She got in and looked at him calmly. She was not surprised. She started the car and pulled out of the parking lot.

"Is there someplace you want to go?" she asked.

"I have a room at the Greenwich Hyatt Regency," he said.

She turned toward Greenwich and for several minutes neither of them spoke.

Then Jonathan said, "Of your sixteen predecessors, only two ever killed."

"Do you disapprove of what I did?"

"Don't acquire a taste for it. It's dangerous."

"I have no taste for it, you may be assured."

"Are you glad to see me?"

"Yes," she admitted quietly.

"I am glad to see you, Lisa," he said. "I mean, this way. You know I am never far away from you. But to see you when I can touch you is . . ."

"Is what, Jonathan?"

"Is important to me."

"Do you mean you are capable of *caring*?"

"Not just capable. I do care."

She frowned. "And that complicates everything," she murmured.

She had to acknowledge to herself that she was glad to see him. He was so strikingly handsome a man that she could be proud to be seen with him; and maybe here she *could* be seen with him, as she could not in Marietta. Though she had lived in Greenwich until she went away to college, she had been gone a long time. It was rare for her to see anyone she knew on the streets of the towns along the New York–Connecticut line. Here she wouldn't have to be furtive with Jonathan. Maybe she could get to know him better.

He was wearing a hip-length black leather coat with a wool scarf at his throat.

"I want you to understand that nothing prevents your taking Communion," he said. "Nothing prevents your praying. The Almighty will hear you."

"He hears the prayers of witches?"

Jonathan glanced away from the road and looked into her face curiously. "Why not? The Almighty hears the prayers of all kinds of people."

"What if I pray to Him not to be a witch?"

"I don't think the Almighty will answer that prayer. Short men pray to be tall, and they don't grow tall. Fat women pray to be thin, and they don't become thin."

"Jonathan . . ."

"You are a witch. Your mother is a witch, and your grandmother was a witch, and so on, back through sixteen generations. As you and the old priest were saying, it is not a matter of will; you did not elect to be a witch; it is a matter of status. It is a status ordained by God."

"I still say that's a heresy."

"It would be if you define all witches as inherently evil. But apparently the Almighty doesn't so define them."

"Then why did He tell Moses—"

"Father William explained that."

"Anyway . . . if I pray to be relieved of this onus, I will not be relieved?"

"I don't think so." He shrugged. "Try it."

"Have you ever prayed to be an ordinary mortal?"

"No. There was a time when I prayed. I prayed once, with all the power I could bring to it. What I asked was so simple. All I wanted was for Jacqueline to be released from her agony, even if God had to do it by taking her life. And He didn't grant my prayer. She died of the torture after prolonged agony. I have not spoken to that God since."

"Are you not afraid of Him?"

"I've been given no cause to be afraid."

"I have been afraid I would offend Him by taking Communion."

"The Almighty won't strike you dead. None of you has ever been struck dead. The Almighty has not even interfered with you."

She stared at the highway. They had now entered the Cross-Westchester Expressway, and truck traffic was heavy.

"How did you come here?"

"I drove, of course. What did you suppose, that I flew on a broomstick?"

"Your car wasn't at the church. So how did you get there?"

"You begin to ask questions you should have asked a long time ago. How did I materialize in your study in the tower? How did I enter Mathilde's dungeon? Why did I go there? I didn't fly to the church on a broomstick, but I could have."

"Can I do things like that?"

"I don't know. Why don't you try?"

"I don't know what to try. For a time I thought you were the source of my powers, that you could give them or withhold them. Now—"

"I only made you aware of them. In fact . . . I am quite surprised at you. I *sensed,* suddenly, that you had the wolf in you. I hadn't sensed it there before, but suddenly I had to believe the wolf was within you. Only the four powerful witches could metamorphose. I think I know why. I think I know what made them so powerful. But you are different. I don't know the source of your power. Not exactly. Maybe there are five of you now, the *five* powerful witches."

She had to concentrate on the traffic. These northeastern highways could be dangerous, especially in winter. For a long time she did not speak. Only when she had turned north on I-95 did she say, "You know, of course, why I am here. Or why I'm supposed to be here."

"To explore the possibility of placing our daughter with an adoptive family."

"Yes. I am supposed to look into the idea."

"I hope you won't do that, Lisa. You will rid yourself of me if you do. Partly, anyway. I will have to be where I can watch over our daughter." He sighed. "Even so, it is an alternative, and if you choose it I will not interfere."

She took her eyes off the road long enough to stare very briefly at him, to try in a glance to read his face, to see if he could possibly be serious.

"Speak straight, Jonathan."

"I want *you* to rear our daughter. I want to be with both of you. But if you choose to place her with another family, where she will grow and thrive, the eighteenth generation, I cannot prevent you. If, on the other hand, your husband tries to kill her—"

"Enough of that, Jonathan! *There will be no abortion.* My daughter is going to have a loving mother . . . even if she doesn't have a loving father."

"I am pleased, Lisa," he said calmly. "If you elect to allow her to be adopted, I will have to . . . influence the choice of parents, to be sure she has a loving mother. She will have a loving mother, of that you may be certain."

"I will rear my own child," Lisa said firmly.

"That choice is yours. I demand that she live. And that she be loved and reared well."

"She will be a witch, of course."

"Yes. The eighteenth. And powerful. I had thought she would be the fifth powerful witch. Now I begin to suspect she will be the sixth."

"At forty-one . . . I wish I'd known my powers years ago. What I might have done!"

"No. You think you would have changed the world? You wouldn't have. The others didn't. Couldn't. Your great-grandmother was powerful. Do you think she could have changed herself into a wolf and thrown herself at the throat of Adolf Hitler?" He shook his head.

Exit 5. She turned off the Interstate.

"Tell me, Jonathan. Who was the knight in armor?"

He shook his head. "Who?"

"The dream you sent me. Mathilde and the man wearing armor."

"I gave you no such dream."

"I dreamed I was with Mathilde. She was telling me some things about using my powers. And the man came toward us in the forest."

"Describe the man."

"Big. A knight in armor, on a horse. He looked like Michelangelo's *Moses*. Mathilde and I turned into wolves and fawned at his feet like puppy dogs."

Jonathan shook his head. "I know nothing of such a dream. You are finding them on your own now."

They sat together in the lobby of the Hyatt Regency, a sort of indoor grove with a stream running between small trees and a plethora of shrubbery; Jonathan had a martini and Lisa a glass of white wine. When they had finished their drinks, he asked her to go to his room with him.

"Why?"

"Because I want you."

"You can have any woman in any room in the hotel."

"I want *you.*"

"You are direct, anyway," she said. "So . . . Why not? I want you, too, if you want to know."

In his room they undressed. She of course wore no underwear, it having disintegrated in the rectory. He interrupted his own undressing to reach out and touch the mole on her left breast. Then he touched a thin white scar below her right breast.

"Lisa, where is the amulet?"

"I don't always wear it. I didn't want to have to explain it to Father William."

"Maybe that was wise," he said soberly.

When he was naked, she ran her hands over his body. Whatever he was, he had the flesh and bones of a twenty-five-year-old. The penis she had feared would be cold, as that of Satan was reputed to be, was erect, its tip glistening with his seminal fluid, already issuing from within him.

"We are not in my house," she said. "We are not in my parents' home. We are not where interruption is possible. We have all the time we want. Let's use it well, Jonathan."

"I have always used it well, I thought," he said ingenuously.

"No. No, you haven't. You have always given me pleasure, but sometimes it was hardly more than rape. You used to come to me and not make love to me not in any sense. You just mounted me like a stud mounting a mare."

He bent forward and put his lips to her left breast. His tongue came out and began to lick the mole. Rapture . . . She had not guessed it was an erogenous spot. As her body stiffened and writhed, she realized this was not just titillation, that this was a phenomenal delight, reaching something in her that was carnal in the extreme, yet more than carnal.

It was what had made women witches!

He moved his mouth and began to run his tongue around her nipple. It was good but not the same.

"Why didn't you introduce that to me before?" she asked.

"It is something newly given you," he said.

Suddenly she was the wolf. She trotted around the room, and after less than half a minute she changed back.

"Lisa," Jonathan said sternly, "you must learn to control that. You didn't mean to do it just now. You must not allow strong emotions to generate the metamorphosis. Your decisions must be rational; the change must be of the will, rationally directed. I am surprised at how rapidly you have developed extraordinary powers, but you are still very inexperienced in using them. Be careful."

She felt sweat on her body. She smelled it. "Jonathan . . . Take me!"

He mounted her as he had done before and plunged into her with primal energy.

"Be a little careful," she whispered hoarsely. "Don't take any chance on injuring—"

"No danger," he said.

She was surprised at how well he prolonged the act. She reached an orgasm, then another, and was approaching a third when he shot his fluid into her.

They lay side by side, staring at the ceiling. Among her thoughts was an amused one that in old movies this would have been the time for cigarettes. That she could have that amused thought was evidence of how very easy their strange affiliation had become.

She had almost ceased to wonder what he was.

Almost.

"Jonathan . . . When she is born, will you disappear?"

"No. Do you want me to? What do you want?"

" 'Uncle Jonathan,' " said Lisa. "She will have her Uncle Jonathan, living nearby in his nice restored house. Then you know what will happen? The man she will know as her daddy will be transferred. We will move, as we've done before, leaving the house and the town. Then what will Uncle Jonathan do? Will he show up and buy a house in the next town? And if he does, how long will it take for the truth to become obvious?"

Jonathan propped himself up on one elbow and looked down at her. "Being what we are has never been a promise of instant gratification," he said. "And despite our powers, we can't solve all problems. I brought lightning and thunder on New Year's Eve, and you remarked scornfully that it was a show; there was no rain. It's sometimes like that."

"I have this dreadful sense," she said, "that all I am to you, really, is a vessel to receive your seed and carry your child, to continue your line."

"It was so, Lisa, at first. I have planted my seed before, when I had to, to be sure there would be another generation. I have done it without love. That is my obligation. I cannot and will not let the line die out. But there is something about you that is different. I am confused. You are not the same as the others. Anyway, the line of descent is not mine. It is yours. It is only male egomania that has traditionally directed descent through the male line. Mothers and daughters are the true line. Certain species of insects and spiders and so on have no further use for the male once he has planted his seed. I have a bigger role than that. I am your guardian. I am the steward of the line."

"Is there any place in the whole scheme for *love?*" she asked indignantly.

"I loved Jacqueline d'Alembert," he said softly. "She was young and beautiful, a virgin when I married her." His voice turned cold and bitter. "She was tortured to death at the command of the beast Jean Chauvin, as you know. I loved Angélique. I found her and loved her all her life. I loved Mathilde. And Charity. I have given love, Lisa. I have received it. It takes a great deal of understanding for a woman to love me, for she has to know I am something different, not an ordinary man."

"A direct answer, please, Jonathan."

"The answer is yes. I love you, Lisa. I love you, and I will do everything I can to diminish the pain of our . . . But do you love me? Or do you hate me? You have the right to hate me."

Lisa shook her head. "No, Jonathan, I do not hate you. I *love* you. May God forgive me, if my love for you requires His forgiveness; but I love you with all my heart and soul and"—her voice broke, and she began to cry—"and I don't know what the hell is going to happen!"

11

"THERE'S AN ODD TELEPHONE MESSAGE FOR YOU," HER MOTHER said to Lisa when she reached home in Chappaqua about six o'clock. "It's from the Pennsylvania State Police. They say it's important you call them as soon as possible, no matter what hour. They're investigating the deaths of two men."

"What could I know about the deaths of two men in Pennsylvania?"

"They said you could call any time. I wrote down what they call a reference number. Call collect, they said. You don't need to make it collect. We can pay for it."

"Pour me a soda or something," Lisa said wearily.

Eight or ten weeks ago she had regarded her own warm kitchen as a sort of refuge, as her mother's kitchen seemed now. It was a woman's domain, which she could decorate as she chose, hanging maudlin plaques or sticking odd notes and bits of verse on the refrigerator door with magnets attached to plastic bugs or plastic groceries. Her mother's refrigerator door, somewhat to Lisa's disgust, was covered with snapshots of her grandchildren. That Benny—a six-years-ago Benny—had a prominent place on that refrigerator door did not pacify Lisa, who found herself, every time she was in this kitchen, confronted by images of the obnoxious brats her siblings had parented.

Kitchen . . . Refuge . . . Sanctuary.

"You're exhausted," her mother said.

Lisa nodded. She sat on a tall kitchen stool, still wearing jeans and sweatshirt, having been naked of them twice today.

"Want to tell me?"

Lisa nodded again. She blinked her eyes and squeezed out tears. "I spent an hour with Father William," she whispered. "Tough talk, Mother. Tough . . ." She shook her head. "He knows now that it's all true."

"An hour?"

"No, I didn't get exhausted in an hour. Jonathan's here. He has a room at the Hyatt Regency in Greenwich. We talked, too. A lot of talk. And—you may as well know—he banged me out of my mind. Twice."

Mary O'Neil poured seltzer over the Scotch and ice she had put in a glass for herself. "You had better be careful about that—for the sake of the baby."

"I won't act on this idea," said Lisa, "but I suspect the baby is invulnerable. I mean, it has special protection."

Her mother turned her attention to the counter, where she sat on another stool and began to slice vegetables for a salad. "I hope you're right," she said dully.

"I suppose I'd better see what the Pennsylvania cops have in mind."

She punched in the number, and in a moment a woman came on the line, identifying herself as, "Pennsylvania State Police, Corporal Higgins."

"This is Mrs. Lisa Hamilton calling from Chappaqua, New York. I have a message to call and give this reference number."

She gave the number; and after a minute filled with the clicks of much switching, a new voice came on the line. A man said, "Lieutenant Raven speaking."

"This is Mrs. Lisa Hamilton calling from Chappaqua, New York. I gave the corporal the reference number."

"Oh, yes. Thank you for calling. I have a few questions, if you don't mind, about something that happened on the highway Tuesday evening. We're conducting an investigation into the deaths of two men. I think all the questions we want to ask you can be answered on the telephone."

"I didn't see any accident or anything."

"No. No. But did you have a flat tire along I-78 Tuesday evening?"

"Yes. I sure did."

"Did a couple of fellows stop their pickup truck and fix it for you?"

"Yes. Two men. They stopped and changed my tire."

"Then you drove on to Allentown on your solid-rubber spare and had a new tire put on at a station called Angelo's Shell Service. Right?"

"Right. They mounted the new tire for me and put the spare back in the trunk."

"And you paid for it with a Shell credit card, which is how we located you. Ford Probe. People saw you along the highway, truck stopped behind you, men changing your tire. Then you pulled into a station and got your new tire."

"All that's right. So what can I do for you?"

"The two men who fixed your flat never got back in their truck. They were killed, both of them, not twenty yards from where you stopped."

"My God! How were they killed?"

"They weren't killed in any ordinary way, Ma'am. They were attacked by some kind of wild animal that tore their throats open, so they bled to death."

"My *God!*"

"We want to know if you saw or heard anything that might give us a clue as to what happened."

After a moment Lisa realized that shaking her head at the telephone was not giving the lieutenant an answer. "No . . ." she said. "They took off my tire and put my spare on for me. I offered to pay them, but they wouldn't take any money. When I drove off, they were just standing there, kind of watching. I saw them in my rearview mirror. That was the last I saw of them. I didn't even get their names."

"So you didn't see or hear anything to give us any idea how they were killed."

"I wish I could be more helpful."

"One thing. Can you describe the two men?"

"Yes. Big fellows. Beards. Quilted jackets."

"Yeah. Well, you may have been lucky, Ma'am. I don't want to frighten you, but I suggest you carry an emergency radio in your car and when you get a flat, lock your doors and call for help. One of that pair had a criminal record for sex crime. He once raped a woman."

"Oh, my God!"

"Well, I don't mean to give you something to worry about. But do be awful careful."

"How did you find me here in New York? Did you speak to my husband?"

"As a matter of fact, yes, Ma'am. I talked to him myself, to find out where to call you. But I told him it was nothing to worry about. Obviously you aren't even remotely a suspect in those two deaths. It's for sure *you* didn't tear their throats out."

"I guess I'm lucky another way," she said. "If someone had shot them, I—"

"Right. But you sure didn't use fangs on them. We appreciate your help, Ma'am. I can't think of any reason why you should hear any more about this."

Lisa fixed her eyes on her mother as she hung up the telephone. It had been amazingly easy to lie to that policeman. Now it would be easy to lie to her mother, to explain what the call was about.

She summarized what the Pennsylvania policeman had told her.

"All right," Mary said a little coldly. "If that's what you want me to believe."

Lisa sipped her soda. "What do you want to know?"

"I want to know if you killed two men," said her mother quietly. "And if so why? And how?"

"What makes you think I might have?"

"An instinct. A sense. A parapsychological phenomenon. What we've talked about. You're radiating strong emotions."

Lisa hesitated for a moment, then said, "I told you about having a tire fail on a dark, remote stretch of highway. They were going to rape me. I was afraid they would kill me afterward, to cover the crime. I was afraid they would kill my baby."

"Lisa . . . Then you did do it! You *killed* two men! *How?* How did you do it? Did you use . . . powers? What kind of powers do you *have,* for God's sake?"

"Let *me* ask a question. Could my great-grandmother have done it?"

Mary put down her knife and poured herself a heavy shot of Scotch. She nodded as she poured. "I don't know, Lisa," she sighed. "She could do more than read other people's cards. I can tell you that."

"Why did you never tell me before?" Lisa asked.

Her mother sighed, then sipped from her drink. "Fantasy stuff," she said. "It's the kind of thing, if you talk about it, people think you're nuts. What would your father think about this conversation? It would be meaningless to your sister, meaningless to *my* sisters."

"What powers do *you* have, Mother?" Lisa asked. "We understand each other now, so don't lie to me about it."

Mary frowned. "First, tell me how you killed those two men."

Lisa raised her chin. She narrowed her eyes. "I tore their throats open. They died of . . . loss of blood? Maybe not. Maybe of sheer terror."

"You tore . . . ? You? How, Lisa? How?"

"I . . . Let's say that I became like an animal. I was given the strength to save my baby. That happens, doesn't it? We hear of women being given fantastic strength when they need it to save their children."

Mary shook her head. "Given the power to kill like a wild beast? No. I never heard of anything like that."

"You remember I told you I sense that the baby is under a special protection, may even be invulnerable. Whatever—whoever—protects it gave me the power to defend it. Gave me the *will* to defend it, even by killing."

Her mother shuddered. "This is too much, Lisa. It cannot be of God. Your great-grandmother . . . No, I can't imagine she could have—"

"Maybe because she never *had* to," said Lisa. "And maybe you could, too, if you had to."

"I couldn't," said her mother, shaking her head.

"Couldn't? Or wouldn't?"

"Couldn't. Sometimes I . . . I see things. I see things I know I didn't see, not in the ordinary sense. I . . . don't think I can do any more than that. I'm not conscious of any other powers. I can't make things happen. Or not happen. I've sometimes wondered about the horse races. I've wondered if Grandmother Kennedy picked the right horses or made her picks win."

"Did she ever do anything more . . . ominous?"

"Lisa, she was fifty-seven years old the year I was born. She was well into her sixties before I became aware of her. I remember only that she played cards exceptionally well and won money at the races. God knows what she did as a young woman."

"Did she teach you anything?" Lisa asked. "Did she ever try to teach you?"

"About powers, you mean? No. She was just a grand old Irish lady. Pillar of the church."

"But she was a witch!"

Mary's lips stiffened, whitened. "It pains me to think she was."

"It pains you to think *you* are," said Lisa. "And that your mother was and that I am. But we *are,* dammit!"

"Do you wish you weren't?"

Lisa closed her eyes for an instant and blew away a noisy breath. It was not a sigh. It was a puff of annoyance and frustration. "Great minds run in the same direction," she said.

"I have never known exactly how to deal with the fact that my mother and grandmother—and I, for that matter, and now you—are not . . . ordinary," Mary said. "I have lived my life avoiding the word 'witch.' I didn't want to hear it. I studied parapsychology, thinking maybe there was a rational explanation for our idiosyncrasy. The truth is, we have no choice, do we?"

Lisa shook her head. "No. Well . . . Yes. Not to decide if we are witches or not, but we have a lot of choice about how we use our powers."

"Where does it come from, Lisa? The power? Is it from Satan?"

"That I don't know. But the authors of *Malleus Maleficarum* said that witches have powers only with the permission of Almighty God. Jonathan himself says he serves a lesser god, one the Almighty could destroy with a gesture if He wished. And therefore we are what we are with God's consent. We are a part of His creation, and we serve His purposes."

"A very nice rationalization."

"Father William doesn't reject it."

Mary tossed back her Scotch and poured another. "Tell me how you . . . Tell me how you killed those two men."

"No. No, I won't tell you."

"Prove to me— Prove to me, somehow, that this is not just foolish talk! Show me a power, Lisa! Show me something you can do."

"Mother, this is not—"

"This conversation is insane. *Insane!* Show me it is not."

Lisa faced her mother, drawing shallow breaths, searching herself for will. Why should she show her mother anything? What could she show her?

Jonathan . . .

Maybe the inspiration came from Jonathan. Whether it did or not made no difference.

Lisa used will. She would not turn into a wolf. There must be something else. She willed what she had seen Charity will.

Only differently. On herself, not on a child in a well. She willed herself to rise from the kitchen stool and float upward. And it happened. She drifted toward the ceiling.

Jonathan had said he didn't ride to the church on a broomstick. Yet he had not driven his BMW. He could move! Well, by God, *so could she!*

"Lisa!"

Her mother was terrified.

Lisa floated down and returned to the stool.

Mary crossed herself and mumbled a prayer. Her eyes glistened with tears.

Lisa picked up her glass.

"Lisa, in the name of God!"

"If it is not with God's help that I do it, at least I do it with His consent. *And so can you.*"

Mary shook her head.

"You can. Do it with God's consent, as I just did. We could not do it otherwise. So do it, Mother. Let me see you rise."

"Lisa, I cannot! You know I cannot!"

"You can," said Lisa. *"Will it!"*

"I . . . don't want to."

"Will it!"

Her mother stared at her dumbstruck, but after a moment she drifted off her stool. She screamed and thrust her feet down, and in a second she stood, feet on the floor.

"You willed it!" she shrieked at Lisa.

"No. You did."

Mary stood at her kitchen counter shaking her head, her fists clenched on the Corian surface. "I want nothing to do with this," she muttered.

"You need not have anything to do with it. But know it. It's there. It's what you are. What I am."

"It's a *curse!*"

"Maybe. But you can't be rid of it. Or . . . actually, maybe you can. Father William says you can. Pray to be relieved of it. Pray that your powers go away. He wants me to take

Communion, then to pray. We can go together, to his church."

"And you will pray to be relieved of your powers?"

Lisa drew a deep breath. "Not until my baby is born. I may need my powers to protect her."

A letter:

Mr. Mountfort presents his compliments to Miss Douglas and begs leave to explain his protracted absence from the great pleasure of her company, it being occasioned by an indisposition his surgeon is endeavoring to cure as rapidly as may be. On the command of his surgeon, he has been from his lodgings but once this fortnight, and that whilst doubly wrapped in wool and carried in a chair, that he might do his duty to the Earl.

Dearest, dearest Molly! I greatly fear that bad is to be followed by worse. Were it not for the indisposition that now rages in me, I should be plagued by naughty merchants making their usual demands. In consequence, not only am I deprived of the delight of your company but am also unable in any wise to respond satisfactorily to your polite request for 45 guineas. Dare I suggest that you apply once more to our generous benefactor, your honorable parent?

Accept, dearest girl, my humble assurance that, given one stroke of *good* fortune, I will expeditiously attend to the matter that so concerns us.

In the meantime, accept, I beg, my profession of deep and abiding attachment. But for this plagued indisposition, I should plead—nay, *demand*—the honor of looking on your gentle face, of touching your divine hands, of caressing your precious parts. Whilst at Divine Service this Sunday, pray for me, for him who cannot leave his quarters even to be present for services. Pray, too, that we may be together again very soon.

I beg the honor to remain, dearest girl, your most humble, obedient, and *devoted* servant,

Charles

Moll Douglas—or Lisa, for they were the same—angrily crumpled the arrogant, lying letter and tossed it into the cold black fireplace.

Damn him! *Indisposition!* Indisposition indeed! It was infection! Disease! Which he had got from some trollop he had picked up in the Haymarket, no doubt. Which, likely as not, he had passed on to her, though she had as yet felt no symptom of it.

Damn him, too, for his impudent indiscretion in sending her such a letter! What if it had fallen into the hands of her mother?

On that thought she retrieved the paper from the fireplace, touched it to a candle flame, and tossed it in again.

Apply to her father for forty-five guineas! She dared not. He would require her to return to the Country and live there for the rest of her life, to marry there, probably to some dull Scot. She might wind up living in Edinburgh, where her parents had lived until her father had had the good sense to throw in his lot with the King rather than with the Pretender and was awarded the estate in Buckinghamshire.

Though the house was only two miles from Windsor Castle and only twenty miles from London, it was still the Country, and she suffered oppressive boredom every day she spent there. Glorious day when she and her mother had finally persuaded Sir William Douglas to buy the house in Town! Now they spent as much time here as they dared, for her mother loved the Town, too. To be compelled to confess to her father that she had lent that knave Charles Mountfort almost her entire allowance for the year—the money that was to have paid for all her clothes, for her tuition in French, for— No! She could not do it!

She had to recover her forty-five guineas, if not from Charles then by some other means. She doubted not that Charles was unable to repay. Her money had saved him from debtors' prison, no doubt. She was compelled to acknowledge, now, that he was a rake and a scoundrel and that she had been a fool to accept him for what he appeared to be.

She had taken him for a gentleman of the Town. Certainly he knew the Town and had assisted her mother and her in identifying the most fashionable places where a young woman could wish to be seen. He had escorted them to coffeehouses and taverns and theaters. He had arranged for them to be received by persons of some note, including James Boswell, Laird of Auchinleck, who in turn had arranged for them to be received by Lord Eglinton.

Sir William Douglas remained in the Country and was not aware that his wife and daughter had made the acquaintance of the Laird of Auchinleck. If he had known that, he would have required them to return home immediately, for the Laird had a dark reputation for excessive drinking and, it was said, for using prostitutes to satisfy his grosser desires. That he had recently published a biography of Dr. Samuel Johnson would not have excused him to Sir William, since Johnson, too, was notorious for his carousals and had been besides a man notably contemptuous of Scotsmen.

Moll's mother had been amazed at Sir William's acquiescence in the girl's plan to live part of the year in London. Grudging though his consent was, he had given it, which she would not have thought possible. Moll herself had been surprised. But not entirely. She had long since discovered in herself a faculty for persuading other people to do what they didn't want to do.

She had— She wasn't sure how to express it. She had extraordinary strength of will. She had discovered in herself unusual abilities to see and understand, to sense thoughts and emotions, particularly in those who opposed her in any way, and even sometimes to exert a force against the will of others, causing them to abandon their opposition.

Having discovered these curious talents, Moll had struggled ever after to develop and strengthen them. She hadn't yet learned their limits, but she found uses for them.

For example, she had wanted a certain handsome chestnut mare broken to harness so she could make a show being drawn to the village in a rig behind so pretty a little horse. Opposition came from her brother George, two years older, who wanted the mare for his saddle horse. In the petulant confrontation that followed, her father had favored his son and ruled that the mare would not be harnessed.

"'Tis, after all, a man's honor to sit his horse well," her father had said. "In a few more years George will be wantin' a great stallion, but for now the mare suits him well. He does make a pretty sight on it, now, doesn't he? Even you will admit that, Moll."

George, astride the mare, had whipped her into a canter around the paddock. The horse had carried the princely lad, dressed in scarlet coat, white vest, white stock, white breeches, black boots, powdered wig, and black tricorne with plume. Moll had thought him swollen with pride.

She had tolerated George's prideful show for some minutes, until, passing her, he had doffed his hat and bestowed on her an arrogant smirk. Then, darkly furious, she had fixed a baleful eye on the mare, which turned and for a moment stared at her eyes, then reared. George, not a skillful horseman, had slipped off backward. He would have taken a simple, painful, humiliating fall on his back in the mud, except that his right boot had been thrust too far forward in the stirrup, where it remained wedged, leaving the young man hanging by one leg. The mare had panicked and run. By the time grooms had caught up with the horse and stopped her, George's leg was broken and his face was bleeding.

"She's to be shot!" he had screamed. "Shot! Now!"

"Noo, George," Sir William had said. "We nae shoot sae pretty a little mare because—"

"Shot! I demand it!" George had screamed. Then he voiced a thought planted in him by his sister. "I will never mount that horse again!"

"Soo, then, Moll has her for harness after all."

One after another, she had won small triumphs, manipulating people's will, sometimes by direct opposition, more often by deception. Even so, she much doubted she could will her father's clemency when he learned she had lost her allowance.

Moll Douglas was an exceptionally attractive young woman: short, a bit plump, with dark curls showing from under her caps and bonnets, a quick smile, laughing eyes, and a white bosom swelling from her low-cut gowns. She had learned she was fascinating to men and had drawn the attentions of a wide variety of them, from blackguards and rakes like Mountfort to dour Scots barristers come down from Edinburgh to visit her father.

It was her hope that London would afford her some great match, by which she could avoid the sort of marriage she supposed her father was arranging for her. If some great lord or some man of wealth and influence applied for her hand, her father could hardly refuse his consent, consign her instead to the dreariness of Edinburgh, or, worse, some squalid Scots village.

Perhaps the Town didn't know what a fool Mountfort had made of her. Perhaps her forty-five guineas had been well spent, since it was through Mountfort, after all, that she had gained some little entrée into the better sort of company.

"Ma'am?"

She looked up from her musing. Millie, the housemaid, stood in the doorway.

"Mr. Roper is belowstairs, Ma'am. He is conversing with Lady Douglas, who asks you to join them."

Jonathan Roper. A very interesting man. He was their neighbor in Bucks, having bought an old stone house on a small tract, where he lived most comfortably, apparently on income from investments. He was twenty years older than she was, at least, and had known her father and mother for a very long time. It was a misfortune, she had often thought, that he was so old, for surely Jonathan Roper was the handsomest man she had ever seen.

"Mr. Roper," said her mother, "has invited us to dine with him at Clifton's Chop House. As I cannot, for reason you know but need not name, I have suggested you alone accompany him."

Moll glanced quizzically at Jonathan Roper. Her mother must have noticed, for she added, "It will be quite proper. Mr. Roper is a good friend of the family."

It was some distance to Clifton's, which was in Fleet Street, so Mr. Roper hired chairs, being emphatic to the chairmen under the poles that the chairs must not become separated from each other. The young lady would have no money to pay the men carrying her, and he, Mr. Roper, would not pay his men if the two chairs were not delivered at the same time at Clifton's.

Moll sat comfortably inside hers, viewing the bustle of the streets through the windows as the chairmen carried her through The Strand, past Somerset House and Saint Clement's. The magnificent dome of Saint Paul's loomed ahead wreathed in fog and smoke, yet gleaming in the afternoon sunlight.

Her eyes were not on that dome but on the carnival of the streets. She had a glimpse of a water seller dipping water from his barrels into the cans a serving woman carried on a yoke. A child trotted beside her chair for a few yards, offering yellow flowers for a penny. Another child sold sprigs of heather. A woman with a basket hung around her neck offered oranges. The carnival separated to let a coach pass—a lumbering, majestic vehicle, as it appeared to Moll, drawn by four matched black horses. She glimpsed the crest painted on the door and wondered what great person rode inside. A milk seller passed, offering dippers of milk from the buckets hung on his yoke. Two whores sauntered by, smirking.

Dr. Johnson was supposed to have said that the man who is tired of London is tired of life. For herself, Moll could not imagine wanting to live anywhere else, which reinforced her determination not to be forced back to Bucks, much less to barbaric Scotland.

Mr. Roper and his guest were received at Clifton's with elaborate deference and were conducted to a table in an alcove, where they had a degree of privacy, though not so much as to cause it to appear that he had brought her here for any licentious purpose. They would dine privately, yet within view of anyone who chose to glance their way.

"I am grateful to you, Sir," Moll said. "I faced a dull afternoon."

"I should not want your life to be dull, even for an hour," he said.

Mr. Roper wore the white smallclothes he favored, which gave him in the Town, she had heard, something of the name of a fop. His coat was of rich plum-colored velvet, and his white waistcoat was ornamented with gold embroidery. He had the aspect of a man who satisfied himself and cared little what name others gave him, as amply evidenced by the fact that he wore no wig but went about showing his own hair. He removed an exquisite diamond-encrusted gold snuffbox from his waistcoat pocket, dipped out a pinch between finger and thumb, and tucked that pinch into his nostril.

"Mountfort is ill," he said rather loftily.

"You know about Mr. Mountfort?"

"Yes. His disease has not been transmitted to you, though you should be more careful in such matters."

"It has not? Pray, Sir, how do you know?"

"I know much about you, Moll. I know that Mountfort was not yet infected when you allowed him your favors."

"You know, then, about the forty-five guineas."

"I do indeed."

"I was a dunce to have given them to him. I will never see it again. But, la, Sir, how do you know so much? Are you a friend of Mr. Mountfort's?"

"I am not, I assure you. I admit no man of his character to my friendship."

"Then, Sir, I inquire again: how come you to know—"

"I follow your affairs rather closely, Moll. Has your mother not told you why?"

"Indeed not, Sir. What should she have told me?"

"That I am your father."

"*Sir!* What do you say? Oh, Lord, I am overcome! It cannot be! How can this be so?"

"Your mother sent you to dinner with me alone so that I could tell you. We had decided it is time you knew. *I* knew it was time when I realized you had fallen into the clutches of so miscreant a rogue as Charles Mountfort."

"But have not you and my mother acted wickedly, Sir? For surely Sir William Douglas believes he is my father."

"Sir William Douglas has always favored his sword and his political intrigues far more than his marriage. Once your two brothers were born, he was satisfied and required nothing further from your mother but an occasional sporting. She is a fine lady with the needs of a healthy woman. I met her needs. You are our pride, born to us when we were near forty years of age. Sir William does not, of course, suspect."

"I am a bastard!" she wailed.

"No. It is the law of England that a child born during coverture—that is, during marriage—is conclusively presumed to be the child of the husband. There are no exceptions."

"Even so . . ."

"Your mother should have told you. I have always watched over you, Moll. I will replace your forty-five guineas. Better yet, if you wish, I can show you how to replace them yourself."

For a thoughtful moment she stared toward the street, where the unceasing bustle was visible through the windows at the front of the house. It was late afternoon, of course, and the sun was setting. The light outside was red and fading. Inside, the servants were scurrying about, lighting more candles. The light inside was warm yellow, and thin columns of black smoke rose above the scores of candles and formed a sooty cloud just beneath the blackened ceiling. The heavy oaken tables were laden with great platters of beef and chops, with potatoes and bread and boiled vegetables. People ate hungrily. Some washed down their meat with ale from flagons. More of them poured from bottles of claret and port.

"So you are my father, Sir. Will you, then, arrange my marriage?"

Mr. Roper smiled gently. "I believe I shall have some influence, though Sir William may not realize it."

"He might want to marry me to Edinburgh, Sir. I cannot endure the thought of it."

"Your hope is to find in London a marriage so fine he cannot object to it. Your mother has explained that to me."

"Now that I know he is not my father, I can say I do not wish to marry a man like him."

"You shall not."

"Whom, then, Sir? What man will satisfy both my . . . both Sir William and me?"

"We will find someone. Indeed, Moll, I have someone in mind."

"And who is that, Sir?"

"Do not ask me to tell you all my secrets at once."

Moll reached for her glass of claret. She took a swallow. "It is odd, Sir, will you not own, that we are so little like?"

For he was blond with pale blue eyes. Her mother had sandy hair.

"You are even more unlike Sir William. But you are like me in ways you do not know."

"Tell me of those ways, Sir, I pray you."

"Are you not aware, Moll, that you have an exceptionally powerful will? Sir William bought the house in Saint Martin's Lane and allows you and your mother to live in it half the year. That is totally against his will. *You* willed it. And he did it."

Moll smiled mischievously. "Then what am I, Sir? A witch?"

Roper pointed at the claret bottle. "My daughter . . . put your hand there, on the table," he said, tapping his finger at a spot six inches from her hand. "Now . . . make the bottle come to your hand, Moll. *Will it!*"

She tipped her head and smiled. Then she stared at the bottle. It moved. It slid the few inches and came into her open hand.

"My God, Sir! Say it is a trick, Sir!"

"Didn't you know you could do that?" he asked.

"We live in the Age of Reason, Sir," she said. "Who would suspect, in this day and age, that a woman might have the powers of a witch?"

"You have them."

"Does my mother have them?"

"In a few small ways. Not like you. What you have just done is only the most insignificant manifestation of your powers. You are one in a long line of mothers and daughters. You are the third to be endowed with great powers."

"Why do I have greater powers, Sir?"

"Because you are my daughter. Your mother is a witch, with power. Being born of her and of me concentrates the powers in you. You have great power, Moll."

"Are you then Satan, Sir?"

"No, though I am pleased to see you are not frightened by the prospect that I might be."

Moll Douglas stared across the chophouse. A strong gust of wind blew out half the candles, leaving the place half dark and the patrons frightened. She stared at the ware on their table, and it moved around. She stared at the big yellow cat sleeping on the hearth, and it jumped up and screeched.

"Careful . . ." murmured Jonathan Roper.

Moll grinned and licked her lips.

12

BOTH WENT FORWARD, OUT OF THEIR PEW AND INTO THE SIDE AISLE to join the line of people taking Holy Communion. Father William Longford himself waited for them. Wearing his green-trimmed ivory-colored vestments, he dispensed the sacramental wafers and wine to the communicants. Lisa was amused to see that, even performing this office, he remained gruff, athletic, abrupt, and a little awkward in his movements. He took an extra moment with Mary O'Neil. He could not have known who she was but perhaps guessed she was Lisa's mother.

When Lisa knelt, he gazed pensively into her eyes, as if the thought suddenly had come to him that maybe he should not give this woman Holy Communion. But he did. She took the wafer into her mouth. He wiped the lip of the chalice with his white cloth. She sipped. And she had taken Communion.

At the door of the church afterward, Lisa took a moment to introduce him to her mother.

"It's a pleasure to meet you, Mrs. O'Neil. Your daughter and I have become friends. I'm glad to see you here this morning, Lisa. I hope it reflects a decision."

"We'll talk with you later, Father."

* * *

It was the custom in the house at Chappaqua to eat the main meal on Sunday early in the afternoon, as soon as possible after the family returned from Mass. Ben should have known this, but he didn't remember, apparently, and he called at the most inopportune time.

"I need to talk to you," he said, a little curtly, she thought. "Are you where we can talk?"

She had gone into the kitchen to take the call. "I suppose so. In the kitchen."

"Your friend Jonathan Roper has flown the coop. Gone. Disappeared."

"Leaving bills unpaid?" she asked.

"No. Not that. Something else. The same day *you* left town, *he* left town. So I want to know something. Is he up there with you?"

"Ben, for Christ's sake!"

"Yes or no will do."

"No."

"All right. What's this business with the Pennsylvania State Police?"

"I had a flat on the highway at night. Two guys in a truck stopped and changed it for me. They put on the solid-rubber spare, so I had to stop and buy a tire as soon as I could. I went to a Shell station and used the Shell credit card. The two guys got killed later. People driving by had seen them changing the tire on a Ford Probe, so the cops checked stations for a Ford Probe that needed a new tire. The police lieutenant was very polite. All he wanted to know was, had I seen or heard anything unusual."

"How were these guys killed?"

"That's odd. They were attacked by a wild animal. Right where they had been when they changed my tire. But I didn't hear any wild animal."

"Have you checked into the possibility of placing the baby for adoption?"

"I talked to a priest about it."

"Why not a lawyer?"

"Priest first, Ben."

"Well, what did he say?"

"He said he'd help me if I decided to do it."

"So what have you decided?"

"I don't think we should try to talk about it on the telephone. I'll come home."

"Which means you've decided no."

"Ben . . . Maybe this is something we shouldn't try to talk about on the phone, either. But . . . Dammit, Ben, why do you hate the baby?"

"Jesus Christ, I don't hate it!"

"Then why are you so determined to get rid of it?"

"Will you give me a straight, simple answer to a straight, simple question?"

"Absolutely."

"Is it really mine?"

She hung up.

Frankie Gerard called on Monday morning. She said she had heard that Lisa was back in the area and asked her to meet her for lunch.

"Off the time clock, Lisa. Not doctor-patient. Friend to friend. I hope you think of me as a friend."

They met for lunch in the restaurant of the Stouffer's Hotel on the Cross-Westchester Expressway. It was plain that Frankie was taking time off for this meeting, since she was wearing blue jeans and a sweatshirt, as was Lisa.

"I'm not sure I made one thing clear before," said Frankie. "I am Catholic. My education in the sciences makes that a little tougher, but I haven't given it up. I've given a lot of attention to your problem. I mean, I've read as much as I could. I'm no longer sure it's a matter of mind. I'm ready to acknowledge it can be real."

"It *is* real," said Lisa. "There's nothing to talk about on that question. Father William knows it's real. My mother knows it's real. I . . . I'm grateful for your offer of friendship, but I'm not sure there's a damn thing you can do for me."

"What you revealed under hypnosis was real," said Frankie. "Maybe you have something more to reveal."

"Would you like to meet Jonathan?" Lisa asked.

"Why— Yes, I very much would."

"That's Jonathan, at the table by the window."

In the silent moment while Frankie was turning to look at Jonathan, while his and her eyes met, Lisa's mind flooded with an impression from Town.

Town. Town. Why Town? Images of London were intruding on her sense of this time and this place, so why was she thinking of Town?

"I shall enjoy the Town a great deal more, now that I know Sir William Douglas cannot force me to return to the Country. He shall never govern me again, Sir. Why should he? He is not my father. And you have shown me I have the power to overcome him. I shall use that power as may be necessary."

"Use your power sparingly, Moll," Jonathan Roper said. "It can cause you great unhappiness."

They were on Saint Martin's Lane, Moll having expressed a wish to walk the short distance home from Saint Martin's-in-the-Fields Church. It was safe, she thought, since she was accompanied by the man she already accepted fondly as her father and since he was wearing a smallsword. Besides, Roper had hired a link-boy to walk ahead of them with a flaming torch that they might not risk the darkness. The streets were by no means safe in the dark. Apart from the danger of being set upon by cutpurses and worse, there was always the strong possibility of stumbling over someone lying on the street or of fouling one's shoes in filth. The sweepers worked all day but stopped at sunset.

Even in this dark lane a whore lurked in a doorway, ready to expose her breasts to a man and solicit his custom.

"Sir, I am determined to prevent my unhappiness," Moll said simply.

"You can control Sir William," he said. "Your mother

can influence him. You can control him. But it will be much better if he is not befuddled. It is better that the existence of your powers remains unknown, even to those on whom you exert them. It is better that you not be thought odd, that you not raise questions you will not wish to answer."

"I shall remember that excellent advice, Sir," she said. "I shall defer to you."

"You will be tempted to do otherwise."

When she reached home, Moll found her mother sitting before a small coal fire, reading and dozing—in what proportions Moll could not guess. She bade her good night without fully wakening her. The bottle of port sitting beside the half-eaten apple on the table by her chair was perhaps the explanation for her drowsiness.

In her own room, Moll allowed the maid to assist her in removing her clothes and dressing in a white nightgown. She dismissed the girl then and locked the door. The curtains were drawn, and the room was stuffy. She pulled off the nightgown and sat down naked in the chair that faced a tiny fireplace, this one dark and cold. Like her mother, she enjoyed a glass of port at bedtime and kept a bottle in her room. She poured a glass. There was a bit of cheese and the stale remains of a loaf of bread in a cabinet, and she put these on her chairside table, too.

No one knew this of Moll Douglas: that she enjoyed nakedness. When she could be certain she was alone and could not be spied on, she often threw aside her clothes, all of them. She read whilst naked. She was often naked when she wrote her letters. She tolerated cold better than other people and was comfortable with nakedness until winter brought its damp chill to London.

She smiled to herself, flexed her shoulders, and lifted her breasts in her hands. They were happy to be released from the rigid stays that shoved them up and out for stylish display: a display she gloried in and depended on to win her attention. Someday a man was going to discover the beauty mark on the left one. A mole, small and dark, it made a piquant contrast with white skin and pink nipple. The man who discovered it was going to see it as a beauty mark, a *natural* beauty mark. He would be beguiled.

Charles Mountfort had seen it . . . and had had so little imagination as to fail to appreciate it. Blackguard! *God damn him!*

God damn him.

Mr. Roper . . . Her father. He *said* he was her father. Actually . . . Yes. He *was* her father. She sensed it. She *knew* it. And he said she was a witch! She had not just the special force of will she had long known she had but also fantastic powers! Use your powers sparingly, he had said, but she had already taught herself that the more she used her powers the greater they became. Anyway, what good were they if she didn't use them?

She had reason to use them.

She sat down on her bed and focused her will. On Charles Mountfort.

His lodgings were in Downing Street, as she well knew. She focused on the rooms she had too often visited: a bedroom and a fine large sitting room above his landlord's family rooms on the street floor. The rooms were neither modest nor luxurious but were the kind of quarters unmarried young men rented, where they lived comfortably. The landlord and his wife and son had seen Moll coming and going and had known for what purpose she visited; but they were circumspect and had invariably averted their eyes and pretended they only noticed her and did not look closely enough to recognize her if they should see her elsewhere.

She saw the sitting room, across a distance, through the dark, through the walls, even.

There he sat. He was ill, as he had written. His parts, exposed by his wide-open dressing gown, were swollen and inflamed. His physick was at hand, and as she watched he took up the bottle and gulped a swig of it.

He was attended by . . . Very likely by the infected strumpet who had given him the disease. She was a fat, pink-skinned, slovenly girl, maybe seventeen or eighteen, with large sagging dugs which she exposed naked to Mountfort, though obviously he was unable to be aroused by the sight of them.

This . . . These creatures. This was the sort of company into which she had been drawn by this poxy scoundrel. No doubt he was regularly attended by whores. Her new father had said the fellow wasn't yet infected when he was with her. *Newly infected* was probably what he meant, for a man of this character had to carry the disease with him every day of his life. She could hope Mr. Roper was right, that she was not infected; but if she was not, it was no thanks to Charles Mountfort.

Moll was angry. She became angrier. In her fury she changed, from plump, pretty, smiling young woman to gaunt, ember-eyed witch, blazing with purpose. No hag, still young, still beautiful but in a wholly different way. From the chest at the foot of her bed she snatched up her cutty sark, the short chemise she wore under her corset, and pulled it over her head.

She pulled back the curtains, thrust open the window, and swept through it, into the air above Saint Martin's Lane. Over Charing Cross she soared, and over the roofs of Whitehall to Downing Street. Her hair flew behind her. The loose cutty sark fluttered in the wind, but she was not cold.

Either by coincidence or because Moll willed it, the little trollop left Charles Mountfort's rooms two minutes before the witch arrived. Moll glided through his sitting-room window without opening the shutter or breaking the glass. In one instant she was not there. In the next she stood before him.

The sick man looked up at the apparition that had so suddenly appeared. He was too weak to be terrified and only stared at her in resigned dread. He did not recognize her and probably took her for the specter of death.

Which for him she was.

* * *

"Of your sixteen predecessors, only two ever killed," Jonathan had said.

Moll did. Moll . . . And against Jonathan's wishes, apparently. That was interesting.

Frankie Gerard stared at Jonathan, who was sitting alone, drinking Scotch, looking at the menu. He wore a gray cashmere tweed jacket, regimental-stripe tie in dark blue and scarlet, white shirt, charcoal-gray slacks, Gucci loafers. He looked up, smiled, and nodded.

Lisa beckoned him to join them. He came to their table carrying his drink and menu.

"Dr. Gerard, may I present Jonathan Roper."

He took the psychiatrist's hand. "I am glad to meet you, Doctor," he said. He sat down. "I feel I already know you, as you must feel you know me."

Frankie Gerard was clearly frightened of Jonathan. She could not conceal it. She pulled back her hand as soon as she could without jerking it out of his clasp.

Jonathan did not trouble himself to conceal his wry amusement. "Dr. Gerard," he said, "if I were a psychiatrist and Lisa were my patient, I would do everything you have done and more to dispel from her mind something that in your frame of reference absolutely has to be a delusion. I bear you no ill will for trying. Really. No ill will at all."

Frankie Gerard found courage. "What are you, Mr. Roper?" she asked in a quavery voice.

"Even I don't know," he said simply.

"Do you represent good or evil?"

"What *is* good, Dr. Gerard? What is evil? Wise men have tried to define those terms for a very long time. All I know is, whoever defines them simplistically defines them wrong."

"What is your relationship to God?"

"As I have told Lisa repeatedly, the Almighty allows me to exist, even as He allows you to exist."

"Did He create you?"

"The Almighty allowed me to be created."

"Then who did create you?"

"The Power that created everything created me. But

213

maybe indirectly, as you were created by will and consent, though your parents were the agents of your creation."

"Who or what was the direct agent of your creation, Mr. Roper?"

Jonathan turned to Lisa. His eyes settled on her with a gaze more loving than she had ever seen from him before. "Lisa knows," he said.

"But *I* don't," Frankie Gerard persisted.

Jonathan laughed. "'Doctor, Doctor, I beg you to stop these insane experiments! You are toying with the secrets of life itself! There are some things man was not meant to know.'"

"Then . . . Are you saying that Lisa has been raised to a higher plane and is entitled to know things the rest of mankind is not entitled to know?"

He nodded. "You could say it that way. Yes. Yes. That's good. I hadn't thought of it quite that way, but that's a good way to think of it."

Frankie Gerard stared at her drink: a Beefeater martini on the rocks. She drew a deep breath. "Mr. Roper," she said in a voice just above a whisper, "is there any way *I* can be initiated into this knowledge? Is there any way I can become what Lisa is?"

Jonathan's pale blue eyes turned hard and unmoving: unnatural. "Lisa," he said, "is the daughter of sixteen generations of her kind. Her blood and mine are mingled through centuries. You cannot be what she is. I should probably erase this conversation from your memory."

"I ask," said Frankie Gerard solemnly, "not to be what the seventeenth generation is, only to be what the first generation can be."

"Why?" asked Lisa.

"The knowledge . . ." Frankie Gerard whispered. "To know what—"

"What humanity does not know," Jonathan interrupted. "Knowledge. You might be sorry to acquire it. How do you know it is not a curse, like the knowledge acquired by Eve, and then by Adam, when they ate the forbidden fruit?"

Frankie Gerard's chin wrinkled as her face turned rigid. "Mr. Roper," she said. *"It is a risk I want to take."*

Jonathan frowned at Lisa, then smiled. "I'll be damned," he said.

When they reached the parking lot, Jonathan climbed into Lisa's Ford.

"I'm not sure we should let her remember that conversation," he said to Lisa as she pulled out of the parking lot and made her way to the entrance to the eastbound Cross-Westchester Expressway.

"Why not see what she does about it?"

He glanced at her and smiled. "You've begun to think like me. Do you know that? Do you know how much you've changed? You've become *devious*, Lisa."

"I've become a witch," she said.

"You were born a witch."

"But I didn't know it. Why did you wait so long to tell me, Jonathan?"

"Not every woman is pleased with the knowledge. Anyway, there was no need for you to know."

"I wish I had known from the beginning. I wish I'd known your motive. I . . . I could have tried to have the daughter with Ben. Couldn't I?"

"I watched and waited a long time for you to do that. Then I saw you were not going to. I could not let the line end."

"You told Moll you were her father."

"I was. After his sons were born, Sir William Douglas had no interest in more children—and little interest in his wife. I was Moll's father and her great-great-great grandfather."

"What are you to me?"

"Most recently I am your great-great grandfather."

Lisa shook her head. "My great-great grandmother was Elizabeth Christina Dugan, who married Timothy Spencer. The line wasn't running out with her. They had several daughters."

"Think, Lisa," he said. "Use your powers if you want to. I

don't have to feed you your history anymore. You can call it up for yourself."

"You've spoken of the four powerful witches. I suppose all of them were your daughters."

Jonathan nodded.

"I seem to have great powers. But I am not your daughter. Am I?"

"As I've told you, Lisa, you have more powers than my other wives. Not more than my daughters, but more than my wives. I have also told you I am not sure why. Maybe the gods have some great purpose for you."

"'Gods.' You use a plural."

"There is one Great Power, which I call the Almighty. There are also lesser gods. Call them angels if it makes you more comfortable. One of them is greater than the others. He is called by many names, just as the Almighty is."

"You cried out to Satan when you were dying in Geneva."

"And he responded. Or maybe the Almighty responded through him. Yes, I think that is the way it was. The Almighty heard my cry but was displeased because I was cursing and renouncing. So Satan was appointed to succor me. Satan was *allowed* to succor me."

"So what did he make you, Jonathan? What are you? Are you, too, a witch?"

"Only females are witches."

"A warlock, then."

"No. That's a fable. There are no males with witches' powers."

"Then what are *you?*" Lisa persisted. "You told Frankie you didn't know."

"I suppose I am an angel."

"Angels are supposed to be good."

Jonathan laughed. "Supposed to be angelic. No, Lisa. There are nine orders of angels: seraphim and cherubim, which are the highest, and so on down to archangels and angels, which are the lowest. None of them are white-robed creatures with wings."

"And which are you?"

"I am not sure. The Almighty might have told me, but I shall never see the face of the Almighty. At least I haven't yet, and I suppose I won't. That is a part of my penalty for cursing it at the end of my life."

" 'It.' You almost never use the word 'God.' You speak of the Almighty, but you don't use the male pronoun for God. You don't speak of 'Him.' "

"I am not sure the Almighty is 'Him.' I don't know. I suspect the Ultimate Power is something else. Anyway, I suspect I have been shut off from ever seeing the face of the Almighty, ever knowing just what it is."

"And I? Will I be allowed to see the face of God?"

"I don't know. But I believe you might. It depends on how you use your powers."

"Even witches can see—"

"Why not? You are not evil. You have been the victims of centuries of slander. For example, you did not become a witch by a coital connection with Satan. You know that. Yet that is the old story about how women become witches."

Lisa smiled. "I wonder what Frankie thinks."

"I don't much care," he said. "I want to spend the rest of the afternoon with you in my hotel room."

"Whatever else you are, you are very much a man," Lisa said with a grin.

"You are my sixth wife," he said. "Only two of them before you ever meant anything much to me. I made my wives the mothers of my daughters, but I didn't always love them, or even respect them. I have loved all my daughters. I expect to love our daughter. I am a little surprised about it, but I love you, Lisa. Something about you is different, very different, and I love you."

"What are we going to do about the fact that I'm married and the mother of a son?"

"So long as your husband does not interfere with the birth of the child," said Jonathan, "I must leave it to you to decide what to do about him."

* * *

When Lisa arrived back at her parents' home in Chappaqua, her body ached from the fervor of what she and Jonathan had done on his bed at the Hyatt Regency. She could not remember when, if ever, Ben had satisfied her so much.

Ben . . . What could she do about Ben? She'd never had an affair before. He'd never had one, she was certain. He had been a good husband to her. She had been a good wife.

Well . . . Within the conventional interpretation of the terms, they had been a good husband and wife. They'd had a conventional marriage.

If she had never ventured outside her marriage, maybe it had been because she had never seen any advantage to doing that, as much as out of any strong sense of obligation. Maybe it had been because she'd never met another man who interested her enough to inspire her to take the risk.

Maybe it had been the same for Ben, too. He was not venturesome. Ben was entirely comfortable in the hierarchical structure of a corporation. It would have smothered her, she always thought, but to him it meant order and security; it meant expectations that would be regularly met. It was important for Ben to live his life as he had planned it. Since an extramarital adventure was no part of his plan—and might have interfered in the regular procession of achievements and promotions that his life revolved around—it would have taken an extraordinary intrusion by an extraordinary woman to tempt him.

That was a terrible confession to have to make—that they had remained true to their marriage vows only because no one had come along who offered sufficient incentive to move them otherwise—but it was the truth.

Jonathan . . .

Well . . . What if one of the witches had appeared to Ben? Say Moll Douglas. There was a minx! What would Ben have done?

Rationalization.

"I know where you've spent the afternoon," her mother

told her as soon as Lisa was inside the house. "I couldn't tell Ben. He's called four times."

Lisa frowned. "What do you mean, you know where I spent the afternoon? How do you know?"

Mary's chin rose, stretching the loose skin of her neck. "You sent a strong signal," she said crisply.

Lisa smiled wanly. "You're using your powers."

"I prayed to be relieved of them. Apparently my prayer has not been answered. They are actually stronger."

"Remember the cliché, 'Use it or lose it.' When you use powers, they become stronger, apparently. Maybe this is the first time in your life you've used yours."

"I'm afraid of them. I always have been. They are not from God."

"We can talk about that later. You say Ben called four times? What does he want?"

"Something's wrong. He's very cold."

Lisa punched her home number into the wall telephone in her mother's kitchen. After three rings, Ben answered.

"What's wrong?" she asked.

"What do you think?"

"Don't play games, Ben. What is it?"

"I know where Jonathan Roper is."

"Oh? Where is he?"

"He's staying at the Hyatt Regency Hotel in Greenwich."

"Really? That's news to me. What makes you think he's there?"

"I'm not stupid, Lisa, and I'm not without resources. I used a directory the company has to get a list of the better hotels in your area, and I called half a dozen of them and asked to speak to Jonathan Roper. Sixth or seventh call, *bingo!*"

Lisa gasped—a gasp that Ben probably heard. The telephone had rung while she and Jonathan were in bed that afternoon. Someone had been on the line and had hung up. If it was Ben—and almost certainly it was—he had heard Jonathan breathless from his exertions.

What could she say? What she said was absurdly weak: "Jonathan Roper is not an uncommon name."

"Right. So it's a coincidence that our Jonathan Roper leaves Marietta the day you leave, and some other Jonathan Roper is staying in a hotel not twenty miles from Chappaqua."

"What do you want me to do, Ben? Come home?"

"I'm not sure I care if you come home or not. All I have to say is, if *he* comes back when *you* come back, then I know something for damned sure."

"You say . . . you don't *care* if I come home or not?"

"If he's going to come back when you do, then don't come back."

Lisa glanced at her mother. "All right, Ben. I'll have to think about it. I'm not sure I want to come back to a husband who's accusing me of . . . Well, name it. What *are* you accusing me of?"

"That's plain enough. And you can break it off. But I want the truth. You can break it off and tell me the truth."

She sighed. "I can't leave today, or even tomorrow. I'll call you, probably tomorrow evening."

"I own, Sir, that I have been mightily discommoded by this knavish adventurer. I have been, indeed, most foolish to lend him money. And now he dies, and the money is not to be had. I am reluctant, Sir, that my father should know how imprudent I have been. Yet I cannot live in London without some little money to buy the small things a woman requires. If, Sir, you could see fit to advance me a few guineas against the next payment on my allowance, I should be most grateful; and I will repay by not drawing my full allowance until you are entirely recompensed."

The banker shook his head. "Be specific, Madam."

"My father, Sir, has authorized you to draw on his account for fifty guineas a year, payable to me quarterly."

"And, my dear Miss Douglas, I advanced you your entire fifty guineas, though only half the year had passed, on your assurance to me that you required the money for the extraordinary expenses of setting yourself up in London for the first time."

"Very well, Sir. I have owned that I gave most of the money to a man I had all reason to believe was honest."

"A hazardous assumption, Madam."

"Indeed, Sir."

She had no doubt of her ability to influence this banker to do as she wished. He was older than she, but not so old as to be unsusceptible to her charms. Indeed, she had noticed that he was emphatically susceptible, as evidence by his eyes, which shifted constantly to the full white breasts pushed up by her stays. Since he wore a powdered wig, as did most gentlemen of quality, she could not guess if he was bald or if his hair was gray; but his complexion was smooth and his features strong. His face was thin. He had a sharp nose and chin. Had not all merchant bankers? He dressed in modest but expensive stuffs, in dark colors.

"If I advance, Madam, it cannot be from your father's account, since his instructions in that regard are strict. It must needs be from the bank itself, or from my personal funds. How do you propose to repay?"

"The next draw on my allowance, Sir, will be twelve and a half guineas. If you advance me five guineas now, I will accept seven guineas, ten shillings, sixpence for my next draw and call the account square. What could be simpler, Sir?"

The banker smiled. "Nothing simpler," he said. "Of course, the bank must require interest."

"My next draw is due in less than two months, Sir. Take my sixpence for it."

The banker chuckled. "About three shillings, Madam, as I estimate."

"Three shillings, then. Have it as you will, Sir, so long as you advance it."

"I shall advance it, Madam, from my personal funds, so you shall pay no interest whatever."

"That is very kind of you, Sir."

"I impose a condition, Madam."

"And what might that be, Sir?"

"That you and your mother, the Lady Amelia, be my guests for dinner today."

"Why, Mr. Osborne! I shall of course be delighted. I can't speak for my mother, but I believe she will be, too."

"I shall call for my coach to take you home," said the banker. "Perhaps you can return word with my coachman as to whether or not your lady mother consents."

"Thank you, Sir. In any event, *I* shall be free to join you for dinner, whether my mother can do so or not. I am confident she will have no objection to my dining even alone with so distinguished a gentleman."

"Very well, then. My coach will return for you at four."

"You have not, I trust, forgotten that we are dining with the Erskine family."

"I am sorry, Mother. I shall be unable. It is the unhappy time of month for me, and besides the usual pains, I suffer from a severe headache. Please express my regrets to the Erskines."

When Samuel Osborne arrived, he was astonished to find Miss Douglas waiting on the doorstep. He would have been more astonished if he had known how she came down from her room without passing through the house.

Then she was surprised, for they did not dine at a chop-house or tavern as she had expected but at his home. Osborne House, too, was a surprise. It was in Piccadilly, not far from Burlington House. The banker, it turned out, was a wealthy man. Moll Douglas was not in his house an hour before she resolved to become the mistress of Osborne House.

In the coach on the way home, he said to her, "Miss Douglas, I should be greatly pleased and honored if you would grant me the favor of a kiss."

"Sir, I would not have you think me a loose woman."

"Madam, I could never think you a loose woman."

"Then, Sir, you have my consent. But let the kiss be brotherly."

It was brotherly for a moment. Then Moll sighed and threw her arms around Samuel Osborne. "Oh, Sir! Oh! Oh! Oh! You quite distract me!"

He needed only small effort to shove down her dress and stays and spill her breasts. He fondled them, then kissed them.

"Oh, Sir!" she whispered. "This is most wicked! You will think me jaded as a woman of the streets."

"Dear, dear Miss Douglas. I own that I am most taken by you. I proceed from affection, sincere and honest affection. You are enchanting, in all your parts. Ah, what is this? A handsome but curious bijou."

He had discovered the amulet. He lifted it and stared at it with intense curiosity, frowning over the woman and the snake.

"La, Sir," she said. "It is an amulet of some considerable antiquity, passed from generation to generation by the women of my family."

"Ancient, I should judge," said Samuel Osborne. "A most interesting object." He bent forward and once more kissed each of her breasts in turn. "And what is this?" he asked.

He had found the mole.

"It is a blemish, Sir," she said.

"Nay, my darling. It is a beauty mark."

He touched it thoughtfully with one finger, then with the tip of his tongue. In a few more minutes Moll was certain she would soon be mistress of Osborne House.

Lisa reviewed the report of the London genealogical researcher. Samuel Osborne, the report said, had been a merchant banker with a countinghouse in Chancery Lane. He and Moll Douglas were the parents of Honor Osborne who married John Trowbridge, from which marriage came Honor Trowbridge who married Josiah Tatum. Angelina Tatum was the daughter of Honor Trowbridge. Moll Douglas was, thus, the great-grandmother of Angelina.

But there the line ran out. Jonathan had said that Angelina's daughter, born to her in jail before she was hanged, died.

The line ran out.

No, it didn't. It couldn't have. Jonathan had said he couldn't allow that.

If she, Lisa, was descended from Moll and Charity and Mathilde, then there had to be a connection between the line descending from Jacqueline d'Alembert and the line descending from Kathleen Finn Dugan. There had to be!

And . . . Of course! She saw it. She didn't even have to use a special power to see it. Jonathan . . . Damn him! He admitted he told the truth only when it was to his advantage.

13

"LISA, I AM SORRY I OPENED A LETTER ADDRESSED TO YOU. I HOPE you'll understand why I did it. Please read it, and then we'll talk about it."

Ben handed her the letter. It was written on small blue notepaper, with a fountain pen, in a handwriting characterized by flourishes and spirals. The postmark was London, U.K. The profile of Queen Elizabeth II was on the stamps. Lisa frowned and read:

Dear Lisa,

You are one of a number of people in Marietta to whom I owe a note of apology. On 12 February I received a call from here, notifying me that my brother was in extremis and might not survive long enough for me to reach his bedside before he expired. (I did in fact arrive just in time and held his hand as he died.) In any event, I was distraught and felt compelled to dash off immediately for New York and JFK airport, without so much as speaking to friends to whom I owed an explanation for my abrupt departure. Please accept my explanation and apology. I hope all of you will continue to be my friends when I return.

In the meantime may I impose on you for a personal favor? Would you be so kind as to speak to Mr. Longfellow on my behalf and explain all to him? Please tell him I wish to continue the work on the house and will settle his account immediately on my return. If he wishes to continue work on the basis of this assurance, I shall be grateful. If he should prefer to be paid first, I shall understand.

I hope to have all matters settled within the fortnight and to return to the States within a day thereafter— probably to find my auto stolen from the lot at JFK. In the meantime, please give my best wishes, apologies, and respects to such of our mutual friends as you may encounter, especially to Ben.

> In haste,
> Jonathan

Ben reached for her hands. "I'm sorry, Lisa. You can understand, can't you?"

She closed her eyes and nodded. But she thought, Jonathan, you have not solved the problem. Cleverness is not enough, you slippery son of a bitch!

She nodded at Ben. "I suppose it did look odd. I mean, there being a Jonathan Roper in the Greenwich Hyatt." She didn't like the easy way lies came to her tongue.

"More than that has looked odd lately," he said. "Are you aware that you've changed, that you are not the same person you were this time last year?"

"I'm pregnant, Ben. Three months. First trimester, as they say. That makes a difference in a woman."

He nodded gravely.

He sat at their kitchen table watching her heat a can of mushroom soup. She had driven in from Connecticut, coming through this time without trouble, and had reached Marietta about nine o'clock. He'd eaten downtown but had agreed to share the soup with her. He was still wearing the three-piece brown suit he'd worn at the office all day, and he was sipping a Scotch and soda.

Lisa tried not to stare at him. But she did, and she was confirmed in a conclusion she had reached as she spent the long hours behind the wheel of the Ford, all the way from Chappaqua to Marietta. This man—this strong, reasonable, literal, and mundane man—could never understand her now, nor could he understand Jonathan or cope with what she was. There was no way he could be a part of this. Which meant . . .

She was faced with a dreadful decision.

"I hope you understand, Lisa."

"Ben . . . The relationship between Jonathan Roper and me is not what you thought. On the other hand, it is not casual. You must understand that."

"Maybe you had better be specific." A note of hostility returned. "Let's be very simple and straightforward, hmm?"

"Think of him as a teacher. He's made me understand things about myself."

"Like that living as a housewife in a small town, married to a plant manager, is not your thing."

"Don't get sarcastic, Ben. That is not the kind of thing he has taught me at all. Nothing like that. Jonathan Roper comes from a world you don't even suspect exists, that I didn't really guess exists. He—"

"Sophisticated. You admire his sophistication."

"Nothing so shallow."

"Oh? He's your guru, then?"

"If you're going to be scornful, dammit, I can't even try to explain."

"Well, you're not making much progress at explaining whatever you're trying to explain."

"All right. Let's start with this: Jonathan Roper and I are distantly related. From many generations back. He has told me things about my family—about my mother's family—that I couldn't have imagined."

"Like what?"

"Well, for example, a woman who was my great-great-great et cetera grandmother killed a man. In London, about the time of the American Revolution. An ancestor of

Jonathan's was her father. She became immensely angry at a man, probably for valid reasons, and she killed him."

"What happened to her?"

"Nothing. She got away with it. The fact that she had done it was never found out. She married a wealthy banker and lived in great style."

"Now, wait a minute," said Ben. "That fax that came from the genealogical researcher in London said that one of the ancestors of—what was her name? Honor Trowbridge? —was a merchant banker in London in the eighteenth century. Is that the same person?"

Lisa nodded.

"Does that mean you're related to the Tatum family, here in Marietta?"

"I'm trying to find out. If I am, it's of course a very remote relationship. But it is possible."

"So you've acquired a new family that includes two women who murdered people."

"It's not that simple."

"Can you believe the tales this man tells? My impression of him is that he's altogether too slick. He's got that reputation around town."

"He's proved what he's told me," she said. "I am more skeptical than you are, but Jonathan has shown me proof of everything he has said."

"Yes. Well, I'd like to see the proof sometime. Maybe I'm more skeptical than you think."

Lisa's thought was that she was not sure he *would* like the proof. She didn't say so. Instead, she just nodded, then said, "I may be carrying some evidence. Just before I left Chappaqua, my mother gave me an old-fashioned letter-file box, one of those with the orange spine and the manila dividers inside. It's jammed full of handwritten letters, written and received by my great-grandmother. I'm anxious to look them over."

She didn't tell him that an image of the file box, with orange spine and spackled paper cover, had come to her last night as she slept in Chappaqua.

"Pursue your own ancestral story," Jonathan had said. "I don't have to spoon-feed it to you."

She remembered having seen the box when she was a girl of twelve or thirteen. She remembered she had resolved that someday she would read the letters in that box, supposed to have been written by Elizabeth Mary Spencer Kennedy, but she had forgotten it in the course of a summer's adventures. The image of that file box had come to her vividly during the night, and this morning before she left, she had asked her mother for it.

"What about the adoption?"

Lisa flared. "You are determined to get rid of my daughter, aren't you? You're not satisfied she's yours, are you?"

"Is she?"

"I won't even address that question."

"You're not the same woman you were four or five months ago."

"The suspicious, hostile man I'm facing is not the same man he was four or five months ago."

"I've been given reason to—"

"Ben, I'm taking my soup and that file of letters up to my study. I'll sleep up there on the couch tonight. Maybe by tomorrow the tensions will have diminished a little."

"If you leave my bed, by God you leave it permanently," he snapped.

"Don't be so sure. Don't be so facile and simplistic. I'm very tired, from a long drive as well as from this discussion. I said I'm going to sleep alone *tonight*. If you want to shut our bedroom door against me tomorrow night . . . Well . . . That will be *your* decision. Think it over."

He was a transparent man, and she was sure he had thought it over and relented even before she had loaded her tray with soup and crackers and a big glass of milk; but he was too proud to say it, so she went to her study and locked the door.

There she closed the blinds and, on some sort of curious impulse, took off her clothes and walked around the room naked, looking at herself in the mirror that stood in one of the eight corners of the room.

She could see Moll in herself. Lisa was taller, but she was the same kind of heavyish, bosomy, dark-haired woman Moll had been. She was—Ben was too prosaic to have said it, so someone else must have said of her—the archetypal woman, broad-hipped, generous of frame, fashioned by the Almighty for woman's elemental role: bearing children. She liked that and had never denied it. Though she'd borne only one child so far, she was proud that she could.

The capacity to reproduce was not, though, the be-all and end-all of a woman's existence. She had other faculties of which she was far prouder. She was exceptionally intelligent. She was smarter than most people. Most people who knew her acknowledged it, so why should she deny it to herself? She had educated herself thoroughly, absorbing more from her college years than most students did; and she had never stopped learning. She had found limited opportunity to visit the great museums and continue her study of art, but she saw what she could. She read constantly. She pondered on what she read. She tried to find among her friends people who could talk about the things that interested her. That was why she liked the spike-haired Pat Irving.

Looking at herself naked in the long mirror, Lisa was content with who she was. She had been content before she learned she was a witch. And now, troublesome though it was in most of its aspects, she had to acknowledge that she was intrigued with her new knowledge of herself. She liked what she was and knew she would never give it up.

She sat down on the couch, still naked, began to eat her soup, and opened the file box.

The letters seemed to be in chronological order, earliest on top. As she read the first letter, her memory changed, and she recalled that she had once glanced over one or two of these letters. They had impressed a child of twelve or thirteen as stilted and boring, and that was why—not because she had forgotten—she had returned the box to its place in an attic cupboard and had not looked into it again.

Her great-grandmother's handwriting had been small, neat, and in the flourishing steel-plate style that had been taught before the Palmer Method came along and made handwriting dull. Elizabeth Mary Spencer had written with a pen with a split nib that enabled the writer to vary the thickness of lines. She had written on blue notepaper with an *S* embossed at the top. Ink that had once been black had faded over the many decades and was now a dull brown.

My Dear Sir:

It is indiscreet of you, Mr. Kennedy, to send me roses, and I should deprecate your so doing, except that they have given me so much pleasure. Please, Sir, do not place a young girl in so difficult a position. Whether or not your addresses are welcome, it is not to <u>me</u> that they should be directed.

Very sincerely yours,
Miss Elizabeth Mary Spencer

Dear Miss Spencer:

I have twice attempted to give you a verbal relation of the contents of this letter; but my heart as often failed. I know not in what light it may be considered, only if I can form any notion of my own heart from the impression made upon it by your many amiable accomplishments, my happiness in this world will, in a great measure, depend upon your answer.

My circumstances are independent, my character hitherto unblemished, of which you shall have undoubted proof. If it is to your satisfaction, I shall not only consider myself extremely happy, but shall make it the principal study of my future life, to spend my days in the company of her whom I do prefer to all others in the world.

Your humble & obdt. servant,
Sean Kennedy

My Dear Mr. Kennedy:

I received your letter yesterday, and as it was on a subject I had not any thoughts of, you will not wonder when I tell you I was a good deal surprised. Although I have seen and familiarly conversed with you on several occasions, yet I had not the most distant thought of your making a proposal of such a nature.

With respect to myself, I freely acknowledge that I have not at present any reason to reject your offer, although I cannot give you any definite answer until I have consulted with my parents.

I must assume you realize that I am my family's <u>adopted</u> daughter and have no idea of my true origins. I remind you of the fact, in case it should seem to you an impediment to our happiness.

As soon as I have consulted with my family, I shall return an explicit reply.

With great sincerity,
Elizabeth Spencer

My Dear Sean:

In my last I promised you should hear from me as soon as might be. I now sit down to fulfill my promise. I communicated your proposal to my parents, who extended their entire approbation and urged me to communicate it to you. "May every happiness attend you," my mother said.

I have no doubt, Sean, that we will enjoy as much happiness in the married state as this life will admit of. You may be assured that you possess my respect and affection. I entrust much to you but doubt not that the exalted principles inculcated in you by our Holy Mother Church will operate on the whole of your future conduct in life.

You may therefore lay aside the tedious formality of courtship and regard and treat me hereafter as your future wife.

Yours,
Elizabeth

Sean Kennedy was of course Lisa's great-grandfather, the flashy Irish lawyer.

Elizabeth Mary was the formidable old lady who could not lose at cards, the great-grandmother Lisa had sometimes sensed was communicating with her.

Use your powers, Jonathan had said. Learn for yourself. Yes . . .

The family called her E.M. and called her mother E.C.— affectionate nicknames that conveniently distinguished Elizabeth Mary from Elizabeth Christina. One of her earliest memories was of being called E.M. She didn't know they were using initials, didn't know what initials were or what a nickname was, and supposed her name was Eeyem. Why not? When they spoke her father's name, which was Tim, it sounded to little Elizabeth Mary like Teeyem. Why shouldn't the daughter of Teeyem be Eeyem?

Another early memory was of finding the lost silver thimble. She had heard them talk about it more than once. It was not a big issue in the house, but a curious question: where could E.C. (Eesee) have mislaid a nice silver thimble? E.M. knew. She had always known, from the first time she heard her mother express annoyance over it. The annoyance was just enough emotion to carry the signal—though little E.M. had no idea of that. She simply knew that the object they were talking about, whatever a thimble might be, lay behind a maroon plush drapery in the dining room. It had fallen off the accumulated things in her mother's sewing basket as she hurried through the dining room. It had rolled under the drapery.

E.M. was happy to retrieve the little object. The truth was, she, too, was annoyed. She was tired of hearing about it: thimble, thimble, thimble. All her life the word "thimble" would faintly nauseate her. She would own many, rarely use one, feel no antipathy to the object, but hate the word.

She had little to be unhappy about in her young life.

All her years she would remember the Christmas of 1876, when she was eight years old. She was taken to a toy store, where she was to choose her Christmas doll from among scores on display in the gaslit shop.

She remembered her father: a tall man with a formidable mustache, wearing that afternoon a camel-hair overcoat and carrying a walking stick. Her mother wore a bustle, of course; they were de rigueur. She wore a fur hat and a fur coat and kept her hands in a fur muff.

It was her own outfit that Elizabeth Mary remembered most vividly. Her hip-length black-velvet jacket was trimmed with ermine at the lapels and the hem. A little cap matched the jacket. At eight, she was too young to wear a bustle, but below her waist in the rear she wore an immense black-satin bow. Her pink skirt was a mass of ruffles. It showed a few inches of pink stocking above her calf-length black patent-leather boots. She was a lady in every aspect but the way in which her mother had arranged her hair. Ladies wore theirs up. Elizabeth's lustrous blonde curls hung over her shoulders and down her back.

The doll she chose that afternoon was in her bedroom the day she died, seventy-five years later. It was a lady doll, not a baby doll: half as tall as E.M. and dressed in a floor-length ruffled dress of white silk and lace.

E.M. had two difficult things to learn.

The first, the more difficult, was that she was her parents' *adopted* daughter. Not only that. They had no idea—or insisted they had no idea—who she really was. They said it made no difference. She was Elizabeth Mary Spencer, as cherished as any other member of the family. They refused to discuss the circumstances of the adoption, except to say she was a tiny infant when she came to them, that she was a child of honorable but unfortunate circumstances, and they regarded as a gift from God the chance to rear her in their home as their own daughter.

They told her when she was fifteen. They said they had promised they would tell her; it was a condition of the adoption. They asked her to forget all about it. As if she could.

The second difficult thing she had to learn was that she was a witch.

She was nearly forty years old before that word ever came to her mind. She was twelve or thirteen before she fully realized that she was very different from other people, that it was not just accident or coincidence that she knew things they didn't know.

As a child she was observant, as most children are, and she had learned very quickly that she should keep her special insights secret. The incident of the thimble had made her a curiosity for a while. She had to listen to the story too many times, and people had looked at her strangely when they heard it. Eventually they concluded that little E.M. had found the thimble because a child playing and crawling on the floor saw things adults overlooked. Good. A facile, rational explanation.

The four-year-old girl knew how she'd found the thimble. She *saw* it. That was all. After that, when she saw something people were distressed about losing, she retrieved it and put it where they would find it.

When she was seven she became aware that she knew what people were thinking. Not all people, not all the time. When their thoughts were reinforced by emotion, they came vividly to the girl's mind. When thoughts were only casually moving in the stream of someone else's conscious, they remained blurred to E.M.; she could gain only impressions of what they were.

She had been frightened one day. Passing along the hall outside the parlor, she had sensed that a heavyset man in conversation with her father was concealing a raging fury. He was talking quietly enough, but he was angry. Not just angry. He was afire with wrath. The little girl had never known anything like it, and she had burst into tears.

Her father had rushed out into the hall and taken her up in his arms. She could not explain why she was crying. How could she tell her father that the man in the parlor was murderously angry?

The heavyset man had stared at her, and she had read the seething rage, directed even at her, for no reason at all.

Little E.M. had repaid rage with fury. Abruptly the blue had drained from her eyes, leaving them almost white, cold, and stone hard. Her seething fury had glittered supernaturally in those hard white eyes, fixed in an unmoving stare on the reddening face of the angry man.

He was terrified. More than that . . .

He grabbed at his throat as if he were choking, tried to rise from his chair and fell back, and croaked gutturally. E.M.'s father put her down and rushed to the man, whose eyes now popped out of a crimson face. E.M. turned her back on him and walked out of the room. When she glanced back, he was recovering. The anger was gone, replaced by fear.

So. So . . . Couldn't her father have subdued the man's hostility the same way?

Apparently not. Of course he hadn't the least suspicion that the man's seizure had come from his little daughter. E.M. put the experience aside in her mind. She would always remember it vividly, but she would never do anything like that again.

Both her parents played the piano. The instrument was not, however, the focus point of their parlor. The settee was. It was a magnificent piece of furniture, round and some eight feet in diameter, with black horsehair upholstery. More than a dozen people could sit comfortably on it, facing any part of the room. In the center was a huge china pot filled with black soil and planted with a variety of lush plants, some of them palms.

At least three evenings a week the family gathered to sing—father, mother, two sons, two daughters. Once a week they would be joined by Father Michael, who would add his piping Irish tenor to the mix of voices. He would lead the family in prayers before he left. The Spencers were deeply religious.

When she was seven, Elizabeth Mary was enrolled at

Saint Catherine's Seminary for Girls. Taken there each morning by her father on his way to his office, picked up each afternoon by her mother or a servant in a hack or the family carriage, she studied under the stern Saint Cat's nuns for nine years. She learned Latin, French, and German, mathematics and natural science, logic and rhetoric, literature and music. She learned to be a lady. She was solidly reinforced in her faith.

It was difficult in those years to conceal her special powers of mind. She could not let her teachers know that she raced ahead of all the other girls in her classes, sometimes absorbing in two or three weeks everything that was to be taught in four or five months. She could not tell the nun who taught mathematics how often she was wrong, how often she misunderstood and imposed on her pupils a misunderstanding of, say, a proposition of Euclid. The nun who taught natural science still believed tomatoes—"love apples"—were poisonous, or if not actually poisonous, at least capable of inflaming carnal passions, and should not be eaten by young girls. Elizabeth Mary ate as many as she could get her hands on one summer, to find out.

Elizabeth Mary relieved herself of the tedium of her classes by traveling in her mind. She traveled to a fantasy world peopled by women named Angélique and Mathilde and Charity. Her imagination painted for her vivid, colorful pictures of places like Amsterdam, cities on the Rhine, and beautiful heaths in Scotland. She fantasized adventures lived by these women in past centuries. She saw their extensive families, their homes. . . . She saw much, but she knew she was shut out of something. As she visited them again and again, she found she could not dispel from the souls of these women—whom she supposed she was creating in her imagination and should be able to make as she wished—a pervasive melancholy. Each of them knew something she did not know and could not discover.

Two of the nuns sensed that they did not govern this young woman. Elizabeth Mary understood what they sensed, because they resented it, and their resentment communicated itself to her. For a time she tried to win them over, smiling, nodding, deferring. Their hostility only grew, and they harassed her. One day when she was thirteen, her impatience with their petty hostility overwhelmed her restraint, and she simply erased their resentment from their minds. They forgot what they didn't like about Elizabeth Mary Kennedy and were thereafter cordial to her.

This was a heady power. Even frightening.

She worried about it. Where did it come from, this power? Was it of God? She prayed for guidance. But she did not confess. She sensed—another one of those insights she almost wished she did not have—that Father Michael would prove totally unable to understand what she was willing to tell him. So she sought enlightenment from God directly, through prayer, without the assistance of the learned priest.

And that, perhaps, was why she received no enlightenment.

Not long after her parents told her she was their adopted daughter, Mr. Roper appeared. He bought a house on the street. He became her friend.

More than her friend. He never admitted it, but Elizabeth Mary came to understand that Mr. Roper was her father. She never dared confront him with it, much less to ask who her mother was and where she was; but insightful as she was, she understood—instinctive knowledge, she knew, was often better than factual knowledge—that this intriguing man was her father. Something terrible had happened to her real mother. Her senses told her that. But Mr. Roper had come to watch over her, now that she knew she was not the daughter of Timothy and Elizabeth Christina Spencer. Somehow he had known when they told her, and then he had appeared.

Lisa had wondered how they met: the lawyer from New York and the girl from Philadelphia. Then suddenly she knew. The image came to her: the tall blond man with the pale-blue eyes, Jonathan, twenty years older. He wore a full beard now; and, as always, he was well dressed in the current fashion. In this image he was not wearing the high silk hat he had worn in Marietta almost twenty years before; instead, he wore a jaunty boater, which now, as the image developed, he swept off and put down on a white rattan table.

They were on a broad front porch, on a tree-shaded brick street. It was summer, and this was Philadelphia.

Five people had gathered on this porch. Lisa recognized the tall girl as her great-grandmother, now perhaps nineteen or twenty years old. The woman sitting in the rattan rocker had to be Mrs. Spencer—whom until now Lisa would have identified as her great-great grandmother.

Jonathan Roper introduced the man standing beside him. "Allow me," he said, "to present my friend Mr. Sean Kennedy, from New York City. Mr. Kennedy represents me as an attorney, relative to some property I have acquired in that city. I asked him to come to Philadelphia to allow me to examine some papers, and I promised him I should introduce him to my dear neighbors the Spencers."

It was evident immediately that the big sandy-haired Irish lawyer was taken with the tall blonde girl, as she was with him. Whether that was natural or was of Roper's doing was not apparent.

Who was he? Whence Sean Kennedy?

His income was $15,000 a year, a princely sum in the 1880s when it was not diminished in any significant way by taxation, when servants could be hired for their room and board and two or three dollars a week, when a man with that income could afford to live on fashionable Murray Hill— that is, in what was then considered uptown Manhattan— could eat in the best restaurants, drink at the finest bars, and travel to Europe as often as he liked. He had inherited a mite, but he was essentially a self-made man, a successful lawyer who commanded high fees. He was a handsome, personable man, as well: big and ruddy and imposing in his carefully tailored suits.

He was not, just the same, accepted in the *good* clubs, not invited to the *better* homes, not in fact welcome at certain sporting events and along certain riding paths. If he had bought a yacht, which he could have afforded to do if he wanted to, he would have been hard put to find dockage for it. He would not have been allowed to tie up at any club dock.

He was Irish.

It was an impediment. But it was no such thing in the eyes of Elizabeth Mary Spencer or of her adoptive parents, who were Irish, too, and were more than flattered to discover that the rich New York lawyer Sean Kennedy was spellbound by the tall, somewhat gawky E.M. Sean Kennedy was infatuated with E.M. from the day they met.

It was as if he'd been bewitched.

He spoke with an Irish brogue.

They were married in the spring of 1888. He took her on a three-month wedding trip to Europe. When they returned they established their home in his house on East Thirty-seventh Street in New York.

So. That was how Jonathan had done it. Maybe when Elizabeth Mary Kennedy thanked Mr. Roper as she lay dying, she meant only to thank him for introducing her to Sean Kennedy. But Lisa doubted that. Because it was obvious now that Elizabeth Mary was Roper's daughter, the fourth powerful witch, and probably he watched over her much of her life.

She was of course the daughter of Angelina Tatum, who had reached the age of thirty-nine without marrying or bearing a daughter. Jonathan Roper had therefore intervened. He had said Angelina's daughter died. She had, yes, in 1951. Jonathan had somehow arranged her adoption by the Philadelphia couple, the Spencers. That wouldn't have been very difficult, once he found the family he wanted. The Washington County Children's Home would have been glad to be rid of the embarrassing love child of the hanged murderess. Then, as Lisa had just seen, he arranged for her to meet Sean Kennedy, his choice for her husband.

Angelina had been the daughter of Honor Trowbridge, who was the daughter of Honor Osborne, who was the daughter of Moll Douglas Osborne. So the line had continued. She, Lisa, made seventeen generations of witches, four of them—now apparently five—unusually powerful. With a certainty Lisa's daughter, the eighteenth generation, would be the sixth powerful witch.

Lisa's thoughts went to Ben, asleep below—or maybe not asleep, maybe awake, wondering and pondering. What role could such a man possibly play in the birth and rearing of the sixth powerful witch?

Well. Maybe. Elizabeth Mary Spencer Kennedy had been reared by Timothy Spencer and his wife. Moll Douglas Osborne was reared by Sir William Douglas and his wife. . . . The others before them . . . Jonathan had not served in the role of father, apparently. He stayed near his daughters and watched over them, intervened in their lives as he saw fit; but he did not rear his children. In fact, she had no promise that he would rear the child she was carrying now.

Lisa was not sure she would accept that way of handling things.

Jonathan returned to Marietta. He paid Mr. Longfellow, and work resumed on his house. Ben began to suspect that the letter from London was a ruse. Jonathan could, after all, have written it in Marietta or at the hotel in Connecticut, sent it overseas by air courier service to a friend in London who posted it back to Marietta. The disappearance of Jonathan on the very day that Lisa left for Chappaqua, followed by his return within a day or so after she returned, was too much of a coincidence.

Lisa maintained her posture of wounded indignation, but it was difficult, knowing that what Ben suspected was the truth. You resented suspicion all the more deeply when you knew the suspicion was the truth. She had learned to lie but not, as the cliché went, to live a lie.

Then Frankie Gerard called. "I've got to see you. I've got

to talk to you," she said. "If Jonathan is there, all the better. He must hear what I have to tell you."

"Can't you tell me over the phone?"

"No. I have to see you in person. I have to see both of you if possible."

"I can't promise you Jonathan will consent to see you."

"What I have to tell you is in his interest and yours and is very important."

She flew in and arrived in time for dinner, four days later. Lisa picked her up at the airport; and, even though she had a motel reservation, drove her to the house on Fourth Street, where she insisted Frankie would be her guest during her stay.

Ben was cordial to her, more cordial than he had been to Lisa since she returned from Chappaqua. He poured wine for her as the three of them sat at dinner in the dining room.

"I am reluctant to say that Lisa needs psychiatric help," he said. "But I'm glad to know you're friends, and I want you to know I will be happy to take care of fees and expenses if she is also your patient."

"That's good of you, Ben," said Frankie. "Actually, we ended the doctor-patient relationship some time ago. I'm here just as a friend, for a little visit, to see this wonderful house Lisa told me so much about, and to see the town."

"Lisa has become a little less rational lately," said Ben. "Maybe it's the pregnancy."

"As her former psychiatrist and her present friend," said Frankie, "I can tell you she's the most rational person I've known in a long time."

Ben stiffened visibly. "Well . . . maybe she has more to tell you," he said.

Probably Frankie had noticed that Lisa was not sleeping with Ben. She would not have guessed, though, that every night Lisa stood naked before the big mirror in her octagon sanctuary and studied her body with growing interest. No external sign of her pregnancy had yet appeared, though her doctor assured her it was real and progressing normally.

Signs of pregnancy were not what she was looking for, actually. She had begun to wonder if a woman who could cause herself to metamorphose into a wolf could not also cause herself to metamorphose into another woman or a man.

Standing before the mirror, intently working her will, she had begun to see her own image blur. But that was all. It blurred a little and then focused again. She willed the wolf. That worked. She changed quickly, trotted around the room a couple of times, and willed return.

Why? What was so difficult? Then suddenly, as if the idea had been sent to her from some distant source, she knew what the trouble was. When she willed a wolf, she had a vivid image in her mind of a wolf. When she willed another woman, she willed only something vague: just "other woman," without definition. And that was what she achieved: a blurred image of a different woman, but nothing more specific.

She stepped to her desk, picked up a photograph Benny had given her of himself and Anne standing on the steps of his fraternity house. Her future daughter-in-law, it seemed. Mousy little girl, clinging to Benny. Or maybe not so mousy. Steel-willed enough, stubborn enough to have an abortion.

Lisa held the picture before her and willed herself to become Anne. And abruptly she *was* Anne. After a smooth, easy metamorphosis, she saw in the mirror a slight girl, ascetically thin, ribs showing on her narrow chest, with almost no breasts, with a concave belly and narrow hips, with a thick tangle of untrimmed pubic hair. Her image in the mirror was fuzzy, until Lisa realized why: because Anne needed the gold-rimmed spectacles she wore, and her vision was blurred without them.

Lisa tried something more. She willed better eyesight. She had willed the healing of the knife wound given her by Gene. Willing a slight reformation of her eyes was not as difficult.

She walked around the room, keeping her eyes turned toward the mirror. She liked her small, flat bottom, her shiny-smooth little belly. She was lithe. With a little more self-confidence, the real Anne could be lithe and graceful. She had the body of a ballerina—and was no doubt ashamed of it.

She turned away from the mirror. Jonathan was sitting on her couch. He, too, was naked.

"It will be fun to do it with that body," he said dryly.

"Could the others do this?" she asked.

"Only one," he said. "Mathilde. She was the most powerful of them all. There was a reason for that, a special reason. Why you should have such power, I cannot understand. It is not from me. It is from somewhere else."

"I know, Jonathan," she said calmly. She smiled. "Well. If I am asked tomorrow if Jonathan humped Lisa last night, I can say no and be telling the truth. Who is going to ask if Jonathan humped Anne?"

"There is something I don't know and cannot understand," he said. He reached out and gently slapped her flat little belly. "Where is the baby? Surely it is not there. And where is it when you are a wolf?"

"You don't know?"

He shook his head solemnly. "I fear for it."

"Apparently you need not. The doctor says it's as healthy as can be. The answer, of course, is that the baby is not flesh and blood. As now, standing here as Anne, neither am I."

Jonathan drew a deep breath and shook his head. "Mathilde could do it. And, now that I remember, *did* do it, while she was carrying children. But I thought the power originated in a special fact about Mathilde. Maybe it didn't."

Anne-Lisa sat down at her desk. "I know I can call up the images of the other witches by myself and learn anything I want to know—as you told me I could. But I would rather hear you tell me. What was special about Mathilde?"

Jonathan slumped and for a long moment stared at the

floor. "Jacqueline died in agony, at the hands of the beast Chauvin. So did I—I, Jean Cordier."

"Roper," said Anne-Lisa.

"Yes. Roper, Cordier, Seiler. They mean the same thing, in different languages. I have also called myself Restarius: the same thing, in Latin. Anyway, I cursed the Almighty and called on Satan at the last. Jacqueline didn't. She is in heaven, among the martyrs. She, too, I will never see, any more than I will see the face of God. That is my punishment for cursing the Almighty."

"Angélique was your daughter," said Anne-Lisa. "Mathilde was your daughter. Charity was your daughter. Moll was your daughter. Elizabeth Mary was your daughter. But I'm not, am I?"

"No."

"I wonder what my father is," said Anne-Lisa.

"Nothing special, I can tell you. A good man but nothing more."

"Except for what comes from you, nothing comes through the male line, then?"

Jonathan shook his head. "So far as I know," he said. "Now I am interested in entering this slender young body you have borrowed."

"'Borrowed'? Do you mean the real Anne is somewhere without a body?"

Jonathan laughed. "She is in bed with your son, in her sorority house room. And he enjoys this body, greatly."

Lisa didn't will an image of that for herself. She took his word for it.

Lisa walked around the room, displaying herself to her mirror as much as to Jonathan. She preened. She was a different woman. Lisa had never preened, wouldn't have even if she'd had the body of a *Playboy* model. She wasn't certain she liked this narcissistic persona. She brought her vanity under control and sat down at her desk, facing Jonathan.

"You must stop lying to me," she said sternly.

"Yes. I am sorry. I had to do it for a while. At least I thought I did. It is useless anyway, now that you have the ability to learn the truth for yourself."

"In any case, you don't know all the answers, do you, Jonathan?"

He shook his head. "No. I don't."

14

THEY MET THE NEXT MORNING IN THE OCTAGON STUDY—LISA, Jonathan, and Dr. Frances Gerard. Ben was up the river at the plant. They had agreed they would have lunch in the dining room of the Lafayette Hotel, downtown, so Frankie had dressed in a gray cashmere suit and a white silk blouse, with a string of pearls at her throat. Jonathan wore jacket, white shirt, and necktie. Only Lisa was still in jeans and a sweatshirt, saying it would take her three minutes to change.

Lisa sat at her desk; Jonathan and Frankie sat side by side on the couch.

"I have come to tell you there is some danger for you," Frankie said solemnly. "I realize that you two have extraordinary powers. I doubt you are invincible. I don't think God would allow that. I think you are subordinate to Him, subject to His will. Father William Longford is convinced of this, too—and that fine old priest has told me that he saw a frightening demonstration of what you can do, Lisa. Even so, he thinks you are vulnerable. He begs you to return to him, to cooperate with him in banishing whatever Jonathan represents and returning to God."

"I have never abandoned God," said Lisa coolly. "Whatever I am and do, I am and do with His permission."

"Father William says that is one of Satan's cleverest arguments."

"Is this 'fine old priest' sending us a threat, Doctor?" Jonathan asked.

"I think there is a sense in which that's probably what he is doing, yes. He told me he is determined to save Lisa. He feels he has the means. He has given the matter a great deal of thought and prayer, seeking the means, and he thinks he has found it."

"Does he plan to exorcise me?" Jonathan asked in a voice that suggested he was amused.

"In a sense," said Frankie Gerard. "He thinks exposure is what you can't stand. He means to confer with the Cardinal-Archbishop of New York and secure his authority and permission to perform a rite of exorcism. They will report the exorcism to the news media. Father William will talk about Jonathan Roper, an agent of the Devil, who has corrupted and threatens eternal damnation to the soul of Lisa Hamilton. Half the news people—no, far more than half—will mock him. But all of them will pursue the story with an intensity and vigor that will deprive both of you of all your privacy, this year and next. He doesn't think you can live with that, Jonathan. He thinks it will drive you away, even if the exorcism doesn't."

Jonathan glowered. "He assumes much to himself," he said angrily.

"He is merely a parish priest," said Lisa calmly. "One of my ancestors attacked and nearly killed a suffragan bishop."

"More than that," growled Jonathan, his pale blue eyes hard and menacing. "With the consent and aid of the Almighty we condemned the soul of Jean Chauvin to everlasting torment."

Frankie crossed herself. "But *he* had earned it," she said. "He would have been condemned without you."

"There have been others," said Jonathan.

"A Scots preacher," Lisa said.

"More than that," said Jonathan.

Frankie rose from the couch, as if she felt uneasy sitting so close to Jonathan as the tension in the conversation increased. "I did not have to come here to warn you," she said. "I have come to help you, for a reason you can guess."

"You still think you want to be one of us," said Lisa. "Did you tell Father William that?"

"No."

"You want our gratitude," Jonathan said. "You hope to influence us by making us beholden to you. You should understand, Frankie, that gratitude is an uncomfortable feeling. People who owe other people gratitude are uneasy with them and don't really like them."

"I can try to cope with you in one of two ways," Frankie Gerard said, her voice strained. "As the saying goes, I can either lick you or join you. Father William is determined to lick you, defeat you. I see you as answering questions that neither science nor religion has been able to answer for thousands of years. It is really inconceivable to me that you can be wholly evil—or evil at all, maybe. This may be Satan's favorite rationalization, but I can't see how God could permit you to exist if He didn't have a purpose for you. And maybe"—Her voice fell, until it was barely audible—"Maybe you represent God's way of revealing new truths."

"That's a feeble rationalization," said Jonathan. "I have possessed the same truths for more than four centuries, and the world is no better for them."

"Did you *try?* What did you do with the truths that are yours? Did you try to communicate them?"

"In my way. In our way. What do you suggest I should have done? Start a crusade? Found a new church? Father William Longford is correct in one way: I do not want public attention—but for reasons he does not understand."

"You'd rather join us than try to lick us, hmm?" Lisa asked Frankie. "Does it occur to you that it's like asking to be allowed to join the British royal family?"

Jonathan smiled and chuckled. "Lisa," he said, "you have become—"

"But what are we going to do about the priest?" Lisa interrupted.

Jonathan's face darkened. "I don't like what he threatens. There are many ways to stop him."

"Why don't we go see him? Maybe we can talk him out of this foolishness."

Dr. Frances Gerard—shaken, trembling, and pale—stumbled toward a stone bench at the edge of the cemetery and there sat and covered her face with her hands.

Lisa herself was nearly as shaken. She had known Jonathan could travel. She had come to suppose she could. After all, they were not flesh and blood—not all the time, anyway. Sometimes they were disembodied.

But Frankie! She was flesh and blood and nothing but. How, then, could she have been transported in an instant from the octagon study on Fourth Street in Marietta to the churchyard of the Church of the Holy Name of Jesus, something like 550 miles as the crow flies? Lisa stared at Jonathan. Some of his powers were greater than hers, surely; for she had no idea how she would have done this. And for a hard moment she wondered if she should not regret all the unnatural faculties that both of them had.

"Now let us have a talk with this 'fine old priest,'" said Jonathan.

He strode into the sanctuary of the church, confident apparently of where Father William Longford was to be found. And indeed he was right. Father William was hearing confession. Jonathan sat down in a pew and with a respectful air waited for the priest to emerge. Lisa and Frankie followed him in and sat down, glancing at each other, wary.

Lisa distrusted Jonathan at this moment. She sensed his anger. She doubted he would kill Father William, but she wondered if he might not erase part of his memory. Or worse. Her great-grandmother had erased parts of the minds of two nuns. She remembered vividly that Charity had utterly destroyed the mind of the Scots preacher.

"Father," said Jonathan in a heavy voice when the

confession was over and the penitent had left the sanctuary, "we are waiting for you."

The priest came out. He glanced quickly, apprehensively, into the face of each of the three. Then he nodded and appeared to calm himself. "Yes. I expected you," he said. "Shall we talk in my study?"

"Why not here?" asked Jonathan. "In the sanctuary. It is the holy place, is it not?"

"There is not much privacy here," said the big, white-haired priest.

"There will be enough," Jonathan said confidently, glancing at the doors.

"Lisa . . ." said Father William. "Dr. Gerard. And you, I assume, are Jonathan Roper."

Jonathan smiled and nodded. "Jonathan Roper. Jean Cordier. Johann Seiler. And I've been known by other names. At your service, Sir."

Father William frowned thoughtfully for a moment. Then he reached down and lifted his pectoral cross. "Are you reluctant to touch this?" he asked.

Jonathan bent forward and kissed the cross. "Not at all," he said. "Father . . . I was *martyred* for the Holy Mother Church, as was my dearest wife. I gave all I had to the Almighty. I surrendered my spirit in agony, as did my eighteen-year-old wife, for the crimes of being married in a church, of hearing Mass, and of sheltering our daughter from the kidnappers who would have handed her over to the heretics."

"Then what are you, Jonathan Roper? *Why* are you? Why do you exist?"

"Can it occur to you that it might be because I demonstrated my love for the Almighty more and better than you ever have? Could it be possible that I am *favored* by the Almighty? As are my wives and daughters?"

The priest shook his head vigorously. "No," he said. "The Church does not, cannot, recognize——"

"Let Lisa explain," said Jonathan.

"Jonathan and his wife were tortured to death, Father,"

she said. "By the specific order and partly in the presence of John Calvin. At the end, Jonathan—then Jean Cordier—in his agony cursed God and called on Satan to succor him."

"And Satan did, I imagine," Father William said solemnly. "Did he not?"

"Yes. He did."

"Which makes this creature a servant of Satan. The great Liar, the great Killer, the great—"

"You know better," Jonathan interrupted. "He is a seraph. A servant of the Almighty, in his way."

Father William focused his eyes on Lisa. "Heresy," he said. "Heresy known and fought through centuries. Lisa, my child, the Evil One makes a persuasive appeal. He made it to the saints of old. Some of them were persuaded and fell. He tempted Our Lord. He is with us always—devious, insidious, cunning. And I fear you have been persuaded."

"Father . . ." said Lisa.

"My child. I have asked you before, and today I ask you for the last time to renounce this creature—" He nodded toward Jonathan. "—and all he represents and all the unholy, unclean powers that may have been conferred on you by Satan. Your *eternal soul* is at stake, Lisa Hamilton! And you must *choose!* Show me your sincere, repentant renunciation of Satan and all his works! Only then can I cleanse you. And then I *will* cleanse you. Without your renunciation and repentance, I cannot."

"What of the child I carry, Father?" Lisa demanded in a thin voice.

"If it is of your husband, as I believe it is, it will be born, will be baptized, and will live in the care of the angels. If it is of this filthy monster, then likely it will drop from your womb when you rejoin God and reject Satan. If it is *his,* it is an impure thing and should not live to pollute the world."

"*Father!* In the name of God! She is my child! You were my friend. How can you—"

"I *am* your friend. Your best friend. Your soul and the soul of your child are at stake. I saw you change yourself to an animal, Lisa. I have no doubt you did it. You didn't hypnotize me. You did it. Can you believe that such an unnatural thing was God's doing? And if it was not His, then whose was it? You *know*, Lisa. You have to know."

"It is of the knight," Lisa said softly. "The man in armor who was shown to me by Mathilde."

Jonathan's head jerked around, his mouth open. He stared at Lisa, startled, and began to shake his head.

"Then you have seen Satan," said Father William. "Did you couple with him?"

Lisa shook her head. "I . . . I worshiped him. I fawned at his feet, as I told you."

"Your soul can still be saved," said the priest. "God forgives everything to those who repent and rededicate themselves to Our Savior."

Frankie Gerard had fallen to her knees and was praying fervently, her trembling lips struggling to form coherent words but stumbling over them.

Jonathan glanced back and forth between Lisa and the broad-shouldered, ruddy, white-haired, black-clad priest. "I honor your vocation, Father," he said. "I deplore the shallowness of your understanding."

"It is between you and God, Lisa," said Father William Longford. "My child, you must renounce Satan and all his works. There is no other way."

"Including the child in my belly, if she is Jonathan's," Lisa said sullenly.

"She is not his," said the priest, shaking his head firmly. "She is the child of your husband."

"She is *not* of my husband. That much I know. So am I to renounce her?"

"Renounce Satan and all his works, whoever and whatever they be."

"If I don't?"

"I suspect Dr. Gerard has explained to you what course of action I expect to take—and that is why you are here. I much doubt that this monster can live under the scrutiny of the Christian community."

"You think you can destroy me?" Jonathan sneered.

"Better men than you have tried. Better men than the petty Cardinal-Archbishop of New York."

"It will be worth any risk. I mean to find out. I place myself in the hands of God, and I shall find out."

"And what about me?" Lisa asked. "And my child?"

"I cannot stand by and allow this great evil to be loosed on the earth," said the priest. "You must make your choice, Lisa. You must make it now. I ask you: do you renounce Satan and all his works, whoever and whatever they may be?"

Father William Longford, his face rigid and gleaming pink, stood and faced Lisa and Jonathan. For a moment they remained seated. Then Jonathan rose. Then Lisa rose. Frankie Gerard remained kneeling, but she stared up.

"Do . . . you . . . renounce? Yes or no?"

"No, God damn you! No!"

They sat in the octagon study. Frankie trembled. For Lisa, transferral from the church to the study had occurred in an instant of which she had been hardly conscious. Frankie had just described it differently: as a horrible tumbling through darkness relieved only by sizzling orange and yellow sparks.

"I tried to communicate something to you," Jonathan said to Lisa. "I mean, just before you damned the priest. Your emotions were so highly charged that you didn't sense what I was trying to tell you. You could have lied. You could have told him you did renounce. He can't read what's in your heart. Only the Almighty and the seraphim can do that."

"To hell with him," Lisa muttered resentfully. "To hell with that narrow-minded old son of a bitch!"

"He may do what he threatens."

"To hell with him," she said again.

"He can make things difficult."

"We shall see."

"Lisa . . ." Jonathan whispered. He shook his head. "Don't kill him."

"I hadn't thought of it."

"I believe you have thought of it. But don't."

"I had supposed *you* would be the one to think of it, the one to do it," said Lisa.

"I can't. Unless *you* sanction it."

"I must sanction it?"

"Yes. Haven't you seen enough to understand?"

"Who sanctioned the death of Josiah Tatum?"

Jonathan shook his head. "She did—Angelina. She wanted him dead. She willed him dead. And once she mustered the will, I gave her the power."

"It was *your* power, working through her."

"But the will was hers."

"My great-great-grandmother . . ."

"Yes."

Lisa wondered— But she was distracted by Frankie, who was on the verge of hysteria.

"You sit and talk calmly about killing a priest!" Frankie sobbed. "You refused to renounce Satan, and you cursed a priest! You have no fear of the Church, no fear of God!"

"Not so, Frankie," said Lisa. "I fear God. All I asked of Father William Longford was that he understand that I, too, am God's creature, as is my daughter, whom he proposed to kill. If my daughter is not my husband's, she was to . . . to drop from my womb, he said. An abortion! Oh, I fear the Almighty, but I don't fear that narrow-minded old priest."

"For a moment there in the church, I thought I might see the hand of God raised against you. I was terrified. I thought I might see—"

"Does it occur to you, Frankie," asked Jonathan in a soothing voice, "that the Almighty's forbearance at that moment might prove something?"

"Does it prove you are closer to God than I am? Closer than Father William?"

"Not necessarily," said Jonathan. "That's not exactly what I had in mind."

Frankie sobbed. "It *does* prove it," she said. "*I* want to be closer to the Throne! You have shown me that you are closer to God than I am. I want— I want—" Her voice broke and she could only shake her head and sob.

"Exactly what is it that you want?" Jonathan asked. "Say it, Frankie!"

Frankie, who stood with her back to a window, her bottom resting on the sill, clasped her hands and stared at them. "I want to be what Lisa is," she said quietly, simply.

"Use the word," said Lisa.

"I want to be a witch," Frankie said. "I want to know . . . the secrets."

"We don't have the power to make you one," Jonathan said quietly, as if he regretted it.

"And if I did, I wouldn't," said Lisa. "I'm not certain yet what it means to me. You might hate me forever for introducing you into something I don't myself entirely understand and that you don't understand at all." She glanced at Jonathan. "I don't think you can abjure. Once you are a witch, you will always be a witch. Even beyond the grave."

Frankie wept softly. "Maybe, then, you can teach me how to do it for myself. Or teach me the truths you possess. All my life I've been torn between religion and science. All my life I've wondered how to reconcile them. All my life I've hungered for knowledge, and I was never sure it wasn't wicked to crave it so much."

"There is no wickedness in that, Frankie," said Lisa.

"Lisa! Do you understand how blessed you are? You're a mother. I'm not. And now . . . this miraculous contact with the eternal! If I could only be allowed to see what you see, even if not to be one of you. *Please!* Lisa. Jonathan . . . give me a glimpse. Teach me! Please!"

Jonathan glanced at Lisa, then glared at Frankie. "I am old-fashioned," he said, his eyes narrowing, his chin rising. "I have lived long. I do not see a woman in the posture of a supplicant. Times have changed, but have they changed so much that a supplicant does not know how to supplicate?"

Frankie understood and dropped immediately to her knees. "I beg you," she said quietly.

Lisa was appalled. Only Jonathan's sharp glance kept her from going to Frankie and offering her hand to help her to her feet.

"I still don't see a groveling supplicant," Jonathan said quietly, without scorn.

To Lisa's astonishment, Frankie fumbled open the buttons of her suit jacket and her blouse, unhooked her bra, and exposed her breasts to Jonathan. Then she threw herself on her belly. She did not crawl. She slid toward Jonathan, her handsome gray cashmere suit wiping dust from the floor. When she reached his feet she clutched them in her hands and rested her head on them. She whimpered quietly.

"Beg Lisa," said Jonathan.

Frankie crawled to the chair at the desk, not lifting her belly or her forehead from the floor. Lisa was stunned and disgusted, but Jonathan raised his hand in a calming gesture. Frankie reached Lisa's feet. She drew off Lisa's shoes and began to kiss her feet—in fact, not just kiss them, but to lick them fervently.

"Mistress . . ." Frankie murmured.

"What the hell have you done to her?" Lisa demanded of Jonathan.

"Nothing. It's what she wants. What you are seeing is a Frankie that was always in her, probably since her childhood, an element of herself that she has painfully suppressed."

Frankie was now sucking Lisa's toes, one by one. Lisa was confused. She wanted her to stop, but she didn't know how to make her stop in any way that was gentle and didn't amount to cold rejection.

"What are we going to do about her?" she asked Jonathan.

He shrugged. "We could do worse than have a servant. She can be useful."

"To do what?"

He smiled. "We can find work for her."

"And reward her with what?"

"Some insight," he said. "Some understanding. That's really all she wants. She doesn't want powers. Just knowledge. Isn't that so, Frankie?"

"I will be grateful, and I will serve you faithfully," Frankie whispered. She lifted Lisa's foot and ran her tongue across the sole. "Please consent. . . ."

Lisa sighed heavily. "I don't know what to say." She drew her foot away from Frankie, as gently as possible. "Get up, for God's sake. I, uh . . . I consent. I don't know what I'm consenting to, exactly, but I consent."

Lisa found it strange to sit at a table in a busy restaurant and have lunch with a woman who half an hour before had been groveling on the floor and licking her feet. Stranger yet, Frankie was not embarrassed; she seemed even to be self-satisfied. She was oddly calm, even serene. Lisa was embarrassed, and she tried to be kind to Frankie, maybe to put the incident out of mind.

Lisa was well aware that Jonathan had done something to Frankie: had done something to her mind. She focused on it. He had spoken the truth, partly. He had done nothing more than bring to the forefront of her consciousness something that had been there all her life. He had acted like a psychiatrist. Irony.

"Do you want a drink before lunch?" Jonathan asked Frankie.

"Yes, I would like a martini . . . if that's all right."

Lisa flared. "Don't do that, Frankie! Don't subordinate yourself, dammit!"

"I am your servant," Frankie said passively.

"That may be, but don't wear it on your sleeve. I don't want people to think we're having lunch with a zombie."

Frankie nodded. "All right. I'll remember. I'll be careful." Then she smiled at Lisa, her eyes moved mischievously, and she whispered, "Mistress."

* * *

Lisa wanted to return to the life of her great-grandmother. She willed a dream, and this time she did not dream as a witness to Elizabeth Mary Kennedy; she *was* Elizabeth Mary Kennedy.

Sean was a fine man: a big, effusive, loving man, a good husband, a good father, a competent lawyer. He expected to be deferred to in his role of paterfamilias, but that was all right; she would have been surprised if he had not. He was a lusty lover, and they produced two sons and three daughters as a first family, then another son and daughter when the first five were all old enough to spend most of the day at school.

He was inordinately proud of his large family. It proved his manhood. Besides, wasn't bringing many children into the world what Holy Mother Church told a man to do? The family outgrew the house on East Thirty-seventh Street and moved twenty blocks uptown. They entertained friends and were entertained by friends. Their name was known in New York.

The problem remained. Sean Kennedy was an Irishman. Many doors were closed to him. The trouble was, many others were open. Saloon doors. The old story was that an Irishman's curiosity would not allow him to sniff the odor of beer wafting to the street from a saloon and not go in to sample the source of that delicious smell. He was fond of whisky, too. It was Irish tradition to be fond of it and to be fond, too, of the good company to be found at the bar.

Elizabeth Mary—who had brought with her the nickname E.M. she had acquired in Philadelphia—enjoyed a nip or three of whisky and a pint or so of beer daily, too. But she had to become concerned with what drinking was doing to her husband.

"It's his judgment that I fear for."

She sat in her electric-lighted parlor in the house on Fifty-seventh Street after dinner, after the children had eaten and had been dismissed to their studies or their beds. She was elegantly dressed, in raspberry-colored silk. Bearing seven children had not thickened her or ruined her health. She remained a tall, slender woman, possessed of a new grace, born partly of the position her husband had achieved for the family, partly of her heightened confidence in what she supposed was a unique status.

Her guest this evening was elegantly dressed, too, as he always had been.

"You see, Mr. Roper—"

She interrupted herself. The serving girl had just knocked but had come on in without waiting for an answer to her knock. On a silver tray she carried a coffee service and a bottle of brandy.

When she had gone, E.M. continued, "You see, when Sean is in his cups he is the hail-fellow-well-met: accommodating, reassuring, and kind. I greatly fear he has signed some papers he would not have signed when he was entirely sober."

"You mean, your husband has endorsed other men's notes," said Roper.

"Yes. Guaranteed them."

Roper smiled. "Does he know that you know?"

"Mr. Roper, need you ask? He does not suspect I know *anything* about his business. I know as the result of doing what you taught me I can do, may the Good Lord forgive me."

"No forgiveness is necessary," said Roper.

E.M. had never been absolutely sure Jonathan Roper was her father. She sensed that he was, believed that he was, but she had never asked, and he had never told her. She had never asked her parents, who probably knew, and they had never told her. He had always been near, a part of her life: an understanding man, always the source of sympathy, with a special and personal affection for her. She supposed he had been compelled for some reason to give her up when she was an infant and then had returned to watch over her like a guardian angel.

She had never dared ask anyone about her real mother.

Her instincts told her she did not want to know what had become of her.

Mr. Roper had been a neighbor in Philadelphia, then a neighbor in New York. Sean, who tended to be a jealous man, had never been in the least jealous of Jonathan Roper. Maybe it was because Mr. Roper was twenty years their elder. He had to be at least sixty.

He was a mystic. That was the best word that came to her mind. He had taught her to focus her attention, to use the special abilities she'd had since childhood. She could discern things other people seemed unable to discern—a very useful ability. She tried not to influence other people by imposing her will on them, but she had sometimes done it—another useful capacity, though she could not help but wonder if it was unholy.

She had to wonder if the woman and the snake on the amulet he had given her were not pagan talismans and unholy. She rarely wore it. She could not have explained it to Sean. She kept it locked in her jewel box.

"How bad is it?" asked Roper. "Is he in danger of losing so much that—"

"It could be a disaster," she said.

"Well. Then we will have to do something about it."

"I dare not intervene in his affairs. That would be worse than—"

"Not worse," he said. "But it can be done without his knowing."

"Are you going to do it for me, Mr. Roper?"

"No. You are going to do it yourself. I will show you how. Tell me the worst thing that has happened."

E.M. crossed herself. "I used the second sight you told me I have and found out that Sean has endorsed the note of a man named O'Brien. O'Brien is a speculator in commodities futures and has made a fortune estimated by some to be as much as sixteen million dollars. It should have occurred to my husband, it seems to me, that a man with a fortune like that should not need a cosigner on a note for half a million. Indeed, the next day, when his head was throbbing, he guessed the truth. And the truth is that O'Brien's fortune is all on paper: good only if all his risky investments go well. And they are not going well."

"Is the note about to be called?"

"I have not told you all. The note is payable to another speculator named Walton. He and O'Brien are co-conspirators. They were looking for a way to take a half-million flier in coffee futures without risk to themselves. They had done the like before, and the scheme goes this way: O'Brien borrows the money from Walton and signs a note. Then they persuade a third man, like Sean, to sign also. Why not? O'Brien's an Irishman. So is Walton. The third man is always an Irishman, too, and usually influenced by drink. If the investment goes well, it goes well. O'Brien makes a profit, which he shares with Walton. If not, Walton calls the note, O'Brien protests he can't pay, and Walton looks to the cosigner for the money lost. O'Brien and Walton cannot lose. If profit is made, the two collect it. In the event of loss, the poor co-signer loses. Sean has guessed the first part of the deal. He has not guessed all of it. And coffee futures don't look so good."

"Where is that note?"

E.M. frowned. She concentrated. Lisa was partner to the sight that came to her. "The note is in Walton's desk, in his office in lower Broadway."

"The problem is simple," said Roper.

"What can I do?"

"Burn it," he said.

"How could I do that?" she asked in a strained, hoarse voice.

"You can, you know," he said. "You can do it now. Come. Let us go downtown."

He drove an air-cooled Franklin two-seater with glaring electric headlamps and was experienced enough with it to maneuver his way expertly among the horse-drawn vehicles on the evening streets. E.M. spent most of the journey holding down her hat. The noise of the engine made conversation all but impossible.

They arrived at the two-story brick building that housed the office of A. Walton & Co., Brokers and Financial Managers. Roper stopped the automobile across the street.

"Start a fire in the attic," he said. "There are still a few people in the building and that way they can get out."

"Mr. Roper!"

"Walton is a criminal," said Roper. "A fraud. That note threatens the well-being of your family. *Start the fire,* Elizabeth."

"I don't know how!"

"Will it."

E.M. stared for a moment at the building, her body trembling a little. Lisa withdrew now and became a witness: a woman standing on the street.

A puff of white smoke erupted from the roof of the little office building, followed in less than a minute by an eruption of orange flame. People on the street began to yell. The people in the building rushed out, some through the doors, a few from the windows. The fire spread at a measured pace at first, but when all the people were out, the fire exploded and engulfed the building. By the time the fire company arrived, galloping gray horses drawing the steam-driven pumps, the building was a pillar of fire, and all the firemen could do was spray water on neighboring buildings to save them.

E.M. watched. Her eyes switched from the fire to Jonathan, then back. "So . . ." she said quietly. "The dreams were of real things that happened to real women."

Jonathan nodded.

"We burn a building. Papers. Records . . ."

"Not 'we,'" said Jonathan.

"I, then. And what does that make me? Never mind telling me. I know. Well . . . I do it with the consent of Almighty God, do I not?"

"You do it with the consent of the Almighty," said Jonathan. "The Almighty made you what you are and consents to what you do."

"Up to a point, I suppose."

"Oh, of course. Your powers are not limitless."

"You are my father, Mr. Roper, are you not?"

He nodded. "I am."

"Tell me about my mother," she said. "I suppose I could find out for myself. But tell me. Was she what I am?"

"No. She was not what you are."

"She was not your daughter."

He shook his head. "She was not my daughter. I offer you a suggestion, Elizabeth. Don't seek the memory of your mother. You don't want to know what happened to her. You really don't."

"Did she suffer?"

"Yes."

"I sensed that. I could feel it."

"Don't pursue her memory, Elizabeth. I beg you not to."

Elizabeth Mary put her hand on his. "You have my promise, Mr. Roper. I will not."

Sean Kennedy might have been fool enough to sign the note while in his cups, but he was insightful enough to realize, only the next day, that he had been cheated. And now, with the paper burned, he was shrewd and devious enough to pretend he could not remember having signed it.

Walton appeared at the house to say he was confident an honest Irish businessman like Sean Kennedy would of course honor a note he had signed, even if it had been burned up.

Sean Kennedy frowned and shook his head. "A note, ye say? In what amount? Ah, and it burned up in yer office fire? That's most interesting. I know I would vividly remember signing a note in such an amount, but I don't remember it. Surely, Mr. Walton, the shock of your tragic fire, with the loss of so many records, has confused your recollection. In any event, Mr. Walton, my client Mr. O'Brien is worth many millions and is a gentleman of honor. I know ye will be at no loss, since he would never have called on me to make good on a note on which I accommodated him. Look to him, Sir, and the best to ye."

Lisa watched as E.M. played the tables at Piccardi's and laid money on the horses and in the course of the balance of the week accumulated a private personal nest egg of more than sixty thousand dollars. She placed it where her husband could not find it and did not tell him of it. From time to time she telephoned her banker and instructed him to invest. A year later her sixty thousand was worth nearly four hundred thousand. She meant never again to see her home and family at risk from anything her husband did while he was drunk.

"Have we all been rich?" E.M. asked Jonathan one day.

"Only those who wanted to be," he said.

Lisa had not willed what she now saw. She wondered if Jonathan had. Maybe it was her "servant," trying to serve.

She knew somehow that it was twelve-thirty, though how she knew it was not clear. For many years she had slept with a digital clock on her nightstand, but that was in the bedroom downstairs where Ben slept alone, and Lisa was sleeping on her couch in the tower. Her wristwatch was on her desk, beyond her sight. Still, she knew what time it was.

Ben was awake. He had been wakened by a knock on the bedroom door.

Now he heard the knock again.

He got up and opened the door. Dr. Frances Gerard was standing there, wearing a robe and nightgown. She was carrying a bottle of brandy and two snifters.

"I'm sorry if I've wakened you. I couldn't sleep and thought maybe you wouldn't mind having a nightcap."

Ben frowned at the bottle and snifters. "Well . . . come in." He checked the time. "I guess it's not so late," he said, suppressing a yawn. He was wearing blue and white striped pajamas. "Uh . . . have a seat," he said. "I'll pour."

She sat down on the bed, not on the chair or on the bench at Lisa's dressing table.

Ben poured generous splashes of brandy into the two snifters. He stood beside the bed and did not sit down.

"Lisa is not my patient anymore," said Frankie. "Just my friend. So I don't know, and maybe I shouldn't ask, why she sleeps on the couch in her study and you sleep alone."

"That's a rather personal question," said Ben, but with a friendly smile that told her he was not offended by it.

Frankie stared up into his face. "I know something about you," she said.

"Really?"

"You're a hell of a man. Lisa told me that when she was my patient. You're a normal man. Not an ordinary man, but a normal one. I imagine you're not very happy about sleeping alone."

"No, I'm not. But it's her choice."

"I know something else about you."

"I'm not sure I want to know what."

"You're wondering what it would be like to sleep with me. At least you're wondering why you shouldn't."

"Dr. Gerard, I'm not thinking anything like that."

"The hell you're not. Look at you."

She nodded at his crotch. The thin cotton fabric of his pajamas totally failed to hide his erection.

Ben sighed. "A man betrays himself."

Frankie shrugged out of her robe. Her nightgown was modest, but it did show something of her spare figure. She clutched a bit of the cloth in her right hand. "If you want this off," she said, "*you'll* have to pull it over my head."

Ben put his snifter aside and tugged Frankie's nightgown over her upstretched arms, leaving her naked. She put her snifter on the table, swung up her feet, and stretched out on her back on the bed. Ben shed the pajamas and came to her.

He was an enthusiastic lover: more enthusiastic than expert, driven by the circumstances to a premature ejaculation. He told her to pour another drink for each of them while he went to the bathroom for a minute, and he promised to repeat.

"You can't stay with me all night," he said when he

returned. "I wish you could. But . . . Lisa sometimes comes down from her tower pretty early in the morning."

Frankie's smile was enigmatic. "She knows, Ben. She knows what we're doing."

"What do you mean?"

"Ben . . . Lisa knows everything. You don't understand about her. She knows *everything.*"

He did not hear the dark solemnity in Frankie's voice. He only shrugged, grinned, and said, "Yeah, I've sometimes thought so."

15

THE GRAY WOLF TROTTED OUT OF THE WOODS INTO THE CLEARING where a woman sat naked on a rock by a tumbling stream. That woman was Lisa. She had just bathed in the stream and was basking in the sun, letting its warmth and the warmth of a summer breeze dry her. She was in her own body: tall, broad of shoulders and hips, with heavy breasts and a smooth round belly. Her clothes lay nearby—together with a pitchfork, so maybe she was a peasant woman who had been working in the fields. A pleasant weariness in her arms and shoulders suggested that she had been pitching hay.

She heard the wolf, then saw it. It circled her, examining her with its yellow eyes. It circled her three times. Then suddenly it was gone and Mathilde stood facing Lisa.

"Moll killed Mountfort for no good reason," said Mathilde without a preliminary word, either of greeting or otherwise. "For not a good *enough* reason, anyway—in our terms." She spoke German, but Lisa could understand. "She killed again, disastrously. After that, her powers diminished until there was hardly anything left of them. She was greatly frustrated. She was the daughter of my father, daughter of my grandfather, but she was no longer favored.

She lived no very long life, either. Your powers have burgeoned since you killed, so you did not incur displeasure. And I . . . My powers grew and grew, and I lived for almost a hundred years. As you have guessed, I killed. More than once. You shall see why."

"I want to see."

"You will."

Responding to Mathilde's gesture of invitation, Lisa metamorphosed to a wolf, a transfiguration no longer accompanied by pain, no longer even requiring any extreme effort. The two of them bounded into the forest.

They moved in time as well as in space, covering more time and more distance than Lisa's senses discerned. As a pair of wolves they prowled the night, not hunting, of course, but terrifying everything that became aware of them. Just before the sun rose they returned to the bodies of women.

They were naked. They remedied that very quickly by stealing clothes from a house where they compelled people and dogs to remain asleep until they had dressed themselves to their satisfaction, eaten a bit of bread and cheese, and walked away, down a lane and onto a broad highway.

"You don't know where we are, so I shall tell you," said Mathilde. "This is Burgundy. The town ahead is Dijon. You will witness what I have come here to do."

"You are going to kill someone," Lisa said somberly.

"I am going to kill someone," said Mathilde.

"Does the Almighty want this person dead?"

"Could I do it otherwise?"

"Yes," said Lisa. "I don't believe the Almighty sanctions every murder."

"Not murders done by ordinary people with ordinary powers," said Mathilde. "But I am not going to attack the man with an ax or a knife."

"Who is he?"

"I will show you."

* * *

It was the gruesome spectacle she had seen twice before, and she was grateful that Mathilde placed her as a witness, not as the chief subject. She was in chains, even so, inside a filthy cell, gripping crossed iron slats, staring at the agony of another victim. Mathilde meant for Lisa to experience enough to understand why she was about to kill.

No matter that Lisa had seen and experienced the dungeon and the torture before, she could not believe the inhumanity that simple people who called themselves God-fearing—not the twisted psychopaths who made the middle decades of the Twentieth Century such a horror—could impose on their fellow men and women. The heavy iron bands around her neck, wrists, and ankles were fastened with rivets and could not be removed except by the black-smith with a hammer and chisel—the same blacksmith who had hammered the thick iron rivets into place.

That the shackles were riveted on her meant that they were not to be taken off, perhaps not until they were pulled off her calcined bones after she was burned. They had long since chafed away her skin, so blood and pus oozed through scabs constantly broken by the scraping of the iron. The links of her ponderous chains were as big around as the palms of her hands, the iron as thick as her thumbs. She was immobilized, helpless. Even so, a chain from her iron collar was locked to a ring in the stone floor of her cell, as though she might at any moment spring to her feet and run. Besides that, the door of her cell was secured with an inch-thick bolt fastened in place by a heavy padlock.

Her cell was a tiny cage, actually, of riveted iron slats, furnished with nothing but a bucket for her slops. It was not big enough for her to lie full length on the floor, and such sleep as she got, she got sitting up.

There were five others just like it around the stone-walled torture chamber. Three other women lay in chains in three of those cages. In the fifth lay a young man who had been castrated before he was brought in. He howled in agony, hour after hour, day and night. From time to time the torturer thrust red-hot pokers into his cage and burned him, to shut him up.

The young woman who was Lisa was weak. Lisa sensed that she was dying. Her name was Agathe.

Agathe's dirty hair was blonde. She was small. Lisa guessed she was twenty-five years old. She sensed also that this young woman was educated, the daughter perhaps of a prosperous merchant. This young woman was more than literate. She knew much of the world. Lisa sensed that Agathe had traveled, had visited—what? The great Burgundy fair? She was naked, without even a rag to hang around her loins. She was filthy and cold and hungry.

Pressing her face to the slats of her cage, she stared at the torture, knowing it would be done to her, too, sooner or later. The other chained women clung to the doors of their cages and watched in terror.

The torturer was an ascetically thin young man dressed in simple brown. The women in the cages cringed from him whenever he walked near them, from fear he might choose them for his next attentions, also from simple dread of a man who would do what he did.

They knew he was not the man who chose the next victim. He did not even decide how much torture would be applied.

The man who made those decisions sat at a table a little apart from the rack, carving a bite of cheese with his knife. He was sleekly fat, dressed like a nobleman, in white silk embroidered with gold thread. In her persona as the woman chained in the cell, Lisa knew who he was. His name was Charles Mirecourt. He had given himself a title: *Marteau des Sorcières*, Hammer of the Witches, derived no doubt from *Malleus Maleficarum*. He was a sadist. To win from him even a little mercy, the women in the cells constantly offered him all they had to offer—whatever he wanted of their bodies, even the most revolting acts—and he regularly accepted. The woman now dying in agony on the rack had debased herself with him only two nights ago—and had earned herself not a crumb of mercy.

That victim—a woman of maybe forty-five years who might have been a sturdy farm wife—lay stretched on the rack, her body distorted by the strain that had pulled her joints apart. Even on the rack she remained chained. She had ceased to scream. She only moaned and whimpered.

"What result, Maître Marteau?" asked a thin old man in the gown of a lawyer, as he entered the chamber in company with another, burlier man, a nobleman wearing a sword and crimson and purple clothes. The man spoke French, but Lisa understood. "A confession?"

"Presently," said Mirecourt. "You may have arrived at just the right time, Maître Boguet."

Henri Boguet! The author of *Discours des Sorciers,* which Frankie had given to Lisa to read.

The nobleman sat down behind the table opposite Mirecourt and poured himself a cup of wine from a flagon. Lisa knew who he was, too. He was the Sieur d'Auxonne—Lord of Auxonne.

"I wish you well in your blessed work," said the thin old man, Boguet, "though I wish it could go more quickly. All over Europe witches are multiplying like caterpillars in a garden. Why, in Savoy there are so many they could raise an army and go to war against a great king. Does this one have children?"

"Two," said Charles Mirecourt.

"Will you burn the children, too?"

"It is not the law here," said the Sieur d'Auxonne. "The children will be bound to stakes and flogged while they watch her burn, so they will never forget."

The old man, Boguet, shook his head. "A great pity," he said. "Those children are likely witches themselves, or likely to become such. It would be best to burn them as well as the mother. It's the only way to stamp out the pestilence. Indeed, I wish all witches were in one great body, so we could burn them all in one great fire."

It was obvious to Lisa that this wispy old man sincerely believed every word he said. That made his statement only the more horrible.

"We don't have a confession from this one yet," said the Sieur d'Auxonne. "Do we, Monsieur le Marteau des Sorcières?"

"We'll remedy that," said Mirecourt brusquely. "Monsieur le Bourreau, are the tongs hot?"

The torturer nodded. After donning leather gloves, he lifted a set of iron pincers from the glowing coals in a large fireplace. The tongs glowed red.

"Pinch off the parts suckled by the Devil," said Mirecourt.

The woman screamed. "No! *No-o-o!* Please, no! I confess! I confess all! I confess!"

The torturer paused with the hot tongs inches from her left breast.

"You confess that you are a witch?" asked Mirecourt.

"I confess I am a witch!"

"You confess that you had carnal connection with Satan?"

"I did! I confess!"

Charles Mirecourt sneered. "Monsieur le Bourreau, it seems she does not want to feel the bite of the tongs. You may return them to the fire."

He grinned, and the torturer grinned. Before he stepped back from the woman, he ran the glowing iron across her breast. She shrieked. Smoke rose from the hideous burn he had given her.

"A confession, gracious lord," said Mirecourt to the Sieur d'Auxonne.

"A confession indeed," said the nobleman. He opened a leather bag he carried on his belt and withdrew three gold coins. He shoved those across the table toward Mirecourt. He laughed as he said to Boguet, "You see. As Marteau des Sorcières, he is entitled to his reward for each confession he obtains. He has become immensely rich. I insist on hearing each confession, so I may be sure of the count."

"I will not falsely certify confessions, My Lord," said Mirecourt. He was grinning, confident that the Sieur d'Auxonne was only gibing him. "If I am rich, it is only because the witches have so astoundingly multiplied."

The Hammer of Witches opened his own purse and handed two silver coins to the torturer.

"A county may consider itself fortunate when it has devoted and skillful men to lead its attack on witches," Boguet said with complete sincerity and great solemnity. "Would that such men were at work in every part of the world. We live in perilous times, my friends, when Satan's servants threaten to overwhelm us."

"We must be efficient," said Mirecourt. "Put her away, Monsieur le Bourreau. Let us talk to another one." He swung his arm toward the cell where the chained Agathe clung to the iron slats. "That one perhaps."

"No, Mathilde!" Lisa breathed.

The dungeon was cold. Lisa partook now of Agathe's memory and remembered that during the weeks she had endured imprisonment in this hellish place she had suffered from the damp cold, to the point where she doubted she would survive, even if—unlikely chance—they found her innocent. She drew a breath. Her lungs rattled.

She knew she would never see her home again, never her father or mother. She wondered if they did not lie in some other chamber of the dungeon. Thank God she could doubt that. The women here, when they lay alone in the dark after the torturer was gone and the fire was allowed to die, talked to one other. None of them knew of any other chambers. If her mother was here, almost certainly she would be in one of these cages.

Agathe knew about half the women here. She had known about half of those who had confessed and been taken away to be burned. Their whole village had been denounced. Hardly one woman had not been called a witch. If her mother had not been brought here, probably she had fled, or had died. One of the women Agathe had watched being tortured was her sister Thaïs, who had confessed—from terror, not pain—as soon as she was put on the rack. She was sent out to be burned within the hour.

Most women endured the torture as long as they could. Surely, they supposed, the fire burning around the stake must be worse. Since Agathe had lain here, not one woman had survived the torture, been determined innocent, and released. Two had died on the rack. Fourteen others had confessed and had been sent out to be burned alive.

Poor little Thaïs, only sixteen years old, had not known what she was supposed to confess. Neither had Agathe when she was first brought here. Only by listening to Mirecourt accept the shrieking confessions of women in agony had she learned what you were supposed to say.

Thaïs had not yet learned when she was dragged to the rack. She had been here only overnight and was put to the torture while she was still clean and pretty, as a show for two guests of the Sieur d'Auxonne. Chained as heavily as Agathe, she had been stripped and spread out on the rack, and the torturer had turned the wheel, stretching her just enough to cause her pain, yet not enough to crack her joints.

As soon as Mirecourt approached her, Thaïs had screamed her confession. She was a witch! The Devil had seduced her! "Mercy, in the name of God! Who could resist the Devil? He forced me."

"And carried you to the Sabbath?" Mirecourt had asked.

"Yes . . . yes."

"By flying through the air?"

"Yes!"

"And what did you see there?"

"I . . . I . . . I saw Satan. Satan was there."

"Did you have carnal connection with Satan?"

" 'Carnal'? I . . . What is it?"

"Thaïs, did you ever see a stallion mount a mare?"

"Yes."

"Did Satan do that to you?"

"Yes . . ."

"Did he present you with a crucifix?"

"Yes."

"And what did you do with the crucifix, Thaïs?"

"I kissed it."

Mirecourt had nodded at the executioner, who turned the wheel one more notch on its ratchet. Thaïs had shrieked.

"Now. What was it you did to the crucifix?"

The girl had shrieked and sobbed. "I don't *know.*"

"You spit on it, didn't you?"

Thaïs had nodded.

And so it had gone. Mirecourt had supplied the confession. The girl had agreed to everything he suggested. It had gone on until one of the Sieur d'Auxonne's guests abruptly slammed his cup on the table, spilling wine, rose from the table, and stalked from the chamber, growling that they ought to have the girl confess to the assassination of King Henry IV. The Sieur had handed Mirecourt his gold coins and ordered that the confessed witch be burned immediately.

Agathe had watched in horror as Thaïs was carried out of the dungeon. Later a woman newly brought to the dungeon said that the executioner had strangled Thaïs before he lit the fire.

Agathe longed for a glimpse of the sun, a moment of the warmth of sunlight. She expected to see the sun just once more, for a short hour, when they carried her to the stake and lit the fire under her. In the meantime she was cold.

Charles Mirecourt was conscious of the cold, too. As the torturer and an assistant lifted the broken, agonized, almost lifeless woman from the rack and carried her to a cell, Mirecourt backed up to the fireplace and warmed himself in its hot glow. He watched, smiling and approving, as the torturer reconnected the helpless woman to a ring in the stone floor. Her knees torn apart by the rack, she could not have risen. Even so, the torturer carefully closed a huge padlock that attached the chain from the ring to the iron collar around her neck. He was equally careful in bolting and locking her cell.

"Let us see if we can earn a few more coins this morning," Mirecourt said to the torturer.

The torturer moved to open the cell where Lisa cowered.

A shadowy figure appeared in the dungeon, on the wall opposite the fireplace. Lisa saw her. The Hammer of Witches saw her. The others did not.

It was Mathilde.

She raised her right hand and pointed at Mirecourt. He stumbled back and fell into the fireplace.

He fell over the blazing logs, his feet stomping in the glowing coals. He howled. His silk clothes took fire instantly and enveloped him in flame. He kicked the glowing hot tongs across the floor, but his effort did nothing to save him. He began to writhe, shrieking and gasping.

No one but Lisa, and perhaps Mirecourt himself, could see the shadowy Mathilde chortling, pointing at the burning Hammer, and bouncing in a joyous little dance.

No one tried to save Mirecourt. The other men approached him cautiously. His violent kicking and thrashing were throwing fiery embers in all directions. The torturer retreated as an ember stuck to the skin of his leg and burned him. Boguet retreated to beat out a small flame that took hold of his gown.

The Sieur d'Auxonne rose from his chair at the table, took a final gulp of wine, and walked closer. The Hammer seemed unable to comprehend what was happening to him, much less to understand what he had to do to escape it. He seemed paralyzed. He roared and shrieked as the flames licked his squirming body.

The ghost of Mathilde had disappeared. Lisa had left the body of the woman chained in the cell and stood invisible outside the cell, watching Charles Mirecourt burn.

The Sieur d'Auxonne put on the leather gloves and picked up the hot tongs. As Mirecourt's writhing ceased and he lay almost quiet on the fire, the Sieur calmly used the tongs to pluck the Hammer's purse from his waist and recover his gold coins.

"I cannot kill them all," the invisible Mathilde said in Lisa's ear, "but I am licensed to do *some* justice. Now, come. You have more to see. We have been summoned."

Lisa hesitated. She wondered if she had at least the power to save the woman whose body she had occupied, whose anguish she had sensed. She looked to Mathilde and pointed.

Mathilde shrugged.

"You can save her. Can I?"

Mathilde shrugged again. "Find out," she said.

Lisa stared at the wretched wraith hanging on the slats of her cage, frightened even by the death of the man who would have tortured her to death. Lisa . . . How was it to be said? Released Agathe?

She turned then and focused a baleful stare on the Sieur d'Auxonne and Henri Boguet.

"No, Lisa," Mathilde whispered. "They are too many. We can't kill them all."

The sun set. Another day was finished. Lisa stopped at a pool in a tiny stream and lapped water, great long drafts of it to slake the thirst of a long run. She sensed the presence of another animal, maybe a fox, lapping the same water, and she drove that animal away with a low snarl.

The moon rose, and the wolves, Lisa and Mathilde, moved easily through gently lighted woodland.

Mathilde stopped. She grunted. She metamorphosed, and so did Lisa. As two naked women, both wearing the amulet, they walked into a grove.

The grove was crowded with other women, as many as fifty of them, all naked. As Mathilde and Lisa walked toward the center, the others fell back and dropped to their knees.

One crawled forward and prostrated herself before Lisa. She was Agathe. She raised her face toward Lisa and clasped her hands before her in an expression of adoration and gratitude.

My God! Had she created a witch? She had told Frankie Gerard she couldn't. So could she?

Agathe crawled back to the group.

Lisa looked at these women. They were of all ages, all sorts, but all of them were marked; all of them bore scars: some had whip marks, some carried grotesque shiny burn scars, and some hobbled on legs long since crushed. Lisa and Mathilde were the only unscarred women in the grove. Lisa could not be sure, but these women seemed to recognize the amulet as a talisman.

But Mathilde had been scarred once. Lisa remembered. She had lain on a dungeon floor, so laden with heavy chains she could hardly move, and she had been scarred, if not from torture at least from abuse. Now she was unmarked. She was a youthful, perfectly formed blonde woman, graceful in her carriage. She accepted the adoration of the other women with a queenly mien, as her due.

Lisa didn't know what year it was. She guessed, from what she had seen, that it was a year during the mortal lifetime of Mathilde Seiler.

In the center of the grove— The knight! Only now he wore no armor. He wore nothing. He presided over the assembly of scarred women, sitting on a throne they had likely built for him of heaped-up rocks. He was, beyond question, the same man she had seen wearing armor; no one who had seen that face would forget it. If his face might have served Michelangelo as a model for the face of Moses, his body might have served as a model for the musculature. The great sculptor had not portrayed Moses as a wispy old man but as a powerful leader in the prime of his years. This man was conspicuously strong, of body and soul. He was haughty, yet magnificent.

The women who had parted their ranks to let Lisa and Mathilde pass kept their eyes on him and doted on him.

Mathilde spoke to Lisa. "Victims. Tortured. Every one of them."

"He is . . . Satan?" Lisa whispered.

"Of course," said Mathilde. "Or the Devil. Whatever you want to call him. The Master."

Looking at him, Lisa could saw a vivid contrast between the Master and the Satan described in the confessions. In the first place, his beard was not coal black but was streaked with silver. In the second place, he certainly did not have a tiny male member no thicker than a woman's finger, as described in the maunderings of Henri Boguet.

Mathilde walked boldly forward to within a pace or two of

the man enthroned on the pile of rocks. Lisa watched, mesmerized. Mathilde and the man were illuminated in the cold light of the moon. When Mathilde was a pace away from the man, she dropped to her knees. She crawled that last pace, lowered her head, and kissed his feet, then lifted her head, seized his big and erect penis, and kissed that, too.

The man placed his hand on her head in a gesture that seemed to bestow a blessing.

Mathilde looked up and spoke. "This is my daughter Lisa," she said.

The Master nodded and beckoned her to come to him.

Lisa dropped down and crawled forward. She reached his feet and kissed each one in turn. Then, as she had seen Mathilde do, she raised her head, took his engorged penis in both her hands, held it up to her face, and kissed it. The confessions had it that the penis should be cold. It wasn't, any more than Jonathan's was. It was as warm as any man's, and in the moment that her lips touched it she felt his pulse.

He put his hand on her hair, and a palpable thrill ran through her. She felt his hands under her chin, lifting her face. She stared into his face.

His eyes were stern, demanding. They fastened on hers, and instantly she was conscious of his hypnotic power. From that instant she could not be sure if what she saw or thought was real or something projected into her mind by him. But there was more in his eyes: understanding, maybe, and maybe warmth. His eyes were impossible to read.

"You have committed yourself to me," he said. "I offer you now the chance to renounce that commitment. It is often given unwisely. It is often regretted. I do not set myself against those who elect to recant."

"I do not recant, Master," she said.

"Then do you want to unite with me, forever?"

"I do, Master."

In his presence it did not even occur to her that joining herself to him might be a fatal error. What was more, she knew how to make the pledge he asked for. She lay down on the ground, spread herself, and he mounted her. He ejaculated after only two or three strokes, then pressed his mouth to the mole on her breast, sucked hard on it, and drew a droplet of milk. Their union was complete.

A mutter rose from the assembled women. They voiced their wonder, their awe, their gratitude for having been allowed to witness the union.

The Master rose and extended his hand to help her to her feet. For a moment he embraced her. "It is forever," he said.

He held her hand and led her out of the grove. The others, even Mathilde, fell back as they passed—Mathilde visibly bewildered. The big man led Lisa through a thicket of brambles, but none of the thorns touched her. They came into a small clearing at the edge of another small, splashing stream.

He stretched out his arm and pointed. A man and woman stood by the stream, staring, apparently thoughtfully, at the water. They seemed to be studying the play of moonlight on the rippling water, as if it conveyed some meaning to them. Her master clutched her arm and restrained her from approaching closer.

He and she stood and watched as the couple made gestures over the water. The water moved in response to their gestures. Lisa had not at first noticed—had not noticed even so basic a fact—but these people, too, were naked.

"Do you know them?" the Master asked.

Lisa shook her head.

The big man smiled broadly. "They are God," he said. "*They* are the Almighty."

Lisa stared. At first she couldn't believe what he said. Then, as she watched, it became apparent. They were not entirely corporeal. Before her eyes they merged into each other and were one, then separated again and were man and woman.

She dropped to her knees and crossed herself. It seemed the appropriate thing to do.

The couple turned and faced her.

They were like two statues by Praxiteles—he the *Hermes,*

she the *Aphrodite of Cnidus:* the ideal young man and woman, flawless, perfectly sculpted in every detail of what each man and woman in the world might hope to be. They were not of marble or of bronze, nor yet were they of flesh, since she had seen them merge and separate; but they were, for the moment anyway, like flesh. Except for their extraordinary beauty, they were different from any youthful couple in one way only: that they were at least seven feet tall. They were in fact like two exquisite Greek statues come to life.

For a moment she thought she discerned a glow from them, but she realized that was more of her expectation than from any strange light she saw. She wished she could have seen them in sunlight, though, rather than in the moonlight, which lent realism to nothing.

The woman gestured to her to rise.

Lisa stood—but stood in as humble a posture as she could contrive.

The man smiled and opened his hands toward her.

God! *God!* Could they be? Could all of theology, Christian or other, have been so wrong as to have failed to know that ultimate divinity could not be male or female but had to be both? Looking at this couple, Lisa could not doubt. They *were* God, male and female together as one. Unless they were a dream, imposed on her by hypnotism or the special powers of Satan, they were God! And . . .

And *let it be so!*

She glanced back at her master. He was smiling, but he was also standing in a respectful posture.

God the Father continued to hold out His hands, in a welcoming gesture. God the Mother held out Hers the same way.

Lisa stepped forward a pace. She was almost close enough to touch them. But she could not. She could not move forward another step. She could not reach out toward them. They continued to smile gently, and she understood she was receiving a benison.

She clasped her hands before her face and respectfully lowered her eyes. When she looked up after only a moment, they were gone. And so was the Master. And so, even, was the stream. She stood alone in the moonlight in a thorny brake.

A wolf trotted through the tangled underbrush and became Mathilde.

"You have seen what I have never seen," said Mathilde. "You have seen what my father-grandfather has never seen. You are favored above us all, Lisa. I don't know why."

Mathilde dropped to her knees and lifted her hands toward Lisa in a gesture of adoration. Lisa looked down at Mathilde and extended her hands. As she did, her eyes stopped on her amulet. It was no longer heavy bronze, nor was the chain. They had metamorphosed. She was not certain what they were now. The chain was perhaps of platinum. The woman and the snake—what they were was impossible. A diamond could not be carved that way. Yet that was what the glittering object seemed to be.

16

"I DO NOT UNDERSTAND," SAID LISA TERSELY. "I DO NOT understand, and I don't like it."

Her study. Midday. Frankie was on her knees before Lisa, her forehead touching the floor. That was bad enough, but Lisa could understand that, maybe. What was totally beyond her comprehension was that Jonathan was, too, though he only knelt and did not grovel. His posture destroyed her comfort.

She herself had been sitting in soft faded jeans and a gray sweatshirt, comfortably glancing over the *Times* crossword puzzle, when they had knocked at the door. In a moment they were both down on their knees like this.

"You have seen the Almighty," Jonathan muttered. "We have been told. Even Mathilde was never privileged to face the Almighty. Even Mathilde could not tell you what it is, who it is. What is more, you have been entered by *him*. Mathilde was, not the others. Their power came from me . . . *through me*. Yours is now entirely independent of me. I am your servant, as much as Frankie is. You have become a queen, Lisa." Even before you showed me the amulet as it now is, I saw a vision of it. A diamond! You are our queen!

"You are wiser than I am, just the same," said Lisa. "You have centuries of experience. You can explain what I cannot. I still need you."

"I am not sure I can explain anything you cannot," he said. "Or help you much now."

"I can't answer the question of questions," Lisa said.

"What is that?"

"Why *me?* Why should *I* be favored? Why should I have greater powers even than Mathilde?"

"Why should any of my daughters have had *any* powers?" Jonathan asked. "The Almighty has reasons."

"I want to talk to Father William," Lisa said.

"Let it be here," said Jonathan. "That is my advice to you. Bring him here."

She transported the priest to the overgrown family cemetery on the ridge high above the wooded land outside Marietta. It was evening. The sun had set, but a glow persisted in the western sky, and they were not in darkness.

She spoke quietly for an hour as they walked through the cemetery and then higher on the ridge, where she had run as a wolf. The glow faded and was replaced by the yellowish light of a rising full moon, then by the whitish light of a high moon.

"You *could* believe all this because you were hypnotized," said Father William. "It could be a great deception practiced on you by Satan to keep you his."

"And you could refuse to believe it because *you* are hypnotized," she said. "That's a facile answer. Maybe you *are* hypnotized, by something different. By a centuries-old tradition that hasn't much basis in fact. Think of what you preach, Father. What evidence have you of its truth?"

"Faith," he said simply.

"Credo quia absurdum," she said. "Is what I am telling you any more absurd than what you believe?"

" 'I believe it *because* it is absurd,' " he translated. "A test of faith. If I believe what the Church tells me, even knowing it is absurd, I—"

"You are perhaps a fool," said Lisa. "The Church has been the home of many good men and women—and many charlatans. Is that not true?"

"Faith is superior to reason," he said stubbornly.

"I have seen a vision of the Almighty," said Lisa. "Couldn't my vision be a new revelation?"

"That is not impossible. It is, though, wholly unlikely, like the vision of Joseph Smith. Do you mean to found a new church? Build a new Zion?"

"New Mormons . . . No. We have enough faiths, enough churches, already."

"Then—"

"When we last met, Father, I cursed you," she interrupted. "I regret that. I withdraw the curse and apologize for it. I was . . . upset. You have to understand how I felt, hearing you talk of my child falling from my womb."

"I did not take your words seriously, Lisa. Your emotions were—"

"On the other hand, you threatened me. I took that very seriously. I *do* take it seriously. Understand, Father, that I will not allow my child to be destroyed. And I am capable of defending her. Whatever my special powers may be, they were given to me to enable me to defend my child. I will use them, Father. Don't for a moment doubt it."

"Now *you* threaten *me.*"

"So be it. I suggest an accord between us. If you see evil done by me, then do what you can to destroy me. If you do not, leave me alone."

"What of your eternal soul, Lisa?"

"My soul is mine. It is not yours. It does not belong to the Church. I know that now. You reminded me that the Almighty has given us free will. So my soul is mine to save or lose, as I will. Your concern for it touches me. To save souls is, of course, your vocation. But this soul *is mine.* I am ready to risk it for what has been revealed to me. If I am wrong, the damnation is mine, too."

"Your soul is not yours, Lisa," he said firmly. "Our souls are God's."

"Very well. I agree. I commit my soul to the Almighty. The only difference between us is that you are certain you know what the Almighty is, while I have seen a different vision."

"You can no longer even use the word 'God,'" he said. "Do you have trouble saying it?"

"The word is restrictive," she said. "You speak of God in three persons. I have seen it in five. If God is the Father and the Son, It is also the Mother and the Daughter, plus the Holy Spirit, which makes five. Or better, It is One, because I have seen It merge."

"Your God is not the God of the Holy Scripture, then, is it, Lisa?"

"Perhaps not. Tell me, do we worship a god or a book? The chief religions, Father, seem to worship books. What will you do if incontrovertible evidence is unearthed in archaeological digs in Palestine that the New Testament is a fraud, a piece of propaganda?"

"Lisa, this unclean heresy will condemn you to the lowest depths of hell."

"All I ask of you, Father . . . All I ask is that you not attempt to interfere."

"What will happen if I do?"

"Since you are certain I am going to the lowest depths of hell anyway, I will add to my sins by destroying a priest."

I want you to see this. I want you to know.

Lisa heard the unvoiced call of Frankie, coming to her in her sleep. A dream . . . Yes. No. She focused on what Frankie wanted her to see.

Frankie was in bed in the guest room. Ben was with her. They slept together every night. Frankie understood perfectly well that Lisa knew that. It was a measure of Ben's naïveté that he supposed—and he *did* suppose; Lisa could read his thoughts—that by cleverly sneaking around in the night, using one bedroom one night, the other bedroom the next, he was deceiving Lisa, at least partly. Ben knew she suspected he was sleeping with Frankie, but he thought he and Frankie had prevented her from really knowing.

He also believed Lisa didn't want a confrontation. Obviously she could come down from her tower any night and see what was going on. That she didn't was evidence to him that she didn't want a scene—also evidence that she didn't really care.

"Watch what I am doing, Mistress," Frankie called. "I want you to know."

Frankie was fellating Ben. He was in ecstasy, squirming under her ministrations. He lay on his back in his pajamas, his penis sticking out through his fly. Frankie was deeply troubled, but she knelt over him on the bed and performed with apparent enthusiasm, at least with great vigor, her head bobbing up and down, his penis slipping in and out of her mouth.

"Tongue . . . *tongue!*" Ben gasped, and Frankie brought her tongue into action, fervidly licking the tip of his penis.

Ben pulled her nightgown up and caressed her bottom.

Lisa watched. She had never done this. The Bible said no. But then, the Bible forbade other things she had done. At least the Church said it did. Ben had never asked her to do it, probably for the same reason. She had thought of it but had never offered. She'd never thought he wanted it. She wondered if he had asked Frankie to do it or if Frankie had initiated it. She searched the vague images being generated in their fervid minds and didn't find the answer.

"It is sickening, Mistress. But I do it for you."

Lisa flared. Frankie's groveling was sickening, too. "I didn't ask you to do that. If you do it, you do it for him. You love him, don't you?"

"Yes, Mistress."

Ben grabbed Frankie by her short hair and held her head down on his crotch. She could not have spit out his penis if she had wanted to. He groaned. His climax came, and Frankie choked on his ejaculate, but he held her in a tight grip and forced her to hold what came in her mouth, or to swallow it. She gulped it down.

"Oh, Mistress!"

"I didn't order you to fall in love with him. I didn't even suggest it. I didn't tell you to suck his cock. I didn't even suggest it. Do what you want about that, Frankie. Make yourself happy. Make him happy. But don't lay any part of it on me."

"I understand, my Eternal Mistress. I will always obey."

"No, by God. You're not obeying. You're doing your own thing."

Ben still gripped Frankie by the short hair on top of her head. He pulled her up by it and kissed her mouth, which was wet with his ejaculate.

"Frankie," he murmured. "God, Frankie! *I love you!*"

Lisa watched and listened. How easy, how convenient, she thought bitterly. Her servant would replace her as wife. A quiet divorce and suddenly Ben would be married to a respected psychiatrist. American Cyanamid would not object. Benny and Anne would not. The town would not.

Jonathan would be pleased. So would the Master. She would bear the eighteenth generation without the impediment of Ben. Even the Almighty would be pleased, probably.

How slick! How superficial and slick! Who could have arranged it? Not the Almighty, who would have been more subtle. Not the Master. Jonathan? No. She had to face it: she had done it herself, however much she might wish she could deny it.

"We can't stay here in Marietta," Lisa said to Jonathan. "We can't live here. The baby can't be born here."

"Au contraire," he said insouciantly.

"All right," she said sternly. "Never mind 'can't.' We *won't* stay here. That is my decision."

He nodded. "It is your decision."

"You are going to be a father to this child, Jonathan," she said. "You are going to live with me and behave like a daddy."

"Ben could do that for us."

"No, Ben can't do that for us. Philippe Robeus did, never imagining that you were both the father and a grandfather of Mathilde. Angus McDougal never guessed he was not the father of Charity. Sir William Douglas was a fool not to have guessed that his charming, virile neighbor was the father of Moll. Only Timothy Spencer was treated honestly. He knew he and his wife had adopted my great-grandmother. He knew he wasn't her biological father. All he didn't know was that her mother had been hanged."

"Ben—"

"Ben knows. At least he suspects. And he has very conveniently—I am sure this amuses you, and probably Frankie, too; it was so simple—fallen in love with his fellatrice. No, Jonathan. You are going to stay near home and be domestic for the next twenty years or so."

"As you command," said Jonathan.

"That I do command," she said. "If I can give you commands, regard that as a command."

He nodded.

"Where are we going to live?" she asked.

"Wherever you wish."

"What will we do for money?" she asked.

"Really, Lisa! How can you wonder? We know what stocks will rise tomorrow and what will fall. We know what horses will win what races. We can sense the locations of buried treasure. We can have as much as we want, without taking it from the mouths of others. If we are not too greedy—don't try to corner the world market in something or other, don't change economic trends and so on—we can have whatever we want."

She smiled. "Elizabeth Mary took it from the hands of gamblers. That appeals to me. To beat the house. To turn their scams against them."

Jonathan laughed. "I have lived so, through many decades. Lately I have scooped money out of Las Vegas and Atlantic City. The operators would kill me if they suspected."

"They would *try* to kill you," she corrected him.

"Yes. Try to. But I go in various guises."

"Money is nothing to be concerned about, then."

"The Horsemen of the Apocalypse are of no concern to us, Mistress," he said. "War, Pestilence, Famine, Death—no concern to us."

"Death?"

"It is not a concern for you. Not anymore. What did the Master tell you? You and he are united forever. Mathilde lives, in a way. I live. You will live."

"Until I come to wish I didn't," said Lisa.

Jonathan nodded. "When that day comes, tell the Master. I believe he will release you. I have thought of it. But I have never asked for my release."

"In the meantime where will we go? Where will the baby be born?"

"As you wish. We shall disappear."

"And go where?"

"Wherever you wish. For myself, I would live in London or Paris, maybe Rome. Or I would live in a hilltop house in northern Italy or in the restored ruins of an Austrian monastery. We will become bored with all of them and will move on. That is our great enemy: boredom."

"We will watch our child grow," said Lisa.

"And *her* child and her grandchild and their children and grandchildren. The line must and will continue."

"It must continue," Lisa agreed.

"I don't know why, Lisa," Jonathan said, "but you are the most powerful of them all. You are their queen. Mathilde agrees. You are favored. You are . . . You are a goddess. You are new in my experience. I am glad, but I don't understand."

"*No!* I was created. I do not create."

Jonathan dropped to his knees. "Forgive me. It was a foolish thing to say. Lisa . . . do you love me?"

"I love you, Jonathan."

"My wives and daughters never have, not since Jacqueline. They thought they did, I suppose, some of them. I don't understand why it is this way, why it is so very different with you. Can you understand why it makes so much difference?"

"Did you love them?"

"I have told you. I loved my daughters. Of my wives . . . really only Jacqueline, in the complete way that an ordinary man can love. Angelique was both daughter and wife. I loved her, too, as best I could. With the others . . . there was purpose. On both sides. I acted to preserve the line. With Anna, who was the mother of Charity"—he shook his head—"it was purely mechanical. She didn't even understand she was in the line of descent. Even when I told her, she didn't understand. Amelia Douglas didn't understand, either. She wanted something better than the old soldier who was her husband, plus escape to the Town." He sighed.

"What about Angelina?"

"She thought her hanging was a proper punishment for her adultery, the death of Josiah Tatum aside. It was no pleasure to make that child. You can buy rubber devices that mimic the act of love with more warmth than she brought to it."

"But it was a joy with me?"

"Oh, yes. I could have impregnated you with one act. But I didn't want to. I wanted to come to you again and again. I don't know why, exactly. You are elemental woman, Lisa. Uncomplicated woman. But only physically. Spiritually and mentally, you are far more."

"Explain something to me," she said. "Do I have any options? Or is it all fixed?"

"You have no option about the baby. It must be born. Other than that— You are a queen."

"After the baby is born, could I return to what I was six months ago? Could I . . . Could I even *forget* all of this?"

"Would you want to?"

Lisa closed her eyes and lowered her chin to her breast. She shook her head.

* * *

The cast-iron gates to the cemetery were never locked. If they had been, she would have entered anyway. The hour was midnight, and Lisa walked among the headstones of the ancient burying ground with the great conical Indian mound in the center.

She heard voices and realized that two people—college students, most likely—were coupling on the ground in a dark spot where stones and shrubbery blocked the dim glow from a distant streetlight. Maybe there were others. She did not want to risk being seen, maybe even recognized. She took off her clothes and hid them among the limbs of a thick evergreen, then metamorphosed and trotted silently through the cemetery as the wolf—dog, they would think.

She reached the mound, an Indian burial mound as much as a thousand years old. It was about thirty feet high and something more than a hundred feet in diameter. Steps had been laid into it on one side, so visitors could climb to the top. The cone was truncated, leaving a flat space at the top where the town kept a small circle of park benches.

Lisa had no need for the steps but easily loped to the top. There in the dark she returned to woman and knelt on the gravelly soil. "Master," she whispered. "I have need of you, Master."

He appeared.

"I am not to be summoned at whim," he said.

"I did not summon, Master. I entreated."

He extended his hand and helped her to her feet. He was not the knight now but a formidable gentleman dressed in Edwardian style: top hat, opera cape, white tie, carrying a stick with a heavy silver head: a wolf. His beard was trimmed much closer to his chin and cheeks. The changes did not disguise him. He was her master, Satan; he could not have disguised himself from her, any more than Ben Hamilton could have. She kissed him.

She was of course naked; her clothes were hidden below. She was cold. He removed his cape, wrapped it around her, and clasped her to him as if to warm a child.

"So, my daughter, why did you call me?"

"To beg for the answer to a question."

He did not wait for her to voice the question. "You are favored beyond all the others," he said, "because you are found more worthy than any of the others. Jacqueline was a very special woman but never a witch. She was relieved of her agony, called to the other side and to her reward, because her courage did not fail her at the end and she did not renounce the Almighty as her husband did. If she had, she might have become the first witch. Mathilde was worthy of great powers and was given them, but she became too fond of killing. You saw her kill Mirecourt, and he was by no means the only one she killed. But the witch burning went on. To stop it we would have had to kill as many witch burners as they were killing women they thought were witches. She cannot kill now, has not been able to kill since her mortal lifetime. She will find someone she thinks deserves death and will beg you to kill, as sometimes she begs me. There is justice in her demands, but the injustices she wishes to correct cannot be corrected by killing. It is not her fault. She is what I made her."

"I will not kill for her," said Lisa.

"You have another question," he said. "Why, with her powers, did Mathilde allow herself to be kept chained in a dungeon, deprived of sleep, and led to the stake? The answer is, she did not suffer in that dungeon. I was beside her. I gave her sleep. But I wanted her to witness the witch burners at their worst. I wanted her to know what she was and why she was to be given great powers, lest when she discovered them she should use them capriciously and for petty purposes. We have given you to see, too, before you realized your powers. Mathilde fully realized hers only minutes before you saw her use them to save herself from the flames. Besides, she had not yet borne a child, so her death would have ended the line—which was really no line as yet but had been fated to be a line."

"She confessed," said Lisa.

"To what was true," he said. "She had joined in union

with me, as you did. The details, about my being cold and so on, were the canon of the witch burners and were included in every confession, including tens of thousands that had not a word of truth in them."

In the cemetery below, a laughing couple frolicked toward the mound. The Master called a bolt of lightning to flash across the sky, followed by angry thunder. The couple ran.

"Jonathan's daughters have been the powerful witches. Charity used her powers to save her daughter from death. She was a good woman, so good that she was afraid of her powers and hardly ever used them again. As to Moll, you saw her faults, and Mathilde told you that her powers were withdrawn. She was frivolous. And then . . . your great-grandmother. She enjoyed her powers. She used them sparingly but wisely. I was fond of her."

"And me?"

"You had to be chosen, of course. The birth of the next generation depends on you."

"I could have borne the next daughter without knowing why I bore her or what she was," Lisa said. "Others have done that, I gather."

"But Jonathan told me you were the best of them all, worthy of trust, worthy to receive understanding, worthy to be given great powers. I studied you. I watched you as more and more was revealed to you. So did the Others, the Almighty. And we decided that Jonathan was right. You are strong and intelligent, Lisa. At first you did what any modern woman would do. You sought to dispel your visions as nightmares, your new knowledge as hallucination. When you couldn't do it alone, you turned to psychiatry. You might have allowed yourself to be narcotized. But you didn't. That was impressive. You sought understanding from religion and did not find it there. When you had to accept the fact that what you were seeing and learning was real, you were able to cope with it. Dr. Frances Gerard and your friend Pat Irving would have been driven to madness. Your strength is in your very simplicity, Lisa, in the direct way you think and act."

Instinctively Lisa clung to him for his warmth, all but oblivious of the fact that he was Satan.

"What is Jonathan, Master? He has begun to call himself my servant."

"What are *you*, Lisa?" asked the Master. "You are what I am, only of a lower rank. In terms of Medieval theology, we are angels. I am of high rank, serving close to the Almighty. Only Joshua, the son of Joseph, called the Anointed One, serves closer than I. You are of lesser rank. Jonathan is of still lower rank. He is a messenger and guardian spirit."

"A witch is an angel?" Lisa asked.

"'Witch' is the name given to my angels. *Sorcière. Hexe.* Those who hate me and give me an evil name give ugly names to my angels. My name for you is the Latin word, *sāga*—meaning 'wise woman.'"

"But we are all creatures of the Almighty," she said.

"And all partake of Them, to one extent or another. Remember this, Lisa: that over the centuries those who constantly cry their name for the Almighty have accused me and my few *sāgae* of every foul crime, though we have never committed the tiniest fraction of the sins *they* commit and practice every day."

"Do you punish great sinners in an afterlife?" she asked.

"Yes, though I do not define 'sinners' as loosely as tradition would have it. Occasionally I punish them in this life. That is a service I perform for the Almighty. But remember this: The universe is the kingdom of the Almighty. I am Their servant. I do not rule a separate kingdom. Hades is Theirs as much as Heaven is."

"After I rear my daughter, what will I be?"

"Nothing less, if you are a loyal servant. You will live a long life. After that, you will live on, still a servant of the Others and of me."

Lisa slipped down to her knees, seizing his hands to kiss.

"A warning, Lisa," he said. "So far, the priest, Father William Longford, has abided by the bargain you astutely made with him. He sees no evil in what you are doing, so he does not interfere. But watch him. He must not be *allowed* to interfere."

"What am I to do if he does?"

"Decide," said the Master.

And he was gone.

Shortly, so was she. She invited Ben to sit down alone with her in her study to talk out their situation. She was surprised at how little emotion either of them could generate.

"When it first occurred to me that Jonathan was encroaching on my marriage," Ben said, "I realized that I could not compete with him."

"You didn't really try."

"Would it have made any difference?"

She nodded. "I think it might have."

He shrugged. "How long would it have been before something else happened? To either of us. I used to wonder what would happen if the company had transferred me. Would you have given up this house and left with me?"

"I never thought of doing otherwise."

"It's not your fault, really," he said. "I guess it was just a matter of which one of us did it first. You found your alternative first, but then . . . Frankie. It could have happened the other way, I guess, if I'd met someone first."

"So . . . it seems kind of easy, doesn't it?"

Ben nodded. "I'm ashamed how easy."

"I'll be leaving in a day or two."

"Where are you going?"

"To Chappaqua for a few days, then I think to Europe. We'll probably live there, for a while anyway. I'll telephone as soon as I have an address."

"What about money?" Ben asked. "What about your half of this house?"

"I don't need money. I don't want alimony. Have your lawyer draw up papers to make the house yours. Send them, and I'll sign them."

"Jonathan is that rich?"

Lisa nodded.

"Well . . . will we never see you again?"

She smiled weakly. "Ben, of course you'll see me again. Benny is our son. I'll come back. But probably not until after the baby is born."

"Good luck with the child. Honestly, Lisa, I've always known it was Jonathan's. Frankie has agreed that I should have a vasectomy."

"You and Frankie should get along well. She's smart. She's younger than I am."

Ben stood. He nodded. His voice failed, and he turned and left the room.

Lisa sat on the couch and wept.

Jonathan materialized. He held her and nuzzled her neck. "I love you," he said. "We will love each other forever."

Father William Longford said a short, fervent prayer, then crossed himself.

She sat on the foot of his bed, having wakened him in the middle of the night in his Spartan bedroom in the rectory of the Church of the Holy Name of Jesus.

"Have you come to destroy me?" he asked.

"Your God would permit it," she said.

"Perhaps we should find out," he said. "That would be a test."

"Father . . . there are many ways to destroy a man. You suppose I might kill you." She shook her head. "I have killed two men, maybe also a woman. I hope they are the last. If you threatened to destroy my child physically, I *would* kill you, but even then, only if that was the only way I could stop you. The truth is, I can stop you in other, less drastic ways."

He smiled. It was a small, faint smile, and she took it for a sneer.

"You want a test?" she asked. "Very well. Let's have one. I will not kill you. But . . . say the Lord's Prayer for me, Father."

"I'm not sure it should be said in the presence of what you have become."

"Say it, Father. Let me hear you say it. Maybe it will have some impact on me."

He glanced up at the crucifix hanging above his bed. He turned down the corners of his mouth, drew a breath, and braced his shoulders. "Our F . . . Ower Faw . . . Awrff!" He drooled. "Jee . . . Hol . . . Ahhh!"

"Do you think you can say Mass?" Lisa asked quietly, sympathetically.

Father William blew breath between fluttering lips. "Holy Mother of God, pray for me!" he cried, articulating perfectly.

"She will," said Lisa. "The Holy Mother who *is* God will hear and grant your prayer—so long as it is not a prayer for *my* destruction!"

"It is the work of Satan!" he protested tearfully.

"It *is* the work of Satan," she agreed. "The Master is a creation of the Almighty and is Their servant, as am I. As are you. I don't ask you to accept a new dogma, Father. I ask you to go on serving as you have always served, for which I am certain the Almighty are grateful. I ask you not to impose on me the unhappy necessity of silencing you."

The priest put his hand on hers. "Do you bring a new truth?" he asked.

She shook her head. "No. A very old one, a truth that has become obscured. But don't accept that from me. Pray for it, Father. Pray for other evidences of the truth. I am certain They will give them to you. You are worthy. You opposed me because you sincerely and thoughtfully believed you should. That will not be held against you."

He blinked. "Should I be grateful to you?" he asked.

She smiled and caressed his cheek. "No, Father. Bless me. Bless my child."

He did.

Epilogue

THE EIGHTEENTH GENERATION WAS NOT BORN IN A HOSPITAL. NOR was she born at home. Nor was a doctor in attendance. The birth happened on the twenty-first day of August, out-of-doors.

Lisa and Jonathan had leased a small stone farmhouse in Cornwall, at the crest of a wooded hill so high that they had a distant view of the English Channel. The house had been remodeled as recently as the 1940s by careful architects who had preserved its eighteenth-century character while giving it twentieth-century amenities. The owners had an eclectic taste in furnishings, which pleased Lisa. The place was comfortable and suited them for now, though it would not be their permanent home.

They bought a Land Rover and drove over the Cornish countryside, exploring. Lisa bought an antique chair eminently in character with the farmhouse—but which they would carry with them when they left.

One day they drove as far as Salisbury, in Wiltshire, and there visited the great Gothic cathedral. They went on to Winchester to see the cathedral there, and doubling back they stopped at Stonehenge in early evening. Lisa was fascinated by Stonehenge and felt attracted to it. Because of vandalism in recent years, visitors were kept a short distance away from the famous stones and were not allowed to wander among them, touching, as they had done for many centuries. Lisa was so much attracted that she insisted on returning at midnight. She assumed her wolf form, entered the compound, and prowled among the stones, sensing a mystic connection, as if something among the stones tried to speak to her. She knew it was a common feeling, one shared by many visitors to Stonehenge.

Oddly—inexplicably—she sensed that for her there actually *was* a connection. She formed a determination to explore later. Stonehenge . . . Why? She had to know.

That was the only time since they had come to England that she prowled as a wolf.

In May she signed the papers sent by Ben's lawyer. By the first of July the divorce was final. Lisa and Jonathan married as soon as they could, so the baby would legitimately carry the name Roper. The country magistrate who performed the wedding noticed Lisa's full belly but made no comment. Only when they applied for the license did Lisa learn that Jonathan held a British passport.

Three weeks later Benny arrived and spent a long weekend with them. Somewhat to Lisa's surprise, he immediately struck up a friendship with Jonathan, who somehow appealed to him. Lisa could not restrain herself from laughing when Benny told her that Frankie was pregnant. In bed, hours later, she secured from Jonathan his unqualified assurance that he'd had nothing to do with it, not even so much as to encourage the couple to be careless.

She placed a telephone call to Frankie, who pronounced herself deliriously happy and did not raise the question of receiving further insights.

On August 21, Lisa and Jonathan decided to take a picnic lunch to a small, pretty ridgetop grove they had noticed during their explorations. The baby was due in a week or so, but she had felt no intimation of its coming soon and felt confident they could easily reach Plymouth, where they had arrangements with a doctor and a small hospital, in case her contractions began.

It didn't happen that way. Lisa gave birth on the blanket they had spread out on the grass for their picnic. Only Jonathan attended her, but she didn't need anyone else; he knew what to do. The birth was amazingly easy. She suffered little pain.

Perhaps she was granted mercy, for she drifted and slipped into a formless dream at critical moments and so felt little. Glancing around when her vision was fuzzy, she thought she saw wolves walking in a circle around the grove, guarding.

Hearing the cry, she reached for her baby. Jonathan was wrapping it in the checkered cloth from one of the picnic baskets. She looked at it.

It was a boy!

How could that be? The doctor back in Marietta had tested her and said it was a girl. Everything, *everything,* was predicated on the baby being a girl!

The baby boy looked up at Jonathan and gurgled, as if there were some small joke between them.

Lisa heard another shrill cry. But the baby wasn't crying. He—

There was another child! She had borne twins! Jonathan handed the little boy to her and then turned to lift the second baby and wrap it in a white cloth. *It* was a girl!

The doctor in Marietta had not said twins. She had been examined by the doctor in Plymouth, and he had not said twins. She didn't understand.

She had not imagined the wolves. They were really there, forming a protective circle, watching with solemn intensity. She had not noticed a pool of clear water in the grove. It had not been there when she and Jonathan sat down to have their picnic. But it was here now.

And then *They* were there: God the Father and God the Mother, just as she had seen them before. Then the Master appeared. The Almighty stood in the water, which covered Their feet and ankles. The Master stood just out of the water. He held cupped in his two big hands a shallow golden bowl studded around the rim with a ring of diamonds.

All were naked. Even Jonathan had suddenly become so. He knelt beside Lisa and helped her unwrap the babies.

God the Mother extended Her hand. Lisa walked forward, carrying her daughter. Jonathan carried their son. They walked to the edge of the pool.

Lisa was grateful now to see the Almighty in the sunlight. In its warm, bright glow the pair were even more splendid in Their perfection, Their statuelike bodies the more magnificent for being more vividly seen. They were like statues, but They were flesh—now, anyway. Their skin was pale, only a little colored by the sun. The Father's body, which had reminded Lisa before of the *Hermes* by Praxiteles, now brought to her mind Michelangelo's *David:* sculpted muscles, narrow hips, oversized hands, plus a face of calm and confident beauty. It was perhaps imagination that caused Lisa to see in the face of the Mother the introspective serenity of the same sculptor's wondrous *Pietà,* though Her eyes were open and She was smiling.

Lisa stood at the edge of the water, holding her daughter in her arms. Jonathan stood beside her, holding their son. The Master held the golden bowl forward, toward the Almighty pair. God the Father lowered His right hand into the bowl and withdrew it dripping with clear oil. He touched the forehead of the baby boy. God the Mother dipped oil and touched the forehead of the baby girl. Then God the Father anointed the girl, and God the Mother anointed the boy.

Jonathan sank to his knees, clutching his son to him but gazing up at the Divine Couple with an expression of intense adoration.

Lisa knelt.

God the Mother dipped oil and touched the foreheads of

Megan Marklin

both of them: Lisa and Jonathan. God the Father did the same.

Lisa knew that if she closed her eyes They would be gone. Even so, she did it. When she opened her eyes, They *were* gone, the Master was gone, the pool was gone, and she and Jonathan knelt nude in the soft grass, holding their children.

304

Afterword

Satan, the Master, has many names.
One is the Great Deceiver.
Was it all a shrewd and elaborate deceit?

About the Author

The author, who calls herself Megan Marklin, lives in Greenwich, Connecticut. She insists her novel is not autobiographical. Even so, there are many parallels between her and her heroine, Lisa. Her description of Lisa is not very far from a word portrait of herself.

Besides *THE SUMMONED*, she has written a series of erotic stories, which prompted her to publish under a pen name. "I'm not sure how my stuff will play with the Symphony Guild."

Her fascination with the supernatural originates in her childhood. "I grew up in a haunted house," she says. "Really. Our ghost was no silly wall rapper, no blustering poltergeist that knocked things off mantels; our ghost appeared to us constantly, filmy and luminescent, sweeping majestically through a hall or down a flight of stairs, always in a hurry. My only regret is that he/she never said anything."

CIRCUMSTANCES UNKNOWN

A NOVEL OF SUSPENSE

JONELLEN HECKLER

He crossed the street slowly and entered Central Park near the boat pond. Children and their parents ringed it, operating remote controls on a fleet of toy sailing ships....<u>Look how they close the circle, these people, making fences of their devotion, shutting him out</u>. In the photograph in his pocket, the family was smiling....Tim. Deena. Jon, age five. Soon, they would pay for the sin of their pride. Soon, they would learn that it all can end in a flash...in flawlessly planned, seemingly accidental death....

POCKET

BOOKS

Available in hardcover from Pocket Books

615-01